HEROICS 101

HEROICS 101

MAGICAL GIRL UNDERGRAD – BOOK 1

Aest Belequa

Podium

This is a work of fiction. Names, characters, places, and incidents are either products of the author's imagination or used fictitiously. Any resemblance to actual events, locales, or persons, living, dead, or undead, is entirely coincidental.

Cover design by KittraMcBriar

ISBN: 978-1-0394-7031-6

Published in 2024 by Podium Publishing
www.podiumaudio.com
Podium

HEROICS 101

PART ONE

1

Casting Call

SATURDAY, AUGUST 30

I was going to kill my idiot boyfriend.

Okay, maybe not. I hadn't decided yet. I could ignore my buzzing phone—the clock read 2:48 a.m.—but I *couldn't* let his texts sit unread, and he knew it.

<Hey, Annie. Can't sleep. What are you up to? - Peter 12:24>
<I miss you. wyd tomorrow night? - Peter 1:13>

His survival was in *serious* doubt. He knew my plans already—packing—but at least the messages weren't from Riverside's greatest supervillain. Yet.

<Feeling bored. Might do something bad later - Peter 2:48>

I groaned, silenced his number, and rolled over. The cool night breeze blew in, filling the room with the smell of freshly watered grass and early autumn flowers. I shut the window. Curling into a ball, I tried to set aside his texts. Maybe I could ignore it all. Maybe he'd decide not to follow through on his threat. Maybe I wouldn't have to suit up and stop him. My eyes drifted closed.

My phone buzzed again. I glared, grabbed it, and jabbed my finger against the unlock button.

<One more time, for old times' sake! Soon my bots will strike the bank! - Professor Panic 3:17>

Maybe not. Shit.
[Casting Call]
[Episode: Professor Panic's Payout Plan! - PG]
[Role: Teen Heroine! Do you accept the role? (Yes/No)]

[Role Focus: Drama+Flamboyance]

I squeezed my eyes shut and screamed quietly into my pillow. The idiot had started an Episode? Of course he'd pull something like this tonight! I hugged my plushie cat, wishing I could just *sleep*.

Then I pulled myself out of bed and felt my way to the door. It wasn't fair. I didn't want to answer the **[Casting Call]**. I wanted to rest—I was heading to college in two days, and I had a busy schedule before then.

I flicked on the light.

I'd been in other girls' rooms throughout high school, but I'd never invited anyone over to mine—except Peter. He understood. It was frozen in time—the perfect early middle-schooler's room. Pink bedding covered my twin bed, and I'd painted my mirror frame a vibrant purple. Posters of superheroines—all signed and old and yellowed from Mom's secondhand smoke—hung on the walls. The cast photo from my senior play sat on my nightstand. And on my pillow lay Tails, a white cat plushie with pink-and-blue star-button eyes and two limp cloth . . . tails.

I didn't have time for this, but someone had to stop Professor Panic and his Panic Pals, and the police couldn't compete with the young Genius's inventions. Or, if I was being honest, his sense of presentation—of Cunning and Drama, which the Style System wanted so badly. Neither could I.

At least, not in my pink footie pajamas!

"Wake up, Tails," I said, pointing at the plushie and accepting the **[Casting Call]**. "There's a new Episode at the bank. We have to go now." If I hurried, I could stop Peter before he did something *really* stupid.

[Professor Panic's Payout Plan: Act One in Progress]

Tails's star eyes glowed and started spinning, and it stretched just like a real cat.

<Oh, Understudy, we're saving the day again? Nya!> Tails's high-pitched voice echoed in my head. **<Remember, you have to do the oath—>**

"I know, Tails. I hate this oath," I grumbled. Quietly. Then I grabbed the cat plushie and held it above me. "I swear on my family, who I love very much, that I'll stand up against Professor Panic, his minions, and villainy all over Riverside! I'll fight for justice, peace, and hope! And I'll never stop 'til evil does first!"

I cringed; I'd made up my oath when I was thirteen, and it was suited for the little leagues—the lowest tier of superheroes. They usually dealt with neighborhood-level threats, like the cartoon superhero shows before Launch Day. But I was eighteen now, and I wanted more than a little-league show. Squeezing my eyes shut, I tried not to be too embarrassed. At least no one could see what came next. My **[Transformation Sequence]**. Even though they might hear it . . .

Choral music swelled, and I winced against the sudden noise and lights. Singing echoed through our trailer—Mom would wake up for sure—but I was committed now. Pink-and-blue flashes flickered across me as I spun, my stuffed cat struggling in my grip. She leaped free and landed on the bed. My foot traced a wide circle onto the shag carpet as I pirouetted. My body glowed brighter and brighter, and I lifted off the ground. White thigh-high tights sprang up my legs, and matching gloves covered my hands to the elbow.

Then the dress replaced what pajamas remained.

Poofy off-shoulder sleeves. A pink bow with a sapphire in the middle across my chest. Two magenta stripes running down the front. Then the skirts and petticoats—blue, white, and fuchsia layers, patterned with white laughing and crying mask buttons. Why did this always take so long? I had things to do! More pink ribbons tied themselves into my hair as a golden wand with a brilliant coral gem at its tip slapped into my left hand.

The song started fading. My boots touched down on the carpet. When I opened my eyes and looked in the mirror, my pupils had gone star-shaped, and my hair was strawberry blonde. A pink-and-white domino mask sealed itself above my nose, completing the Costume. The music cut off, the flashing lights stopped, and everything quieted.

Except for my mom's sleepy sounding mumbles! "Anika, what was *that?*"

I froze. My heart pounded, and I swallowed nervously. If my mom walked in right now, it'd be a disaster! "Oh, [**Beep**]," I whispered.

[**Rating Warning #1! Episode Rating - PG! Censor in Effect**]

Whoops!

"Don't fear Magical Girl Understudy is here I swear to defend the weak against evil and uphold truth and love," I murmured in a long, breathless string of words. Who'd made this oath, anyway? Oh right. Younger Annie. "I'm fine, Mom. I couldn't sleep, so I got on my tablet to watch a video or two. Go back to bed."

Mom didn't say anything. I tensed. I needed a moment to think.

I could untransform, but that'd take too long. I didn't have time for two more [**Transformation Sequences**], not to mention finding a place to do them discreetly. Peter would do something terrible way before I finished all of that.

Or . . .

<**You could try the window, Understudy. It's what I'd do, and you'd get outside right meow!**>

It'd be faster, for sure. And I'd be on my way to stopping Professor Panic.

I made my choice—the window it was. I popped it open and coughed. Wisps of smoke rolled into the room and through the gap under the door.

Then I quickly pulled the screen off my bedroom window and stuck a leg through. I listened as Mom staggered down the hall, hacked a smoker's cough, and knocked on my door.

"Annie, why does it smell like smoke in here? Are you smoking? Come out here and talk to me!"

"We'll talk in the morning, Mom. I'm tired." I yawned, threw my other leg over the window frame, and hopped into the dirt yard our dog used to tear up. Then I ran, weaving through her trailer park's twisting streets and sprinting toward the cottonwoods along the Winter River's banks.

If Mom went back to bed, everything would be fine. Probably. And if not, I'd get in trouble for sneaking out two days before I left for college. What was the worst that could happen? Grounding? Keeping me home from the mayor's speech? Taking away my phone? Peter could still talk to me without it—he'd made some gizmo to do it in middle school. Texting just made things easier—except when he did it at one in the morning, the jerk!

I had more important things to worry about. Tails purred and looped between my legs as I caught my breath—or tried to. The smoky smell filled my nostrils and stung my eyes. Whatever Professor Panic had planned, it probably involved the fire, which meant I needed to go faster.

"[**Starwave Sail**]," I shouted, jumping and spinning into the air. A translucent pastel sailboard shimmered under my feet, catching me before I could hit the ground and rocketing forward on a glowing pink-and-blue contrail. I rode it above the river-bank toward a bright orange light downtown, sail flapping in the wind next to me. I leaned back, pushing the board's nose up, and windsurfed into the sky over Riverside. Tails sprinted along, her plushie body extending and compressing as her legs churned at nothing.

The first chrome camera drone met me before I crossed the river, humming through the air behind me. A moment later, a pack of blue-steel Panic Pal robots zipped by, playing the villain's stupid theme song as they gnashed their metal teeth and spun in the air. I turned to follow them toward the bank, my glowing trail lighting up the sky over Riverside with proof I was on my way!

[Show-off! +1 Flamboyance Point]

The little message in my peripheral vision got me thinking. Was I close to a Flamboyance skill roll? If I was, I could roll an upgrade to one of my skills, a useful new power for my build, or something that just . . . sat in [**Skill Storage**] until the end of time. I had a few of those already; I could only equip six powers. Flamboyance was also special because it was my [**Signature Skill's**] style. I pulled up my point total.

▶ Flamboyance - 45

I was! Maybe I'd roll something that'd finally let me use my **[Signature Skill]**. I'd been sitting on **[Adaptive Armoire]** Rank 0 for a while, but either Tails didn't know how it worked, or the stuffed animal wouldn't say. It didn't matter. If I played the Teen Heroine role right tonight, I'd have a new skill to roll by the Episode's end—maybe even by the time Act One ended—especially if I could force a Short by stopping Peter.

Could I force the System to make this a Short, or would the System demand a full Episode? I'd never tried it before.

I closed my point total and returned to tracking the Panic Pal bots toward Carver Street.

My hometown sprawled below me. The road and the town's brick-and-wood buildings ran straight beneath me, their restaurants and shops closed for the night. I recognized Mario's, the pizza place where Peter had taken me before prom. I'd paid. He hadn't paid for a date since I decided his cash was villain money. A few seconds later, Riverside High's gravel track zipped by. I'd never competed past sixth grade. It wouldn't have been fair.

I saw the flickering lights and glued my eyes to two things as I dove.

First, the bank. Fire trucks, ambulances, and police cruisers surrounded it, and a crowd of bystanders had gathered—Extras in the Episode, though they didn't know it. As I watched, a team of firefighters manning a hose hustled away from the front door. A moment later, the faux-stone pillars collapsed, along with the roof, blocking it.

The sailboard angled for the ground, disappearing as it touched the parking lot. I ran, sprinting to bleed off momentum, and skidded to a halt on the asphalt.

[Show-off! +1 Flamboyance Point]

A firefighter jogged up to me, screaming, "The bots grabbed people! They're stuck inside!"

I nodded and said what I knew the audience expected. "Don't fear; Magical Girl Understudy is here! I'll get them out. Just keep fighting!"

[Intense Line! +1 Drama Point]

But most of my mind focused on the message I'd seen while flying in.

The message Peter had scorched into the grass outside the bank. The message for me.

One last time for old times' sake?

2

One Last Time for Old Times' Sake?

Clearly, this wasn't just another Episode. Peter wanted this to be about *us*.

I pulled my gaze from the smoldering letters. The air smelled like gasoline and charred wood. I stared at the burning bank as part of the atrium fell with a crash.

So did my stomach. I balled my fist around my wand until I felt my fingernails through my gloves. Peter had gone too far. I'd kick in the doors, drag him and the hostages out, and see him arrested. His army of lawyers wouldn't save him this time! I just had to get inside first.

"Understudy! Thank God you're here!"

I spun, cringing. It wasn't a line, but it *felt* as corny as one.

The man running at me filled out his bright yellow fire suit. A helmet covered his hair, but no mask or face shield hid his oversized walrus mustache. "We're losing the building, and we've got bots and hostages in there!"

I bit back a sigh. Peter—no, Professor Panic—was in there. Or at least his robotic minions. And I couldn't focus on him. I had to save the Extras instead—that was clearly the goal for Act One. There'd be no Short this time.

The silvery chrome camera drone hovered high overhead somewhere, but I had no illusions that it would miss a thing. "That's terrible! Professor Panic will pay! How long do they have, Chief Thatcher?"

[Intense Line! +1 Drama Point]

He shrugged. "Could only be a couple of minutes if they found a safe place. Could be longer if they're in the vault. Can you do anything?"

"I can. You think the safe is . . . safe?" I asked.

"Yeah, it's safer than anywhere else in there. They'd have air for hours if they got inside, and it's watertight and airtight. And I'm sure that Genius Professor Panic wouldn't do something like this without a way into the vault. He's too smart for that."

"I'm going in. I'll get them into that vault. Keep a window open for me. [**Starwave**

Sail]!" I jumped onto the magic sailboard and flew toward the building. Below me, firefighters started dragging a second hose forward. Chief Thatcher directed them and the first hose team toward the bank's front and left side. I disappeared behind the building before they could start spraying. The chrome camera drone followed closer now that there weren't Extras around to spot it.

<I'm always up for jumping through a window,> Tails said, swishing her . . . tails around as she hopped onto the grass. A moment later, I joined her. The plushie cat hissed and stalked away from the inferno. <But in this case, it's too hot for me. Good luck in there, Understudy!>

I waved goodbye to Tails and stared at the back door. As I reached for the handle, I had an [Inkling]. Busting a window would feed the fire more air but also give me a safer way out. I wasn't trying to save the bank—just the people inside, and Peter, if I could get through to him quickly enough. I stepped back and looked at the second-story window.

"That's pretty high up," I thought out loud. "[Starwave Sail]!"

I leaned back as I flew through the air, making a long, wide loop over the bank's parking lot and the firefighters below. Then I turned sharply and dove right at the building. I had to get closer to make the shot.

Closer to the window. Closer. Now!

My hand flew off the sailboard's handle and pointed toward the window, fingers wrapped around the gold-and-tourmaline wand. "[Stellar Ray]," I shouted. A beam of solid, pale blue light punched through the window, shattering it. I threw myself off the sailboard a second later and tucked into a ball. Glass crunched as I hit the floor with an "Oof," rolled once, and hopped to my feet. My superhero damage shield had protected me.

[Bull in a China Shop! +1 Badass Point]
[Show-off! +1 Flamboyance Point]
[Good Thinking! +1 Cunning Point]

The chrome camera drone followed silently, floating up into a corner. I'd made it into the bank.

I hacked and coughed from the smoke. Judging from the last time Professor Panic used fire, the smoke wouldn't slow me down too much. It would make fighting harder inside, though. Especially if—

"HE'S COOL! EVIL! SMART! ALL-ORGANIC!

CLAP YOUR HANDS FOR PRO-FESS-OR PANIC!"

—that happened.

I barely had time to think about how dumb that lyric was before the first Panic Pal flew around the corner.

With friends.

The flock of blue-steel bots swerved into the burning hall behind it, metal-fanged mouths chomping and green headlights searching through the smoke. One blasted Professor Panic's theme song from a speaker, the hip-hop beat nearly drowning out the fire's roar, while the others dove toward me.

"THE FACTS ARE IN, THE TRUTH IS OUT, PANIC'S THE BEST! HE PUTS RIVERSIDE TO THE ULTIMATE TEST!"

"[**Beep**] it, Professor Parsnip! Turn your bots off and surrender!"

[**Rating Warning #2! Episode Rating - PG! Censor in Effect**]

I screamed in frustration. I didn't have time for this! The bot swarm buzzed toward me, and I ducked under it. One caught my back with a long, spindly arm, knocking me to the side. I jumped, spinning midair, and aimed for the one playing the music.

"TELL EM, PANIC PALS, WHILE WE'RE ALL JUST CHILLIN'! WHO DO YOU THINK IS THE ULTIMA—"

"[**Stellar Ray**]!"

Even though [**Stellar Ray**] didn't punch much harder than a boxer's fist, the Panic Pal's case wasn't very thick—just a few sixteenths of an inch, if that. Plus, it didn't have a long cooldown—only a few seconds—so I could spam it if I missed a shot.

But I didn't need to. The light beam caught the bot dead in the headlight, and it crashed through the wooden floorboards and into the bank's main floor. "Ha! One down!"

[**Dramatic Damage! +1 Drama Point**]
[**Stylish Shot! +1 Flamboyance Point**]

The others collapsed on me before I could fire another [**Stellar Ray**].

I found myself in a punching contest with the Panic Pals, and I didn't like it one bit! Each bot was only the size of my head, but I couldn't get any distance with three of them attacking me.

Trying not to . . . panic . . . I flailed and punched one in its single green "eye." It snapped back, eye shorting out, and skittered along the floor.

Two thin steel limbs slammed into my chest, and spiky metal jaws closed over my glove. I winced and sucked in a breath. The magical cloth held against the bite, but I'd have a bruise from the slams tomorrow!

[**HP 5/6**]

We rolled across the scorched floor. Fists, feet, and metal arms flew. One of the bots broke free from the scrum and popped open its speakers.

"HE'S COMING FOR YOU, AND IT WON'T BE FUNNY!
GIVE HIM YOUR PHONE, YOUR KEYS, AND YOUR MONEY!"

I kicked the other Panic Pal. It went spinning and crashed into a wall. I stuck my wand out again, screaming, "[**Stellar Ray**]" at the biggest threat: the speaker-bot. As the beam slammed into it, I rolled away from the others.

[Dramatic Damage! +1 Drama Point]

Crack!

The weakened floor gave way under my weight. I crashed into the tellers' counter, feeling the air whoosh from my lungs. Broken bots and wood flooring panels rained down around me. I took a deep, painful breath and pushed myself up off the shattered counter, ready to fight the rest of the Panic Pals. Luckily, superhero damage took most of the fall. It wasn't a full shield. The fall still *hurt*. But I could power through injuries that would stop an Extra in their tracks.

[HP 4/6]
[Dramatic Damage! +1 Drama Point]
[Gritty Recovery! +1 Grit Point]

One last bot descended, keeping its distance from me. I watched as it fled for the stairs. The speaker started up again as soon as they'd left my line of sight.

"YOU THINK THAT YOU'RE TOUGH? THINK THAT YOU'RE MEAN?
PROFESSOR PAnic's the best you've ev . . ."

I grinned painfully as the bot fled and the song faded. A few seasons back, Peter had kidnapped a rap group by hijacking their tour bus. He'd led me on a high-speed chase while he forced them to record his theme song. "Panic Prof and the Beastly Boys," the Episode had been called. One of my favorites, even if nineties hip-hop *sucked*.

The last bot lay motionless beneath a beam. I glanced at it just long enough to confirm it was toast, then took stock of the blazing room before I could accidentally become toast, too.

The odds of becoming toast were getting higher by the second.

Acrid, plastic-smelling smoke from burning desks and half-melted rolling chairs rushed through the hole I'd made in the ceiling. The drive-through's windows had shattered; the fire roared as it greedily ate the cool night air. The carpet smoldered, and wreckage from the atrium covered the lobby's front half. Another floor panel crashed down, shattering behind me on the tellers' counter. Flames licked at the counter's base, and stacked paper lit up.

I needed to keep moving. The Panic Pals had headed toward the stairs, so the hostages were probably downstairs by the vault.

I followed them down. Smoke pooled at the bottom of the stairs, and steam hissed up as fire hose water heated up around me. I felt like I'd descended into a mist-covered fantasy world, but one whose acrid stink made me cough and choke. The fire's roar faded to a background whooshing. After the deafening battle above, it sounded like silence.

Safe-deposit boxes sat half-open, their contents strewn across the floor. Pearl necklaces, gold bracelets, and promissory notes lay scattered everywhere. Had Peter even *taken* anything?

Muffled crying caught my attention. Then another sound interrupted it—a cough. The hostages were on the other side, near the vault! Or maybe . . . in the vault. That'd be convenient. The door hung open on the far side. Pushing through the smoke, I started talking toward the single green light in front of me. "Professor Panama, I presume?"

No response to my disparaging nickname. I loved those nicknames, and I had dozens of them. I never called him Professor Panic. Ever. The hostages started squirming, though; I could hear them moving.

Oh well. We'd both always been dramatic, and the chrome camera drone hovered just above me. Time to give the viewers what they wanted. "You can't beat me, Professor. If you turn off the bots and come out, we can save these people from *your* fire. Together. The jury will like that."

[Intense Line! +1 Drama Point]

The single green light grew brighter as I picked my way through the mess of safe-deposit boxes.

"Or we could fight, and I'll have to destroy your bots, disable your super-suit, and make you give up. Again. Lives are at stake, Panda. Do the right thing for once. For me."

A yawning circle taller than a person loomed in front of me. Inside, in the back, the single green light cast a pallid glow across a half dozen sitting and kneeling silhouettes. I peered at the light through the gray-black smoke.

Then a second emerald light flicked on. And another. And another. And two more, glowing like a cartoon mouse's ears.

"Professor Panic can't come to the phone right now, Magical Girl Understudy," a synthetic voice monotoned. "Please leave a message after the bang!"

3

Please Leave a Message After the Bang

BANG!

A wave of hypercompressed air slammed into my chest. The force flung me through the safe-deposit box room and smashed me against the stairs.

"Ow," I groaned, picking myself up off the ground. The ringing in my ears was already fading, and I could hear . . . screaming? I shook my head to clear it and readied my wand.

[HP 3/6]
[**Gritty Recovery! +1 Grit Point**]

The Extras—the hostages, that is—screamed. And with good reason; LABRAT was terrifying.

"Professor Pancake sent you, LABRAT? He was never here at all, was he?"

The [**Laboratory Assistance Bot–Retrieval, Aggression, Terror**], Peter's masterpiece and lieutenant, unfolded itself to its seven-foot height and stomped forward on its two legs, crushing jewelry and papers beneath its three-toed feet. Its arm cannon whirred as it charged for another shot. It stared at me as it spoke in its digital monotone. "Of course not. He knew you'd come, but he grabbed these chumps off the street to get you inside! The professor planned for everything."

If LABRAT and the remaining Panic Pals wanted a fight with the hostages at risk, I'd have to be faster and stronger. "Luckily for you folks, I'm a [**Hometown Heroine**]! I'll have you safe in no time," I shouted. A faint blue glow surrounded me, weaving around my body like a nimbus. It'd last twenty seconds, and I'd be—

"No, she won't!"

BANG!

—faster than usual while it did. I spun to the side as LABRAT's cannon fired again. This time, [**Hometown Heroine's**] speed buff let me dodge. Instead of hitting me, the shockwave spun me around a second time before I steadied myself in a crouch.

[**Graceful Dodge! +1 Flamboyance Point**]

I waved my wand. "[**Stellar Ray**]!" The light beam clipped LABRAT's blue-colored steel torso just below its pincer arm, but most of it went past the man-shaped robot. The Extras' screams redoubled as the bright blue light sliced over their heads. It also hadn't hurt LABRAT much.

"You're willing to hurt the hostages to destroy me? Bold, Magical Girl Understudy!"

For a second, I froze. No. I wasn't willing to get the hostages hurt. I lowered my wand slowly. As long as LABRAT stood between me and them, I couldn't use it anyway. This fight had just gotten a lot more complicated, and I wasn't sure I had a plan for the—

[**Inkling**] activated, urging me to dodge right.

I dodged right.

BANG!

The airburst slammed against the wall in front of me, shattering deposit box doors and throwing them across the room, but I'd pirouetted clear. Sometimes [**Inkling**] let me predict attacks. Other times, it helped find clues. But I didn't have much control over when it activated, and it'd never happened more than twice in an act.

[**Intuitive Moves! +1 Cunning Point**]

"Panic Pals, get her!" LABRAT yelled. One . . . two . . . three bots flew into the room. The first two charged me, while the last opened up with its best weapon—its speakers. God, I hated those damn speakers.

"HIDE YOUR RUBIES, YOUR DIAMONDS, YOUR PEARLS!
PROFESSOR PANIC'S IN THE HOUSE, BOYS AND GIRLS!"

"That line's the worst one! [**Stellar Ray**]!"

[**Dramatic Damage! +1 Drama Point**]

I blasted the bot as it flew away from the Extras. I sprinted toward the two remaining Panic Pals before the speaker-bot hit the ground. With [**Hometown Heroine**] ticking down, I quickly ran down the first one, springboarded off the wall, and windmill-kicked it in the eye.

I ran toward the next bot as that one spun crazily.

BANG!

An airburst punched into my side, flattening me against the wall. I held back a curse; I'd tunnel-visioned on the annoying Panic Pals and lost track of LABRAT! I picked myself up and kept chasing the Panic Pal, but this time, I kept an eye on the hulking bot standing by the vault door.

[HP 2/6]

I caught up with the chomping, flailing Panic Pal just as the buff from **[Hometown Heroine]** ran out. I grabbed it and kicked off from the wall, launching myself toward the Panic Pal—and LABRAT! It spun, trying to bring its compressed air cannon around to blast me. Eddies of smoke whirled behind me.

BANG!

LABRAT's airburst missed me by inches, whipping my hair and bows back and forth. The bot couldn't change angles fast enough, and both the Panic Pal and I slammed into its arm. The Panic Pal bounced right. I skidded left.

Toward the vault door.

I sprung to my feet, readying my wand. LABRAT struggled to its feet and stepped toward me. Its air cannon swung from a few wires, hissing as air rushed through the severed tube. It reached its pincer arm across, cutting its own arm off. The cannon clattered to the ground. A moment later, a three-toedd foot crushed it. "So, Magical Girl Understudy, you have chosen destruction?"

"Yeah! Yours!"

[Badass Line! +1 Badass Point]

I readied another **[Stellar Ray]**. But I didn't need it. As the robot started walking forward, the ceiling above it collapsed, burying it in floor tiles, half-burned chairs, and the check-writing desk. Its clawed arm pushed free and flailed around, trying to move the heavy, flaming desk off itself, but it wasn't going anywhere for a while. I let out a sigh I hadn't realized I was holding. Time to focus on the Extras.

I ran into the vault as LABRAT continued to struggle with the desk. Four hostages sat on the floor, none of them bank employees. I had no idea where Peter had found them, but a couple smelled like booze. Had he picked them up from a bar? Either way, they needed help.

I pulled the duct tape slowly off the first one's mouth and wrists. "Have . . . well, a little fear. You're in a burning bank. I'm Magical Girl Understudy, and I have a plan! Get yourself the rest of the way free, then start helping the others. I'm going to make sure you're safe and— What is that?" Something on the ground caught my eye, distracting me.

"The big robot put it there. There's a note, too," the woman said shakily. She rubbed her wrists and ripped off the duct tape holding her ankles together, shivering. "What's your plan? How are you gonna get us out?"

"I'll lock you in the vault. The fire department can bust you out in a couple of hours. Chief Thatcher said it was fine," I said, distracted. A pair of green-tinted safety goggles sat on the vault floor in a pile of bills.

Peter's goggles.

With a note.

To the victor goes the prize. Try these out to shield your eyes.

He'd left his goggles here. For me! He really did care, even if he was an absolute ass about showing it! I scooped them up and put them on over my forehead.

"Magical Girl Understudy, I'll break you, and then I'll break that vault!"

"Gotta go!" I said to the freed hostage and ran for the vault door. Sure, I could close it from the inside, but LABRAT had gotten in once. It'd break in again. I had to deal with the robot—after I made sure the Extras would be safe.

The check-writing desk rocked and teetered as I pushed on the bank vault's massive door. It thudded shut. A second later, a terrible metal-on-metal screech filled the air. I spun the vault's handle and turned to face LABRAT.

[Hostage Rescue! +1 Drama Point]

I peered through the pooling acrid smoke, coughing. The desk rolled to the side, and green lights in LABRAT's head and unbroken limbs straightened slowly until the robot towered above me. The light made glowing spheres of green in the swirling smoke. LABRAT stomped toward me. It had ripped off the rest of its damaged arm, but the crab-pincer one snapped open and shut.

"**[Stellar Ray]**!" I swung my wand at the menacing machine, but its torso armor took the light beam without a scuff. "Ugh, I hate fighting you so much, LABRAT!"

"I hate you, too, Magical Girl Understudy," LABRAT monotoned back at me. It stepped toward me, swinging its claw. It clacked shut on my arm, and the robot flung me into the corner. "It's in my programming."

[HP 1/6]

Picking myself up, I brushed off my dress quickly. "I'll be your **[Hometown Heroine]**," I said, running as the robot clunked around behind me. The blue buff kept me in front of the damaged robot while I thought.

I couldn't fight LABRAT. One more hit, and I'd start getting hurt, not just taking superhero damage.

And I couldn't just run away. If LABRAT got the door open, the hostages would be in serious trouble.

I needed a solution before **[Hometown Heroine]** ran out and LABRAT caught up. I came up with one. But it was pretty dumb. Peter had programmed the robot to hate me. So maybe it'd hate me enough to follow me away from the vault.

Hey, it was worth a shot!

I gained distance as my blue halo faded, then I skidded to a stop among the jewelry and promissory notes. I glanced up; the floor had collapsed on top of LABRAT, and there had to be a gap. Maybe one big enough to . . .

There.

LABRAT lumbered toward me, but it'd never make it in time. "**[Starwave Sail]**!"

I shouted, immediately leaning back as the sailboard popped up under me. The board rocketed up. I jumped, throwing myself toward the jagged hole in the ceiling. The sailboard vanished almost before it'd fully appeared. I went flying back up into the lobby, somersaulting through the air. The floor greeted me, and I rolled, arms flailing.

[Dramatic Escape! +1 Drama Point]
[Show-off! +1 Flamboyance Point]

I picked myself up. No HP loss. No Grit point gain. And no sign that LABRAT was following me. I took a deep breath, grabbed my wand, and peered over the edge. The robot stared up at me, mouse ears glowing. I stared back, wiping smoky sweat off my face. Time to get LABRAT up here, away from the vault door.

"Hey, bolt-brain, get up here! A fair fight, just you, me, and this burning building," I called down at it.

The robot just stared. Its gaze dropped to the vault door. Time for desperate measures.

"Unless Professor Pantry programmed you to be chicken! Bawk bawk bawk!" Tucking my hands under my armpits, I strutted around, clucking at LABRAT and bobbing my head like a pecking hen. At the same time, I tried to shield my reddening face from the circling camera drone. Taunting a robot? What was I thinking? How was that supposed to work?

But it did.

LABRAT stopped moving. Its gaze turned toward me. "Professor Panic has directed me to tell you that he 'didn't build any scaredy-bots.'"

"Coulda fooled me!" I waited for it to run for the stairs. I wasn't that lucky.

The giant robot's arm locked in place at its side. Flaming jets poured out of its feet. I watched, dumbfounded, as LABRAT's glowing green eyes grew even with mine.

[Play Stupid Games! +1 Drama Point]

I groaned. This was so unfair! I just wanted to stop Peter and go back to sleep! Then I ran for the left front window, wand in hand, and threw myself into the hoses' spray. "[Starwave Sail]!"

As I tore across the bank's lawn on the sailboard and Tails sprinted after me, LABRAT crashed through the window frame. The plushie cat only had one question.

<It flies now?>

4

It Flies Now?

It flies now!"

It flew now.

My sailboard soared over Riverside, leaving the burning bank in its pink-and-blue wake.

Tails sprinted alongside, chubby plushie legs churning the air. **<What are you going to do, Understudy? What are you going to do?>**

"I don't know, Tails!"

LABRAT flew now, and that changed my whole plan. I'd been ready to fight it in the lobby until it'd gotten good and fixated, then figure out a way to lure it outside and **[Stellar Ray]** it until I found a weak spot from the sky. But clearly, it was already fixated. And it flew now.

At least LABRAT had seemed slow back at the bank.

I looked back, sending my sailboard arcing in a lazy turn right. "Uh, Tails? Is LABRAT getting closer?"

Tails flipped over onto her back, somehow keeping pace as she looked behind her over her stomach. **<Nya, that oversized lunch is catching up!>**

Somehow, the foot-mounted thrusters on LABRAT's . . . feet kept pushing the robot faster and faster. Flames framed its glowing green eyes and mouse ears as it rocketed toward me. Worse, the stupid camera drone that hovered in front of me had a friend. A second one followed LABRAT, filming from right behind the robot.

Whoosh!

The huge robot roared over my head, clipping the windsail's mast and sending me into a spiral. "Watch where you're flying, LABRAT!" I yelled.

"Check your mirrors!" the robot monotoned after me. Was it . . . laughing? Then it zipped past in a cloud of smog.

I pulled the handle. The windsail slowly righted, and I watched LABRAT's long, wide turn as it wheeled around to attack me again. I kept watching as it turned slowly.

Really slowly. I started laughing. That idiot! "He built boosters into LABRAT's feet, but Professor Pancreas didn't include good turning! We're diving low!"

My sailboard sparkled its way into an alley behind Carver Street. For a second, it was quiet. Then LABRAT's rockets rattled windows and kicked up dust behind it as the massive robot tried ramming me.

I waited, looking over my shoulder. Just a bit closer.

"Don't forget, I'm a [**Hometown Heroine**], and this is my hometown!"

I whipped the handle and leaned hard to the right. The whole sailboard jerked over, turning so fast that the blue glow around me kept going for a split second before it caught up with my move. I pulled back, braking the windsail as LABRAT careened past me, trying to slow down or turn around.

Then I flipped around and pulled back into the alley. Behind LABRAT.

"[**Stellar Ray**]!" My shot caught LABRAT's right foot, and the rocket sputtered. Its leg expanded in slow motion. I saw fire between the panels.

Then it exploded.

Blue-steel shrapnel ripped into the alley's brick walls. Car alarms went off on Carver Street as glass shattered. LABRAT slammed into a wall, reddish dust choking my view. I heard a thunderous crash as the robot bounced off another wall. The robot careened through my windsurfer's nose before I could dodge. It fell to the ground.

So did I.

"God [**Beep**] it!" I shouted as the magical windsurfer came apart. I spun toward the dirt alley below and skidded across the dirt, kicking up glass bottle shards and chunks of cardboard.

[**Rating Warning #3! Further Rating Violations Will Result in Point Penalization!**]
[**HP 0/6**]
[**Good Thinking! +1 Cunning Point**]

"Ooowwwww," I muttered, picking myself up. My HP had been at zero for the slide's last few seconds, and no amount of brushing off would fix the scrapes on my knees or the rips in my tights. I had to try for the cameras, though. Tails bounced gracefully to a dumpster top and started licking her foot while staring right at me. Unlike my brushing, her efforts actually cleaned something. "Stop it, you show-off," I groaned.

<No.>

"I . . . hate you so much, Magical Girl . . . Understudy."

I spun, dropping into a fighting stance with my wand out. LABRAT was still active! But where was it? I saw a faintly flickering greenish light from around the corner. Cautiously, I crept toward it, my wand ready for a [**Stellar Ray**] as soon as I saw the bot. Tails stalked behind me, back arched, standing as upright as she could.

Something popped loudly around the corner. I jumped and gasped. Tails hissed. Then LABRAT's voice monotoned from out of sight. "Looks . . . like you won this round. But . . . do you have the courage to . . . finish . . . the job?"

I stepped around the corner, wand at the ready. "[Stellar Ray]!" I shouted before I'd even gotten a good look. The blast caught the bot's torso in a massive tear in its armor, and it shut down. Not that LABRAT had been functional anymore. Its torso had leaked oil before I'd blasted it, and most of its green lights had shattered. The last one slowly faded as the camera drones got one last shot and disappeared.

[Merciless! +1 Badass Point]
[Dramatic Damage! +1 Drama Point]
[End of Act One! Act Two in Five Minutes! Skill Rolls Activated!]
[Alias - Understudy] [Archetype - Magical Girl] [Community Rank - 1/3]
[HP 0/6]
[Styles and Skills]
▶ Archetype Skill - Transformation Sequence
▶ Badass (6)
▶ Cunning (33)
▶ Inkling 1
▶ Drama (15)
▶ Stellar Ray 1
▶ Hometown Heroine 1
▶ Flamboyance (51) (Skill Roll Available)
▶ Signature Skill - Adaptive Armoire
▶ Starwave Sail 1
▶ Grit (16)
▶ Rejuvenation 1

<Good job, Understudy,> Tails said. <You sure showed that bot who was the best flier. And you're at fifty points in Flamboyance.>

"Roll the skill?" I asked, looking at Tails. She nodded, and I pumped my fist. "Roll the skill!"

[50 Flamboyance Credits Used. Rolling Skill!]

I watched as the System message's letters started spinning faster and faster, like a slot machine. Some disappeared, while others seemed to change or rearrange themselves. I tapped my foot on the dirt. Why did the Style System's rolls always take so long?

Letters started falling into place, and I squinted, trying to read them.

[Rank-Up! Adaptive Armoire 1! Store a Costume for our Transformation Sequence. Switch between them for unique skills.]

"The missing piece? Yes!" I cheered, reaching down to pet Tails. "But I still don't know how to use [**Adaptive Armoire**]. How do I *get* a Costume?"

For all that the [**Signature Skill**] was supposed to be my *thing*, I'd never gotten to use it. I'd been fighting down a skill this whole time, and I still felt walled off by the System. The slot machine feel might be fun for the audience, but as a super, it just felt . . . frustrating sometimes.

<I wonder if Professor Panic's Signature Skill needed to level before it was useful as well, and he just got meow-re lucky than you did on his rolls?> Tails asked. She purred and pushed her squishy head against my shredded thigh-highs.

"Oh shit. Peter." I was on a break. I could talk to him. Maybe I could talk him down. I searched through my Costume until I found my phone. "How much time do we have?"

<Two minutes, thirty-five seconds.>

"That'll be enough." I scrolled through until I landed on Peter Adkison and pressed Call. The phone rang once. Twice. Three times. Then it picked up.

"So, you've beaten my LABRAT, Magical Gir—" Professor Panic said in his manic-sounding voice.

"Shut up, Peter, we're on break for a couple of minutes! Why does it fly now?"

Peter responded slowly, without the edge that Professor Panic had. "Why wouldn't it fly now?"

"Dammit, we had a deal about 'no flying robots'!"

"Well, what about your surfboard? It lets you fly, so why can't LABRAT? And the Panic Pals fly."

"They do, yes. It's a sailboard, and it's a power."

"LABRAT is a power, too. Or at least I used a power to make it."

<One minute, Understudy,> Tails interrupted.

I took a deep breath to steady myself. He wasn't wrong. It probably wasn't fair that I could fly and he couldn't. No! Wait! That wasn't the point I needed to make. I was angry about getting woken up, this whole stupid Episode, and how Peter had acted the last few weeks. Not about LABRAT.

"Peter, I destroyed LABRAT again. It's in the alley behind Allan's Hardware and Mercantile if you want to send some Panic Pals to collect the parts." I kept talking through his interruption. "I'm finding you, and we're discussing boundaries. You can't throw a super-fit just because I don't answer your texts in the middle of the night! You know I have to respond if there's an Episode. This isn't fair to me, and it's really out of hand. I just wanna go back to bed, but I can't because of you. Just . . . stop this Episode before I have to fight you again. Please."

<About twenty-five seconds,> Tails said.

Peter paused, then coughed into the phone and started talking, voice speeding up. "Well, Magical Girl Understudy, you're welcome to *look* for me if you want, but I assure you, Professor Panic is hidden better than you'd think. I'll *see* you when you figure it out." I waited while he laughed maniacally, rolling my eyes. When he'd finished, I kept saying nothing until he coughed awkwardly and kept going. "Y'know what? Forget the hints. Did you . . . find my goggles, Annie?"

"Yes. I'm holding them right now. It means a lot that you gave them to me, hun." It really did. It was a cute gesture, and one I'd cherish for a long time.

"It's nothing, really. I just really like you, and since we couldn't do sports in school, I never got a letter jacket for you. I know you like gifts, and I wanted you to have this one. Besides, I'm wearing the Mark Four version right now!"

For a moment, I just stood there. Anyone watching would have thought I looked like an idiot, staring at my phone, jaw agape. How could he do that to me? "Peter, that's so rude! A gift like that's supposed to mean something, not be a way to recycle your old stuff! I'm going to kick your—"

[Professor Panic's Payout Plan: Act Two Beginning]

"Bye."

I hung up and tucked my phone away. The five-minute—or shorter—intermissions didn't leave time for a good conversation, and what we'd said hadn't made me feel any better. Not at *all*. Well, maybe a little. But not much! Peter meant well, he really did, but he could be so clueless! I'd known he was worried about . . . us . . . when I went to college and he stayed in Riverside, but we needed to talk about it, not have Episodes about it.

Ugh! Boys!

I walked down the alley, trying to blink back tears of frustration under my domino mask. Honestly, I didn't know where Peter was hiding, so I figured I'd just patrol for a bit. I was way too annoyed to fly right now. I couldn't deal with him, and a power I didn't understand, *and* Professor Panic's antics all at once. Not at . . . I checked my phone. Four in the morning.

I pulled his stupid Mark Three goggles down over my eyes. It might have been dumb, but just like the other girls at school who'd gotten hoodies or letter jackets from their boyfriends, I'd finally gotten something of Peter's to wear. I couldn't walk around Riverside wearing Professor Panic's eyewear in broad daylight like they could with a sweater, but all the same, it felt nice to do it now.

I opened my eyes, expecting to see the world tinted in green.

Instead, I saw an address. But before I could read it, the world started spinning, condensing into an infinitesimal point past the horizon. Tails's purring lowered in pitch until its drone filled my ears. I wobbled on my feet and screwed my eyes shut under the stupid goggles. But I still saw the System message.

[Welcome to Rocko's studio. System Disabled. Now arriving Backstage.]

5

Now Arriving Backstage

Aaaayyy! Annie DuPont! How's my favorite little leaguer? Mid-Episode wardrobe change and [**Signature Skill**] upgrade, eh? We can do that! The viewers will ogle all over it—ratings through the roof!"

I opened my eyes and pulled the goggles off. Sweat poured down my face—between the heater blasting warm air and my footie pajamas, I was hot! And I wore my pink footie pajamas again; Backstage wasn't a place for Costumes. This wasn't my first time Backstage, of course. The first time, I'd been thirteen and soaking wet from the Riverside Tube Float. A swimsuit and shorts were also way cooler than PJs.

And standing in front of me, all three feet of them, was Rocko.

The Ilneat was covered in short black fur that shone with oil; it reminded me of the otters I'd seen on a field trip to the Tokyexico City Zoo. Their narrow black eyes darted back and forth between their desk and me, even as their mouth smiled wide, revealing four wide, sharp teeth like a gorilla's. They carried a cigar in one of their delicate grasping hands while two stronger squeezing hands grabbed each other behind their back. And, of course, they wore a tie and sport coat but nothing else. Not even an auto-translator.

Rocko didn't mind the heat. Ilneats liked it hot and humid, and since they'd saved humanity from extinction on Launch Day and helped clean up the fallout, I'd just have to put up with it.

Rocko had gotten me a role as a super with my own show—even if it was little league. And they'd helped me learn my powers to catch up with Peter—he'd gotten his a few months before me. As much as I hated to admit it, I liked the greasy little gorilla.

Plus, they were *technically* my boss.

I caught a glimpse of the room—superhero Costumes on racks behind a clear wall, cigar smoke wafting from somewhere below me, and a massive machine idling in the corner—before they pulled me down into an armchair. "I saw on the tube. You got the [**Adaptive Armoire**] level during the break, and the goggles from Peter! This is great, DuPont! We're real close to taking the primo morning kids' slot! Your [**Signature Skill's**] gonna push *Small-Town Super* over the top!"

"Rocko, you're in my bubble."

"Oh. Sure, sure!" The personal space invader clambered off the chair arm, smoking the whole time with their grasping hands while their squeezing hands lowered themselves onto the floor. Rocko—Ilneats always used cartoon nicknames to keep to human naming conventions, and they preferred the nineties for some reason— knuckle-walked to a mountain of ice and pulled out a water bottle. They kept talking the whole time in a ridiculous Yorkston accent. "Look, kiddo, with those goggles and [**Adaptive Armoire**], we can build you a new Costume! Pataki, get back here! DuPont needs a new super-suit."

I took the offered water bottle and dumped half of it on my head, shivering. Then I drank the rest while another Ilneat clunked their way back to the gigantic, idling machine. The heat really drained me; I felt more exhausted than I had after fighting LABRAT.

The room was way bigger than I'd thought on my first visit; it was practically a warehouse, and its clothes racks and shelves held thousands of variations of every super-suit I could imagine. Magical Girl Stella-Lunar's pure-white dress. Mister Felsic's volcanic gloves. Even—I cringed just thinking the name—Lord Destructo's horned helm and mace. The Backstage had it all.

Safely behind a plexiglass window, of course.

Pataki glared at Rocko, carrying a cigarette, then rasped, "Okay, DuPont, stand on the platform. Feet on the *Xs*, squeezing hands straight out from your body, grasping hands . . . missing . . . as usual. You'll feel some tickling. Don't move. I'll take the goggles." Unlike Rocko, Pataki *did* use a translation device, but their voice still sounded like a sixty-five-year-old smoker's. All the smoke in the air wisped around as fans blew.

I handed the goggles to Pataki, who set them on a shelf next to the machine. I climbed inside it and did as the Ilneat instructed. The machine started spinning, forming a hard-light model of me near its center. Without my pajamas on. Or anything else. I blushed and looked away.

"I said, 'Don't move.' We'll have to take a new head scan, DuPont. Keep still."

I looked back at hard-light Anika, embarrassed. At least they'd blurred out the . . . private bits. I started talking to Rocko, as much to distract myself as to learn anything. "So, ratings are up, huh?"

"Oh yeah, kiddo! *Small-Town Super* is really close. You're most popular on the nursery worlds—Ilneat-Three, especially—but it's about to make Rocko Pictures a *lot* of money. We're talking action figures, plushie Tailses, and Panic Pal robot kits! I'll be able to pay off my house!"

The machine scanned my face while I stood silently and listened to Rocko go on and on about merchandising. Most of it wouldn't ever get sold on Earth, but my contract as a superhero gave me a small cut of whatever sold on-world. Ilneat rules about contracts with minors were pretty lax—I had enough money for college squirreled away in accounts across the planet, thanks to Rocko's company, and the investment terms looked more than fair.

"Step out of the scanner, DuPont," Pataki drawled, interrupting my thoughts and Rocko's rambling. "We will now begin building your new Costume. Let's start with a standard Magical Girl dress and tights, then work from there."

"Not yet." I didn't want to look at the naked hard-light projection anymore, but this was my chance. "I'm ready for the minor leagues, Rocko. I hit eighteen two months ago, I'm going to college, and Professor Pancake's gimmick is getting . . . old. I'm not *Playpen Patrol*. I'll run into *serious* supervillains at Tokyexico University, and keeping a PG rating is going to be—"

"Annie, Annie," Rocko interrupted, slinging a clutching hand over my shoulder as they stood on a chair arm. "Look, Annie, your whole archetype is kid friendly. There ain't many Magical Girls in the minor leagues unless you count Dark Girls, and only Stella-Lunar's got a contract in the majors. Villains like Dark Girls don't bring in the profit for studios *or* supers. Not funny enough, too much angst. Just stick with Rocko, and we'll get that primo kids' timeslot together, okay?"

I drummed my fingers as a clone of my Costume appeared over the hard-light model. "Why can't I try the minors, though?"

"Two reasons. First, you're contracted to finish at least one more season of *Small-Town Super*, and we can't change the show's content rating right now. We'd never financially recover from that. And second, you've been working hard, but have you ever seen minor leaguers fight? Let's add a lab coat. She's gonna be copying Professor Panic."

"Yeah, I've watched them— What do you mean, copying?"

"Well, not copying, but using some of his powers while cosplaying him. What did you think [**Adaptive Armoire's**] Costume storage was for? Stuff you made up? Nah, you need part of a super's Costume, and it has to be *given*. You'll get some of Prof. P's powers as a finale for Season Five and tease even more fantastic Costumes for Season Six. It'll be a hit, 110%! [**Adaptive Armoire**] could even get you to the major leagues one day if you build it right."

"Lab coat added. Rocko, I'm gonna give the whole outfit a Professor Panic color scheme."

"Nah. Just the goggles, lab coat, and some glowing lights like on his bots," Rocko said. "Keep the rest of the outfit just like Understudy's. It'll sell better."

"But you just said I couldn't try the minors! Now you're saying it's a major-league power?" I couldn't think straight—not against Rocko's logical leaps. I struggled to keep a yawn down.

Rocko barely glanced at me before looking at the Costume-in-progress. "Annie, you struggled with LABRAT back there. How long do you think you could hold out against, say, Big Fish? Or a metamorph Bruiser? Minor leaguers are loose cannons."

Rocko looked like they were thinking, then turned away from me. "Still, we could work toward a minor-league show after this season. [**Adaptive Armoire**] needs a lot of work. Costume hunting, leveling up skills, and then playing catch-up with your peers. It's a slow-burn skill, but it's top-tier if you're up for the work. You might be in the minor league by the end of the year. There's rumor about an opportunity. Then it'd be the big bucks for both of us!"

I bit my lip and chewed on it. Tokyexico University was supposed to be my big break in theater *and* superhero work. Now it'd be entirely on me to make it happen. It wasn't the big win I'd wanted from Rocko, though. I opened my mouth to argue, yawn, or agree. I wasn't sure which it'd be.

My eye caught the TV screen behind Rocko's desk. "Is that live?" I asked.

"Yep." Rocko turned up the volume so we could hear.

I watched in horror as a swarm of Panic Pals crashed through a window on Carver Street. One of them played a speech by Professor Panic himself. "If the so-called Protector of Riverside doesn't come out from hiding, I'll have to call up more of my pals! My Panic Pals! Magical Girl Understudy, you have until four thirty! You'll have to *look* hard to find me. *See* if you can do it by then." The speaking bot flew off after the rest of the swarm, heading for Black's Shoe Store.

"I have to go," I said. Black's Shoe Store was one of my favorites! And Peter needed to be stopped before he . . . actually, maybe it was too late for "before he did something stupid." Peter needed to be stopped.

"Yeah, you do," Pataki drawled. "Suit's done. I'm uploading it into the System for you. Put on the goggles, start a **[Transformation Sequence]**, and pick Lab Assistant Panic. You'll need to do *something* that the Costume-giver did to activate it, so think about that."

"Get that **[Adaptive Armoire]** running and make us a mint, Annie! Go get 'em, tiger." Rocko sat at their desk. They pushed a button, and my vision collapsed to a pinprick. "Do well at college, DuPont!"

[System Enabled. Episode: Professor Panic's Payout Plan: Act Two in Progress]

<Welcome back! I hate to be the purrer of bad news, but Professor Panic is looking for you. You might want to hide right meow!> Tails crept out from under the dumpster, covered in filth. She started cleaning herself, seeming unconcerned with the news she'd just given me.

"I have a better plan." I pulled off my domino mask and slid Professor Panic's goggles down over my eyes.

"SHE'LL SAVE THE DAY . . . SHE'S . . . uh . . . A PRETTY GOOD MECHANIC!

EVERYONE CHEER FOR LAB ASSISTANT PANIC!"

Yeah, this rap stuff was harder than I'd thought. I jumped, spun, and jazz-handsed on the last line. The whole world flashed green in my eyes. When it cleared, and I'd landed on the ground, I looked down at myself.

[Rejuvenation Activated: HP 3/6]

Most of my Costume was the same. Pink-and-blue dress, thigh-highs, and boots. But a green-glowing circle covered the center of my chest, two more glowed from the garter clips holding up my tights, and even more shone on my boots. I twirled. The lab coat flared out behind me as I spun, then fell perfectly into place when I stopped.

[First Signature Skill Activation! +1 Flamboyance Point]

I felt a lot better, too, physically, at least. I'd gotten a Rejuvenation out of the switch—maybe I could use that to my advantage later. I got a pair of Rejuvenations in each act, but they'd been hard to use with full **[Transformation Sequences]**. Switching between Costumes would let me fight longer if I could disengage from the fighting for a bit.

Mentally, though . . .

"Alright, Tails, it's time to take over Riverside!" I gasped and put a hand over my mouth. Had I really just said that? "Wow, these Costumes really get into your head, don't they?"

"Tails is no more. TA-1LZ is fully operational. Battery at 87%. Recommend a stat check."

I looked at the mecha-kitten standing on the dumpster.

"Calculating a 93% chance of new powers associated with LAP designation."

[Costume - Lab Assistant Panic]
[HP 3/6]
[Styles and Skills]
▶ Archetype Skill - Transformation Sequence
▶ Badass
▶ Cunning
▶ Speed-Hacker 0
▶ Drama
▶ Hypercompression Cannon 0
▶ Hometown Heroine 1
▶ Flamboyance
▶ Signature Skill - Adaptive Armoire 1
▶ Stored Costumes: (Understudy)
▶ Maniacal Reveal 0
▶ Grit
▶ Rejuvenation 1

"A **[Hypercompression Cannon]**! Like LABRAT's? Alright!" I started to activate it. Then I stopped. Randomly firing Genius tech down Carver Street *probably* wasn't a good choice. "Okay, I'm really going to have to work to keep a heroine's headspace here. Mwahahaha!"

"Preliminary calculations estimate your villainous breakdown glass at 63% full—"

"Mwahahahaha! Stuff it, TA-1LZ. It's time for my [**Maniacal Reveal**]! [**Starwave Sail**]!" I jumped into the air while spinning. Then I slammed into the ground. "Ow. Why don't I fly now?"

Of course Lab Assistant Panic didn't have [**Starwave Sail**]. I'd have to correct that—or find a replacement power—after this Episode.

I trudged down the alley and onto Carver Street with TA-1LZ following me. Peter was out there, and I couldn't fly, but that was okay. I'd show him! I'd show them all! "Ahahahaha!"

"Revising earlier numbers. 89% and rising."

"89% is a B-plus!"

6

89% Is a B+!

<So, what did we learn?>

"No Lab Assistant when there's no one around to fight?"

<Yes. And?>

"The Lab Assistant Panic Costume is evil?"

<Try again, Understudy.>

"Okay." I yawned and thought momentarily while we walked down Carver Street. I wore my Understudy Costume; whatever the Lab Assistant Panic Costume had done, I was *not* ready for it. I'd deal with Professor Panic as Understudy—or wait to shift into the Lab Assistant Costume when I found him.

"If this is what Professor Panini feels when he suits up, no wonder he's a villain. It's like the Costume was in charge, not me. That poor guy."

<Close. Inside you are two cats, Understudy. One is evil. Pride, anger, fear, and jealousy. The other is good. It's your willingness to fight for hope, peace, and joy, and to stand up against villains like Professor Panic. The two cats are always fighting—hissing, spitting, scratching, and biting. And which one will win is the one you feed. You started feeding the evil cat as soon as you put on the Lab Assistant Panic Costume. With fish and chicken, nya!> Tails licked her lips with a plushie tongue.

"So, everyone has two cats inside them? That sounds uncomfortable," I joked. But it made sense. The LAP Costume hadn't given me a supervillain's attitude. Or if it had, I'd fed it—made it bigger and stronger than it should have been. I'd *enjoyed* not being Magical Girl Understudy, Protector of Riverside. And I'd only caused a little property damage before Tails talked me into switching. But if I'd only fed the evil cat a little, what about Peter? How much had he fed his evil cat?

"So if there are two cats inside me, are there two cats inside Professor Paltrow?"

<Nya, just two robots. And they're both pretty bad!>

"Har har. I guess my **[Maniacal Reveal]** will have to wait." I looked around at the shattered windows and broken street signs. I'd done a number on Carver Street, but most of it was Professor Panic's fault. Probably. After all, it was his responsibility. He'd started the Episode. Everything I'd done so far had only one purpose: to stop him.

Speaking of which . . .

I held up the goggles. I'd seen an address earlier, before the trip to Backstage, but I hadn't had a chance to read it. And I'd had other . . . priorities . . . as Lab Assistant Panic. But now I could see the lettering. It was definitely Peter's handwriting. I held them up to a streetlight so the pen strokes were backlit. "600 West Calvin Avenue? That's the high school. Let's go!"

I windsurfed into Riverside High's parking lot and landed the sailboard, running along the asphalt toward the front doors before doing a spin for the camera. The towering green-and-red alligator painted on the gym's outer wall stared at me. Below it, a door hung off its hinges, its steel bulk twisted by whatever had slammed through it.

[Show-off! +1 Flamboyance Point]

I sprinted inside. We'd had some big fights at school—either in the building or on the football field. It all depended on whether he meant the Peter/Annie screaming match sophomore year that'd been the talk of the school for weeks or the Panic/Understudy fight later that same night that'd wrecked the stadium just before homecoming.

I bet he meant the screaming match. If I was right, he'd be in the band room. Or at least inside. We'd kind of fought everywhere.

Riverside High was a post–Launch Day building, shiny and fresh. Green exit lights glowed over the door I'd just dashed into, and LED runners along the gym's edge led to the main hall. I ran through the hall, looking for the band room.

BANG!

I whirled, my skirt flaring. I saw a Panic Pal. It . . . waved at me through a window?

Then it smashed through, along with two of its friends.

"HE STEALS FROM RIVERSIDE WITH COMPLETE DISREGARD! MAGICAL GIRL UNDERSTUDY, BE ON YOUR GUARD!"

I groaned in frustration. My sympathy for Peter was running out.

"How many of these bots did he build?" I looped the goggles around my wrist as a trio of Panic Pals zoomed around the corner. He'd clearly been working full-time on his robots, which made sense. I'd quit my movie theater job a few weeks ago, and his dad had given him time off from his apprenticeship at D.A.C. Drillworks, the industrial drill firm the Adkisons owned. And I'd been busy getting ready for college.

Had he spent the *whole* time building bots?

The first Panic Pal dove at me, limbs flailing and teeth chomping. I spun, skirt flaring, and kicked. The kick caught it in the eye, and it slid across the hall with a *ting* sound.

Before I could finish my pirouette, though, the second bot clamped around my wrist. Its teeth gnashed against my glove. I flailed my arm, trying to dislodge it. I slammed it onto the ground a few times before it let go. But when it did, something was hanging from its teeth.

"My goggles! Give those back!"

As I lunged for the goggles, the bot scooted backward. It stared at me, its green eye glowing almost contemplatively. Then it flew off, followed by the speaker-bot.

"**[Stellar Ray]**!" I shouted. The beam of pale azure light speared into the speaker-bot. It exploded, but the thief-bot dipped into the hall before I could wave my wand again.

[Drama Skill Takedown! +1 Drama Point]

I sprinted after it, skidding to a stop outside of Mrs. Abercrombie's drama classroom. Even the bot's faint green light had disappeared.

"Augh! I needed those!" I had to get those goggles back. If Rocko and Pataki were right, the Lab Assistant Panic Costume wouldn't work without them. And more importantly, they were a gift. From Peter, my idiot boyfriend.

I stepped into Mrs. Abercrombie's room. Something had destroyed the old *Midsummer Night's Dream* sets; chunks of castle walls and fairy forests lay scattered everywhere, and prop boxes formed drifts like snow. I plowed through a pile as tall as my hips and stood below a short set of stairs. Mrs. Abercrombie's room backed up to the auditorium. Could it have gone through there? **[Inkling]** said yes, so I followed its lead.

[Good Thinking! +1 Cunning Point]

The first door in Mrs. Abercrombie's backstage led to the girls' green room. As I peered inside, I had a suspicion—not an **[Inkling]**, but a hunch—that the Panic Pal was hiding inside somewhere. I sorted through the Costumes and props piled on every surface. Nothing. Then I started checking under furniture. Nope.

Had it opened a door? I cracked open one of the dressing stall doors. Something pushed against it, trying to hold it shut, but I overpowered it. I saw a faintly glowing green inside. "Got you!"

[Good Thinking! +1 Cunning Point]

"HE'S BEEN CALLED A CON ARTIST! A SOURCE OF STRIFE!
BUT PROFESSOR PANIC IS LARGER THAN LIFE!"

I raised my wand. "I take back everything I've said about your theme song, Professor. That has *got* to be the worst lyric I've heard."

The Panic Pal rushed me. Its arms flailed back and forth, thudding against me, and I grabbed for my goggles. I couldn't use both hands without dropping my wand, and it couldn't bite me without dropping my goggles. I slammed it down into a pile of rubber swords. It slapped my face, but I held on.

Then it poked me in the eye.

[HP: 2/6]

I let go, obviously. What else *could* I do? It'd poked me in the eye. As tears soaked my domino mask, I searched for that damned robot. This wasn't funny anymore.

Its green glow guided me toward the stage itself. I ran toward the light. "I'm a **[Hometown Heroine]**, and you're going down!"

The bot buzzed through the air away from the stage. I only had one option, so I gathered myself, sprinted to the edge, and leaped through the air. My fingers scrabbled for the goggles.

They missed. But I caught hold of the Panic Pal's legs instead.

As I crashed toward the ground, the Panic Pal jerked out of the sky. The bot slammed into the first row's seats. Bot parts went everywhere, and I heard something crunch.

[Flashy Move! +1 Flamboyance Point]
[Dramatic Assist! +1 Drama Point]
[Brutal Takedown! +1 Badass Skill]

I winced and picked myself up. When I arrived at the bot's mangled remains, though, I breathed a relieved sigh. The goggles were fine. Totally fine.

Better than me. I transformed to Lab Assistant Panic long enough to trigger a **[Rejuvenation]**, then immediately switched back. Did it feel like cheating? Yes, but it worked.

[Rejuvenation Activated: HP 5/6]

I wound them back around my arm and strode out the door toward the football field. He'd be there. He had to be.

"Professor Parley!" I stopped at the painted gator in the center of Riverside Stadium. "This is it! Come down from that announcer's booth and surrender!"

"LADIES AND GENTLEMEN! TONIGHT'S BIG GAME IS BETWEEN THE CHALLENGERS—MAGICAL GIRL UNDERSTUDY AND HER CAT— AND THE HOME TEAM! GIVE IT UP FOR YOUR GAAAAAAATORS!"

The stadium lights came on. Bot after bot smashed through a paper sign with the Gator logo crossed out and a stick-figure LABRAT drawn over the top. Once the swarm of bots had lined up on one side of the field, Peter's voice echoed across the stadium again.

"EVERYONE CHEER!"

The sounds of lackluster, unenthusiastic cheering filled the stadium, and with the stadium lights' help, I could see that Peter had filled the stands with hostages.

I didn't have time to save them, and they weren't in danger, so I squared up against the bots. The police were on their way, anyway. "If I beat your football team, will you please be done? I'm so tired of this!"

"YOU ALREADY KNOW THE ANSWER! MAYBE! PLAY BALL!"

I knew I was playing into his game. I knew he wanted me to fight the Panic Pals instead of ripping him out of that announcer's booth. But I didn't have much choice.

So I ran toward the bots, and they flew toward me. I fired off a trio of [**Stellar Rays**] before we collided.

[**Drama Skill Takedown! +1 Drama Point**]
[**Drama Skill Takedown! +1 Drama Point**]
[**Drama Skill Takedown! +1 Drama Point**]

"FIRST DOWN, UNDERSTUDY! GET IN THERE, BOTS!"

I could hear the desperation in Peter's voice even through the loudspeaker. Good. I'd dragged myself through a burning bank, across town, and even back to school because of him. For him. He deserved to be—

"Oof!"

The remaining bots piled on top of me, limbs flailing. One smashed into my side. I grunted. Another caught me across the face. I groaned as the blow caught my jaw.

[**HP 4/6**]

"I'm the home team now! The [**Hometown Heroine**] team!" I shoved and pummeled the bots as the neon-blue halo surrounded my body. One exploded. Another one shut down as I stomped on it. Then I ran free.

[**Merciless! +1 Badass Point**]
[**Badass Takedown! +1 Badass Point**]
[**Dramatic Assist! +1 Drama Point**]
[**Gritty Recovery! +1 Grit Point**]

<Nya! Hiss!>

Had Tails just . . . said, "Hiss"? I glanced back. She was dodging—and occasionally not dodging—a bot's limbs. The hits did little to her other than poof into her plushie body. A vicious blow sent her flying toward the end zone with a loud yowl.
"FIELD GOAL! THREE/NOTHING, HOME TEAM!"
"[Stellar Ray]!"

[Drama Skill Takedown! +1 Drama Point]

I only had time to fry the pun-bot before the swarm caught up, and I had to keep running. I dashed into the end zone, threw myself into the air, and kicked off from the goalpost. As I flipped over the machines, I took stock of the battle—er, football field.

Tails careened through the air, locked in a deadly grappling match with one of Peter's bots. Tangled together, neither could avoid the uprights. The bot exploded over my head as Tails leaped clear. I whirled and kicked, knocking two more bots out of the sky with one kick.

[Cunning Assist! +1 Cunning Point]
[Stylish Strike! +1 Flamboyance Point]
[Stylish Strike! +1 Flamboyance Point]

<Understudy! The booth!>

I looked over just as something crashed out of the booth and tore through the sky. It was Peter! He flew now, too? "Flying is my thing, not yours!" But sure enough, Peter flew through the predawn sky on a black-and-blue moped. How he'd gotten that thing going, I had no idea. He was a Genius, though.

The Panic Pals were still chasing me. I turned to fight them as Peter disappeared down the street, heading out of town.

<Just follow him! The bots don't matter, and you're almost out of time!>

I hesitated, blasting a bot with a **[Stellar Ray]** as I thought. She was right. I'd been sleeping in, and that'd buy me some time, but the mayor knew the Protector of Riverside was leaving. He'd scheduled a farewell speech for ten o'clock. If I got home in the next hour, that gave me just a few hours to nap, sneak out again, and transform for his speech.

I did know where he'd be going, though.

[Good Thinking! +1 Cunning Point]

[Drama Skill Takedown! +1 Drama Point]

"Sorry, Pals, I've gotta go! [**Starwave Sail**]!"

[**End of Act Two! Act Three in Five Minutes! No Skill Rolls Available!**]
[Alias - Understudy] [Archetype - Magical Girl] [Community Rank - 1/3]
[HP 4/6]
[Styles and Skills]
▶Archetype Skill - Transformation Sequence
▶Badass (9)
▶Cunning (37)
▶Inkling 1
▶Drama (23)
▶Stellar Ray 1
▶Hometown Heroine 1
▶Flamboyance (6)
▶Signature Skill - Adaptive Armoire 1
▶Stored Costumes: (Lab Assistant Panic)
▶Starwave Sail 1
▶Grit (17)
▶Rejuvenation 1

As I windsurfed on pink-and-blue waves after Peter's moped, sirens sounded below me. Good, the police *were* coming for the hostages. They'd probably be able to handle the few Panic Pals that I'd missed. Right now, I had bigger fish to fry.

I'd failed to stop him or end the Episode early, but I could still close out the last act with a win. If I was right, Peter was flying toward where high schoolers went to make out and drink beer. I'd been there with Peter a few times, though never as Magical Girl Understudy. I got on my phone and called a special number. When it picked up, I started talking.

"Collidus. We're running an Episode. I know it's early, but I'll need your help. Head to Flat Top Hill.

7

Flat Top Hill

Flat Top Hill loomed over Riverside, bald and proud. I'd lost track of Peter on the way up, but he had to be there. I knew it for two reasons. First, he'd taken me up here on a few dates. After prom once, and when we had time off over the summer. We'd spent a lot of time up on Flat Top, looking down at the town, drinking cheap beer, and listening to his stupid nineties hip-hop. He'd be here.

The other, more subtle clue was the giant drill surrounded by rickety-looking metal scaffolding spewing smoke into the sky.

[Professor Panic's Payout Plan: Act Three Beginning]

I landed in the gravel parking lot, wand already at the ready. The moped sat there, hissing and popping as it cooled. The drill's racket filled my ears, and I smelled the stench of burning oil on the morning breeze. Tails stalked behind me as we walked toward the drill's scaffolding.

"That's far enough, Understudy." A new set of hisses and screeches joined the drill's sounds as a nine-foot-tall set of blue-and-black power armor stepped toward me. Its helmet opened, revealing Peter's shock of blonde hair, goggle-clad eyes, and buck-toothed smile. "You've fallen into my every trap, played into my hands perfectly, but there's only one way this can end. With me taking over Riverside and you defeated!"

"God da—er, for goodness' sake, Parsnip. This isn't about whatever you're planning. This is about us! About you and me." I knew Rocko would edit this. "Shut down the drill, step out of the power armor, and we can talk through this. Together."

[Desperate Plea! +1 Drama Point]

I didn't think it'd work. Peter never surrendered as long as he had his tech. So when his visor shut with a clang, I dashed toward the drill.

"Not so fast!"

Whump!

Peter's arm lashed right into my path like a snake. I tried to duck too late and ran into it, cartwheeling through the air and slamming into the gravel butt-first. The power armor's fist drove toward me, slamming into my stomach and driving the air out of my lungs.

[HP 3/6]

As the fist slammed down again, I rolled out of the me-sized divot in the gravel. "Alright, Panini, let's . . . let's both take a deep breath here," I said, sucking in air. I ran, putting some distance between me and the power armor.

[**Gritty Recovery! +1 Grit Point**]

"I take your breath away, huh?" Peter laughed, his power armor exaggerating the motion. I had to admit his banter was better than mine. "Well, let's air things out!"
Bang!
An airburst, just like LABRAT's arm cannon, washed across me, tumbling me back toward Flat Top's edge. Of course he had a [**Hypercompression Cannon**] in the hard suit's chest! I dug my fingers into the gravel, nails bending—if it weren't for superhero damage, they'd have torn off—and stopped my tumble.

[HP 2/6]

The drill's whining changed, and it coughed gray dust across the hilltop as it dug deeper and deeper. I got ready to move. "You're a villain, Professor Pacific! And I'm the [**Hometown Heroine**] to stop you!"
"Then it's time for my [**Maniacal Reveal**]! Ahahahaha!"
I cursed under my breath. No one could fight during a [**Maniacal Reveal**]! Rocko's camera drone zoomed in on my face, blocking my vision. If a reveal wasn't running, I'd be at a serious disadvantage. Then Professor Panic started his monologue.
"You see, Magical Girl Understudy, this town is mine. Soon, you'll be . . . gone . . . and no one will stop me then. I could have just waited until you left. A week, maybe two—it wouldn't have taken long. But you've been a wonderful rival for me—"
"You're such scum, Professor," I interrupted.
He laughed. "Yes, I am. But I'm your scum. As I was saying . . . you've been a wonderful nemesis for me. So I wanted to give you one more chance to stop me. This drill will reach Riverside's underground sewage treatment plant in ten minutes. From there on, I will control whether toilets flush, sinks drain, or showers turn into baths!"
My laughter interrupted him again. "Really? That's the stupidest evil plot I've ever heard, and you kidnapped a *rap group*."
"You think so?" For a moment, Peter's voice came from the power armor, not Professor Panic's. I could hear how crestfallen he was. Then he coughed, and the

Professor was back. "You think so, but you haven't seen how desperate people get without working plumbing. Besides, if you want to stop me, you'll have to get past my FEAR 2.4 Power Armor! Ahahahahaha!"

I felt the **[Maniacal Reveal]** fade as Peter burst into almost hysterical laughter. I started my own maniacal laughter even as his stopped. I couldn't match up to the FEAR armor in melee—my beatdown earlier had made that clear. And if the armor was anything like LABRAT's, I'd be crit-fishing. That'd take too long, and his ranged attack made it a bad choice, but I had other options.

"PROFESSOR PANINI THINKS HE'S HOLDING A TRUMP!

BUT HIS LAB ASSISTANT WILL SEND HIS ARMOR TO THE DUMP!"

[Rejuvenation Activated: HP 5/6]
[Signature Skill! +1 Flamboyance Point]

With my goggles on and my lab coat flaring behind me, I held up a hand. "Ahahahahaha! You've fallen into my **[Maniacal Reveal]**, Professor! You see—"

"What the **[Beep!]**?"

I smiled, fighting down evil laughter. It was so nice having someone *else* get a rating warning. And the confused look on Peter's face? I . . . well, I couldn't see it, but I could imagine it. "You see, Professor, you're not the only Genius in Riverside. Not anymore. I'm you, but better, and when I've disposed of you as an unworthy rival, this town will be mine!" I blushed. Look, I know it was cheesy, but that's how **[Maniacal Reveals]** go. "Now, do me a favor and get out of town. Or even better, surrender! Ahahahah!"

[Sinister Speech! +1 Flamboyance Point]

Bang! Bang!

Our **[Hypercompression Cannons]** fired simultaneously, sending dust clouds across Flat Top's flat top. I threw myself to the side and landed on the gravel. With **[Hometown Heroine]** running, I was fast enough to dodge Peter's. His power armor was too slow to avoid mine, though.

When the dust cleared, I could see it didn't matter if he dodged. The armor was intact.

"Is that it? Your new Costume is no threat to my power. All it is is dust in the wind." The FEAR armor stepped to the side, between the drill and me.

I was way faster than Peter, but there wasn't a way past him. Not at his current speed. I started up **[Speed Hacker]**, watching as the world reduced itself to ones and zeros. I switched a few around randomly, smiling. It was a good thing Peter hadn't fought a Cunning hero before.

Bang! Pshhhhhhhhhhh!

The power armor swayed as a burst of hypercompressed air surged toward me. I sidestepped, and it pushed off Flat Top's side harmlessly. Peter's suit leaked air from an automatic valve that'd opened when he shot, though.

[Good Thinking! +1 Cunning Point]

Whuff!

I laughed as a breeze from the FEAR suit's cannon passed over me, ruffling my hair, lab coat, and skirt while I posed. "Oh dear, P, is the pressure too much? It's okay for your suit to have performance issues, you know?"

He roared and started charging toward me, steel fists clenched and iron boots shaking the hilltop. Or maybe that was just the drill.

As he charged, I could feel **[Hometown Heroine]** fading. The ridiculous **[Maniacal Reveals]** had lasted too long! "Never fear, Magical Girl Understudy is here! I swear to defend the weak against evil and uphold truth and love." I spun as he charged, jumping into the air and letting the transformation take over. I hadn't been able to switch back before, but with the cannon disabled, I had a second.

When I landed, I was back in my Magical Girl Costume and ready to fight.

I took a deep breath. Then I exhaled, pushing the Lab Assistant Panic persona away. I didn't care what Tails said; the LAP Costume *had* to impact my thinking. I wasn't *that* power hungry.

"Incoming!" I turned to face a wall of steel heading my way.

I didn't have time to run. The only option was to take the hit. I braced for impact. "Here I come to save the day!"

Something purple and yellow slammed into Peter's armor, knocking it aside.

I winced. "About time you got here, Collidus!"

The purple-and-yellow blur stopped moving for a second. An early teenage boy stared at me from behind a pair of ski-style goggles. "You called, and I came running! It's Saturday morning, and I'm here to hero!" He posed, hands on hips and chest puffed out.

The steel fist that slammed into him ruined the effect. But it was still cute for a couple of seconds.

Collidus was my sidekick and the only other superhero in town. He'd only contracted with Rocko a year ago, and so far, his superpowers seemed limited to being really fast. That, and not getting hurt if he was going fast enough.

"Ow!" Collidus said as he scraped across the gravel. He picked himself up. I knew he didn't have the Hit Points I did yet, but he would soon. His build was a combination of Grit and Badass. "So, what's the plan here?"

I paused. "I'm having an **[Inkling]** that stopping the drill is most important. You get around the Professor. I'll keep him busy."

[Good Thinking! +1 Cunning Point]

"Got it." Collidus started running. His legs blurred as he accelerated. Then he ran right toward the drill, past the FEAR suit's grasping arms, and slammed into the scaffolding. He flew through the air, finishing his arc maybe thirty feet up, then bounced across the ground and back onto his feet. "It's too bad I can't play sports. I'd have been the best running back ever!"

The impacts hadn't hurt him. He'd been going too fast.

Peter started to turn to defend the drill. I couldn't let that happen. "[**Stellar Ray**]!" I shouted, waving my wand. The light beam didn't do much to his armor, but it did get his attention.

Caught between defending his drill but accepting my attacks or dealing with me first, Peter hesitated.

"Wheeeeeeeeeeooooooooooo!" Collidus slammed into the scaffolding again, causing a horrible creak. This time, when he bounced off, Peter ran toward his landing spot and punted him down the hill.

I ran to the edge, watching my sidekick bounce and tumble down the slope. He flew off a cliff and plummeted toward the ground.

"Eh, he'll be fine." I shrugged and waved, turning toward Peter. Collidus had taken worse falls. He'd be fine—probably—and he'd earn a ton of Grit points on the way down, but he was out of the fight for now. "We have unfinished business to take care of and then a serious talk."

The power armor suit nodded. Its fists went up.

A screeching sound split the air. We both whirled as the scaffolding tipped and teetered. Had Collidus caused enough damage? Would I have to finish it off?

I didn't have time to find out. Peter charged toward me as fast as his armor would go. "Ann—Understudy! Time to finish this!"

8

Time to Finish This

[**Inkling**]. I should dodge toward Peter.

I hadn't considered that option. But as the FEAR Power Armor's fist reeled back to launch a haymaker my way, I realized it was perfect. I'd get inside his reach. Maybe even behind him.

I lunged toward Peter. His fist rocketed over my head, ruffling my hair. Then I slid between his giant suit's legs, rolling back to my feet. I waved my wand toward him. "[**Stellar Ray**]!"

The beam of light clipped his shoulder, but the armor stayed intact. I wasn't getting anywhere without crit-fishing. And I couldn't do that without—

[**Good Thinking! +1 Cunning Point**]

As he spun around, I realized something.

I didn't have to fight him. I was past him. I could destroy the scaffolding and stop the drill. Then I could worry about the power armor. "[**Hometown Heroine**]!" I dashed toward the scaffolding. Closer. Closer . . .

I could see the weak spots from Collidus's ramming attacks. I aimed. "[**Stellar Ray**]!" The beam hit a half-shattered weld. It popped. The whole tower groaned and squealed.

I was going too fast, though. There wasn't time to slow down. I gritted my teeth and raised my arms over my face. I slammed into the scaffolding tower and lost control.

[HP 4/6]
[HP 3/6]
[HP 2/6]
[**Bull in a China Shop! +1 Badass Point**]
[**Gutsy Choice! +1 Grit Point**]

I pushed on the labyrinth of steel and wood on top of me. The whole tower had come down—with me under it! It was no use, though. I couldn't move it all. Not before . . .

Crunch!

[HP 1/6]

Peter's fist slammed into my face. Not for the first time, I thanked the Ilneats for their System and superhero damage. Then he grabbed my arm, pulled me out of the rubble pile, and threw me toward the edge.

[HP 0/6]

As I skidded across the gravel, my mind wasn't on the massive bruise I would have on my butt or my scraped-to-hell hands. It wasn't even on the pain in my wrenched shoulder.

[Hometown Heroine] was still running. The drill was gone. And Peter had tossed me away from his armor.

I'd won.

The FEAR Power Armor stomped toward me. It was too late, though. I picked myself up and started running. Once I had enough distance, I turned quickly. "**[Stellar Ray]**!" The ray caught Peter's power armor in the chest. It didn't do any damage, but I hadn't expected it to.

Peter kept coming, stomping closer and closer. I fired off another **[Stellar Ray]** and ran again. This time, I hit an elbow. I wasn't sure, but the arm might have been moving a touch jerkier.

"Stay still, Understudy! Come closer so I can hit you with my power fists!"

"I don't think so. I can stay out of your reach and fish for hits that'll cripple your FEAR armor. Face it, Professor Pander. You've lost. **[Stellar Ray]**!"

I didn't see if my light beam hit. I was already running. But I heard—and felt— the power armor take three more steps. Then it stopped. Something hissed, and I glanced over my shoulder.

Peter, all one hundred forty pounds of him, climbed out of the power armor. He grinned sheepishly at me. "Alright, Magical Girl Understudy. I can see when I'm beaten. The FEAR armor isn't fast enough to catch up, and you got lucky with your hack earlier. I, Professor Panic, Terror of Riverside and your archnemesis forever, surrender."

A camera drone hovered over us. I looked straight at Peter. "I hope you learned a valuable lesson today, Professor Pacific?"

"Oh yes. The FEAR 2.5 power armor will be more focused on speed."

"No, no, not that one!" I looked at the camera drone. "That crime doesn't pay!"

Yeah, it was cheesy, but no cheesier than a Saturday morning cartoon. Besides, we were little-league supers, and *Small-Town Super* knew its audience. One of the chrome camera drones started zipping off, heading toward Rocko's nearest teleporter, which meant I could stop worrying about this Episode and start worrying about my talk with Peter.

[Episode Finished!]
[Episode: Professor Panic's Payout Plan! - PG]
[Penalties: 3x Rating Warnings - No Penalty]
[Episode Finished! +5 of each Style Point]
[Winner Winner! +2 of each Style Point]
[Season Finale! +1 of each Style Point]
[Role Focus: Drama+Flamboyance - Goal Met! +20 Focused Style Points]
[Alias - Understudy] [Archetype - Magical Girl] [Community Rank - 1/3]
[HP 0/6]
[Styles and Skills]
▶ Archetype Skill - Transformation Sequence
▶ Badass (18)
▶ Cunning (48)
▶ Inkling 1
▶ Drama (52) (Skill Roll Available)
▶ Stellar Ray 1
▶ Hometown Heroine 1
▶ Flamboyance (36)
▶ Signature Skill - Adaptive Armoire 1
▶ Starwave Sail 1
▶ Grit (27)
▶ Rejuvenation 1
[50 Drama Credits Used. Rolling Skill!]
[Rank-Up! Hypercompression Cannon 1!]

I saw something moving in the corner of my eye. Tearing myself away from the end-of-Episode menu, I turned. Peter was poking around at his armor's legs. "Professor, step away from the armor!"

He hummed and kept fiddling with the joint, tightening bolts and adjusting gizmos. Where had he gotten tools from, anyway?

"Uh, Peter, can you hear me?" I reached out and touched his shoulder.

He jumped and turned toward me, shaking his head and blinking. I could see his green eyes dilating under his goggles. Then his body shivered; he'd gone full Genius mode that fast and was coming back out of it now. It was getting worse. "Sorry, Annie, I was just . . . thinking. If I tweak the actuators at the knee joint, I could move some more motor functions up the FEAR's thighs. That'd let me lighten the limb itself, which could lead to even more speed in the legs."

I let him ramble on about his suit improvements. Truthfully, now that I had him here as a semicaptive audience, I wasn't sure how to start the conversation. I played with a loose bit of hair that'd escaped—probably after he'd thrown me across the hilltop. Did I just tell him he couldn't text me after ten? What would we do for boundaries when I went to Tokyexico University in a couple of days? Would he be reasonable about it? What if we had another screaming match? I didn't want to leave Riverside on bad—

"I'm sorry."

Uh, what? This wasn't how this conversation was supposed to go. I stopped playing with my hair. "It's . . . fine?" I facepalmed mentally. It wasn't fine. It was *really* far from fine. I took a deep breath and tried again. "No. It's not fine. I'm . . . I don't know?" I sat in the dirt, hands pulling my knees to my chest. For all the righteous frustration I'd felt, actually *talking* to Peter about it felt awkward.

"Scared, Annie? You're scared about college? What it'll do to us—and to our show?"

"Yeah." I started sniffling, and tears ran down my cheeks before I could stop them. I stiffened as Peter put a hand on my shoulder. Before I knew it, I was shouting. "Mostly us. I've been trying to get you to talk about this! So many texts, and even calls! Calls! But you just deflect and deflect! We need to figure this out, and it's like you don't want to! I haven't slept in nights from nerves, and your messages at ungodly hours of the night are *not* helping!"

A siren whined faintly from the bottom of the hill, then another. The cops were coming.

I sniffled and pulled myself into a tighter ball. "You know what? Forget it. We don't have time to talk about this now. Just promise me something, okay? No more Episodes until I leave? Then you can fight with Collidus all you want."

Peter opened his mouth, then looked at my face and closed it. He nodded. "No more Episodes, Annie. I'll let you sleep. Can I just say something, though?"

I bobbed my head up and down, squeezing my eyes shut.

"I don't know what long-distance is gonna be like. I'm sure we'll have a lot to figure out, and I'm sorry. I've . . . I've been scared too. It's been easier to pretend nothing's gonna change for the last few weeks. That's why I haven't wanted to talk about . . . us." Peter sat down next to me and put an arm around me. He pulled me closer—or tried to.

"Noodle arms." I laughed into my knees and leaned into it. The police sirens' wails grew louder as we sat for a moment.

Peter kissed the back of my neck. I shivered a little and wiped a tear away as he kept talking. "We won't have time for this talk this morning. They'll pull up in thirty seconds. But, Annie, I'm with you, even with the changes we've both got coming." He stood up and held out a hand.

I took it and let him help me up, even though he was shorter—and probably weaker—than me.

I gave him a quick kiss. "The usual, then? See you after Rocko's people spring you and pay for damages?" I had to fix my face before the cops showed up. Magical Girl Understudy didn't cry. Even if Anika DuPont did. Sometimes.

"Yeah. I'll swing by to help you pack. We can talk a little then, if your parents don't hear. Love you, Understudy."

"Love you too, Professor Pantry." I squeezed his hand, then grabbed his wrist.

"Can't you just call me Professor Panic? Just once?"

"No."

We waited near the gravel parking lot as a half dozen patrol cars wound up the hill. They surrounded us in a half circle, and officers poured out, handguns drawn. Peter held up his hands and got on the ground; this wasn't his first rodeo.

I started talking as soon as I saw the sheriff. "Not to worry, Sheriff Harris. Justice prevailed. Professor Panpipes has surrendered. He planned to break into the sewage treatment plant and take it over."

"Well, that's the stupidest evil plot I've heard in a while, and I was in one of the chase cars when he kidnapped that rap group." The police boss peered out from below his hat, staring at the power armor, practically salivating. "Is that . . . Genius tech?"

"Keep your hands off it! It's retina-locked and DNA-coded to melt down if any of you Extra scum so much as step inside. No test drives!" Professor Panic went off, quickly pulling himself back into character. "I want my lawyer contacted and at the station by the time we arrive."

"You'll get your lawyer," Harris growled. "Hell, he'll have you on the streets again in a couple hours. But one of these times, you'll mess up, and we'll have you. Good work, Magical Girl Understudy. We'll take it from here."

"Alright, Sheriff. If you need me, you know what number to call. [**Starlight Sail**]!" I hopped onto my sailboard and surfed off through the morning sky as the sun crested the hills across from the Winter River. I'd had Peter set up a spoofed phone number chain that linked to my cell phone for Sheriff Harris to use, just in case I wasn't around when an Episode started.

I landed near the Winter River, some cottonwoods and willows between me and the trailer park. "Magical Girl Understudy reporting! Mission success! I'm signing off, but kids, remember—good always triumphs as long as your heart is pure!" The final camera drone peeled off as my Costume faded away in a burst of stars, hearts, and comedy and tragedy masks.

I checked my phone: 5:10. Plenty of time to sneak back in through the window—or even the door, if I was really quiet. I started walking, then stopped. "Shit." I covered my mouth, but no warning popped up. The Episode was over.

But now I had a new problem: crossing the trailer park in my pink footie pajamas!

I started walking, trying to stay out of the main road. A few folks glanced at me with puzzled looks, but I ignored them. It wasn't the first time I'd been . . . eccentric. I was a theater kid, after all.

My window was still hanging open, and I pulled myself into the brilliantly pink bedroom. I yawned and collapsed into bed. I was out within seconds, even as Riverside woke up around me.

PART TWO

9

Keys to the City

And so, as we move into a new era without our greatest protector, Riverside thanks you for your service. *I* thank you for your service, Magical Girl Understudy. You've kept the town safe . . . mostly . . . from Professor Panic's plots."

I held back a wince at *mostly*. Sure, it was true. We could see the burned-out bank from the podium Mayor Albright was talking on. But I was standing behind him, in full Costume. So I had to stay the positive, friendly Magical Girl that Riverside had gotten used to.

The mayor kept on talking and talking. I had no idea how he'd been elected, as dull as he was. I bit down a yawn. It didn't help that I hadn't slept the night before or that I'd had to get up an hour beforehand to "volunteer at the animal shelter." I'd often used that excuse to get out of the house so I could transform.

Someone elbowed me in the side. "Hey, Under Girl, I assume you won?"

"Shhhhh!" I scolded Collidus out of the corner of my mouth. "Everyone's watching. And of course I won."

"Now, miss, if you'd step forward to receive a gift from the Riverside City Council and myself?"

As I stepped toward the podium and shook council members' hands, I looked around for the gift. If I had to guess, I'd say—Yep, that. I groaned mentally when two elementary-aged kids approached the podium, struggling with the gigantic key's weight.

"On behalf of the City Council and the Mayor's Office"—he was definitely verbally capitalizing those words, the pretentious, political jerk—"please accept this ceremonial Key to the City. Know that you'll always have a home here, should you choose to return. Now, if you'd kindly say a few words?"

"Uh, sure!" I strode to the mic. I had an [**Inkling**] of what I wanted to say, but I'd be lying if I said I'd prepared for this. I was ready to bumble through a short speech and be done, but that wouldn't be very in character for Magical Girl Understudy, would it? I took the mic from Mayor Albright, coughed into it once, and held it up to my face. "Hi, Riverside! I know there are some nerves about me going off to college—I have them, too, believe me! Professor Panda lost, and we arrested him, but it's only a matter of time until his lawyers get him off the hook. And without me, there's probably some fear that no one will be able to stop him."

By the nods among the small crowd, I knew my words had struck home. Of course they had. Carver Street was in shambles. The school was closed for a while so people could fix the stadium and theater room. And the bank was definitely, 100%, a lost cause. The fire department had rescued the hostages from the vault, though, so I'd won that round!

"Today, I'm asking you not to fear. To trust in the power of good"—I cringed a little, but kept going—"and to believe that evil can be stopped. Collidus is young and a bit reckless, sure. He *did* bounce down Flat Top earlier today. But he's got a pure heart and the bravery of a superhero twice his age. Please, citizens, trust that he can keep Professor Panic from ruining our wonderful Riverside. I know I do."

[Good Thinking! +1 Cunning Point]
[Inspiring Speech! +1 Drama Point]

There, I thought. That should make them happy. Right?

Not right. Faces still looked concerned. Someone looked over their shoulder at the bank and whispered to their neighbor. I had to keep talking.

"Besides, uh, I'll be back and better than ever in December for winter break! And if things get bad, I'm sure I'll get a call, and I can be there in no time. I'll always be your **[Hometown Heroine]**, just a **[Starwave Sail]** away." I jumped onto the sailboard, grabbed the far-too-heavy key to the city, and zipped off over the city as everyone cheered.

[Show-Off! +1 Flamboyance Point]

Well, not everyone.

A blonde-haired boy in the back kept his arms folded over his chest. He glared at me and the stage as the mayor took the mic back from the podium where I'd tossed it. How had Peter gotten out of jail so quickly? He must've contacted his lawyers in advance. Which meant he'd known he was going to lose. I grinned stupidly as I sailed down Carver Street and took a right at the river. "How cute can he get?"

<I don't have an accurate answer to that right meow. If you shifted to Lab Assistant Panic, I'd be able to give you a data-based response, though.>

"No, that's okay." I landed. My parents were expecting me back from the animal shelter soon. Luckily, Collidus and I had an agreement. I'd spent half an hour playing with his cats, so my street clothes were covered in fur. I'd contacted Rocko a few days ago to let him know I'd be using my powers today for a few hours but that there was NO Episode to film. It was just public relations. But that time was over now.

I untransformed back into a tank top, short canvas shorts, and sandals in a flurry of sparkles, stars, and masks.

I sat on my bedroom floor a few hours later, a mountain of bras and panties around me. I grabbed a handful of underwear and shoved them into the duffel, groaning as my stuffed cat stared at me from the bed. Mom and Dad had been right. It was too much. "I should have packed days ago."

Now my bright pink bedroom was covered in notebooks, laptop accessories, and clothes. So many clothes. I'd packed for summer camp once; Rocko's studio had paid me for my first year with a trip to a camp that'd turned out to be for super-kids. But this was different. This was . . .

A nightmare.

I had no idea how I'd fit everything I wanted to bring. For example, the purple-framed mirror. I'd had it since I was eight or nine. I'd learned to use makeup in it—one of Dad's favorite stories to tell strangers. It'd always been embarrassing, but I loved that mirror. And it was too big.

The dorms at Ash Hall were supposed to be prefurnished, so my bed wasn't coming either. But would my bedding?

Come to think of it, how much space would I have? The Ash Hall page on the college's site didn't say, but I'd be sharing with another girl. And that was only if I couldn't get into Rho Theta Chi Kappa. Should I try to join the sorority right away and get out of the dorms? Or should I wait? Joining the sorority would be great for my social life, but a mess as a superhero.

"Augh!" There were just too many questions! And I hadn't had time to answer them.

"Uh, bad time?" Dad stuck his head through the door. He wore a white tank top over his beer belly and black athletic shorts. I looked up, then at my pile of underwear in horror. He laughed. "I've seen it all before, Annie. I used to change your diapers, remember? But if you think it's embarrassing for guys to see, I'll just tell Peter you're taking care of your intimates. We'll have some man time."

"Auuugh! Dad, get out!" I slammed the door shut and desperately shoveled my underclothes into the duffel. Why was Peter here? Couldn't he have waited? I froze. No, he couldn't have. We'd agreed on today. He wasn't breaking any rules or pushing my boundaries. He was just . . . being Peter. I doubled my efforts.

"Hey, Pete, did I ever tell you about Annie's first time trying out makeup?" Dad's voice drifted through the door.

"No, actually, Mr. DuPont. How'd that go for her?"

I tuned out Peter's voice and started zipping up the bag. He could help me pack other stuff. *Any* other stuff. Hell, he could even see my underwear, on me, when I wanted him to. But not right now.

"Peter, it's Garret. And I have pictures. I keep 'em on my phone, just for moments like this."

"Let's take a look," Peter said. "Ahahahaha! Can you send that to me, uh, Garret?"

Okay. That was enough. I shoved the door open, stomped to the living room—red-faced and furious—and grabbed Peter's hand. "Actually, Dad, I'm ready for him. You'll have to share the picture later. Much, much later."

I dragged my boyfriend down the hall and slammed the door shut.

"Door, Annie," Dad shouted.

"Fine!" I cracked it the tiniest bit.

Peter held up an escaped bra, waggling an eyebrow.

I snatched it from him, hissing, "Give me that! Peter, we didn't really finish our talk earlier. You're scared of me going to college—"

"And of me taking over some of Dad's drill business. What do you want me to do with the laptop?"

"Put it in the backpack with the books on my bed. Thanks." I started pulling shirts off hangers and folding them. "You're taking over some of the business, then?"

"Yeah. He noticed I'm kind of a Genius when it comes to electronics, so I'll apprentice with the software people for a month, then take over the program. It'll be a good gig, but Dad's pretty sure I'm going to 'save the company.' And I know I can, but I don't know if I can without . . . you know? Either way, I agreed to take a gap year to help out. Tough decision, but you know how family is."

I nodded. "So we're both scared here. I'm gonna be in a new place, and you'll be here. I'm going to be busy a lot. I can do texts in the evenings. Honestly, any time during the day is probably fine. How hard could the Post–Launch Day History of North America be? But unless I say otherwise, I need my sleeping time."

Peter packed a paper pad into my backpack next to the laptop. "Alright. I want video chats. Once a week at minimum. Two would be so much better. And are you going to visit on the weekends?"

"Yeah, I'll come down when I can." I stopped, looking at the evil grin on Peter's face. Then I whispered, "No. Absolutely not. No Episodes for at least the first quarter. And take it easy on you-know-who, okay?"

His phone buzzed. He opened it and snorted. "This was you? Half your face is lipstick! Ahahahaha! This is the most adorable thing I've ever seen! I'm gonna post it."

"No, you're not!" I grabbed at his phone. We wrestled for it, rolling in the clothes piles. A hand went somewhere it shouldn't have, and I squealed.

"Kids, behave in there," Dad said from the living room.

I froze and moved his hand, blushing, then continued wrestling for the phone.

I got the phone eventually, but not before Peter tapped the Lock button. I tossed it onto the bed and sat on it, red-faced and breathing hard from our wrestling match. "If I can't delete the pic, you can't have your phone. Then my phone buzzed on the makeup stand.

"I got it!" Peter shouted. He grabbed the phone and sat down next to me. His fingers deftly punched in the unlock code, earning a glare before I snatched it from him. "What? I'm a Genius. Of course I know your password."

It was an email from Tokyexico University. I skimmed through it. "Blah blah, check-in process for the dorms. Policies on pets—no pets allowed. I wonder if Tails counts? Blah blah blah, no drugs and alcohol, and beware. Beware what? Oh, apparently, bike theft is the second most common crime on campus. Behind supervillain-related crimes."

"That's a big category."

I kept reading. Then I laughed and handed my phone to Peter. As he read, he started laughing, too, until we leaned against each other, too out of breath to support ourselves.

Please be aware that the Student Supervillain Society, a legitimate student organization, usually plans an Episode sometime during Orientation. Tokyexico University Student Superhero Association members will be on hand to contain their colleagues and rivals. Incoming freshmen, we ask that you not interfere.

To clarify, incoming freshmen, whether Extras or supers, are not to interfere with the SSS's Orientation Episode. Dr. Mays and the TUSSA have it under control.

Helen Barber
Vice President of Student Services
Tokyexico University

Peter handed the phone back and slid a hand under my butt for his, earning a squeak and a glare. Then he looked at me, pocketing his phone. "You're totally gonna interfere, right?"

10

You're Totally Gonna Interfere, Right?

Absolutely not!"

"Why not? Make a name for yourself on campus. 'Annie, the freshman who saved the day.'" Peter stood up and snatched the phone from me. "Look, it says, 'We ask that you not interfere.' That's permission to get involved."

"Only you would think that, Peter. If they're asking me not to get involved and they have a plan to deal with it, I'm going to respect that plan." I returned to folding shirts and stacking them on my bed next to the duffel bag.

"But, hun, you're sick of the little league, right?" Peter sat back on the bed, fiddling with his phone. His voice had dropped to little more than a whisper.

"Yeah, but they have a whole club and a professor. They don't need my help."

"I wonder what Dr. Mays's power is, anyways," Peter asked. He typed away on his phone, wrinkling his brow. "I mean, I don't know what I expected. His bio doesn't have any references to his superpower. It just says he's a former top-fifty major leaguer. His first name's Ken and he teaches Team Compositions—whatever that is—and Superpower Ethics."

"The first one sounds . . . incredibly boring. In any case, Dr. Mays and TUSSA have it under control. For you villains," I hissed, keeping my voice quiet in case Dad was listening, "it might be easy to move up by breaking the rules, but we heroes know they're there for a reason!"

"Hey now, we follow rules! They're just not the same ones everyone else follows. So, here's what you do." Peter grinned and typed away on his phone. "You sneak away during Orientation, make a splash with your very annoying powers, and then join TUSSA. Or, even better, you use that cool Professor Panic—"

"Lab Assistant Panic. Lab Assistant!"

"—yeah, whatever. Put on the Panic Costume, let the hate flow through you, and help the villains win. That's a fast track to the minor leagues."

I rolled my eyes and shook my head. My phone buzzed in my hand. I had a new notification. About a new post on Followbook. From Peter. "You didn't!" I unlocked the screen and went to Followbook.

And there I was, in all my nine-year-old glory, lipstick and mascara covering my face and way too much blush on my cheeks. With the words "My beautiful girlfriend, Annie" written underneath. My cheeks burned. So did the rest of my head. I glared at my idiot boyfriend.

"Peter, take it down!"

"Hey, I'm home." Mom coughed once from the kitchen. "Are you packed? We've gotta get the wagon loaded. We leave tomorrow morning at first light."

"I'll take it down later," Peter said. "Let's get you packed up."

I glared at him and picked up the duffel. "Fine. Leave it up for now. Maybe it'll get you some comments for once. Go . . . deal with the books and stuff. They go in that box." I'd give him something to do if he was going to be a jerk. Something I didn't want to deal with.

I set the duffel on the bed next to the mauled shirt piles I'd so meticulously stacked, unzipped it, and started loading clothes into it.

So many clothes.

We ate boxed mac and cheese, a rotisserie chicken Mom had brought home from the grocery store, and frozen veggies. Peter sat across the table from me. Every once in a while, he'd bump a foot into mine. I smiled stupidly every time.

The chicken tasted okay. It was still hot from the store and tender enough that we didn't need knives. Mom was being polite and not smoking during dinner. She cleared her throat. "So, what are your classes, Annie?"

"Hmmmm," I stalled, chewing. When I'd signed up for classes, I'd done it by myself, and I hadn't told Mom and Dad what I was taking yet. I swallowed my mouthful of carrots and peas. "Post–Launch Day North American History, Algebra, Biology, Ilneat-Human Relations, and, uh, Intro to Drama."

I looked at Dad's face. He nodded slowly and chewed on a piece of chicken. Mom wasn't quite so polite. "You're serious about the theater thing, huh?"

"Well, yeah," I said. I tapped my fork on the table until Mom glared. "I think there's a lot of room for actors post–Launch Day. The Ilneats think we're cute or something. Wasn't their whole thing about superpowers just them wanting more superhero movies? Maybe they like other human shows, too."

"I still think law is the way to go," Mom said. "It's been twenty years. Most precedents or whatever have been set in superpower law, and it's not like there's no one to defend. I mean, Professor Panic has legal problems almost weekly—"

Peter ducked his head down, pretending to have dropped something on the floor. I snorted into my water.

"You can laugh if you want, Anika, but it's true. I bet he's paid those shark-faced lawyers hundreds of thousands over the last five years since he showed up. You could be tapping some of that money."

I snorted again. Peter was very, *very* engrossed with finding whatever he'd dropped on the kitchen floor. "Mom, the guidance counselor at school said I should follow my dreams on this one, and I did well at playing Hermia last school year. I know I can do it. I can be an actress."

"I don't know, Dot," Dad said.

I bristled a little at the unexpected betrayal and the pet name. This was supposed to be a serious conversation between three adults. Four, if you counted Peter, which I did. Sometimes.

Dad kept talking. "I think your mother's right. If you play your cards right, there's a lot of potential for a good, solid career that isn't drill fabrication or waitressing. Not that there's anything wrong with waitressing, Claire."

"No, Garret, it's alright. I get what you're saying." Mom sighed. I sighed, too. They were ganging up on me. "You have a chance neither of us did growing up, Anika. We had to go to work right out of high school. I didn't even graduate. But you can get out of here thanks to that scholarship. What was it?"

"The Daggett and Norbert Annual Full Ride?" Peter poked his head over the table, finally rejoining the conversation. "I was so mad you got it, Annie. I worked my butt off in the lab for months on my experiment. Not that I would have used it, but I wanted to beat you."

"You always do," I said, "and yet you so rarely win."

"Anyways, yeah, the . . . Daggett and Norbert Annual Full Ride," Mom said. She raised an eyebrow as she said it; the names were from her childhood. Two raccoons or beavers or something? "You need to look at the future, not just what you want to do. Someday, you'll have a family to take care of. Unless you stay with Peter and he takes over the company, your partner's probably not going to have the income to take care of everyone on his own."

"What your mother's saying, Dot, is that you're going to have to make a choice. I'll support you in whatever choice you make, but there's one that's better for your future and one that's more fun right now. We think studying law and going into superhero rights and responsibilities is the best path for you. You're already taking some of the right classes for it, so you don't have to change anything this semester. Just decide by January, okay?"

"Alright," I said, shoving a forkful of boxed mac and cheese into my mouth. I'd already decided. Or maybe the System had. Either way, I was a super, which meant acting wasn't just a viable career path. It was the *best* career path—except for Geniuses like Peter and a few other archetypes. I already had a job. At least, if I could make it to the minor leagues, I did. I didn't want to be stuck with *Small-Town Super* for the rest of my career as Understudy.

Not that I could tell my parents that. They didn't know. They *couldn't* know. And this conversation was going nowhere. "Peter, you're going to keep working at D.A.C Drillworks, right? Are you working in the same department as Dad?"

Peter stared at me for a second. I raised an eyebrow. He struggled to swallow the extra-large bite of chicken he'd been chewing, and I burst out laughing. So did Dad. Mom rolled her eyes; she was way too serious to think it was funny.

Once everyone had recovered, Peter took a big drink. "Uh, probably not. Garrett, you're in fabrication, right? I'll be in software. I have a knack for it. At least, Dad thinks I do. So I might be designing the tools you'll use by next year, but I probably won't spend much time in fabrication, which is a shame because putting stuff together sounds much more fun than designing a computer program. Hey, do you think you can show me around the fabrication floor sometime? I'd love to see it in action."

I took a deep sigh of relief as the conversation drifted toward machining and tech—stuff Peter knew a lot about. I kicked him under the table once when he started to glaze over and go Genius mode, but other than that, I could just relax.

Well, relax and eat my mac and cheese.

"Bye, Mrs. DuPont! Bye, Garret!" Peter opened the front door. Everything was packed. I had a change of clothes hanging in the bathroom, and the spare sheets were on the bed. In the end, I'd decided to take the bright pink bedding. My future roommate would just have to deal.

I followed Peter out into the late-August night and shut the trailer door. We stood there for a few seconds—long enough to make it weird. "Thanks. For, uh, taking over the conversation. It was getting awkward. They don't get it."

"Of course they don't," Peter said. He reached out, then second-guessed himself.

So I did it instead. I reached out and grabbed a hand. I pulled him in for a hug.

He returned it, then pressed his lips against mine. We stood there for a while, framed in the porch light. His hands stayed high on my back, and I could feel him shaking just a tiny bit. After what felt like an eternity, I felt him pulling away. I didn't want to let Peter go. I wanted to hold him a bit longer. But then he was standing just out of reach, arms awkwardly at his side.

He was really blurry.

I sniffled and touched my eye. My hand came back wet. Then I was sobbing. And Peter was sobbing. We hugged again, dripping wet spots on each other's shirts. "Hey, Peter, we'll make it work. We've got a plan, sort of. That's more than we had when we started out, right?

"Yeah, it is," Peter said. "I'll be busy soon. Maybe work will make the distance easier."

My eyes started to dry up as we stood there stupidly on the gravel outside my trailer. Peter cleared his throat, but I could tell it wasn't Peter anymore when he started talking.

"I'm gonna miss you, Understudy," Professor Panic whispered. "Two video calls a week. Promise?"

"Yeah, I promise. We're going to be okay." I didn't know if that was true or not. But I knew I had to say it.

"Love you, Magical Girl Understudy."

Professor Panic untangled himself from my arms. He stood there, looking miserable.

"I love you too, Peter," I said. We hugged one more time, but quickly, and then he walked away.

I watched until he went around the corner. Then I went back inside, into my room with the spare sheets. And there, sitting on my bed, was an envelope. A real, honest-to-god envelope.

I opened it. Before I could get to his letter, though, I read the first four words on the folded stationery.

Love You - Professor Panic

I folded it up and shoved it into my shorts pocket. Then I flopped myself down on the spare set of sheets on my bed and tried to shut my eyes. Tomorrow, I was going away to college.

11

Going Away to College

Sunday, August 31

I buckled my seat belt, and the decrepit station wagon cranked, chugged, and finally started up. I was crammed into one corner of the back seat with a mountain of stuff towering around me.

My stuff. For my new life away from home.

We backed onto the trailer park road, Mom at the wheel and Dad in the passenger's seat. Mom turned on the radio to some oldies station, and a simple melody filled the car. The car struggled, but picked up speed, heading for the on-ramp to the raised highway through the mountains. I pulled out the letter.

Love You - ~~Panic~~

I'd crossed out the rest of the name with eight pens and markers so my parents couldn't read it. I wasn't going to be responsible for outing Riverside's Greatest Villain. Not me!

Hey, Annie,

This world's an ugly place. And yeah, I have something to do with that in my role, but you're so beautiful, and I want you to know that.

I slipped something into your backpack. Don't worry. It's not a trap. This time. It's a gift and a promise. It's a blueprint for something to remind you of me with the clearest instructions I could write. Build him in your dorm room or somewhere private. When he's done, he'll answer to Lil Pal unless you rename him. He's a camera drone—I got the idea from one of Rocko's that crashed during the "Professor Panic Provokes the Police" Episode. He'll be fun for video chatting.

I snorted. Rocko had bitched about that drone for most of Season Two. He hadn't even made a profit off that Episode, the damn things cost so much. Peter's first Panic Pals had shown up shortly after that, but he'd denied taking the drone until Rocko got tired of asking. That was the first time Professor Panic had won an Episode, too.

I know I've been an ass the last few weeks. We talked a little about it at your place, but with your dad around, it was hard to say what I wanted. You were the only person in Riverside who got me, Annie. Not just as a nemesis and constant foil, although the Battle of Carver Street was pretty fun, wasn't it?

Yeah, it was. It'd pushed me to my limits. Season Four had been quiet. Just a few Panic Pal attacks, the time the cheerleading squad went missing, and an attack on a school board meeting. I'd almost started to think Professor Panic was calling it quits. I'd been wrong. Fighting LABRAT and Professor Panic's FEAR 1.5 power armor at the same time would have been too much except for **[Starwave Sail]**, which I got during the Act Two intermission.

Collidus is going to be an excellent rival for me. Rocko talked to me about it. You'll still be the star of Small-Town Super, *but you're on hiatus until the summer. I'm supposed to push him hard whenever you're gone, so don't come back too often. But do come back, at least until more supers show up in town.*

But he won't be able to replace you. Not in my heart. You got what it was like more than anyone else. And I'm scared. I haven't been this scared in a while. Probably since I told you who I was after our first date. I was so afraid you'd hate me. But you got it. And it felt so comfortable to be understood. No one else in town can give that to me. I'm so unprepared to be alone.

Sorry. Anyways. I just wanted to let you know that I already miss you and haven't even left your house yet. I'll text you tomorrow while you're riding over to Tokyexico.

I'd go through hell for you,
Peter

I folded the letter back up and tucked it into my backpack. I wasn't gonna cry. But I got it. I hadn't been this scared in a long time, either. I wasn't ready for this. Going away to college was scary, even when you were a superhero. Especially as a superhero.

"Hey, Dot, how you doing back there?" Dad turned around in his seat as we pulled onto the highway. His eyes locked on mine, soft and caring. "It's tough, leaving someone behind. And college isn't easy, either."

"Yeah." I shut my eyes. I didn't really want to talk about it. They couldn't possibly understand. "I didn't sleep last night. Again. I'm gonna close my eyes until we get there."

"Alright, Annie." Dad leaned over the center console and ruffled my hair. I usually hated when he did that, but right now, it felt nice. Comforting, even. I closed my eyes, put my head on my backpack, and tried to fall asleep.

[Casting Call]
[Episode: Haze-Matt's Escape from Almhurst! - R]

[Role: Hapless Sidekick! Do you accept the role? (Yes/No)]
[Role Focus: Drama+Grit]

"Arewethereyet?" I said, jolted awake by Mom's sudden braking and the **[Casting Call]** that'd popped up. My wide eyes caught sight of the massive concrete wall and steel gates. And the line of traffic waiting to get inside. And the message on the display over the Tokyexico City's entrance. "I guess not."

Attention Travelers: We are currently experiencing a major-league Episode. Please be patient and remain calm.

"No, Annie, we're not there yet. We *should* be, but the gate's locked down." Mom rolled down her window and lit up a cigarette. "The GPS says we're only about five miles away. But who knows how long that'll take?"

"Oh." I stared at the **[Casting Call]** as the car crept closer to the security booths just beyond the gateway. Most cars pulled off to a wide parking lot next to the wall.

"Think it's a Front Range mutant? Those things are terrifying," Dad said.

"Nah. They'd be hustling to get us inside, and the superheroes would be outside if it was megafauna or an insect swarm," Mom said.

I nodded as if agreeing with her. The one nice thing about Riverside was that it was too far from the Front Range for mutated megafauna. We got a few snakes from the canyonlands and occasionally a scythetooth, but for the most part, all I'd had to fight was Professor Panic. So I didn't know much about Front Range mutants—at least, not firsthand. They'd featured prominently in some of the Man vs. Nature Episodes, though.

The car crept forward, and Mom shut off the music. A guard—a minor leaguer, maybe—stuck his head in the driver's side window. "Three adults? Okay, we can't let you in. We've got an Episode running, and it's the kind where you'll be at risk the moment you drive in. The whole district's on—"

Mom flipped open her wallet and passed him a card. "I get it. I'm okay with the risk. Check-in is in twenty minutes, and honestly, this isn't our first rodeo with Episodes."

He stared at the card, eyes flicking from Mom's face to Dad's, and then to mine. Then he nodded slowly. "Alright, I'll let you in, but you must acknowledge that you'll be Extras from the moment you drive through the gates. My team and I can't vouch for your safety."

"Understood. We'll be fine." Mom took her card back and slipped it into her wallet, then tossed that into her purse before I could see what it was. I flopped back onto my backpack, disappointed. How did *Mom*, of all people, have something to get through lockdowns?

"You've never seen anything like this," the superhero guard said. "Maybe on TV. But Haze-Matt is a danger to everyone on this side of Tokyexico if the Triad can't stop him fast. Do you have air filters installed?"

"Of course," Dad said. Air filters were standard-issue equipment to cross the mountains. After Launch Day, a lot of the radioactive air settled in the big, open meadows between the peaks, and since no one lived there, it hadn't gotten cleaned very well.

"Alright, put out the cigarette and roll the windows up. Where's your destination?"

"Tokyexico University," I said. "I'm moving into the dorms."

"You'll be heading straight for the fighting. Take a left. You'll avoid the worst of it, then turn right. Don't roll the windows down or open the doors unless your car leaks. If that happens, run for the nearest building and don't breathe until you get inside. The only thing more toxic than Haze-Matt's powers is his personality." The superhero waved us through the gate, and we drove under the massive walls.

The buildings were like fingers reaching for the sky. I stared through the window at canyon walls of glass-and-steel skyscrapers towering over me. It'd been a sunny day all through the mountains, but the streets felt cold and dark. We took a right, heading south next to the wall, and drove right into the most incredible thing I'd ever seen!

A trio of identical men in red-and-gold super-suits shot through the air into a sickly-green fog bank. I wrinkled my nose at the ammonia odor even through the car's filters. As one, they flipped backward and launched a barrage of energy beams at a hulking figure in a tattered plastic bio-suit and gas mask. I pressed my face to the glass as the street exploded in front of us.

"Shit, shit, shit!" Mom yelled, swerving around potholes that hadn't been there a moment before.

The [Casting Call] blinked. I watched as even more greenish smog filled the concrete canyon. Tree leaves browned before my eyes, and I watched rust creep up a traffic light. I shook my head and declined it. Whoever Haze-Matt was, all I'd be able to do was inconvenience him. Maybe. I didn't have any resistance to poison in my build, and the last thing these major leaguers needed was a little-league sidekick getting herself into trouble.

Besides, I had a front-row seat for the action.

Haze-Matt pulled a rotating gun from . . . somewhere . . . and started filling the air with darts. One red-suited hero crashed to the ground, twitching and spasming, then another. They both vanished. The last started corkscrewing, mouth moving like he was talking to someone.

A woman in a red speed skater's suit popped out of a glowing portal a moment later and dashed toward Haze-Matt on curved, bladed stilts. "Wow! Tele-Portal," I said, staring out the window. I had a poster of her in one of the boxes in the back. Not a signed one, though.

She fired a massive cannon at the villain's feet, then at a skyscraper. Two portals connected, dropping him through the ground and out the skyscraper's side. He vomited smog from his hands and landed back on the street, but his gun crashed into a bus stop.

A mech roared upward from below the street, engines screaming as it pushed through the asphalt with a horrible tearing sound. But its massive speakers were louder. "CITIZEN, GET CLEAR! GO, GO, GO!" It spun up two shoulder-mounted fans, blowing the corrosive miasma away from us. "ATTENTION, HAZE-MATT! UNDERDELVER IS HERE! SURRENDER NOW!"

Mom floored it as the gigantic mech stomped toward Haze-Matt, claws gnashing and flamethrower sparking. We whipped around the corner, and something behind us exploded.

Everyone stayed quiet as Mom pushed the station wagon to its limits, ducking into alleys while the GPS shouted instructions at her. When we finally got onto a major road, she sighed. "Okay, I think we're clear."

"Wow," I said. With Mom relaxing, the floodgates opened. "Major-league super-heroes go hard! Did you see the lasers? And that mech-suit was way bigger than Professor Panic's stuff! Do you think the car is okay from the smog? We weren't in it for very long. It's probably fine, huh?"

I wasn't ready for that level of heroics. I had a cool light beam, not road-breaking lasers and clones. And Underdelver's mech put anything Peter would be building in the next few years to shame. Its arms alone outweighed the FEAR 2.4 power armor. I tried to look back through the wall of dorm stuff we'd packed in the back, just in case I could catch one more glimpse of the fighting.

Nothing.

I sighed and slumped down in my seat. I wanted to know who'd won. More importantly, I wanted to know how long until I could be one of those heroes.

Mom took an off-ramp into an open area at the wall's base. Shining glass buildings stood in grass fields, and manicured trees and shrubs lined the narrow streets. We drove under a sign—Tokyexico University Welcomes Incoming Freshmen and Returning Students—and followed the GPS toward Ash Hall. My stomach was in my throat, and I couldn't stop fidgeting. I'd made it to Tokyexico University and couldn't wait to start exploring my new home.

12

Exploring My New Home

Name?"

"Anika DuPont," I said, smiling at the bored-looking frat bro at Ash Hall's door. I set down my backpack and waited while he flipped through the spreadsheet on his clipboard. He scanned the first page, brow wrinkling under his backward cap. Then the second. Then back to the first. I fiddled with a loose bit of hair. Mom and Dad were already unloading the station wagon.

"You're . . . sure your last name is DuPont?"

I struggled not to roll my eyes for a second. "Uh, yeah. I'm supposed to be in Ash Hall. I filled out the paperwork online and got the confirmation email and everything." I looked over the top of the clipboard, which got a lot easier when he spun it in his hands so I could actually read it. Sure enough, there weren't any Anikas or DuPonts.

I grabbed my phone and pulled up the email. It confirmed that I had a shared room in Ash Hall. The frat bro held out his hand, and I gave him my phone.

He looked at it, nodded, and then sighed, handing it back. "There's always something like this. Every year. Every single year. I'll see if I can help you through it. I'm Barry. Are those your parents over there?"

"Yeah," I whispered. My chest felt tight. I tried to take deep breaths, but it wasn't working. "Mom, Dad, there's a problem with the dorm. I dunno what to do, but Barry says he might be able to help."

Mom bustled over. "I don't understand how there could possibly be a problem. The scholarship included room and board in the Ash Hall dorms. We signed up last month. I watched her fill out the paperwork." She looked like she wanted to say more, but between a hand squeeze from Dad and Barry's apologetic look, she realized she was talking to a college kid, not someone in charge. So she opted for a different tactic instead.

"Who's your boss, Barry? I want to see whoever's in charge."

Barry looked like he wanted to put his face in his hand. I had no such reservations and facepalmed so hard it stung. Mom was such a *Karen* sometimes.

"Okay." Barry flipped the papers on his clipboard and read the last page. "There's a protocol for this. So, 'Beaumont Administrative Building, Fourth Floor, Office 438.

Ask for Camilla Rogers.' Honestly, it's bureaucratic college junk. The protocol even says, 'If the student in question has people with them, tell the student to sign up for a campus tour.' So, uh, Mr. and Mrs. DuPont, BAB 408, Camilla Rogers. Miss DuPont, the campus tours start at the Student Union Building. It's the wide two-story in the center of campus with the arches. You can't miss it. If you see the superhero statue, you've gone too far."

"Thank you," Mom said. "I'll make sure Mrs. Rogers knows you were as helpful as possible. Garret, you go with Anika on this tour. I'll deal with the dorm room."

"I can handle campus alone, Mom," I grumbled.

"Claire, if we can't trust Annie to find her way around campus by herself, we can't leave her here, can we?" Dad ruffled my hair again. This time, I flushed and pulled away from it. "You'll be fine, Dot. We'll meet back here in an hour to unload."

"Oh no, Mr. DuPont. All the rooms in Ash Hall are full. The school has to find alternative housing for Annie. That's why you're going to Mrs. Rogers's office."

"Oh. Oh, okay." I started leaving as Mom's face turned livid and she dug into her purse for a cigarette. As I hurried away from Ash Hall, I looked back at the building that should have been my home.

Its wooden siding looked old, almost like it was a couple of years past due to be replaced. At only six floors, it was short compared to its towering neighbors but dwarfed anything I'd seen in Riverside. A few other freshmen trickled in and out of the door, carrying their stuff inside. I looked forward toward the Student Union Building. I'd have liked to get to know the other residents, but adventures awaited.

My phone buzzed.

<Hey Annie. At campus? Bet your dorm's super cool. Send pics - Peter 1:45>
<Hiya. Problem with the dorms. I'm going on a tour of campus while M+D figure it out - Annie 1:45>

I kept walking toward the campus's center, where Barry had pointed.

<Why take a tour? Explore on your own. What's the worst that could happen? - Peter 1:46>

What *was* the worst that could happen? I could get lost, for starters. The school was way bigger than Riverside. There'd been maybe ten thousand people at home. The school was advertised as having dorm space for twenty thousand incoming students. So getting lost in the dorms alone was likely. Or the Orientation Episode could start.

I opened my phone.

Please be aware that the Student Supervillain Society, a legitimate student organization, usually plans an Episode sometime during Orientation.

Yeah, the Episode could start. If it did, I'd need to be ready. For what, I didn't know.

<I'm gonna wait for a group. I'm not a TUSSA member yet. Getting involved is asking for trouble - Annie 1:48>
<Your funeral - Peter 1:48>
<Tell me when you get your new room - Peter 1:49>
<You got it! <3 - Annie 1:49>

I slipped my phone into my pocket and headed for the Student Union Building. Sure enough, a table with a banner reading Student Ambassador Tours stood next to the sliding glass doors. No one was lined up, so I waved and grinned at the girl behind the booth. She stopped chewing on her bubblegum and stared at me with mascara-covered eyes. "What?"

"Are . . . you doing tours here?" I got a better look at her. Platform Doc Martens, black skirt, fishnet top over a black tank top. Even her hair was black—except for the green highlight on her bangs.

"Sign says we are," she said, kicking back in her chair. "Next one's in ten minutes. Why don't you go inside and get a drink? It's too hot to be out here unless you have to be like me."

I nodded and turned. "Thanks. I'll be back."

She didn't respond. Instead, she reached for a handheld game console and flipped it on. She didn't want to talk, so I dipped inside the Student Union Building.

It was *cold*! I shivered as the air conditioning vomited freezing air into the cavernous main room. Dozens—maybe as many as thirty—tables lined the room's edges, each covered with brochures and swag. Rho Theta Chi Kappa, Omega Beta Theta, and a dozen other fraternities and sororities had tables. I grabbed a PΘXK pamphlet and shoved it into my backpack. Then I saw two tables at the far end of the room.

The first had put a banner across the table reading SSS: Where Supervillainy Grows Up! while the other read What Can TUSSA Do For You? Neither table had any neighbors—both the nearest tables had scooted as far away as they could. And with good reason. The students at both booths were suited up, wearing masks, and looked ready to rumble at the first sign of provocation.

"Uh, hi." I walked to the TUSSA booth and grabbed a pamphlet. If the email hadn't made it clear, these guys were clearly the heroes, and I wanted to know more about them. The cover included a hand-drawn version of one of the super students sitting behind the table. "I'm just looking for information."

"Sure you are," the superhero said, winking. He stood up and stuck out a hand. "I'm Ikenga, president of the Tokyexico University Student Superhero Association. I foretold you'd come."

"Pfft, whatever, Kingy!" A man cleared his throat, and I looked at him. He wore a full tuxedo and black domino mask. "Let me tell you all about *the superior super society* and, of course, me. I'm Monologue, head of the Student Supervillain Society. I founded this club at the end of my freshman year in response to the TUSSA becoming less and less accepting of *alternative* super lifestyles. Why don't you take a pamphlet while I tell you about our creed?"

"Uh, sure?" I looked around, noticing everyone staring at the man behind the SSS booth. And I'd been staring, too. I hadn't even realized it, but I hadn't moved the whole time he'd been talking. I shook my head to clear it. So did Ikenga.

"Monologue, if you're going to use your powers, I'll start using mine as well," Ikenga said. "Otherwise, stop."

"Go to hell, Kingy!"

"What'd I ever do to you, Logs?"

"You know what you did!"

I grabbed an SSS pamphlet, not so much because I had any interest as to defuse the tension. Then I dashed toward the bathroom. I ducked into a stall, sat down, and dropped my pack between my legs. The time was 1:56, so I grabbed the TUSSA pamphlet. Wonderful. I had four minutes to read.

Founded by superpowered students looking for others like them, the Tokyexico University Student Superhero Association welcomes all System-positive students who seek to make a positive difference while on campus. Perks of joining TUSSA include:
Belonging and Understanding
Legal Representation
*Access to the TUSSA-Cave**
Networking opportunities with Tokyexico's greatest heroes
We're proud to be sponsored by Dr. Mays, the head of the Superpower Studies department on campus. Although he also sponsors the Student Supervillain Society, please make no mistake; Dr. Mays is on our side!

Something about that statement struck me as odd. I reached for the SSS pamphlet. But just as I touched it, a System message popped up.

[Casting Call]
[Episode: The Annual Orientation Episode - PG-13]
[Role: Masked Vigilante! Do you accept the role? (Yes/No)]
[Role Focus: Flamboyance+Cunning]

"Oh shit," I muttered.

"You okay in there?"

My face flushed hot. "Yeah, I'm fine." Then I went for my phone.

<Hey, P. The Episode is happening. - Annie 2:00>
<Interfere! This is your big break! - Peter 2:00>

<Uh, no. I'm gonna stay in this bathroom until it's over - Annie 2:01>

"Are you sure you're okay in there? You've been in there since before I came in."

"Uh, yeah." I flushed the toilet to emphasize just how okay I was. Then I thought about it. No one in the bathroom had seen me come in. I could transform right here and join the fight against Monologue and the rest of the SSS's supervillains. Ikenga and TUSSA would be right there, and I'd be on my way to joining their club. It would be my big break, just like Peter said.

<Fine. I'm doing it. - Annie 2:02>

I shoved my phone into my pocket, accepted the [**Casting Call**], and started digging through my backpack for Tails. My phone buzzed in my pocket, but I ignored Peter for now. I pulled out books, a paper pad, a small pillow, and a mouse for my laptop. I felt around in the empty backpack. Then I checked the other pockets: pens, pencils, and the framed picture of the *Midsummer Night's Dream* cast.

[**The Annual Orientation Episode: Act One in Progress**]

But where was Tails? My phone buzzed again, and I pulled it out.

<Before you run off to be a heroine, I put Tails in your duffel. - Peter 2:03>
<She wouldn't fit in your pack. - Peter 2:04>

"AUGH!" I screamed. I started shoving stuff back into my backpack, chest pounding. I stuffed the jumbled mess down, punched the pillow into place, and yanked on the zipper.

"Yeah, you're not okay, honey."

"Of course I am!" I shouted, torn between embarrassment and panic. I was *not* okay! I'd just signed on for an Episode, a *minor-league* Episode, and I couldn't transform! I was a Masked Vigilante . . . with no mask!

13

No Mask

What do I do? What do I *do*?"

"Honey, I *know* you've been in a bathroom before. You've gotta take care of *that* on your own," the girl who'd been talking to me said with a laugh. She finished washing her hands, and I heard her pull a paper towel from the dispenser. The tearing sound stopped suddenly. "Hey, do you hear screaming?"

I paused halfway through putting on my backpack. Now that she mentioned it, I did hear something. Screaming. And crying. Lots of crying. "Yeah. Yeah, I do."

I took a deep breath. Okay. I was in an Episode with a role. There were known villains outside the bathroom. And I couldn't use **[Transformation Sequence]** without Tails. Which meant none of my other powers were on the table either. I'd need to avoid Monologue and any other villains.

So, it was time for a plan.

Part One: Leave the Student Union Building. Easy enough. I'd join the running, crying students. It had to be chaos out there, and I could pretend to be an Extra.

Part Two: Get to Ash Hall. I could run there, grab Tails, and find a private place. Maybe somewhere by the wall? We'd parked close to it already, between Ash Hall and the warehouses.

Part Three: Transform and kick butt. Simple enough.

The crying sounds stopped suddenly.

"Hey, Toilet Girl, we should leave."

I opened the stall and slung my pack the rest of the way over my shoulders, trying to look scared and sniffly. "Yeah. I'm Annie."

"Callie." The tall black girl in volleyball shorts and a workout top smiled quickly. Then she pointed at the exit. "You're a new student, right? This isn't my first Orientation Episode. Just stick with me, and you'll be fine."

She reached out to grab my hand, then stopped. Her nose wrinkled, and she frowned. "You should wash up first."

I washed my hands quickly, not bothering to dry them, and ran toward the door behind Callie. We poked our heads outside. Flipped tables and scattered pamphlets greeted us. Dozens of students stood in the atrium, staring at the young man in his tuxedo. Callie and I found ourselves caught staring, too.

Monologue was . . . [**Monologuing**].

"Yes, that's right, bask in my glory! I, Monologue, have returned! Once again, I shall rule over Tokyexico University with an iron fist. Speaking of which . . ." He raised a walkie-talkie. "Iron Fist, how's the bookstore going? Okay, five minutes to finish up. Don't you all move! As I said, I, Monologue, rule over your hearts and minds!

"Now, don't be alarmed. Even as we speak, my trap has been sprung! My lieutenants roam the campus, robbing your parents and friends. But I, Monologue, the Overlord of Oration, will claim the true bounty!"

He walked through the crowd, reaching into bags for wallets and talking the whole time. He'd pull the money out and then return the wallet. "My powers are beyond your comprehension—thanks for the twenties; I'll actually be able to *afford* books this year—and my skills exceed any before me!" He grabbed my backpack and dug through it.

"Your tribute to the great Monologue is wanting! Laptops are far too heavy. Where are you hiding your—*oof!*"

A satchel slammed into him, knocking him into the stairs. My backpack went flying. Monologue got his feet under him, but another bag flew across the room and clocked him in the head. A blue-haired girl in a very, *very* tight blue catsuit pointed a finger gun in the air, then at the door. I didn't know the sign, but the meaning was clear—get out.

Huh. Yeah, running seemed like a good idea. And with Monologue not talking anymore, I could actually move. I scooped up my backpack as the assembled students sprinted every which way. Callie grabbed my hand and started dragging me toward the door.

"Not so fast! You! [**Cry for Me**]! What was the name of your first dog?"

"B-B-Bubbles!" I choked out, tears already running down my cheeks. A villain in dripping mascara popped a bubblegum stick in her mouth. That was the last thing I saw clearly—tears filled my eyes. Then I felt her grab my arm, and I stumbled, sobbing, for the stairs.

"Bubbles is fine!" I shouted, lifting my arms triumphantly.

Wait a second, I thought. Something was wrong here. I tapped my fingers against the *very* comfortable armchair's arms. I'd had Charlie, and before that, I'd had Raven. But . . . there wasn't a dog before Raven.

My arms fell. "There never . . . was a Bubbles, was there?"

"You figured it out. Good job. Right on time, too."

I blinked away tears as a pair of black eyes swam into view in front of me, followed by a face I swore I'd seen before. I blinked again. Nope. The hair was wrong:

bubblegum pink. Whoever it was, her face was way, *way* too covered with runny mascara. It was caked on so thick it almost looked like a mask, and it streaked down her face in long tear lines. "Now, if you'd answer a few questions for the Sultan of Speeches here, I won't make you remember *Bridge to Terabithia*."

"Thank you for the introduction, Tearjerker. Now, I won't say too much about myself. As you already know, I'm Monologue, the greatest villain Tokyexico University's seen since Mindstorm, and champion of supervillain rights on campus. I could go on, but I won't." Monologue paused. "But, as an old video game villain said, I *could*. End [**Monologue**]."

A weight lifted from my mind. I hadn't thought a single thought the whole time he was talking. But now I could. I started going for my backpack, but Tearjerker cleared her throat and grinned ferally. "Not unless you want the end to *Toy Story 3*. Don't fucking try me."

I sighed in frustration. So did Monologue. "You only get one F-bomb in a PG-13 Episode, and I was *saving* it," he whined.

I sat back down in the comfy chair. As I looked around, I realized Tearjerker had dragged me upstairs. The room made it tough to get my bearings. Its walls had wooden siding halfway up and pictures of the university's campus and stadium in frames. A ballroom, maybe? The far side, though, was solid floor-to-ceiling glass. A few other students stood around in Costumes near the window, looking at the campus.

Callie sat next to me, also in a chair. Unlike me, she kept sobbing about *Charlotte's Web* or something. I didn't think the book was that sad, but she was definitely having big feelings.

A plan started to form in my head. One that went back to junior year at Riverside High, when I'd only barely gotten a chorus role in *Into the Woods*. I'd play the Extra. "Alright, I'll tell you what you want to know. Just keep her away from my feelings."

"Good . . . good." Monologue steepled his fingers. He bent down and stared right into my eyes, eyebrows furrowed. "Now, why did you stop by the TUSSA table first?"

I couldn't help it. I started laughing. "That's what this is about? Did you kidnap me just so I could answer *that*? I went to their table first because their banner sounded nicer. That's the only reason. I don't know the first thing about superheroes or super-villains. I was just killing time before the next tour started."

Tearjerker leaned over and whispered something to Monologue. He nodded, stroking a nearly invisible goatee. "Okay, that checks out. It's strange, though, that you'd go for the super tables so quickly. Most students ignore our clubs. Those who don't are usually looking for work-study, and our offer is better than TUSSA's. Tearjerker, check her bag. Closely, please."

Nope. Uh-uh. I grabbed my backpack and clutched it to my chest. "Why do you want my stuff?"

"Because, *random* student, I don't think you're random at all. I think there's a reason you came to our tables. And I think there's evidence in your bag! You're a super. Come, join us, and together we can rule the campus."

"No way. I'm no super," I lied, "and your pop culture references are lame."

"Oh, come on, kiddo," Tearjerker said. "Remember what happened to—"

The ballroom doors crashed open as a bench catapulted into the room, slamming into Tearjerker. The blue-clad super rushed in, tapped a chair, and sent it on the same path as the bench, then started grappling with the mascara-covered villainess.

A second later, the black superhero she'd talked to at the TUSSA table pushed through the door with a massive, red-tinted man in a toga. "Everyone, freeze! The Tokyexico University Student Superheroes are here!"

"It'll be a trap, Milo. Lockless will try to get you to follow her," Ikenga said to a red-tinted hero in a toga. The other hero nodded.

"Book it! It's the coppers!" A wiry girl in a black-and-white striped ball gown fiddled with a door. She tapped it with her cane. It popped open, and she ran through it.

The hulking red Roman ignored her and stomped toward a man with metal fists.

I'd seen enough. I had no business being in the middle of an Episode right now. I ran for the door, but Monologue started talking.

"Enough! I, Monologue, the Tyrant of Talking, say enough!" He turned toward the springy blue girl, who stopped beating up Tearjerker for a second and stared intently at his lips. It wasn't the vapid expression everyone else in the room had. Her brow wrinkled, and she dropped Tearjerker to study his face more closely as he kept going. "Springlock. You can stop me, or you can stop Tearjerker. You can't do both. Which one will—whoa!"

Springlock wrapped him in a crushing hug and flung herself—by her shoes— toward the glass windows. They crashed through the window and out of sight.

That was my cue! I started running straight toward the shattered window. I was going to leap to freedom. Hopefully, there was grass down there. Or a bush. Without superhero damage to protect me, I didn't know if I could take a full concrete hit.

The rest of the room burst into action, too. Punches and kicks flew everywhere, and Tearjerker yelled to make herself heard. "Ikenga, [**Cry for Me**]! Remember the time in *The No—*"

Everyone froze. Tearjerker midsentence, trying to take Ikenga out of the fight. The boxer and Greek wrestler midfight. And me, in the middle of jumping out the window.

Four adults had teleported into the room. They were obviously superheroes by their Costumes, but I'd never seen most of them in a single Episode before.

The first and second, a young man with a trimmed blonde goatee in a silver super-suit and a blonde woman in a black-and-white spiraled catsuit, were frozen, just like us. The third, a woman in a pantsuit with a glowing, shimmering bubble around her, started casually walking toward me. She was careful not to touch anything, especially the frozen supers. And the fourth . . .

Well . . .

"HI, DOCTOR MAYS HERE FOR . . ."

14

Hi, Dr. Mays Here For...

". . . amazing Xerlan Powder! This stuff snuffs out strange smells! Under the clutching arms? Zapped! In the sleeping rooms? Solved! It's 100% biodegradable and 100% safe for Ilneats of all ages!"

I tried to blink. But I couldn't move a muscle. All I could do was listen to Dr. Mays . . . give an infomercial? What kind of power was this? He was desperately reading the back of the box, trying to get more information on the product. Had he never seen it before?

"See this superhero? Whoo-ie! He's spent too much time in the gym and didn't have time for a shower. But with Xerlan Powder, he won't have to worry about knocking them dead with anything but his powers." He tossed a little powder onto Milo's armpits. It sizzled for a second.

Then the super in the pantsuit reached out and grabbed my arm. Her shimmering bubble ran across me the second she touched me, and I started moving toward the window, just like I'd been before Dr. Mays's advertisement. "Easy there, kiddo. Why don't you take a walk with me? You don't want to see all this."

She was wrong. Whatever Dr. Mays was doing shouldn't have been fun to watch. It was just an ad. I stopped moving toward the window. But I couldn't stop laughing.

"That's not all Xerlan Powder is good for, though! You can . . . put it in food? Yep, you can put it in food!"

I tried to resist the superheroine's pull as Dr. Mays dipped a finger into the Xerlan Powder, stuck it in his mouth, and started coughing.

So she let go, and I froze instantly again.

After a few seconds of being frozen, she grabbed my hand again. "Ready now?"

I nodded.

"Great. Put this on." She handed me a cheap, store-bought domino mask with an elastic band around the back as we walked out the ballroom's doors. "I'm Dr. Jackson. You'll be in my Superpower Ethics course, but with the Orientation Episode running, I figured you'd be happy to meet me early."

[End of Act One! Act Two in Five Minutes! No Skill Rolls Available.]

The bubble fell off me as she let go, but I could still move this time. I took a deep breath and slipped the mask on over my head. "I have a million questions. I'm not even *signed up* for Superpower Ethics! And what kind of power was that? How do you know I'm a super?"

"Not here, not now. We'll wait for the other professors, but for now, know that we know who you are, Anika. Or should I say, Magical Girl Understudy?"

That shut me up. My shoulders slumped, and I stared through the ill-fitting mask at my feet. I hadn't even been on campus an hour, and I'd already been outed. "Are you going to tell anyone?" I asked, voice small.

"Yes. The Ilneats who run the university studio already know, but we *must* register you with the deans. Otherwise, any damages you cause are on you, not our department. So I'll tell Dr. Mays, Warp Tennyson, and Mindstorm—"

"Wait, that was Mindstorm? The supervillain? You work with *Mindstorm*?" My phone buzzed in my pocket, but I ignored it. Some things were more important than Peter. Mindstorm had been *the* villain in Tokyexico—or possibly the whole North American circuit. Only a handful of heroes could keep up: Mister Felsic, Golden Goose (but she could beat *anyone*), and Stella-Lunar (Eclipse Form only, not Star or Moon).

"Yeah. She retired a few years ago. She's *fine*. If she weren't, that'd be too bad, because she's the one who identified you."

The rest of Dr. Jackson's team ran out the door. "Okay, commercial break's over. Let's get moving. Warp Tennyson, are you ready?"

"Yes." Everyone reached out to touch the silver superhero, and suddenly, our surroundings changed. I could hear poetry for a moment as Warp Tennyson finished his recitation.

Then the nausea hit me.

"Bathroom's that way. When you're finished, go to office number 743 and . . . find a seat. *Do not* talk to anyone else in there, okay?" Mindstorm said. "We've got a few more drop-offs to make, then one of us will . . . explain all this and get you registered."

I heard the poetry going again as I staggered toward the bathroom.

I opened the door to office number 743. The sounds of a dozen conversations stopped within a second of the latch clicking, and when I looked inside, I saw a dozen masked and helmeted faces staring nervously at me from folding chairs. But as soon as they realized I wasn't one of the professors who'd told them *not* to talk to anyone, the chatter picked right back up. Four doors sat around the edge of the waiting area, labeled Mays, Jackson, Tennyson, and Mindstorm.

[Guest Appearance Canceled! No Longer Cast in the Annual Orientation Episode]

There were only two seats left. Both were on either side of someone in a kangaroo fursuit. They'd covered it in an orange-and-blue hoodie and gray sweatpants that must've been 4XL or bigger, and matching orange track shoes with . . . claws covered their feet. I paused, shrugged, and sat down to their left. Whoever they were, their power wasn't even the weirdest I'd seen *today*.

"Hi . . ." The voice inside the suit was being modulated. I had no idea if the person inside was a boy or a girl.

"Hi."

"Who are you?"

"An—" I remembered I wore a mask, which made me technically in-Costume. "Magical Girl Understudy."

"Fursona." I could almost hear the person in the suit cringe.

"Ah. That makes sense." I sat quietly, ignoring Fursona and looking at the other super students around the room. A surprising number of them were in store-bought domino masks, though a few had their full Costumes on. One boy made a spark dance across his knuckles as he talked to a gigantic girl eating a sandwich. She laughed and took her final bite, then ate the napkin, too.

"So . . . cape or cowl?" Fursona asked.

Now it was my turn to cringe. "I've never heard anyone call it cape or cowl outside of the earliest Episodes. Magical Girl Understudy . . . stands for hope, justice, and peace. So, I'm a hero. What about Fursona?"

"Uh, I'm not sure. I just got contracted a week ago, and they haven't . . . found a role for me," the fursuit said. "Probably a hero."

I looked at the suit. It had a thin neck, gigantic ears, and a surprisingly fluffy tail for a kangaroo. "So, why a kangaroo?"

"That . . . is an excellent question. I have no idea. I was in my uncle's basement with my girlfriend, and we found it. The System hit me with the contracting message when I tried it on. So, of *course* I said yes. I didn't realize my powers were gonna get tied to the suit. So then Jessie dumped me once she realized I was *keeping* the suit, and I had to carry it home, aaand I'm oversharing again. Sorry."

Jessie sounded like a bitch, but the door clicked before I could tell Fursona that. The professors and a pair of green-looking students came in.

"Alright, aspiring young supers. We'll call you one at a time. First up is Fursona with me," Dr. Mays said, "and Flare with Dr. Jackson. When you're done, see Dr. Mindstorm. Tennyson, you know what to do while we're waiting?"

"Sure do. I'll be back soon." Poetry swelled, and Warp Tennyson disappeared.

Fursona stood up. "Well, I guess this is it." They gulped audibly through the voice modulator and hopped to Dr. Mays's door. The selected students vanished into the offices.

I stayed in my seat, twiddling my thumbs. A few kids made whispered small talk, but with the offices occupied, the waiting room quickly grew silent. Tennyson teleported back several times, handing a gizmo to one student or a folded Costume to another. I wondered if he'd come back with Tails one of these times.

"Yo, Magical Girl Understudy," the boy with the sparks said from Dr. Jackson's door. "You're up!"

I stood up and walked over while he held the door. Then I stepped inside.

"Have a seat."

I shut the door and flopped into an overstuffed armchair on one side of the desk.

Dr. Jackson sat in a computer chair on the other side. She typed on her computer for a minute. Then she cleared her throat. "Alright, would you prefer to be Anika DuPont or Magical Girl Understudy for this meeting?"

Did I get a choice? "Just Understudy is fine."

"Noted. Now, Understudy, I want to apologize for the way today started. We designed Miss Barber's email as a brainworm with Mindstorm's help. It plants the idea of interfering with the SSS's Episode in supers' heads, which makes identifying you in person easier. We already knew Anika DuPont was Understudy from the Ilneats—Rocko is thrilled to be working with the university—but it's easier if supers reveal themselves early in the year. It gives the clubs a way to identify you.

"Now, with the apology out of the way, we have a choice of issues to tackle. The most commonly asked about is the dormitory problem, followed by our change to your schedule. But we also have to cover what you can and, more importantly, *can't* do on Tokyexico University's campus. And finally, there's power registration."

My mind whirled. The Orientation Episode was a setup? My professors had canceled my dorm room? And they were messing with my classes? "Mom and Dad were going to deal with the dorm . . ." I started.

"No, they weren't. They're on a run-around between different offices until we get things hashed out here. Typically, we offer super students their choice of lairs and secret bases around campus. For example, when Dr. Mindstorm studied here a decade ago, she had a bunker under a certain building on campus. And Lightbeam had a tower penthouse. They're a step up from a typical student's dorm but also have some responsibilities. You'll get an email about those." Dr. Jackson turned the computer screen so I could take a look. "Now, we have several varieties to choose from. Does your power set support flying?"

"Yeah. I can summon a sailboard and ride it." All the choices blew me away. Genius lairs below the technical buildings, a hidden treehouse somewhere by the agricultural college, and even an underwater lair in a pond. She couldn't tell me where any of the hideouts were for security reasons, but Dr. Jackson told me everything else I wanted to know.

In the end, with her guidance, I chose a flat on the top floor of Walnut Tower. It'd be subtle enough that I could have an occasional unpowered friend over. It wasn't decorated and hadn't been used the year prior. But it had soundproofing, a secret room for my superhero stuff, and a wide balcony for takeoffs and landings. Plus, like, an *actual* kitchen and a bathroom I wouldn't have to share.

"Now." Dr. Jackson cleared her throat. "We have some minor scheduling adjustments. You're dropping Biology to pick up Superpower Ethics with me. It'll appear as Biology on your transcripts, though. It's part of the minor or associate's degree in Superhero Studies program at Tokyexico University. The rest of the program is Archetypes and Builds, Combat Styles, Team Composition, Extra Public Relations, and Episode Manipulation. That last one comes much, much later, though."

I thought about it. I was so thrilled to have my own apartment that I'd have agreed to just about anything. As I was about to say yes, though, Dr. Tennyson slid through the door. "Your familiar was, by far, the hardest thing for me to get. Next time, keep it with you." He tossed Tails to me, and I caught her.

"Thank you, Tennyson." Dr. Jackson cleared her throat again. "We'll do a quick overview of expectations, and then I'll send you to Dr. Mindstorm. She'll take care of your super student registration."

Super Student Registration

As a super student, you'll need to choose whether to join the Tokyexico University Student Superhero Association, the Student Supervillain Society, or remain a vigilante," Dr. Jackson said. She cleared her throat and typed for a moment. "Given your current show with Rocko Productions, you'll want TUSSA, but there are advantages to all three."

"I'm definitely joining the . . ." I paused. I was 100% a hero. For sure. But . . . "What are the advantages of joining the SSS?"

Dr. Jackson laughed. "Some students don't catch that. You're in real danger, though, of getting typecast. Lots of little-league heroes get stuck there because the Ilneat producers want their shows to be successful. I'm sure you're hearing something like that from Rocko. Most of us did at some point. Going rogue during your college years can be an excellent way to force a transition to the minor leagues. It does have risks, though."

She cleared her throat, holding up a hand. "You probably saw their booths today. TUSSA and the SSS put on a couple of events throughout the year for recruiting. You shouldn't feel pressured to choose until they reach out to you. Now, are you ready to hear about your other responsibilities?"

I tried to listen but was too busy thinking about the apartment—and, more importantly, my options. I'd never considered going Dark Girl, but it made a lot of sense now that I thought about it. It'd be a scary possible future. Dark Girls ended up in some pretty crazy situations. Still, Rocko wanted me for *Small-Town Super*, but if I didn't fit the casting anymore, I could move up to the minor leagues.

"So, to sum up, you'll need to participate in at least one Episode each semester, you're required to complete a minor or associate's in Superpower Studies by the time you graduate, and you'll work as an intern—a sidekick or lieutenant—with a major-league hero or villain once a month starting in October, if you can get hired. If you choose to join TUSSA or the SSS, you'll also need to maintain good standing with them. As a vigilante hero, that requirement doesn't exist, but going solo has its own difficulties and dangers. Any questions?"

"Yes, actually," I said. "How do I get into my new apartment?"

"Right." Dr. Jackson dug into her desk and found a set of two key cards and two physical keys. "Since you're a super student, your apartment serves as your fortress of solitude, as it were. You'll need the key card and physical key to get in the first time. After that, you can keep it as secure as you think it should be. There should also be a set of keys in the kitchen drawers somewhere. That'll get you into the stairwell to your balcony."

"Thanks. One more. What does your power do? Why do you go by Dr. Jackson?"

Dr. Jackson grinned. "My power disconnects me from the System, along with anyone I'm touching. Superpowers don't affect me. Dr. Mays and I have been partners for almost a decade. He's a great sidekick. But I keep my name because, effectively, I have no superpowers. And neither does anyone I'm touching if I choose not to let them.

"That should about do it. Other information will be in an email. Dr. Mindstorm's office is next door for registration. On your way out, could you call Gourmet in? Thank you." Dr. Jackson held out a hand, and I shook it.

"Thanks for the apartment, Dr. Jackson," I said. I had a lot to think about and not much time to do it. I headed for the door.

"Gourmet, Dr. Jackson is ready for you," I called.

The girl who'd eaten the sandwich and bag stood up. She had an empty can of soda; as she took a quick bite of it, her skin, jeans, and pleather jacket took on a metallic hue. So did her domino mask.

"Thanks." She pocketed the can and stood up. "Hey, do you want to grab dinner later?"

"Uh, no thanks." Something about her seemed off. I decided it was the bite mark missing from the can. "My parents are dropping me off, so we were going to get something."

"That's too bad. I'm starving, and you look like a snack! Haha!" Gourmet walked toward me, and I made room for her to go past. The look in her eyes made me shiver. She wasn't flirting. I squeezed Tails to my chest. Then she was past me and inside Dr. Jackson's office.

I opened the door to Dr. Mindstorm's office and quickly shut it. "Sorry, Fursona," I muttered.

"It's fine. They were just . . . leaving," the professor in the hypnotic spiral suit said.

As Fursona walked past me with their head down, I gulped and stepped into the villain's lair. The door shut behind me, and I was alone with a major-league supervillain.

"Do not sit, Anika Jane DuPont, aka Magical Girl Understudy," Dr. Mindstorm said curtly. She slid a form toward me and pointed at one spot after another. "The school says I have to get permission from students before I do this, so . . . please sign here. Here. Here. And initial here and here. It's a release from liability if I damage your mind."

I looked up from where I was signing my name for the second time. "Wait, what?"

"Look, the quickest way to register you is for me to share your mind while you're accessing your System. It's painless . . . unless you resist." She yawned, looking vaguely irritated. "Please don't resist. Someone always does, and then it's weeks of therapy for *both* of us. You for a snapped mind, and me for relapsing. Are you done yet?"

I paused. Nothing about her attitude screamed threatening. More . . . bored out of her mind. So I quickly signed and initialed all six pages while Mindstorm explained what each spot was for. I slid the paper back to her. "What now?"

<[Transformation Sequence],> Mindstorm's voice echoed in my head.

<Wait, what? What's going on right meow?> Tails asked.

My body held up Tails. "I swear on my family, who I love very much, that I'll stand up against Professor Panther, his minions, and evil all over Riverside! I'll fight for justice, peace, and hope! And I'll never stop 'til evil does first!"

<Quit being embarrassed. This isn't even in the top fifty worst sequences I've seen. Magical Girl Honeycomb has it much worse. Not that she goes here, but I've seen it.>

I wasn't *embarrassed*. I was so far beyond embarrassed it wasn't even funny. If my **[Transformation Sequence]** embarrassed me by myself in my bedroom, it was utterly humiliating to be watching it with a professor in my head. It went on and on, the spins, choral music, and light show seemingly endless.

When it finally stopped, I breathed for a couple of seconds. "Is that it?"

<Oh, you sweet summer child. No. [System Menu].>

[Alias - Understudy] [Archetype - Magical Girl] [Community Rank - 479/523]
[HP 6/6]
[Styles and Skills]
▶ Archetype Skill - Transformation Sequence
▶ Badass (18)
▶ Cunning (49)
▶ Inkling 1
▶ Drama (3)
▶ Stellar Ray 1
▶ Hometown Heroine 1
▶ Flamboyance (37)
▶ Signature Skill - Adaptive Armoire 1
▶ Stored Costumes: (Lab Assistant Panic)
▶ Starwave Sail 1
▶ Grit (27)
▶ Rejuvenation 1

<Nya, nya! You can't be doing that!> Tails's voice echoed in my head. <That's private!>

<Calm down, cat. I just need to take a look at a few abilities. Most of these are generics. Oooh, you're under-leveled—small town, not much opposition? Monthly stacking Style Point penalties? Don't bother answering. [Adaptive Armoire] is interesting, though. Let's take a closer look.>

[Costume - Lab Assistant Panic]
[HP 6/6]
[Styles and Skills]
▶ Archetype Skill - Transformation Sequence
▶ Badass
▶ Cunning
▶ Speed-Hacker 0
▶ Drama
▶ Hypercompression Cannon 1
▶ Hometown Heroine 1
▶ Flamboyance
▶ Signature Skill - Adaptive Armoire 1
▶ Stored Costumes: (Understudy)
▶ Maniacal Reveal 0
▶ Grit
▶ Rejuvenation 1

<Okay, you're all registered. Untransforming now,> Mindstorm's voice echoed in my head, then in my ears, as I swapped back to my street clothes and the cheap mask. "We'll do this again at the beginning of classes next year. I know you're considering moving up to the minor leagues, but you're behind most of your fellow students. If I were you, I'd focus on sidekick work with some higher-end heroes. Now, I've got about a dozen more supers to look at today. Your parents are in the lobby. And just in case you're worried, I'm bound not to share anything I've learned today outside of registration information. Your secrets are safe with me. All of them."

I took the elevator down, Tails stuffed into my backpack with her head and front paws sticking out—Peter had been right about not having enough space. Muzak played softly in the background, and a poster in one corner showed a superhero—the same one who'd cloned himself to fight Haze-Matt—with his thumbs up. Lightbeam.

Be the People You Want to Be!

I rolled my eyes and fidgeted with a strand of hair. That poster seemed . . . forced. But it had a good point. Back in Riverside, I'd been the best. But looking at my System Menu, I had to admit the truth. I'd been a small fish in an even smaller pond.

But Tokyexico was the ocean, and some of the supers here were sharks. Or octopi. Or . . . I don't know, whales? Whatever, the point was that I wasn't a big deal here.

I still felt shaky from Mindstorm's mind control. I'd agreed to it, of course, and she hadn't done anything malicious. The paperwork had even warned me I'd feel shivery and sick for a few minutes. But even so, it didn't feel great. I made a mental note not to goof around in any class Mindstorm taught.

My phone buzzed. I pulled it out and checked it.

<Understudy, just checking in? How's the Episode? - PP 2:16>
<Are you winning? - Peter 2:47>
<Not even close.> - Annie 2:47>
<I didn't have Tails. I got kidnapped. The professors had to save me. - Annie 2:48>

I put the phone back in my pocket. It buzzed again, but I ignored it. It was Peter's fault. I might have been a small fish in the ocean, but I could have done *something* if I'd been able to transform. He could wait a minute for more details.

So. What kind of person did I want to be? Dr. Jackson had given me a choice between heroics, villainy, and vigilantism. And while Dr. Mindstorm—the greatest villain Tokyexico had known for *three* seasons—had recommended I stay a little leaguer, she hadn't *told* me I couldn't try. I started planning. Then the elevator dinged, and the doors opened.

"Annie! We have exciting news!" Mom said. She squeezed me in a gigantic hug. "We got you a dorm room!"

"I know. I got the keys," I said, digging in my pocket for them. "When the supervillains attacked, a professor took the tour group to her office to stay safe. We worked stuff out there, and I grabbed the keys on the way down. Do you know where it is?"

"Sure do, Dot," Dad said. "They told us to wait for you here, but the lady who finally helped us gave us a map to Walnut Tower."

"Great! Let's go!" I started running toward the door, parents following.

We walked back to Ash Hall. Occasionally, something crashed nearby as a superhero and supervillain fought each other, but for the most part, it seemed like the Orientation Episode had run its course. And I hadn't done a single thing. How could I, with no transformation? Being a Magical Girl *sucked* sometimes!

But at least it wasn't as bad as in anime. Those girls had it *rough*!

Mom drove the car down a winding street to the base of a towering building near the wall. I peered out the window. The windows grew wider near the top, and a wide railing crossed the dorm building's edge. "Do you know the room number?" I asked. Dr. Jackson hadn't actually told me, and the keys didn't say.

"Sure did," Dad said. He pulled out the map and read a handwritten note on it. "Looks like it's near the top. Walnut Tower, Room 1301."

16

Walnut Tower, Room 1301

You're *sure* we're not paying anything for this, Claire?" Dad asked.

Mom shook her head. "Ms. Rogers said it was vacant, and they had Annie's application on record. TU claims they don't know how her room got double-booked, but those imbeciles sure are paying for it now. No charge."

I shoved the physical key into the lock, slid the key card in, and turned the handle. The door hummed for a second. Then the lock clicked open, and I opened the door to paradise.

I'd stayed in a hotel once on a class trip to Tokyexico City in seventh grade. We'd gone to see the Pre-Launch Museum and the zoo. Emma and I had shared a room on the sixth floor. I'd spent most of the evening sitting on the incredibly soft couch just watching the sunset over the wall, then climbed into the ridiculously comfortable bed; I'd bounced on the mattress a few times. It was so springy! I'd fallen asleep before my head hit the pillows—three of them!

It was the most luxurious night's sleep I'd ever had. It'd taken me weeks to get used to my old mattress again.

"You're absolutely sure we're not paying for this?" Dad asked again with a nervous laugh.

I totally got it. Walnut Tower, Room 1301, made the hotel feel like my old bedroom. And I was going to explore every inch of it! It was, after all, my bat-cave! My fortress of solitude! My Stark Tower—okay, that got blown up, so bad example, but still—it was mine!

I ran through the combination living room/kitchen and down a hall to a bedroom with expansive, floor-to-ceiling windows covered in blackout shades. The bed was almost as big as my bedroom in the trailer, and when I jumped into it, the comforter and sheet swallowed me whole.

"What a fabulous room!" Mom said. She sniffed the air and nodded approvingly. "It's been cleaned in the last day or two as well. Smell it."

I flailed free of the bed's feathery jaws and sniffed. Sure enough, the cleaning supplies' sharp, hospital scent filled my nostrils, and I sneezed. The whole place smelled disgustingly clean. Not like home at all, where the mix of trash that I hadn't taken out and cigarette smoke dominated the double-wide.

I pulled out my phone and started snapping pictures. Peter's message had sat unread and unanswered, so I took a look. The pics were for him anyways.

<I'm sorry! I didn't think you'd need her today, or if you did, you'd be close - Peter 2:48>

<It's fine. I forgive you. Check this dorm room out! I'll explain later! (eight images attached) - Annie 3:21>

A door had Dad's attention. He fiddled with the handle, thumped on it a few times, and read the label. "Maintenance, huh? Well, I guess a place like this would have its own cleaning supplies."

I stared. That door *definitely* wasn't for maintenance. It probably led up to the railing-lined roof where my balcony was, and to my secret lair. Mom and Dad couldn't find those. No way. I had to distract them.

And more importantly, I wanted to check those places out myself!

"Yeah, Dad. It would." I slipped into the kitchen and started opening drawers. They had silverware—actual silverware, not a few plastic sporks like the hotel—and inside one drawer, I found a letter with a key taped to it. I folded it up while Mom checked out the bathroom and shoved it into my ever-fuller pocket. Then I skipped to the bedroom. "I'm going to start getting organized. Mom, Dad, could you bring things up from the car?"

"Sure, Dot," Dad said. He followed me into the bedroom and wrapped me in a bear hug before I could unzip my duffel. "Hey, kiddo, I'm proud of you. No one on my side of the family's ever been to college, and Mom's sister only made it through two years before Launch Day. You're gonna do great things here."

"I know," I said. I believed him, too. I might be under-leveled compared to the other superheroes in town, but I knew I could catch up with a bit of work. Or a *lot* of work. I'd be the best Magical Girl in the minor leagues soon. Maybe even up there in the majors with Stella-Lunar! And, uh, classes would go okay, too, I guess, since that's what he was talking about.

He let go, grabbing a key card from the kitchen table, and he and Mom disappeared. Finally, I was alone. I had time to explore the *rest* of the apartment—three or four minutes, even.

Or did I?

Sure, I could sneak up onto the roof or the balcony, wherever it was. And I could check out the *obviously cool* secret rooms hidden behind the maintenance door. But if Mom and Dad came back, it'd be tough to explain why I'd been back there. Maybe even impossible.

Or I could . . . wait until later. *Ugh.*

Just a peek couldn't hurt, right? I pulled the key off its tape, tucking the letter under the bed's too-cozy pillows. I'd stick my head in and take a quick look.

I hustled to the door, unlocked it, and stared at . . . a big, empty room with a flight of metal stairs in one corner.

Really? That was it? I shut the door, then opened it again in case some previous superhero had a power that changed it or made it weird. An internet site I'd found once was filled with stories about doors that opened to strange places. Maybe it was like that?

No luck. The answer had to be in the letter. I shut the door and headed toward my room, but the door hummed and clicked before I could dig it out.

"Hey, Dot, help your mom with this stuff!"

"Alright!" I hurried over as my parents came in. Had they unloaded the *whole* car? I helped Mom set down the stack of boxes she'd somehow maneuvered into the elevator. "Is there anything left down there?"

"Not really," Mom said. "Now, what do we *need* to take care of, and what can wait? We'll take you out to dinner—our treat—to celebrate this new chapter in your life. Then we have to go. It's a long drive back to Riverside."

"Sushi, really?" Dad asked.

"Yep! We're not in the city every day," Mom replied as we parked the car outside of No More Mr. Rice Guy Kaiten-Zushi, which the internet had marked as the Japanese restaurant nearest to Tokyexico University. "This is a chance to expand our horizons and try something new."

The drive across campus had been uneventful, aside from a **[Casting Call]** for a minor-league Episode the second we'd left. Part of me wanted to accept, but I was *definitely* out for dinner with my parents, and I had a lot to do before classes started tomorrow, so I'd declined. I followed my mom and somewhat reluctant-looking dad toward the kitschy-looking doors and stepped inside.

A soft buzzing and clattering almost drowned out the even quieter music. I stood and watched as tiny plates with a roll of sushi or fish and brown sauce slid by a large table in the room's center on a conveyor belt. Mom waved us to an open booth with one end flush to the clattering belt off in a corner.

After a minute, a waitress walked over. I took a quick look at her and started staring at the sushi plates as they marched past—I wasn't quite sure, but she looked a *lot* like the girl who'd run out of the restroom with me during the Episode. The one who'd called me Toilet Girl.

"Hi, I'm Callie, and I'll be taking care of you all tonight! Have you ever been to a Kaiten-Zushi restaurant before? No? That's totally fine. I'll explain how it works. You'll be experts in no time. Sushi, sashimi, and other food slides by on the conveyor. You just grab what you want, eat it, and stack the plate up. I'll calculate your bill by the plates you took. They're all labeled, so you know what you're getting into."

I watched something go by with rice, seaweed, and fish. I had no idea what it was called, and it passed too quickly to see what was in it. "Is there a menu or a list of what things are?" I asked, still staring as the conveyor belt pulled dish after dish into a gap in the wall beside us.

"Yes. I'll get your table one. Each dish is also labeled, like I said. I'll start you off with some water. If you have any questions, let me know!"

<Hey, Annie. All moved in yet? I can't wait to visit you. That room looks really cool! Let me know when you want to video call. - Peter 3:57>

<Will do. I'm out with my parents, but I'll be free to text later tonight. - Annie 4:01>

"What's your plan with Peter?" Mom asked as she grabbed a plate with a bunch of grapes and a few slices of orange-pink fruit that smelled ridiculously sweet.

I blushed and tucked the phone away. "We're going to video call a few times a week, and I'll visit him when I come home. He might . . . he might also try to come here, but it depends on his schedule with the company. We'll make it work." Hopefully, I didn't say out loud.

But Mom read it on my face anyway. "Alright. Clearly, not something you want to talk about. I hope things work out for you two. You're good for him, and he'll be good for you once he grows up a little. *If* he grows up a little. They don't always." She glanced at Dad, who'd harpooned a California roll and shoved it into his mouth.

I snorted as he struggled to chew the entire thing all at once. But soon enough, I found myself fiddling with my hair and watching the food go by. It all looked great, but my stomach wouldn't stop churning. I'd gone from the top-rated super in Riverside to the bottom 10% in Tokyexico City. And, while I'd gotten through high school just fine, I'd struggled with a bunch of classes I'd need to graduate college. Algebra. History. Even some of the stuff on Ilneats. Sure, I knew one or two: Rocko, Pataki, and a couple of others from the studio. But that didn't mean I knew anything *about* them.

And I'd be away from home. I'd never *been* away from home for this long. It'd be at least a month before I got back to Riverside. Back to my *real* bedroom—the one that smelled like cigarettes and barely had room for my twin bed.

"Mom . . . Dad . . . what if school doesn't go as well as we hope? What if it's all too hard and I need to come home for a while?"

Mom paused halfway through dipping a roll in a dish of salty-smelling soy. "Then you'll come home, and I'll pull some strings at work. You can get a part-time job waitressing until you're ready to find something more serious. Anika, you're supported and loved, and we're not just cutting you loose in the big city, okay?"

"Okay," I said, still feeling sick.

"Dot, you're gonna do just fine. Keep doing your best, just like you did all through high school. It's gonna be scary for a few days. But remember that everyone in Walnut Tower and your classes are in the same boat you are."

I rolled my eyes.

He stared at me until I stopped. "They are. No one here's ever lived away from home before. Make some friends, be yourself, and work hard. That's all there is to a place like this."

I nodded. He was speaking as if he had experience with college, even though he didn't. Then again, maybe he'd done something similar when he moved to Riverside.

He reached across my space and grabbed a plate. "Now eat this. You're a mopey grump when you haven't eaten, and all you've had today is two waffles at breakfast. We'll drop you off at your apartment after."

"Thanks, Dad," I said, pushing back tears. I popped the sushi into my mouth after drowning it in soy sauce. He was right. Food *did* make me feel better. And I had to keep my energy up. I had a lot to do once they left—like getting ready for my classes, making sure I knew where to go, and of course, exploring a secret base!

17

Secret Base

Bye, Mom! Bye, Dad!"

Mom flipped the headlights on and backed the station wagon out of its parking space. Hands stuck out the window, waving at me. I waved back, heart dropping and stomach in my throat. I waved until the station wagon started moving forward. Until it went around the corner. And until it disappeared down the road, heading back toward Riverside.

It was a long drive home. I'd told them to text when they arrived, but I'd probably be asleep already. I'd call Dad tomorrow, though.

My phone buzzed. I ignored it and looked around instead. I wasn't the only student saying goodbye to their parents. Lots of cars pulled out of the lot, and other students were tearing up like me.

Oh yeah, I definitely cried. Outside of a few field trips and sleepovers, I'd never spent a night away from my parents. Now I had weeks—at least—before I'd see them again.

I headed for the elevator, slipped in, and pressed the 13 button. But I wasn't alone. Other students piled in until I found myself squished between a well-muscled guy in a football jersey and a tiny Asian girl.

She grinned at me awkwardly. "Hi."

"Hi," I said.

She peered up at me through thick glasses for a moment, then looked toward the front of the elevator. The elevator started rising. Then it stopped, and a handful of people got off, including the hulking jock. With a bit of space to move, I pulled out my phone.

<Let me know when you're available. - Peter 6:45>
<Heading back to my room. Parents just left. Gonna explore and text you. - Annie 6:46>

Part of me didn't want to talk to Peter while I was exploring. But really, I'd be grateful for the company, even if it were digital.

More and more people got off on every floor. Finally, we hit floor 11, and the elevator emptied, except for the girl who'd said hi to me.

"Uh, I'm Su-Bin. I'm in room 1232."

"Anika. You can call me Annie, though. Room 1301."

"Wow, all the way on the top? You must be a big shot, Annie," Su-Bin said. "I heard those apartments cost a fortune to rent. Not that the 1200s are bad at all."

I shook my head. I didn't want Su-Bin getting the wrong impression about me. Or worse, the right one; keeping my superhero status a secret had to be priority number one! So I started talking.

"Actually, no. I'm from Riverside. I grew up in a trailer park, and I got into TU on a full ride, or I wouldn't be here. Right now, my apartment's kind of a mess, but when I've got it looking the way I want it, why don't you come over?"

"You want to be friends?" Su-Bin asked.

I nodded. The elevator dinged, and the doors opened.

"Sure, I'd like that. I could use a friend around here. This is my stop, but I'll see you later, Annie. Room 1232, okay?"

I nodded again. "Room 1301."

Then she stepped off, leaving me alone in the elevator.

"Dammit. We should have traded numbers," I muttered once I was safely inside my room. I hung up a shirt and skirt for tomorrow—first impressions are important, you know—and tossed Tails onto my bed. Then I got my backpack ready, checked my phone for my schedule (Post–Launch Day North American History at nine, Superpower Ethics at eleven, and Intro to Drama at two), and made sure I had my laptop and notebooks.

Then I was ready.

I pulled out Dr. Jackson's letter.

To the Occupant of Room 1301,

Congratulations on choosing a flight-power-compatible secret base/lair apartment. Your base has a connecting staircase to the roof and a balcony area that is yours. We strongly recommend you only go up there in your superhero suit, as the fall would be deadly without your powers. Additionally, should you decide to team up with another student hero or villain, there is an elevator from the basement up to your room. It requires input from you in order to start; just listen for the buzz. It will arrive in your secret base.

As with all secret bases and lairs on TU's campus, you'll notice a space that appears to be nothing more than an empty room. In this apartment's case, it's hidden behind the maintenance closet door. We strongly discourage you from decorating it or moving too many things into it in the first week. Instead, spend time in it while in your superhero or villain persona, and it will change itself to match your preferences.

For those uninterested in the technical aspects behind this room, attribute it to Fang Swee's power. If you're interested, please read on.

I stopped reading. I didn't care why it worked. If the room wanted me in my Costume, I'd be in my Costume. I grabbed Tails. "Come on. We've got a room to explore!"

One **[Transformation Sequence]** later, I unlocked the maintenance closet and peered inside. The bare linoleum floor and plain drywall greeted me again. This time, I stepped inside and looked around.

The room wasn't much—certainly no bigger than my bedroom. Uh, my new one, that is. "Hello?" I shouted.

". . . ello . . ." The room echoed back at me. What it lacked in aesthetics it made up for in acoustics! I looked around for something—anything—that made part of the room stand out. But its plain white walls and fluorescent lights just looked . . . boring.

<So, what's with the fancy apartment, anyways? - Peter 7:03>
<No clue. Some professors gave it to me as a 'secret base' - Annie 7:04>
<Oh, I had one of those - Peter 7:04>

I sighed and headed for the stairs. Peter *loved* to rub his secret lair in my face. I'd spent so much time in Season Five running Investigative Episodes to figure out where he made so *many* Panic Pals. I'd narrowed it down to "under the D.A.C. Drillworks' main building" or "below the treehouse in his yard," but then summer ended. I shrugged. It was Collidus's problem now.

<Yeah, well, this one's better than yours. - Annie 7:05>

The steel grate stairs led up to a door, which I opened and stepped through. Sure enough, I had a large, expansive balcony to use as a landing pad, with smooth concrete and steel railings around the edges. I walked to the steel bar and looked at the sprawling campus. A few students walked down the wide cement sidewalk that wound from one end of Tokyexico University to the other. A couple other dorms reached the same height as Walnut Tower, but most of the other buildings were much shorter. Even from my thirteen floors up, I could tell that the skyscrapers in most of Tokyexico City dwarfed anything on campus.

<Uh-huh. Sure. I'll tell you what. You promise not to tell Collidus where it is, and I'll show it to you next time you're in Riverside. - Peter 7:08>
<Only thing is, you have to trust me! - Professor Panic 7:08>

I laughed. Trusting Professor Panic was pretty tough!

<I trust Peter. Is that good enough? - Annie 7:08>

While I waited for a response, I turned to the west. The wall covered the mountains we'd driven through to get here.

The wall.

Back in Riverside, we hadn't had to worry much about megafauna. A few made it across the mountains or trickled in from the desert, but nothing outrageous. I wondered why Tokyexico City had such a problem with them that they needed a wall. Migration patterns, or just the number of people in one area?

On the other hand, the sunset over its top was stunning. Bright-pink-and-orange clouds seemed to scrape against the wall's silhouette and brush against the towers cresting its summit. I watched as the light faded into a deep purple.

<It'll have to do, Annie. If you play the damsel in distress, we'll have plenty of fun! - Professor Panic 7:12>

<"Oh no, I've been kidnapped! What does Riverside's Greatest Villain have in store for me?" - Annie 7:13>

<Exactly! I'll blindfold you and sneak you into my lair - Professor Panic 7:13>

<That way you can't find it later - Professor Panic 7:14>

<"I have to escape before I find out!" ;) - Annie 7:14>

I laughed again, feeling a little heat in my cheeks, and headed downstairs. *That* game was a lot of fun when Peter and I were in the mood. As I passed through the empty room, I paused. The lights seemed dimmer. And were the walls a touch more . . . pink? "Well, that was fast. I wonder what it's making?"

I'd see tomorrow morning, at least in part. Right now, I had some serious thinking to do. I ducked out the "maintenance" door, untransformed, and grabbed the pamphlets off my bedroom floor. Then I curled up in bed and read the Student Supervillain Society's brochure.

Do you fear a life unlived? Does your power set lend itself to nefarious acts in the dark? Did your producer fast-track you to EVIL?

The Student Supervillain Society might be for you!

We offer perks like:

Rent-a-Hench - Have a job that needs some muscle? Our Rent-a-Hench service gives you no-questions-asked labor when and where you need it! Available in low-powered and unpowered varieties.

Networking - The best villains—from yesterday, today, and tomorrow—have connections with the SSS! Working with us opens doors for future henching and lieutenant work with villains like Longshot, Haze-Matt, and many others!

Episodes of all ratings - Are you a little-league villain? An up-and-coming minor leaguer? Or even a future major-league city dominator looking to make their break? We offer assistance plotting the perfect Episode to make superheroes sweat—and make you rich!

Looking to start a career in supervillainy? Come to our informational meeting on Wednesday, September 2, at 7:30 p.m. in the Student Union Building's Oak Room.

No power? Still want to participate? Sign up for our Rent-a-Hench program and get paid today. Work-study is available for those who qualify.

Well . . . if I were picking a club to join just based on their perks, I'd go with the SSS. Rent-a-Hench seemed a lot more useful than access to the TUSSA Cave, whatever that was. And other than that Monologue was a self-centered egomaniac (which, honestly, might just be his power talking) the villains I'd met so far didn't seem any worse than the campus heroes.

But could I actually *be* a villain?

I mean, I definitely *could*. The perks were terrific! Plus, it'd force Rocko to move me up to the minor leagues, which I wanted more than *anything*. But I'd grown up a hero. And not just a hero, but a Magical Girl—the one superhero that needed to swear a stupid oath every time she wanted to access her powers. Going evil would be hard. Maybe even impossible.

I had to ask an expert.

<Hey, could I cut it as a villain? - Annie 7:28>
<Ahahahahaha! - Peter 7:28>
<No - Peter 7:29>
<Why not? Dark Magical Girls happen all the time! I could do it! - Annie 7:29>
<No, you couldn't. Being a villain isn't just about style or schemes. It's about being willing to destroy, threaten, and hurt to get what you want. And you don't have that, Annie. That's one thing about you that you won't be able to change. And it's something I like about you - Peter 7:31>
<Oh. Yeah, that makes sense. - Annie 7:32>

Well, the expert had spoken. And Peter thought it'd be a bad fit. But was he right?

No. I'd *been* Lab Assistant Panic. Not acting, and not using her powers for good, but in it to beat Professor Panic and become Riverside's *new* greatest villain. And it'd been natural. Easy. Peter was wrong; I could definitely become a villain. I had the style and the schemes, and I knew if I was Lab Assistant Panic long enough, I'd be willing to hurt my friends, sacrifice my allies, and betray those I loved to win.

That was the trouble.

It'd be easy to let Lab Assistant Panic run the show for a while. But while he was wrong about whether I could do what it took to get what I wanted, he was *right* that I didn't want to. I'd keep the Lab Assistant Panic Costume around. It had some unique powers. But I wouldn't become a Dark Magical Girl to speed-run to the minor leagues.

If I couldn't cheat my way to the minor leagues, I'd have to get there the hard way—through old-fashioned *work*. I'd rush my three classes, and then, after Intro to Drama, I'd start looking for little-league Episodes to star in. Or even sidekick in a few minor-league Episodes near campus.

After all, I had a lot of catching up to do!

PART THREE

18

Day One

I'm Rebecca Smith, and I'll be your instructor for History 143: Post–Launch Day North American History. You should have gotten a syllabus and a questionnaire in your email this morning. Please take a few minutes to complete the quiz and familiarize yourself with the course description and grading policy. There are physical copies of both if you're currently laptop- or phone-free."

Teaching Assistant Smith sat behind a tall, wide desk, typing and clicking away at the big desktop computer. I looked around as I dug out my laptop. The lecture hall was packed with students. Dozens of boys and girls—maybe as many as one hundred—all as tired-looking as me, dug for their computers or got out their phones. I saw screens light up in front of me, then I opened mine and found the email. I clicked the two links and started up the quiz.

1. What year did Launch Day happen? A. 1996 B. 2021 C. 2019 D. 2017

Well, it must have been at least twenty years ago, but let's see. Mom and Dad were in their forties. So *A* was too early. Let's go with *C.* When in doubt, *C* wins out!

2. Why did multiple countries launch nuclear weapons on Launch Day? A. Because one country launched theirs, and the rest followed their MAD doctrine. B. A terrorist attack pushed different countries to use theirs. C. Artificial intelligence chose to launch. D. I have no idea.

Definitely *A.* Had to be on this one; I knew it from high school.

I clicked to the survey's next page, then the next one. Then the next one. By the time I'd answered question 39 *(What was one economic impact of the post–Launch Day deal with the Ilneats resulting in superpower propagation and limited radiation cleanup?)* I wasn't even trying to get questions right. I was just trying to get through the damn survey!

Some students clearly had a similar idea. One was even watching a superhero show on his laptop—with earbuds in! There was no way he'd finished already, not if he was trying! Was this what college was supposed to be?

Finally, I finished question 50 *(How did Ilneat actions on and after Launch Day privilege certain cities, especially those in the former United States and Canada, over Asian and European population hubs?)* and submitted the survey. I looked around—a few people I'd seen in the Walnut Tower elevator were in History 143 with me, but not the tiny Korean girl I'd talked to. And not anyone I'd seen in the Department of Superhero Studies office.

Reading the syllabus proved to be both incredibly informative and impossibly redundant. Informative because I learned that fully 50% of my grade rode on a pair of five-page papers and the final exam in December, and that Teaching Assistant Smith wasn't taking attendance. And redundant because . . .

"Now that everyone's gone through the survey and some of you have familiarized yourselves with the course contents and objectives, let's ensure we're all on the same page. Specifically, page one: Course Goals. Dr. Beauregard wants me to make it very clear to you how important this course is for understanding the world we live in, so . . . 'History 143's stated goal is to understand North America's unique position from both human and Ilneat points of view, to comprehend the circumstances that led to Launch Day and the Superhero System Apocalypse that came after, and to come to terms with our unique role in the galaxy post–Launch Day.'"

I rolled my eyes. If Smith read the entire syllabus, this was going to be the most boring class period I'd ever sat through!

Sure enough, Teaching Assistant Smith read the syllabus until 9:50, when class got out. Those of us who'd braved her monotone tapped the cowardly movie-watchers on the shoulder and woke the weaklings who'd succumbed to boredom. As one of the survivors, it fell on me to wake up the sports star sitting next to me, drooling on the desk.

"Hey. Hey! It's over. You can leave now," I muttered in his ear. "The teacher definitely knew you were asleep, though, so you might want to do better next time."

"Oh, uh, sure," he said, picking his head up. "Hey, I'm Avan."

"Anika."

"I've got an hour or so before my next class. Wanna get a coffee at the SUB?" Avan packed up his bag and slung one strap over his shoulder. The unzipped bag teetered dangerously close to spilling his computer and books onto the lecture hall's floor.

"I'm flattered, but I have a boyfriend back home," I said. I yawned. "Besides, I have to get ready for my next class."

"Just coffee, not a *date*, Anika. But yeah, I get that. Some other time, then," Avan said, raising an eyebrow, and headed for the door.

I followed him and headed toward Walnut Tower, away from the Perkins School of History. The fresh air outside helped me wake up, but really, the coffee sounded phenomenal. If I'd had more time or knew where the Mister Felsic statue that marked the Department of Superhero Studies was, I'd have taken Avan up on the offer just for the pick-me-up.

Dr. Jackson had emailed late last night, and I'd read it when I woke up. It was tersely worded—just a few short sentences.

Hello Students,

Superhero Ethics will be below the Mister Felsic Statue. Arrive in your superhero personas. Books, laptops, and notebooks are unnecessary until further notice. To find the Mister Felsic Statue, consult a map of the campus.

Dr. Catherine Jackson

"Alright," I said to myself. "That's enough time to swing by home. Then I have, what? Two hours at lunch?" I consulted the schedule on my phone. Sure enough, I'd have time to grab a quick bite, maybe an energy bar and a shake, and then start scouting out possible Episode locations.

I struggled not to drift off as the elevator carried me to my thirteenth-floor apartment. Another class as boring as Post–Launch Day History, and I'd be finished. I texted Peter just to complain.

<Hey, Peter. History class is awful. Hopefully, it's just day one problems - Annie 10:03>

<That was the Launch Day one? That sounded awesome. Bummer - Peter 10:04>

<The teaching assistant just read the syllabus. And there was a test - Annie 10:04>

<Sounds pretty miserable - Peter 10:04

<Shouldn't you be working instead of texting? - Annie 10:04>

<Eh. My dad owns the company. I can slack a little :) - Peter 10:05>

As soon as the door shut behind me, I dropped my pack and pulled Tails out. She had a commanding view wherever I went, with her head sticking out between the zippers, but I'd need her a little more engaged to get ready for Superhero Ethics. "Tails, wake up!"

<Oh, what time is it meow? That class even put me to sleep!> The gray cat swished her tails and spun her eye buttons as she stretched in my arms.

"Doesn't take much to get you napping. The next one will be better. I hope. I swear on my family, who I love very much, that I'll stand up against Professor Panther, his minions, and evil all over Riverside! I'll fight for justice, peace, and hope! And I'll never stop 'til evil does first!"

[**Transformation Sequence**] completed, I dashed for the maintenance door and opened it to . . . something.

A pair of lightbulbs seemed to have extruded from the wall—bits of drywall still stuck to them—and two more were clearly about to break through. At least, judging from the drywall-pimple shapes and locations, I figured they were lightbulbs. A mirror had formed under the lightbulbs, and below it was a makeup stand with different bottles, trays, and brushes. And the walls were . . .

Well, the walls were definitely pink. Maybe even *too* pink. "Hey, could you tone it down a bit?" I asked no one.

The other thing that caught my eye was a wooden door, labeled "Rocko Productions" under a star with the Ilneat's smiling face superimposed on it. I reached for the handle—Fang Swee's power seemed to be creating a Backstage dressing room for me, with direct access to Rocko's studio.

<I don't think there's time for a Rocko visit,> Tails interrupted, batting at my boots. **<Not until later, unless you want to abandon your schedule?>**

"Alright, alright," I said. As I jogged up the stairs, which had covered themselves in fuzzy white carpeting, I kept thinking out loud. "I'd guess we want to be a bit stronger before we talk to Rocko anyways, huh?"

<If you want to make the minor leagues, then yes, I'd recommend that.>

I ran out the door toward the balcony's edge. "[**Starwave Sail**]!"

My phone said the Mister Felsic statue was on the far side of the Student Union Building, so I did a half circle around Walnut Tower to get some elevation and started sailing. Students packed the main sidewalk, and I took a moment to mentally thank Rocko or the System for making sure I had a flight power. The kangaroo hop-walking through the crowd certainly didn't look like they were having as much fun as me right now.

I zipped over the Student Union Building's roof and, sure enough, saw a twenty-foot-tall granite statue of a hulking man in a superhero Costume wearing two stone gloves that seemed to glow. His chin looked like it was chiseled from stone. I mean, it *was* chiseled from stone, but it was square and solid, too. Three rock pillars loomed over him, and standing near his feet were a few of the super students I'd met the day before . . . including Gourmet and an excessively fit pair of twins with crew cuts in magenta-and-green Costumes.

[Show-off! +1 Flamboyance Point]

I landed in a run around the cement circle, winded and grinning, then spun onto a concrete bench. I hadn't earned any points from my Guest Star role in the Orientation Episode, so even that one felt great! "Hi, I'm Magical Girl Understudy, here to save the day in the name of—"

"Hey, it's the snack! Hi, Snack!" Gourmet interrupted. She wore a loose-fitting brown-and-gold super-suit with plenty of room to move in and wide boots—almost snow boots, but not quite.

"Hi. Magical Girl Understudy is here to save the day in the name of—"

"Yeah, I don't think anyone here cares, Snack," Gourmet interrupted again. One of the boys snorted, while the other elbowed him in the side.

". . . truth, love, and justice . . ."

The twins wandered over, muscles rippling under their Costumes, and I found my eyes wandering to their arms and six-pack abs. Damn. Then the first stuck out a hand. "Punch."

"And Grapple," the other said, sticking out his *other* hand.

"It's a pleasure to meet you, Miss Unders," Punch continued.

I shook both hands, all crossed up trying to make the right connections.

"Me too! I'm here too!" Fursona hopped over, somewhat out of breath, even through the voice modulator. They gasped for breath and panted, hands on their sweatpants-covered knees. "Am I late? Did we start already?"

"No. We're waiting on a few more."

I looked around as Dr. Jackson walked out from a ramp below the massive statue. She held a clipboard, which she checkmarked five times. "We'll wait until all twelve of you are here for this session. Six heroes, six villains. Then we'll get started right away with the group work!"

Everyone groaned, including me. Everyone, that is, except for one person. Fursona practically hopped with excitement.

"I love group projects!"

19

I Love Group Projects!

Welcome to Superpower Ethics," Dr. Jackson said. "Come on in. The Department of Superhero Studies conducts most of its classes below Mister Felsic here, in the Aspen Building."

We followed her into the tunnel below Mister Felsic and filed into a . . . movie theater? One of the fancy kinds, with the La-Z-Boy chairs you could move and adjust. The room had space for about fifteen. "Dibs on the front row!" Gourmet shouted and pushed past Punch and Grapple. She jammed herself into a chair and started reclining it.

"Well, you all may as well get comfortable. I'll explain the lesson once you've picked spots," Dr. Jackson said. She took the front-right seat.

I sat toward the middle, figuring it'd give me some space. Most kids back at Riverside were either front-sitters or back-sitters. So it shocked me when Fursona plopped themselves into a chair beside me.

Their kangaroo face glanced at me and then the gigantic screen in the front of the room. "Guess Superpower Ethics is a movie class?"

"Looks like it. I wonder what we're going to watch?" I asked.

"Probably something boring, like a history of superheroing or something."

"Yeah." Every class I'd ever had that used movies only showed documentaries, except for theater classes. We'd watched professional theater troupes perform every play we learned—but only after we performed it ourselves first. We weren't trying to be a professional production of *A Midsummer Night's Dream*, and comparing our performance to a professional's before we'd given it was a recipe for disaster. But after we closed on the last night, we'd have a pizza party and watch the pros. It'd always been a ton of fun.

Once everyone was comfy, Dr. Jackson cleared her throat. "Today, we're going to watch an Episode. As we do, I want you all to look for problems in the hero's and villain's behavior choices. What do you think they did wrong, and what could they do better?"

She hit play as a dozen voices started chattering, and almost as many hands shot up.

"No questions at this time. This is best as a blind run."

The lights dimmed. A familiar-sounding theme song started playing. I grinned in spite of myself; it was a classic run of *Magical Girl Stella-Lunar!*

In it, the white-clad Magical Girl hunted her archrival, Lord Destructo, through Big City's slums, looking for either his lair or the villain himself. I braced myself for the scene where he tore through a dining room. I *knew* Dr. Jackson wanted to talk about it. It had to be. Kids and grandparents fled as the armored overlord slammed through the table, Thanksgiving food splattering onto the camera drone.

This was where she'd pause it. Lord Destructo was endangering children, and nothing *happened* after this scene. They fought, and she won, but he escaped to his lair before she could use **[Total Eclipse]** to neutralize his power.

Instead, I found myself staring, wide-eyed, as Stella-Lunar fired a **[Moonbeam]** right through the dining room. Then another, and another. It wasn't until the fifth beam ripped through what was left of dinner that Stella-Lunar entered the room herself, and she didn't check to see if people were okay. Instead, she smashed through the wall and tore after Lord Destructo.

"Okay, that's probably enough to start," Dr. Jackson said. She pressed a button on her chair and froze the screen on a turkey leg that'd been forcibly separated from the bird. "So, what went wrong here?"

Fursona spoke up first. "Lord Destructo put Extras in harm's way deliberately."

"Oh, bullshit," Gourmet said. "You saw the beginning of the Episode. He was straight-up fleeing from Stella-Loser, and she forced him into a no-win situation. He had no choice but to tear down that wall and deal with whatever was behind it."

"Right!" A man's voice spoke up from the back of the room. "This wasn't Stella's first rodeo. She knew that engaging in a residential area put people at risk."

I cleared my throat. "I've . . . never seen this version of 'Black Thursday' before— that's the Episode's name. But if I remember right, this was both Stella-Lunar's and Lord Destructo's first major-league Episode, so they both went all-out for the first time."

"Right." Dr. Jackson hit play again. The two supers fought down the hall, laser beams and giant mace tearing into cinderblocks and shredding ceiling tiles. A well-placed **[Maximum Starlance]** caught Lord Destructo in the chest. He flew through the stairwell, clipped a pipe with his spiked armor, and crashed through the outside wall in a cloud of dust.

Alarms went off across the building as Stella-Lunar used **[Starflame]**. The explosion rocked the camera drone as the shot filled with fire—far more than Stella's spell should have created.

Dr. Jackson froze the screen again. "Twenty-five people went to the hospital because of this Episode. No one died, which was a miracle. It cost over eight million dollars to fix the apartment—the Ilneats took care of some of it, but a lot had to be handled by us. Raise your hand if you've ever caused property damage."

Eleven hands went up.

Fursona hedged, raising theirs halfway. "Does punching my bedroom wall count? I haven't had an Episode yet."

"No, I'm talking about damage as a powered person. Everyone who's had an Episode. How about injuring Extras?"

Eleven hands. During a main street duel with Peter's FEAR 1.3 armor, I'd clipped a few people with a [**Stellar Ray**]. It'd taken a week or two to get back in the dress after that.

"Dr. Mays and I have injured *dozens* of Extras. Our bill for property damage is in the millions. And, speaking candidly, we're *absolutely* the safest duo in the major leagues. I bring up the 'Black Thursday' unedited footage on day one because neither Magical Girl Stella-Lunar nor Lord Destructo had a solid code of conduct prior to that Episode. Both did in their future fights, and injury counts stayed at no more than eight. Property damage fell off as well, especially in residential neighborhoods. Frankly, shit happens out there. Extras don't always stay out of the way, and sometimes they get hurt, but villains don't usually need a reputation for wanton violence, and heroes *never* do."

She turned off the screen. The lights came on, and the tiered seating slowly lowered until we all sat on the same level. "This course is pass/fail, dependent on whether you and your teammates can create a code of ethics that superheroes, supervillains, and later, unpowered Extras can agree to and live by. Each of your teams will consist of two villains and two heroes. Heroes, you'll work with each other on at least one Episode each month, either as hero and sidekick or in another capacity. Villains, the same thing applies to you. Ideally, you'll face off against each other, but that's not required."

Dr. Jackson pointed to Fursona and me. "Magical Girl Understudy, you're with Fursona. Gourmet and Theseus are your villains." She assigned the other super students to their teams. Somehow, Punch and Grapple stayed together and paired up with the boy who made sparks and a villain in a . . . bread cape.

Dr. Jackson cleared her throat once she'd finished with the last team. "One piece of advice. Don't share your powers with your counterparts. Your codes should be broad enough to cover lots of powers and specific enough to avoid confusion. Later in the year, I'll have some Extras join us to see how your codes of ethics work in a more mixed environment. For now, though, focus on your wants, needs, and what you think are your responsibilities to Extras and each other."

"Fuck me," Gourmet said, reaching for a snack as we moved our chairs around to make a circle. "Alright, let's get the basics out of the way. How do you feel about killing?"

I couldn't read Fursona's face, but from their posture, they were horrified.

"Like, up close and personal, or from a distance?" Theseus asked. "Either way, I'm always armed and dangerous!"

Gourmet snorted into her yogurt container.

I rolled my eyes. "Maybe we could start a little more basic than killing. What league are you guys in? I'm a little leaguer, but I have my sights set on something bigger."

"Little league," Fursona said.

"Me too." Gourmet scooped the key-lime-pie-flavored goop into her mouth. She did *not* change color.

"I'm a minor leaguer. I'm head and shoulders above you all!" Theseus quipped.

"Alright, alright, calm down."

"Fine, you're right. It's time to put our heads together and get serious."

For the next ten minutes, we argued back and forth over points that *should* have been simple, easy wins. Like "How much murder is okay?" (none) and "Should rival heroes and villains talk outside their Episodes?" (I said yes, obviously, but the others were mixed). Tempers grew heated; I could tell by how Gourmet bit into her yogurt container and how Theseus was stretching. His shoulders bent at an impossible angle, almost like he was trying to rip his arms off.

"I think that's enough group work for now, class. Remember, you'll need to participate in an Episode this month with your partner, so think about how to find one that suits your unique powers and talents. I'll see you all on Wednesday." Dr. Jackson stood up and walked to the door as we filed out.

Code of Conduct: September 1
We will not ~~harm threaten~~ endanger ~~civilians~~ Extras ~~needlessly~~

Fursona and I walked out from under the Mister Felsic statue. "So . . . Magical Girl Understudy, am I your sidekick now?" they asked. I thought I could hear a hint of teasing, but the modulator made it hard to tell.

"Not formally, no. I think we'll need to talk to Rocko to get that formalized. For now, Collidus should still be my sidekick."

"Who's Rocko?"

"Oh, you'd like them. Rocko is my producer. Everyone has one, and someday soon, when I've got a few more Episodes under my belt, I'm going to make them move me up to the minor leagues. I'm close, I think." I explained how the leagues worked, how producers made shows, and how to deal with camera drones. "You ignore them for the most part unless they actually get in your face. Then you have to say something on-theme like 'Evil will never prevail as long as hope remains!'"

A few passing students looked at us funny, and I blushed before I remembered I was talking to a kangaroo suit. They weren't looking at *me*.

"Anyways, you'll sit down with your producer soon. I'll put in a good word for you with Rocko, and maybe you can sidekick for me for a while. Or we can be partners."

"I'd . . ." Fursona froze for a second, thinking. "I'd rather be a sidekick for a few Episodes first, but I'd like to be partners, too. I've never actually been in an Episode. I'm not even sure I have a producer. Did I mention that before?"

"You might have back at the theater or something. I have to get ready for my next class, and you aren't allowed to know my secret identity, so I'll see you later!"

"I have one more, too. Bye." Fursona hopped away, moving surprisingly fast, and I summoned my **[Starwave Sail]**, drawing some oohing and aahing from the passing students. I took off and started windsurfing away, looping through the sky and over different buildings so it'd be hard to see which one I was aiming for.

Then a Casting Call popped up.

[Casting Call]
[Episode: Short: Wet Noodle Robbery - PG]
[Role: Street-Level Backup! Do you accept the role? (Yes/No)]
[Role Focus: Flamboyance+Badass]

I accepted the role and turned the sailboard, ducking so low it brushed the tree-tops, and zoomed toward a frozen fursuit in the distance. I had to get Fursona involved in this Episode! A Short would be perfect for them, *and* it'd fill our Superpower Ethics class requirement for the month.

[Short: Wet Noodle Robbery: Act One in Progress]

When I landed, Fursona's goofy cartoon eyes stared at me. I opened my mouth, but before I could, they started talking, the words rushing out.

"Hey, I got my first **[Casting Call]**! Street-Level Sidekick!"

"Accept it! This'll be quick!" I said.

"Okay, I got it!"

I ran down the street toward an art gallery with a blaring alarm, Fursona following me. It looked like a simple job—and it would be since it was a Short—so it was time for Fursona's first Episode!

20

Fursona's First Episode

What's the plan?" Fursona asked.

A camera drone dipped down to meet us and hovered before us as we ran—well, I ran and they hopped—toward the gallery. It hovered in my face, waiting for me to say something inspiring. Something fans of *Small-Town Super* would like.

More importantly, Fursona needed some confidence builders. The kangaroo superhero had *no* idea what they were doing, and it showed in how their fur-covered head turned from one side to the other like prey looking for predators.

That wasn't the hero's role. We were here to hunt villains.

"Why don't we see what you can do, Justice-Roo? You go in through the door. I'll circle around back. We'll catch the supervillain in a trap with no way out. It'll be great!" Unless they could fly, of course. Though . . . if that were the case, I'd need to be outside to chase them down on **[Starwave Sail]**.

[Good Thinking! +1 Cunning Point]

"Alright, will do!" Fursona hopped to the door and kicked against the lock. "**[Double-Kick]**, go!"

The glass door shattered after the first of their two kicks, and they fell through it. They picked themselves up, brushing glass off their fursuit as I ran toward the back of the building.

I dashed around the storefronts, hoping to pick the right direction as Fursona flushed the villain into the alley. Unless they were Badass-focused, Fursona could probably hold their own. And if they were, I'd be there soon. Not that I'd fought any Badasses, with one exception for a brief cameo appearance. But I knew the theory. They were the heaviest hitters, but intelligent tactics always won out. Unless they didn't.

A white delivery van filled the alleyway, its back door open near the art gallery's service entrance. I squeezed by, nodding at the driver. "Sorry! Superhero business. Stay where you are, and we'll keep you safe."

The driver narrowed his eyes at me, almost like he was trying to identify me.

"Oh right! I'm Magical Girl Understudy, here to save the day in the name of hope, justice, and love." I did a little twirl; the fans loved that, and the camera drone was on me. "We've got a villain inside, so give us a few minutes, and you can return to work."

[Show-off! +1 Flamboyance Point]

The driver reached up to his dash, started the van, and said, "Another one of *these*? We're gonna be *so* late." He revved the engine and started backing out of the alleyway. I sighed in relief. Even if he'd been rude, having an Extra on-scene always added a little bit of pressure to an Episode, and Fursona didn't need—
CRASH!

[HP 5/6]
[HP 4/6]

The van's grill slammed into me, folding me around it like a banana. Or a football player getting tackled. Or . . . look, it hit me hard, and I folded. Then my head hit the windshield, and the van stopped, throwing me against a dumpster.
I saw the door open, and a dark-skinned man maybe a year older than me got out. I couldn't see his face under the helmet he'd just pulled on—just his mouth and chin. Was he . . . a supervillain, too? What was his power? Driving vans? He didn't seem like a supervillain, and I was a little winded as I tried to get my footing, but I knew blasting an Extra on purpose wouldn't cut it in the little leagues.
He spoke into a microphone hanging from his headset. "Hey, Jun—Jumper? There's another Magical Girl out here . . . No, it's not her . . . Yeah, I hit her with the van . . . Again? Are you sure? I *swear* if you call me 'Minion' again, I'm *done* helping you . . . Alright."
He hopped back in the driver's seat, cleared his throat, and said, "Hey, I'm sorry. She's making me, okay?"
"Uh, what?"
Before I could ask more, the Extra slammed on the gas.
CRASH!

[HP 3/6]
[HP 2/6]

As the van crushed me against the dumpster, I realized I had to defend myself. **[Stellar—]** oof!" The van crashed into me again, its grill hanging by one bolt, and drove the air from my lungs.
CRASH!

[HP 1/6]

"[**Stellar Ray**]!" I blasted a light beam into the van's engine as it backed up to slam into me again. It lost power and coasted to a stop against a brick wall. The driver stumbled out and started running. I dashed toward him, grabbed his collar, and spun him against the van's side. "What the [**Beep**], man?"

[Rating Warning #1! Episode Rating - PG! Censor in Effect.]
[Badass Takedown! +1 Badass Point]
[Dramatic Damage! +1 Drama Point]
[Gritty Recovery! +1 Grit Point]

The man raised his hands and tried to back away from me. "I surrender! Jumper made me! According to the rules, you can't hurt me now unless I resist or run, and you can't take off my helmet!"

Suddenly, it clicked. This guy was a henchman. I dusted off my skirts and groaned in frustration. "Is he telling the truth, Tails?"

<Yes. It's a Section Six. Since he's surrendered, you can't even give him a scratch in a PG Episode.>

I sighed. A henchman had knocked off five of my Hit Points. Five! And I couldn't even do anything about it since he knew the rules. "Alright, 'Bob,' you sit here against the wall. Tails, if he moves, he's not protected anymore, right?"

<Right.>

"Alright, if you move, I'm coming after—"

The door burst open, and a woman in a green hoodie, tan jumper, and running shoes crashed into the alley. She took one look at the minion and tossed a framed painting at me. "Crap, sorry, S. I'll spring you later, don't worry!" Then she started run-jumping away, bouncing off the brick walls.

Fursona hopped out the door a second later, turning their helmet back the right way. "Stop right there! The Marsupial of Justice is on the case!"

The supervillain—Jumper, I assumed—started laughing and let herself slide down the wall. "Okay, kid, first of all, your powers are a copy of mine—"

"They are not!"

"—and second, I already have to deal with Honeycomb. You, teach your furry friend some better catchphrases!"

I didn't have time to figure out who Honeycomb was because Jumper bounded away, actually managing to gain height with each jump.

"I'll get her! I almost had her in there!" Fursona took off, fur disheveled from their fight in the art gallery. She was faster than Jumper, but if the supervillain got onto the roofs, she'd lose the "Marsupial of Justice" anyway.

"**[Starwave Sail]**! I'll keep an eye on her!" I leaped into the air and pulled back until I saw Jumper and Fursona far below me. The supervillain had hopped up onto a roof. She sprinted across the black tar surface and threw herself off the edge. Instead of falling, she rocketed through the air and landed on the other side of the street. She turned and waved to Fursona.

"**[Stellar Ray]**!" I swung around and waved my wand. The beam went wide, scorching a spot into the roof beside her.

"Hey, chill out, okay? You owe me a new van."

"Uh, what?" I landed, running across the tarry roof until I was only a few yards from Jumper.

[Show-off! +1 Flamboyance Point]

"You heard me. That engine's probably totaled, thanks to you! It took me months to buy that piece of . . . junk, and you just blasted it. Now I'm gonna have to explain to a mechanic how it broke—if I'm lucky!" Jumper said. She started walking toward the edge.

"Hey, wait up! You're a villain, aren't you? Why didn't you just steal the van?"

"Jumping to conclusions, aren't you? Oh, we tried that. Neither of us knew how to hotwire a car, so we had to actually buy one. Look, forget the van. Let's get on with this, okay?"

I looked. Sure enough, the camera drones had caught up with us. "In the name of love, justice, and hope, surrender!"

[Dramatic Line! +1 Drama Point]

"Nah."

Jumper heaved herself off the roof. I summoned my **[Starwave Sail]** and took off after her. I caught a flash of blue and orange far below—Fursona looked to be following along by looking up and tracking my sailboard. They gave a quick wave, and I returned it.

When I looked back, Jumper was gone.

"She went inside!" I yelled and landed on the roof. I forced the roof door open with a kick. There had to be dozens of doors in the building—it was an apartment— and I had no idea where she could have vanished to.

[Show-off! +1 Flamboyance Point]

I had an **[Inkling]**, but even that only brought me down a floor. And that was just another dozen doors to choose from. I started knocking. "Hi, I'm Magical Girl Understudy. I was chasing a dangerous supervillain, and she disappeared somewhere in this building. Have you seen her?" I knocked over and over, but there weren't any leads.

[Good Thinking! +1 Cunning Point]

The camera drone swung around me, seeming to mock me as I checked the last door on the floor. I gave my speech, and the man who'd answered said that he'd seen her. She'd pushed her way into his apartment, waited a minute, and then jumped out the window. The police were on their way, but he'd seen her run off.

"When?"

"Must've been at least three minutes ago," he said.

I groaned in frustration and rubbed my temples around my mask's edges. "Thank you, citizen. I need to find my sidekick before they get themselves in trouble." I started down the stairs. I'd made it two flights when my ears filled with a buzzing sound.

A moment later, another Magical Girl started running up the stairs. She was younger than me—maybe high school-aged—with brown hair. She skidded to a halt on the landing below me. "Magical Girl Honeycomb has arrived in the hive!" She said it loudly, but her tone felt . . . off. Like she wasn't really buying it—the poor girl.

Her Costume explained some of it. A green-and-orange flower skirt that didn't quite match her black-and-yellow flower bodice. Fairy wings that looked decorative, not functional. And a pair of yellow flowers on a headband.

"Hi, Honeycomb," I said. I held out a hand, and she shook it. "I'm Magical Girl Understudy. I tracked a supervillain named Jumper here, but she got away."

"She got away again?" Honeycomb looked distraught. Her eyes glistened with tears, and she sat down on the steps and put her head in her hands. I reached down to touch her shoulder, and she stiffened. "She's supposed to be my nemesis, but she just runs away. I *really* could've used a win here."

"Well, we got her minion. Wanna go see?"

"S! Yeah, I've been trying to snag him too. It's tough going solo, though."

Oh, believe me, I understood that from fighting Peter. "He's back behind the art studio. He crashed his van into me. Three times."

"He *what?*" Honeycomb asked.

"I mean, it's fine. Superhero damage, you know?" We picked up Fursona on the way out and explained to them that the villain had gotten away.

Sure enough, when we got back to the van, S was waiting, along with the painting's twisted frame. He'd sat down right where I told him, whistling and chatting through his headset. The second he saw us, he crushed it under his feet. The helmet stayed on, though.

"I'll take it from here, Magical Girl Understudy! Unless you want to make this short a full Episode?"

Did I want to? Yeah. But Intro to Drama was in just . . . twenty minutes? "No thanks. It'd be fun, but I have classes soon! Good luck, though, Magical Girl Honeycomb!"

"Evil Bee-ware, Magical Girl Honeycomb is here!" She seemed in much better spirits with *someone* in custody. "I'll wait for the police here. This'll really help me out with Ed!"

[Episode Finished!]

[Episode: Wet Noodle Robbery! - PG]

[Penalties: 1x Rating Warning - No Penalty]

[Short Finished! +3 of each Style Point]

[We'll Call it a Draw! +2 of each Style Point]

[Role Focus: Flamboyance+Badass - Goal Partially Met! +10 Flamboyance Points]

[Alias - Understudy] [Archetype - Magical Girl] [Community Rank - 477/523]

[HP 1/6]

[Styles and Skills]

▶ Archetype Skill - Transformation Sequence

▶ Badass (24)

▶ Cunning (56) (Skill Roll Available)

▶ Inkling 1

▶ Drama (10)

▶ Stellar Ray 1

▶ Hometown Heroine 1

▶ Flamboyance (56) (Skill Roll Available)

▶ Signature Skill - Adaptive Armoire 1

▶ Stored Costumes: (Lab Assistant Panic)

▶ Starwave Sail 1

▶ Grit (33)

▶ Rejuvenation 1

I had no idea where Fursona could be, but I was going to be late for Intro to Drama!

21

Intro to Drama!

I ran down Walnut Tower's stairs, backpack thumping against my back. It wasn't ideal, but if I didn't get lost, I'd make it to the Doyle Building and slide into Room 305 with seconds to spare. Tails's head poked out of the backpack, bouncing against my neck with every stride I took. But even though I was running full-out, scooters and skateboards still whipped past me.

"I've gotta get one of those," I mumbled.

"Walmart! Fifty bucks! There's a sale right now," one of the scooter riders said as he zoomed past, wheels clattering on the concrete.

"Thanks!" I kept running. Sometime soon, I'd try to learn a shortcut. Or not do Episodes between classes. But for now, I followed the sidewalk. I didn't want to get lost or anything. That'd just make me even later.

That wasn't all I was thinking about, though. Two Skill Rolls? How had that worked out?

[50 Cunning Credits Used. Rolling Skill!]
[New Skill! Card Curio 1! Free-associate information from your surroundings and a card reading]
[50 Flamboyance Credits Used. Rolling Skill!]
[New Skill! Spotlight Strike 1! Follow the limelight and deliver high-damage melee attacks]

The first skill didn't seem like it was much of an upgrade from [Inkling]. Being tied to another item—a deck of cards, no less—sounded frustrating, too. I remembered having my Lab Assistant Panic goggles stolen and having to chase the Panic Pal around Carver Street. But I was stuck with it, so I shoved it into [Skill Storage] for later. I'd try it out if I got the tools for it. And if I went up against someone like Jumper again.

The second one seemed more suited for my build and theme.

One problem with my powers so far was that I didn't have many ways to deal damage. I could [Stellar Ray], of course. And I could hit and kick things. But up against something like the FEAR 2.4 power armor, I'd had to take out Peter's ranged weapon and then fish for critical spots until he surrendered. That wouldn't work against anything tougher than the FEAR 2.4. Heck, it wouldn't work against the next FEAR model he made.

But **[Spotlight Strike]** could change all that. I'd have to test it out, but it seemed like it'd do the part of a Badass power and give me higher damage output. That was a big deal since I rarely even got Badass points; I'd barely even gotten any when it was a Role Focus. But I only had six power slots. I dropped **[Rejuvenation]** into my **[Skill Storage]**. Then I thought about it. That skill was invaluable in longer Episodes. I'd go without **[Hometown Hero]** instead. Fighting without the speed boost could be challenging, but I needed to see what **[Spotlight Strike]** did.

I'd be able to redo my build between Episodes anyway.

The Doyle Building turned out to be the Doyle Auditorium and an attached building with smaller, studio-style classrooms. I sprinted up the stairs, taking the steps two at once, and skidded into Room 305 just in time.

The professor cleared his throat. "I'm Dr. Carlton, but most of you'll call me Carl, so we'll go with that. Syllabi are up front. If we could get those passed around, that'd be wonderful. Thanks. The first thing to know is that, yes, you will be acting in Drama 101: Intro to Drama."

A few students stood up and left.

Carl laughed. "There's always a couple, every single year."

He clapped his hands. "Alright, then! Yes, you'll be acting in here. We'll do play readings every other week for the first half-semester, then we'll pick one play via ranked-choice voting—we're not *savages* here—and then perform it once by the end of class. That's a good chunk of your grade. We will also watch *Macbeth* on Friday, October 24 in the main auditorium. Clear your schedules. If you absolutely cannot make it, the show runs from the nineteenth through the twenty-eighth. If none of those dates work, I'd recommend you join your colleagues who don't want to act."

"I don't think he's reading his own syllabus," a girl beside me whispered. Her glasses were framed by wavy black hair, and she flipped to the second page, shaking her head. "Yeah, this isn't accurate. The date on the top is two years old."

My hand went up. "Dr. Carlton?"

"Please, call me Carl. It'll be easier for everyone."

"Okay. Carl, nothing you just said is in the syllabus."

"You're absolutely right. I'm not fond of syllabi. The department says I need to have one, but every year's class is different, and things change throughout the semester, so why plan for something I know won't happen?

"Now, this class is about understanding theater, which in itself is a way to understand the human condition—and, we've learned in the last few decades, a universal condition as well. By the time you pass Intro to Drama, you'll understand the process of creating a play, from writing to set design to choreography. You'll be better theater and television viewers. And most importantly, you'll better understand how theater influences culture, both in human cultures and in Ilneat space." Dr. Carlton was waxing about his subject—teachers did this all the time, and it was a chance to tune out for a bit.

"I'm Anika. Call me Annie," I said. I held out a hand to my classmate.

She paused, looked me up and down, and then grabbed it for a handshake that felt both quick and hesitant. "Hi, Annie. I'm Bianca. Do you . . . have much experience with theater?"

"Yeah. I was in *A Midsummer Night's Dream* last year in high school. It was a blast. I got to be Hermia, which was pretty cool."

"What's with all the Shakespeare plays, anyways?" Bianca asked. "They're all anyone wants to talk about, other than musicals."

"Now, I want to talk a little more about the performances we'll be reading this semester," Dr. Carlton continued.

I leaned over to Bianca and whispered, "He's done waxing. Tell you after class."

"So, anyways, most modern plays all try to hit these similar plot beats. It's an audience comfort thing as much as anything else, but once you know about them, you can start seeing them everywhere. But only in the modern stuff," I said. The class was out, but Bianca and I stuck around. We sat and talked on a Doyle Building couch. "I think that's why everyone likes Shakespeare now. It has similar plot beats to modern stuff, but there's something a little off and nostalgic about it. At least, that's how *Midsummer Night's Dream* felt."

"Huh. I've never looked into it. My parents said I should take a drama class to learn to be more outgoing." Bianca stood up, putting her copy of the useless syllabus in her gigantic, overfilled backpack. "I record all my classes. I can send you a copy so you know what to expect from the class. If you want."

"Yeah, that'd be great." My stomach growled. I'd skipped lunch to do that Episode and was paying for it now. "I'm going to check out the dining hall. Wanna come with?"

Bianca looked like she was really thinking about it. Then she adjusted her glasses. "No thanks. I'm about peopled out for the day. Plus, I have to turn these recordings into something usable. Give me your number, though. I'll text you when they're done, and you can come over to my place then."

"Sure. Hand me your phone." We traded phones. I punched in my number quickly and waited while she clumsily tapped away at mine.

Then mine buzzed.

"Don't worry about that. It's probably my boyfriend," I said.

"Oh." Her typing stopped. Then she kept going. "Nah, the notification said it was an email from one of the professors. I bet I have a dozen of those. Maybe more. I got two or three while we were in class."

She finished up with her number. Then we said our goodbyes and left the building.

Which made the walk to the Student Union Building awkward.

"So . . . why'd you choose TU?"

"Oh, my parents think I'd be good in bioengineering, so they helped me pay for it. And then I got a good scholarship that covers a lot of the dorm room. It's over on the far side, though. Chestnut Tower, ground floor. Room 103, if you ever want to swing by to say hi." Bianca pointed.

"Oh. I'm on the top floor of Walnut Tower. Why'd they name all the buildings after trees, anyways?"

Bianca shrugged. "This is my turn. I'll see you later." She walked down the sidewalk from the dining hall toward the dorm towers near the wall. I watched her go for a moment, then shook my head and headed for the Student Union Building. Whether she wanted to eat early dinner or not, it was nice to have a friend.

The cafeteria was packed. I took one look at the lines and shook my head; I might have a meal card with three meals a day in there, but I was also a superhero with my own show. I could afford to spend twelve bucks on a burrito in the Rams Cafe next door.

While I waited for the breakfast burrito to finish cooking, I checked my email. Sure enough, Dr. Jackson had sent one with super student email addresses for Gourmet, Theseus, and Fursona. I typed them each in as contact info. Then I grabbed my burrito, slid my card, and went to find a seat.

There were a few more emails below Dr. Jackson's, and I skimmed them as I put hot sauce on my burrito. The fresh-cooked (or reheated, I hadn't paid much attention) bacon smell filled my nose. I took a bite and opened up an email from Dr. Mays that was actually from Ikenga—the hero who'd fought Monologue during the Orientation Episode.

Subject: TUSSA Membership

Greetings, Magical Girl Understudy,

Dr. Mays helped me get in touch with you. You're on the list of new heroes on campus, and I wanted to be the first to inform you about the Tokyexico University Student Superheroes Association's fall membership drive. With all the new super students on campus, we want to make sure you know all the opportunities, like mentoring support and secret base advice, that TUSSA offers.

Since I know you're curious, we'll be hosting a barbecue at my place on Hickory Hall's roof on Thursday at 5:30. We'll be lit up for you fliers, and there's an elevator in the basement for any ground-pounders who want to be subtle about things. Dr. Mays will be there to make sure things stay in control—mostly. You know how super parties can get.

Looking forward to seeing you there!

Ikenga

President, TUSSA

I finished up my burrito, wiped my mouth with my shirt, and headed back to Walnut Tower. I'd just about gotten to my room when my phone buzzed again. This time, it was from an address named *Fursona.SH@tokyexicouniversity.student.edu.*

Subject: Episode Questions
Hey Understudy,
Can I come by your place? I have questions about today's Episode. And about Ilneat producers. And a lot of stuff.
Thankies,
Justice-Roo

I smiled and stepped into my apartment. It'd be my first friend over, even if we were both in Costume the whole time. My first friend over other than Peter since seventh grade.

Subject: RE: Episode Questions
Yeah, come on over. Walnut Tower super elevator.

With my message sent, I started my [**Transformation Sequence**]. I'd start by introducing Fursona to the person who'd helped me learn the ropes.
Rocko.

22

Rocko

The intercom on the wall buzzed, and I pressed the button to read the message.

<Hey, it's the Marsupial of Justice! Let me up XD>

I laughed. Whoever Fursona was, they were *determined* to stay on theme. I tossed my phone on my bed, pressed the button to start the secret elevator, and hurried into my base.

And what a base it was becoming.

It felt like an extension of Rocko's studio, and if I was right about the other side of the door, it was. Fang Swee's power was turning it into a star's private green room. With the lights that'd grown around the mirror, the rack of Costumes (currently with only Lab Assistant Panic on a hanger, but with plenty of room to grow), and the comfy vintage couches and chaise lounge, it was nearly perfect.

Nearly. The walls were, of course, blindingly pink, which was not befitting of a private green room. Or *pink* room, I supposed. I had half a mind to ask the power to change that, but before I could, I heard a ding, and the wall opened up.

"Have no fear—ow, my eyes! Understudy, this room is . . ."

"Painfully me?" I laughed. The room *was* pretty bright. "We don't have to stay in here, but the rest of my place isn't organized yet. I haven't had much time. I was hoping to do some of that this evening, but . . ."

"Oh! Sorry!" Fursona stood by the door, shifting in their Costume. "I didn't realize . . ."

I sighed. This meeting wasn't going how I imagined it, and I had to refocus it. "It's totally fine. Why don't you sit down and tell me what's on your mind?"

I sat on one of the overstuffed blue couches, expecting Fursona to do the same. Instead, they looked around, flopped down on the chaise lounge, and sprawled out with their tail over the back in a "paint me like one of your French girls" pose.

When they saw me staring, they shrugged. "The tail gets in the way of sitting. This is much more comfortable." They cleared their throat. "Alright. Question. I looked you up after our Episode, and you already have a sidekick . . ."

"Yeah. Collidus. He's back in . . . he's back in the small town I came from, though."

Fursona took a deep breath. "Right. Collidus. So, how would I become your sidekick? Officially, I mean. Like, I don't wanna get in the way if you have a good thing going back home, but I thought we did okay together, and I really need someone to show me the ropes and—"

"Okay, so—"

They kept going. Were they even stopping to breathe? "I don't even know how to get a producer, and I have no idea how to talk to an Ilneat, and this whole superhero thing is way too complicated for me and—"

"Stop. Take a breath," I interrupted, standing up and putting a hand on their . . . snout? Muzzle? What was a kangaroo's mouth called, anyways? I waited for a second until they nodded. "Okay, sorry. One step at a time. You have powers. How have you never talked to an Ilneat?"

That was the wrong question. "Look, I was in a fursuit, and my girlfriend started breaking up with me the second she realized I was keeping it, and I had a lot going on. I declined the call. And then I kept meaning to contact Finster—I think that was their name—but I couldn't figure out how."

I cut them off before they could get rolling again. "Well, you're a vigilante right now, so it's a good thing I'm going to get you in touch with Rocko. They're my producer."

"Alright." The kangaroo rolled onto their stomach and blew out a nervous raspberry. Then they sighed. "What are Ilneats like?"

"They're, uh, businesslike and high-energy. Rocko is all about *Small-Town Super* and making it big. My first meeting with them was . . . weird."

Yeah, weird. I'd been summoned while tubing, just after meeting Tails. In fact, had I gotten an opportunity to decline Rocko's invitation? I wasn't sure I had. Instead, I'd been dripping wet in a swimsuit and life jacket. I hadn't been thrilled, especially when my parents eventually found me on the beach after I signed on to *Small-Town Super*. And I couldn't explain where I'd been to them, either.

"Look, just understand that Rocko and Pataki are invested in your success as soon as they sign you on, okay?"

"Okay. So . . . do you want to be my sidekick?" the kangaroo asked, then facepalmed. I couldn't see their embarrassed face, but the way Fursona looked away from me said a lot. "I meant do you want to let me be your sidekick oh my god Fursona you're so stupid." They buried their face in their paws and started rocking back and forth. "Goddammit, Fursona. Pull yourself together. Deep breaths."

As they talked themselves around, I reached out to touch a shoulder. Then I hesitated. "Yeah, I'd love to have you as my sidekick."

"Really?" Before I could react, I found myself wrapped in a gigantic hug. It was like hugging Tails, except instead of embracing a nice plushie stuffed animal, the plush was wrapped around me. Fursona bounced up and down with me trapped by their fuzzy arms. The hops were so high they rattled my bones. "I haven't felt this happy since Jess said she'd go to dinner with me!"

I pried myself out of their grip and brushed myself off. Then I leaned against the couch and crossed my legs. "Well, I am pretty cool, and we did work well together. Plus, I've been trying to get Rocko to move me up to the minor leagues, but that won't happen as things stand. If we work together, maybe we can both make it, and that'd be pretty cool!"

"It would be," Fursona said. "So, are we going to see Rocko now?"

"Uh, yeah, we can see Rocko now if you want," I said. Then I sat back down. "But first, you should have some water. Dealing with the Ilneats is thirsty work."

"Oh, I've got a bladder in here." They paused as I blinked at them, about to make a joke. "Not like that! It's one of those old CamelBak things. My uncle must've installed it in here since it's hard to eat and drink without taking the helmet off."

"Perfect. Oh, uh, sorry in advance. Ilneats like it hot." I put my hand on the door. "Ready?"

". . . Dammit. Ready."

As I pulled on the door handle, my vision pinpointed and swirled.

[Welcome to Rocko's Backstage. System Disabled. System Enabled. Now arriving at Costuming.]

"Aaaaaaayyyyy!"

Somehow, Rocko's greeting never got old, even though something *was* new here.

"Do you have any idea how hard it is to keep you in Costume on a translation like this, Understudy? The System does *not* like letting you keep your powers over here!"

I winced as the Ilneat movie producer got way too close to me. "Hi, Rocko. I need a favor."

"If it's about joining the minor leagues, not yet! There's no way I could swing it with the network. No way! The slots are all full." Rocko puffed their cigar and grinned. "Anything but that, though, Miss Understudy! You know 'Professor Panic's Payout Plan' did it? Top ratings for two whole nights, especially on Ilneat-Four. They had to play it a second weekend! Two weekends! We made it, girl!"

Then their eyes fell on Fursona, and they started cackling and wringing their clutching hands. "Ahahaha! You're Finster's missing hero! What a great day for Rocko Productions! Now listen here, Yiffy—"

"Absolutely not," Fursona interrupted. I'd never heard anyone object to something so strongly in my life, and I made a note to ask them what "Yiffy" meant later.

"Fine, *Fursona.* Doesn't matter. The point is, this is huge! Pataki! Pataki, where are you? Get in here, take the, uh, what do you call yourself? Like, a catchphrase?"

"The Marsupial of Justice or the Justice-Roo?"

"No, no, no, that's not gonna cut it. I'll have the folks in the back work on something better unless you and Understudy can figure it out." Rocko pointed at

Pataki with three fingers, smoking up a storm with the last one. "Take Fursona, take that suit, and give it some flair. Something better than sweats!"

"Alright, alright," Pataki drawled. "You and Miss, uh, Understudy clear out, alright? We're not compromising identities here."

"Fine, fine, we're goin'," Rocko said. As they led me out of Costuming, they turned around and grabbed a hand with both their right ones. "Do you have any idea how big this is, girl?"

The door shut behind me, and Rocko sat in a waiting room chair. I sat beside them, coughed from their cigar smoke, and shook my head. "Look, Rocko. I need a favor. I'm not asking for a ticket to the minor leagues, but I need a new show, okay? Collidus can have *Small-Town Super*, but I need something in Tokyexico, and I need Fursona as a sidekick."

"Yeah, sure, whatever you want, kid. Listen, I only got to contract three supers at a time, and that's you, Peter, and Collidus. And Finster's been harshing my mellow because two of theirs made minor league—as if they didn't have every advantage over you. But then they didn't sign their new one, and no one knew where they went. Finster's been losing their mind—their mind! And you show up with them outta nowhere? It's like the heist of the century! On accident!"

I rolled my eyes. "Rocko, my favor?"

They handed me a bottled water, and I gratefully drank while they talked. "Look, kid, I'd almost say yes to a minor-league role if you wanted it—we could try sidekicking you with, uh, Bulker or someone tough for a while. But a new show and sidekick? For what you just handed me? Done! We'll call it, uh, *Heroics 101* or something."

I beamed. I glowed. I was . . . I was really happy. It wasn't the minor leagues—and Rocko was right. I hadn't handled Jumper. Jumper, who hadn't even fought back. I wasn't ready for that yet. But dammit, I could frontline a new little-league show, especially with a brand-new sidekick.

Besides, everyone loved animals. They'd be a hit. I just knew it.

"Alright, it's a deal. *Heroics 101*." We shook hands on it. Lots and lots of hands. "So, *Small-Town Super* made it big, huh?"

"Oh yeah. Lunchbox sales are through the roof anywhere they use lunchboxes. Action figures—the FEAR 2.4 is a best seller—and of course, Tails plushies. The TA-1LZ one is trending on four planets. We'll need you to shoot one last Episode, though. A series must have its finale!"

We talked about the show until Pataki stuck their head back in. "Good news and bad news, Rocko. The good news is we got the Costume designed. It'll be a day to make it, though. The fursuit's a little different-shaped than most heroes we bring in."

"Fine, fine. Wait here, DuPont. I gotta sign up your new sidekick!" Rocko hustled back into Costuming. The door shut, and all I could do was twiddle my thumbs and wait. And think about how cool *Heroics 101* would be. Sure, it'd still be PG, but Fursona and I could make it work. We had to.

Eventually, a very bouncy Fursona hopped out into the waiting room. "Understudy, I did it! I'm officially a signed superhero!"

"Whoa, whoa, whoa! You're a signed sidekick in the little leagues. Don't go getting a big head yet," Rocko said. "Understudy, you're the best. If you ever need anything—*anything*—give me a holler! I'll see you two later! Good luck, and find some fun Episodes!"

"Bye, Rocko." I herded a way-too-excited Fursona back over to my door. Sure enough, it had a little star with a comedy and tragedy mask on it and my name. I opened it and stepped back into my hot pink green room.

[System Enabled]

"So, what's first? Fighting bad guys? Stopping crimes? We've got so much to do I can't wait!" Fursona blurted as soon as the door had shut. They wrapped me in another gigantic hug, and this time, I let them. "Thank you so much I'm so excited!"

"Nah. We need to survive the first few days of classes," I said. Then I realized something. "Hey, did Ikenga email you?"

"Who's Ikenga?"

"That'd be a no, then?" I cracked my knuckles. Or at least, I tried to—that was a Badass superhero move, or at least for people who knew how to crack knuckles. "Well, let me tell you about the TUSSA barbecue!"

23

The TUSSA Barbecue

So, yeah, I'll be here at five! Thanks for everything, really. I couldn't do it without help, and I was so nervous about asking for—"

"It's fine. We're teammates now, and teammates help each other out. I used to go to Collidus's house just to hang out with his cats," I said. I ushered Fursona to the elevator door. "Look, I need to call home and stuff. I'll see you tomorrow."

"See you tomorrow. Thanks again, Understudy!" Fursona didn't stop talking until the elevator doors closed. When they finally did, I blew out a big breath as my whole body relaxed. I hadn't realized how much Fursona's anxiety had gotten to me, but I felt physically lighter now that they'd left. Hopefully, they'd chill out.

I left my secret base with a final thought—pastel pink, not hot pink, please—and headed for my bedroom. The duffel sat untouched on the floor, with my clothes still in it. I sighed. I needed time to unpack. Now I had a couple of hours. But I really didn't want to. Instead, I grabbed my phone, untransformed, and flopped into my bed's comfy embrace.

<Three New Messages>
<One Missed Call: Dad 5:17>

My heart pounded. I'd told Peter I'd be available in the evenings; sure enough, it was evening. I couldn't wait to tell him all about my first day at TU!

<Work sucks so much. Made a deal with Collidus, though. - Peter 5:15>
<He gets a week Panic-free. - Peter 5:16>
<Hey Dot! Call us when you can and tell us about your big day! - Dad 5:19>

I ignored the message from Dad. Talking to my parents would take all night, and even though Mom worked the morning shift at the diner, she might not be home yet. Sometimes, overtime just happened to her.

<Phrasing. - Annie 5:53>

<You're not gonna believe this, but I already had an Episode! And Superpower Ethics seems cool so far! I've got new friends—Fursona from S.E. and Bianca from Intro to Drama! - Annie 5:54>
<That's great. Got time for a video chat? - Peter 5:55>
<Not tonight, babe. I gotta get all this unpacked - Annie 5:55>
<Feel like I got hit by a truck too. Good to text though - Annie 5:55>

With a groan, I pulled myself back out of bed. Actually, I *had* been hit by a truck, and then I'd gone to class afterward. I shook my head and flopped the duffel onto the bed. Superhero damage was weird sometimes. I hadn't broken anything, and I might not even have bruises, but boy, could I feel whatever S had done with that damn van. I wandered to the closet, found some hangers, and started hanging up shirts and blouses.

<Alright. So, I'm 'learning' the computer program Dad uses at the shop. It's so simple. The modded r-pies in the FEAR suit run more complex programming just to keep it standing. I am SO BORED at work, and it's only the first day. - Peter 5:58>
<History, Powers, and Drama, right? Which one's second best? We both know Powers is #1 - Peter 5:58>

I started typing Drama, then thought about it. Post–Launch Day History was definitely the worst class, based just on the first day. But was Superpower Ethics actually *better* than Intro to Drama? After a day of Ethics, I had no idea what was in store for me in that class. But Drama . . . actually, Drama was similar, only without the possibility of spontaneous Episodes.

<Yeah. Drama's the second best. The professor seems scattered but fun. Dead Poet's Society, maybe? Hopefully - Annie 6:00>

I finished hanging the shirts and jeans and putting my shorts in a drawer. Then all that was left was the underwear. I dumped my panties and bras onto the bed and started sorting them.

<I see, I see. So, you're sure no video call tonight? - Peter 6:02>
<Yeah, I'm sure. So much to do - Annie 6:02>
<Oh - Peter 6:03>

The pantie pile grew until I ran out of them and shoved them into the top drawer. Then I started clasping bras and setting them carefully into the drawer next to the underwear. When I'd finished, I collapsed on the bed.

Something was missing, though. I'd just slept in my clothes last night, but I needed out of my class clothes. My pink footie PJs hadn't made the trip!

<Hey Dad. Classes are good. Unpacking now. I'll call later. Seen my PJs there? - Annie 6:07>

<Yep. On the bathroom floor. We'll wash them for you. - Dad 6:08>

I sighed. Of course, they'd still be home. My evening routine was ruined! How was I supposed to sit around in my pajamas without pajamas?

<Disaster. No PJs. My life is over - Annie 6:09>

<Nah. Check the boxes. Packed you something - Peter 6:10>

I hurried out to the boxes, and sure enough, a sealed plastic package sat at the top of the second one. When I opened it, I grinned.

<This is not something I can wear with guests over, Peter - Annie 6:13>

<Nope, but I bet it's comfy. Try it on - Peter 6:14>

I did. The pink satin nightie went down to my knees—surprisingly low for something meant to be sexy. And it came with a pair of loose shorts, which I put on. Maybe with those, I *could* have a guest over. But probably not—it showed a *lot* of cleavage. I stepped into the bathroom, posed, spun, blew kisses in front of the full-length mirror, and snapped a quick selfie. I couldn't video-chat with him until I had something clean and organized for a background, but I could at least let him know I appreciated his gift.

<Thanks, Peter. You're the best! - Annie 6:18 (1 image attached)>

<Of course. Quick video call? - Peter 6:19>

<Tomorrow night, I promise. I'll even wear this, okay? - Annie 6:19>

<Alright. Pinkie promise? - Peter 6:20>

I sent Peter a quick picture of my pinkie—with a bit more cleavage than necessary, to make the point clear. Then I dialed my dad's number. "Hey, Dad! Yeah, I'm just emptying boxes right now, but Intro to Drama seems like it's going to be a blast. Oh, Biology? Yeah, it's okay, I guess."

Tuesday, September 2

"Hey, Understudy, you ready?"

"Of course I am! Let's go."

Honestly, I was pretty beat, and I wasn't sure how I'd handle the barbecue *and* my promise to Peter from last night. Algebra was . . . algebra. If there was one class I could rely on to feel just like a Riverside High course, it was math. There just weren't that many different ways to learn it. And Dr. Harvey was definitely a "sit in rows and work problems" kind of teacher.

Worse, I'd been wrong about Post–Launch Day History being the worst class. Ilneat Relations looked like it'd be infinitely more boring. I'd signed up thinking that "Professor Quailman" *had* to be an Ilneat name, since it fit all the conventions they used, but it was not. Instead, Dr. Douglas Quailman just happened to have the most unfortunate name in the post–Launch Day world, and his voice was a full-on monotonous drone. By the time the hour-and-a-half-long class finished, I'd found myself missing Teaching Assistant Smith and struggling not to yawn.

And I still had a barbecue and a video date to go—and couldn't cancel either of them.

I stepped onto the elevator right into a quick plush hug, and we rocketed toward the basement. "How do you get over here without being seen, anyways?"

"Maintenance tunnels between the elevators. I bet one even connects to the Mister Felsic statue. They're all pretty well-labeled, and a lot of them feel pre-Launch Day. Now come on, we're gonna be late!"

We hurried through the tunnels, following the sign toward Hickory Hall. When we arrived, the elevator had a pair of familiar-looking boys inside. One saw us and held the door.

"Hey, Underoos and the 'roo," Punch said as we hopped on. "Ikenga's party? Us too. It should be lit!"

"I heard he has live music. What a mad lad, having live music in his secret base!" Grapple hit his twin on the shoulder. As the elevator rose, they roughhoused the whole time. I rolled my eyes, then laughed when Grapple pinned his brother against the door, only for it to open and spill them both out onto the floor, where a wrestling mat had been placed perfectly to catch them.

As they untangled, I looked around the room. Incense smoke wafted from a dozen burners scattered around, filling the air with a cloying smog that hovered like the cigarette smoke in our double-wide. Art covered the faux-stone walls, paintings that appeared to move as I stared at them. And a ghostly figure pointed up the stone stairs toward the roof.

I followed the obvious direction. The party wasn't in Ikenga's secret base. It was upstairs.

Ikenga waited at the landing. "I knew you four would come. That makes all who will. The others have chosen vigilante work for now."

"How do you know?" Fursona asked.

"My [**Signature Skill**] affords me prescience—a powerful ability, though less forceful than Milo's bulk or Springlock's . . . unique skills." Ikenga gestured to the party. Electronic music—not live—pulsed across the balcony, and a pair of coolers stood by the railing. "You will, of course, take a drink from the cooler on the right. After all, Dr. Mays is here, and it'd look bad for a school function if we got underage heroes drunk."

I nodded. I'd gotten buzzed with Peter on Flat Top Hill before, but with a professor watching, I'd pass tonight. Instead, I grabbed a grape soda and popped the tab.

The superheroine who'd saved me from the SSS's Orientation Episode—the one in the blue catsuit and helmet—waved from the grill, where she grilled while a toga-clad wall of red muscles hung out and signed to her.

I strolled over. She didn't know I was the same girl, but it seemed polite. "Hi, I'm Magical Girl Understudy, and this is Fursona."

The Greek wrestler's hands blazed as the grill mistress looked at him. Then she looked at me and started signing. The toga-clad hero translated. "Hi. I'm Springlock. I can read lips, but it's easier if Milo interprets. Welcome to the club."

"Thanks! So, what does TUSSA actually *do*?" I asked. "The pamphlet wasn't very informative."

"That's *another* thing the SSS is doing better than us," Springlock signed, frowning. "TUSSA doesn't offer Rent-a-Hench or anything *cool* like that. We've got a great mentoring program for heroes looking to make the minor leagues and a community hideout that requires membership to know the location. Plus, most of the crew knows sign. You'll learn it too if you hang out with me for long. It's also useful for being sneaky and dramatically revealing your whole team at the right time."

I'd stopped listening after the mentoring program. A route to the minor leagues? I was in! "Tell me more about the mentoring."

"Yeah, I'm interested in that, too," Fursona added. "I've got a great mentor already, but learning from more than one person can't hurt, right?"

Springlock started signing, only for Milo to interrupt her as the music changed. They signed back and forth, then she kissed his cheek and hurried over to the gigantic speaker sitting on the roof. She sat down on top of it and started moving with the bass.

Milo took over the grill, popping his neck. "That's her favorite song. She'll be back. Can I get you anything here while we talk mentors?"

"A burger would be great!"

As he served, he started talking. "Most TUSSA members are solo heroes, and then there's the Quartet. Ikenga, Springlock, Hephaestus, and me. We don't take on mentorships, since we're already a full team. But Sara-N-Dipity over there? She's looking for a sidekick for some entry-level minor-league work." He handed me the burger and looked at Fursona, eyebrow raised.

"Oh, no thanks. I ate before I came. Tough to eat in this suit."

"So, which one's Sara-N-Dipity?" I asked.

Milo pointed at a blonde woman in a sequined sport coat, sitting at the table and flipping an empty soda bottle. It landed on its rim every time. "That's her. She manipulates probability. It's just luck."

At that exact moment, the song went silent, and Sara-N-Dipity stared right at Milo.

"Oh, shit," he muttered.

The blonde stood up and shook a fist at him as the music continued. "It's not luck, dammit!"

24

It's Not Luck, Dammit!

Sara, it's just luck," Milo said, holding his oversized red hands and spatula up placatingly.

"No, it's not." Sara-N-Dipity stood up and strode over to the grill. She threw her bottle in the air. "I'm running the numbers constantly. There's a 1.5% chance of landing the bottle on its rim each flip, but my power lets me change that to a 75% chance. It's just numbers, not luck."

"If it swims like a duck and quacks like a duck, it's a luck," Milo said as the bottle landed on its rim again. "Er, duck. You just came up with the math argument because you didn't want to be *Rabbit's Foot*."

"It's not. It's really, really not," Sara muttered as she returned to her hot dog. I watched her glower at Milo. She seemed intense. But all the same, I wanted that minor-league sidekick gig.

I grabbed my burger and slid onto the bench across from her. Fursona stood behind me, waving their tail. I opened my mouth to talk, but before I could, Punch and Grapple stepped over the bench and sat down on either side of me.

Punch spoke first. "Hey, we heard you're looking for a sidekick. Take us."

Sara-N-Dipity snorted into her hot dog bun. "*That's* your pitch? Listen, I'm middle-of-the-pack minor leagues, moving up toward the majors. You're, what? Bottom 10%? Let's hear what you bring to the table first, then discuss your position. Besides, Miss Magical Girl here was first. What's *your* deal?"

I breathed in, looking up at the evening sky. What *did* I bring to the table? "Alright, I'm Magical Girl Understudy. I'm a freshman. My old show, *Small-Town Super*, had just made it big in the little-league circuit when I left, and—"

"Don't care. Don't want a biography. What do you bring to the table, Understudy?" Sara took a bite from her hot dog. "'Whad maphes oo sfeshial?'"

"I can transform into other supers. Kind of," I hedged. I only had one transformation I could show them, and the middle of a superhero barbecue might not be the time for Lab Assistant Panic to make an appearance. "I only have one—"

"Show me," Sara said. Shit. When I hesitated, she grinned. "Consider this a tryout. I have to know what you can do if you're gonna be my sidekick."

I sighed and put on the goggles. "Hey, everyone, don't kick my butt, okay?"
"PROFESSOR PANIC THINKS HE'S SO TOUGH!
BUT HIS LAB ASSISTANT'S THE ONE WHO'S REALLY BUFF!"
With a spin and a flash of green, I stood next to a dozen heroes who definitely outranked me. In my villain Costume.

I tried to keep my mouth shut. I really did. But it blurted out before I could stop it. "Alright, TA-1LZ, what's the plan for campus domination? Oh, shit. Sorry, the Lab Assistant Panic Costume is based on my pathetic excuse for a rival from home."

"Evil Breakdown chance currently at 66%, Understudy," TA-1LZ said. "Recommendation: shift back before this becomes a *problem*."

I started to shift back, but Sara held up her hand. "So you're copying your nemesis's suit? What else does it do?"

"Ahaha, I'm glad you asked! It's time for a [**Maniacal Reveal**]! By stealing my . . . nemesis, yeah, that word works! By stealing my nemesis's suit, I've also stolen his powers! I can hack anything . . . simple. I have an air cannon! And I can switch back to my outfit at any time!"

"Alright, alright, tone down your power uses before we get an Episode here," Sara said. "Go ahead and change back while I talk with the boys."

I nodded and switched back with a sigh of relief. I hadn't meant to be that loud, but as I returned to my Understudy Costume, I saw everyone's eyes on me. Most relaxed after a few seconds, but Springlock kept staring at me for almost a minute before she grabbed the spork she'd been hovering in the air, ready to fling at me. Then she stood up, pointed off to the side, then at the ground in front of her.

I stared for a second while she repeated the sign.

"Come here," Milo said as he joined Springlock.

"Oh. Yeah, that makes sense."

I hurried over, abandoning my burger as Punch started talking. "Our powers are simple. Grapple holds people real well, and I punch 'em."

"But like, with powers. It's not just beating people up. We use our powers to do it," Grapple said.

Springlock's hands flew as Milo interpreted. "Odds are Sara won't pick anyone tonight. Don't be disappointed. She'll want to see you in action sometime before she picks. And don't take this the wrong way, but she's a support-and-investigation hero. She needs some firepower to help her out. Punch and Grapple offer that firepower."

"So I don't have a chance, then?" I asked, slumping.

"That's not true. She might take you on one Episode and them on another to compare your skill sets. Just hang in there. Also, next time someone asks you to go villain in the middle of a hero party, maybe don't?"

"Yeah," Milo said, pointing at himself to show he was talking, not Springlock. "You were one power use away from a major hero beatdown there."

"Oh. Oh yeah, I thought about that, but Sara-N-Dipity asked, and I don't have another Costume right now, so I showed her what I had." I shrugged and sipped my soda. "So you think she'll pick those two?"

"Yep. They fill her weaknesses way better than you do right now, and Sara's a right now kind of person. She's ridiculously good at solving mystery Episodes, and she hard-counters Lady Lockless, but she can't hold up against villains like Iron Fist or Bruiser. Even Tearjerker has better fight moves than Sara," Springlock signed, "and *she* can't fight her way out of a wet paper bag."

"I can fight. Maybe not as well as them, but I have some combat powers. And I can build for others if my partner is supportive. I'm used to being a solo or with a sidekick, though, so I like having flexibility." And I'd only gotten to the point where I *had* builds recently. I wondered if I could build Lab Assistant Panic to be more of a thinker and Understudy to be a combat Costume. That'd let me flex more.

Then I had an idea. A brilliant idea. "I have to talk to Fursona, but thanks for the conversation!"

Fursona stood near the table, listening as Punch and Grapple took turns talking Sara-N-Dipity through their most recent Episode. I sidled over. "Do you have any parts of your Costume you'd be willing to get rid of?"

"Uh, no?" they said. "I don't know how my power works yet, exactly. What if I need the whole thing to get my speed, strength, and jumping? I don't wanna lose my powers. Why do you ask?"

I explained my **[Signature Skill]** while I ate my burger. "So, since I can copy lesser versions of other supers' powers, I was thinking about doing that with yours. But I understand if you don't want to. We barely know each other, and it took my boyfriend giving me his goggles before I even got my first **[Adaptive Armoire]** Costume." I held up the goggles.

"Oh, you can date other supers? I hadn't thought about that," Fursona said as Ikenga sat down next to us.

"Yes, but I'd caution against it." He sighed. "Especially those on the other side. Break-ups can be . . . messier . . . than dating an Extra. On the other hand, you don't have to lie about who you are. That feels nice until it doesn't. Until it gets in the way. Also, it's a little rude to ask supers for parts of their Costume. It's like asking for a part of them."

I had the good sense to nod, and focused on my hamburger while Sara talked with Punch and Grapple. They chatted for a bit before she stood up on the table.

"Alright, attention, supers! I've decided to let probability and mathematics guide me in choosing my sidekick." Sara-N-Dipity said. "There's 50% chance of Understudy, and 50% of Punch and Grapple."

She tossed the coin up into the air. I watched, holding my breath as it clattered onto the table. It bounced, then tipped, then rolled off. It stood upright in a crack between two bricks.

"Dammit," Sara muttered. "Fine. Here's the deal. You have three weeks to find an Episode, win it, and report back to me. I'm LuckyGirl777.SH@tokyexicouniversity.student.edu. Don't email me unless you think I'll actually be impressed. And ignore the email. They get assigned to us. We don't pick them!"

"You were going to let luck decide when you could have had us?" Grapple flexed. "Seriously, it's not luck. It's probability!"

Fursona and I hung out for a while, drinking soda and talking with the other superheroes. I found myself distracted the whole time—what would I do for an Episode? I got the feeling that wandering the city looking for a **[Casting Call]** might just get me in trouble.

Maybe the villains from Superpower Ethics would be interested. They were teammates, after all. We could plan it out together—Peter had never done anything like that. He'd always liked to surprise me, and surprises were fun, but it would have been nice to have *some* idea of his thoughts. And as classmates, they might actually *do* it. You know, for a grade?

Eventually, I decided to let it go for now. I'd talk it over with Fursona later—and maybe Gourmet and Theseus, too.

Instead, I listened to Ikenga talk about the TUSSA Cave. Apparently, it was an underground fortress below one of the academic buildings, filled with gizmos and machines built by Hephaestus, and TUSSA had its *real* get-togethers there. The kind they didn't tell the professors about—like celebratory parties after important Episodes and league promotions. "I'm sure we'll have one or two of those this semester, minimum," Ikenga said.

"We also run TUSSA vs. SSS Episodes. If you join up, be ready for them. There's usually one or two every semester."

Finally, as the sun set, I stood up. "Well, it's been a great time, but I've got a thing tonight, so I need to get back home." In truth, I didn't want to. Talking with Springlock and Milo had been a blast, and I was having too good a time just being "me" to want to leave. But I'd promised Peter, and I needed to follow through.

"Before you go, please sign up for TUSSA, Magical Girl Understudy. You too, Fursona. We're always looking to keep our ranks up, and you'll be fighting on the side of justice and righteousness," Ikenga said. "There's also a job fair coming up. A superpowered one. More information will come via email."

"Don't you know I'll sign it?" I asked as I signed up for the Tokyexico University Student Superheroes Association.

"I try not to use my powers for *too many* trivial things. The more I use them, the messier the future gets. Thank you. We'll email you the location of the TUSSA Cave and information about the other perks we offer." Ikenga shook my hand and pointed back to the stairs.

I hurried down the tunnels toward Walnut Tower, clearing my mind off superhero stuff. The video call with Peter awaited, and after that? I could start thinking about the next Episode.

25

Thinking About the Next Episode

Hey, Annie," Peter said from my computer speakers. "That was a lot of fun. Love you lots."

I nodded and walked over to where I'd tossed my nightie. As I slipped it back over my head and searched for the matching shorts on the floor, I tried to tell myself the tease had been fun and meaningful. Fun, definitely. I'd enjoyed every second of it; my face still felt hot, and I couldn't stop panting. And he'd definitely enjoyed it, too. But now that it was over, I realized something had been missing. I couldn't put my finger on it, but . . . something.

I heard him zip up his pants and clear his throat. "So, have you had a chance to build Lil Pal yet?"

Shaking my head, I grabbed the laptop and flopped onto the bed. I ran my fingers through my hair; it would be a tangled mess tomorrow, but I had some time before Algebra in the morning. I could deal with it then. "I've been busy, Peter. I've had classes and . . . stuff . . . constantly. I'll try to work on it soon, though, I promise."

"Promise me you'll take a look at it tonight? At least unpack it. I made the design as simple as I could, and the instructions and tools are all in the box. You could build it in an hour or two this weekend if you wanted to."

"I know, babe. I'll take a look before bed. I need to get to sleep soon, though. Love you," I said, yawning. It wasn't a lie, either. I'd been exhausted since before the barbecue.

"Love you, too."

I shut down the computer and sat in front of the black, empty screen for a bit, half-dressed for the night. Why did time with Peter suddenly feel so empty? Was it just *how* we'd spent the time, or was something wrong with *us*? The text conversation yesterday had been fine. It felt normal. Right, even.

Something had to change.

<Hey, the next time I'll be able to video call is probably Friday night. Can we watch a movie together or something? - Annie 10:25>
<Sure? Goodnight! XOXO - Peter 10:26>

<Don't forget the lil pal! - Peter 10:27>

I sighed and pulled myself off the bed. After a few minutes' search in my still-packed boxes, I found the little cardboard box labeled *Lil Pal.* I dumped it out onto the end table next to my bed and stared at the tiny parts and instructions. The whole time I brushed my teeth, I thought about it. I didn't have the energy for sciencing right now, not even as Lab Assistant Panic. Lil Pal was tomorrow's problem.

As I fell asleep, the dull green eye on my end table stared at me accusingly.

Wednesday, September 3

"Now that you've seen what Mister Felsic's before-and-after codes of conduct look like, let's break into our groups and discuss how you can apply the lessons he learned between 'Magma Mia' and 'Basalt and Battery.' Keep in mind that while he had a code prior to 'Magma Mia,' the Park Street disaster caused a month of reflection, from which he created the 'Basalt and Battery' code. And . . . break!"

Gourmet yawned as we slid our chairs into a circle. We were back in the Superpower Ethics classroom—that theater with the comfy armchairs—where we'd just watched clips of Mister Felsic burning down a small town and then, two months later, regulating his powers to produce only devastating damage rather than the total destruction he was more than capable of. Dr. Jackson had us analyzing the changes in his codes so we could use them in ours. But I had a better idea.

"Okay, team, I need your help. I'm trying out for a sidekick position with a minor leaguer, and I need an Episode to make it happen."

"Sounds good. I'm in," Fursona said. "The code of conduct exercise is boring anyways. It's not like any of us can actually cause Felsic levels of damage—or even Magical Girl Stella-Lunar—and we won't be there for a while."

"Actually"—Gourmet grinned evilly—"I ate a building once. It took a few hours and was just a storage shed, but I could probably squeeze in a few more bites."

"Liar." Fursona crossed their arms over their chest. "Someone would have stopped you in a few hours."

"Well, yeah. That's why it took so long!"

"I'm not at Mister Felsic's levels of destruction," Theseus said, "but I can handle myself just fine."

"Okay, so, about my Episode. Are you villains in? I kinda need you." I tried to steer the conversation back to the Episode instead of bragging about our powers and feats of strength . . . or digestion.

"Nope. I'll have no hand in elevating a potential rival to the minor leagues." Theseus grinned and reached for a pencil and paper. "The last thing I need is to give the competition a leg up. Something I noticed about Mister Felsic's pre–'Magma Mia' code is that it played loose with the word *unnecessary*. If I were building a worthless villain code, it'd be full of words like that. They sound good, but they don't mean anything."

Gourmet opened her mouth, staring at me. Then she closed it and shook her head. "Theseus is right, Snack. We'll talk about the Episode later. Meet me at the Student Union with the Wombat there, and you're buying lunch."

I sighed. I had no idea how much Gourmet could eat, but I'd be willing to bet feeding her wasn't cheap. Still, she at least sounded interested. "Fine. Right after class, though. I have an hour or two to get ready for my next one."

"Great, now if you're done wasting time, let's keep an eye out for other useless words in the Mister Felsic code of conduct. I'll read it. You three write as you hear them," Theseus directed, pointing at us. "I swear to value the lives of innocents whenever possible—yep, that's one—in my pursuit of justice. Though my powers are great, I shall avoid unnecessary—two—destruction and loss of life. The realities of my powers notwithstanding, I shall strive to use the minimum powers possible while being sure to stop my opponents . . ."

As Theseus droned on and on, I couldn't help but think ahead to the Episode . . . and to getting Gourmet on board with it. What would she want? I shrugged. Whatever it was, I'd do my best to get it for her. We needed her—otherwise, whose ass would we be kicking? Jumper's?

I narrowed my eyes, thinking about the evasive supervillain. If it came to a fight with Jumper, we'd be ready for her noncombativeness. This time, she wouldn't get away.

"You're taking this really seriously for a villain," Fursona said, jolting me back to the conversation. "I mean, why bother? You're expected to blow stuff up, destroy buildings, and threaten people."

"Sure," Theseus said, nodding and shrugging at the same time. "And believe me, I could get away with the minimum, too. My power would let me. But I'm looking at a career lieutenant position with someone big, and none of the big names take villains without codes anymore. None of them at all. The degree is a foot in the door, too. So please, can we focus on how Mister Felsic made his language less ambiguous?"

"How does that even work?" Fursona asked.

"Vils like McHammer and Lord Destructo run tight ships. They don't even take henchmen without a two-year in superpower pre-law, and getting in with them as a lieutenant? Better have a degree. Now let's get to work."

By the time class ended, the four of us had the first two tenants of our code more or less figured out.

Code of Conduct: September 3

We will not ~~endanger harm threaten~~ endanger ~~civilians~~ Extras ~~needlessly~~
Destruction of ~~non-government residential~~ non-corporate/non-government property is ~~to be kept to a minimum not necessary~~ not okay

Fursona tagged along with Gourmet and me during our lunch meeting. I watched, stomach plummeting, as she ordered five of the burritos I'd had a couple of days prior. I ordered a slice of pizza from the next shop, paid for *all* the food, and sat down.

"This is pretty good!" Gourmet said around a mouthful of eggs and potatoes smothered in ultra-hot sauce. "Now, Episode. What's the catch?"

"There's no catch, Gourmet. I need an Episode so I can try out as Sara-N-Dipity's sidekick. We need an Episode for class, so I figured I'd ask you before I tried out some random villains. It's in everyone's interests to participate, so I don't get why Theseus isn't interested," I explained.

"Because he's minor league. He'd be guest starring, and he doesn't think he'll have the pull from your show—what's it called?"

"*Heroics 101*. We're still looking for our first Episode."

"Hey, ladies? Should we be talking about this in public?" Fursona asked, glancing around at the nearby tables. I followed their gaze. Sure enough, lots of nearby students stared at us, and some backed away from Gourmet as she grinned at them, tortilla caught between her teeth.

Gourmet laughed and took a bite from the paper her burritos had been wrapped in. "Nah. We're not talking specifics here, so there's nothing to report. Besides, what are they gonna do, arrest us? Hey, Underoos, ever been arrested?"

"I got brought in for questioning once, after my first Episode." The police hadn't gotten Rocko's message about superheroes, and they brought us both in. After they heard about it, Rocko'd cleared things up; I got a get-out-of-jail-free pass as long as I was a hero, and Peter . . . Peter got the lawyers.

"That'd be a no, then. Look, Wombat—"

"Kangaroo!"

"—Wombat, the police can't detain me for long—I'd either eat my way out or wait for the lawyers—and they won't even arrest you." Gourmet sighed and burped, breathing out a bit of fire. I wondered, not for the first time, just how her power worked. "Mojo Jojo, my producer, even said to surrender to the cops. It's got to do with the Ilneat/Human Treaties, Section Five. It gives villains certain degrees of immunity as long as they're acting in Episodes, not as vigilante villains. Instead of getting stuck in Almhurst, most of us get a slap-on-the-wrist fine that the studios pay for, and we're back on the street."

I nodded in agreement. "It's true. Professor Panic never spent more than three nights in jail. The record was fourteen minutes, but he'd contacted his lawyers before the Episode started."

"Oh." Fursona stood back and thought for a bit.

"So, Gourmet, are you in?" I asked.

Gourmet finished her burrito wrappers. "I'm in—gimme a week or two. I'll email you when and where, and I'll see if I can convince Theseus to show up, too. Just remember . . . you'll *owe* me. Thanks for the appetizer. I'll see you in class, Snack!" She stood up, burped again, and left.

"Yes! We're going to have an Episode!" Fursona cheered. "I'm gonna go get ready for my afternoon class."

"What are you taking, anyways?" I asked.

"If I told you, you might figure out my true identity, and I can't have that, can I now?" Fursona asked. Then they paused. "I mean, it's a secret identity, and I figured it was supposed to be secret from everyone, but the department knows who I am, and my producers know who I am, so maybe it's not a big deal, but what if—"

"No, it's fine." I laughed. "I don't need to know. See you later. Or maybe we can hang out tonight sometime?"

But by the time Intro to Drama was over, I knew I wouldn't be hanging out with Fursona or anyone else because, at the end of Intro to Drama, we got bad news.

26

Bad News

What kind of monster gives homework in the first week, anyway?" Bianca asked as we sat on the couch in the Doyle Building.

"Calm down. It's not even the full play. He just wants us to read through a couple of scenes. It's no big deal," I said.

"No big deal? I've never read a play before. I don't know *how* to read one, and I don't know why my parents signed me up for this stupid class anyways."

"Didn't you say . . ." I started asking.

"Yes. I said I got signed up because they thought it'd make me more outgoing." Bianca's eyes narrowed behind her glasses, and she crossed her arms over her chest. "Please just let me bitch for a minute. This isn't my strong suit, and I could really use some help."

"Okay." I stood up and held out a hand. Maybe I *was* going to be hanging out with someone. "Why don't you come over to my place? I'm done with my classes for the day. We can pick through *The Importance of Being Earnest* together. It'll be fun. We can find the silly parts to read."

"Oh, if you're done, that sounds great," Bianca said. Something about her self-satisfied expression told me that maybe, just maybe, I'd fallen into a trap some-how. She grabbed my hand and let me pull her to her feet. "You know, I haven't been to someone else's dorm yet. What's the thirteenth floor like? My scholarship was only good enough for a solo room, not a top-floor place. I hear those are pretty fancy—like, for the super wealthy."

I started walking, dragging Bianca along until she let go of my hand. "It's a nice place, but I didn't get it because of my family or anything. I got a full ride here, and it came with a room in, uh, Ash Hall. But there was a paperwork issue, so they gave me an open one in Walnut. They weren't going to use it anyways."

The lie seemed smooth enough, but Bianca gave me a *look* for a moment before she shook her head. "Okay, Annie. Whatever you say. Just help me through this homework."

We walked back to Walnut Tower, chatting about high school the whole time. She'd grown up in Tortuga West, a city on the southeast tip of North America. By the time we got to my dorm, I practically oozed envy. "You got to play soccer? And swim? I didn't get to play sports!"

"No? You look like an athletic type of girl to me," Bianca said. She eyed me critically. "You'd have made a good keeper in soccer—nice and tall, with long arms. I was a midfielder, and I swam butterfly and breaststroke. I wasn't, like, a star or anything, but sports were fun."

She stared off wistfully until we hit Walnut Tower's double doors. Then, as we waited for an elevator, I heard a vaguely familiar voice behind me.

"Annie, hi," said the tiny Korean girl I'd run into the night I moved in.

I looked at her, struggling to find her name. However, I'd met so many people in the last four days that it wasn't happening. "Sorry, I know I met you in the elevator, and you live on floor twelve, but the name's just not in there, haha." I tapped my temple playfully as we climbed on board.

"Oh! Yeah, you remember me. Su-Bin Pak," she said.

"Hi," Bianca said. "Bianca. We're going to Annie's room to study for classes."

"Oh, I'll join you if you don't mind?" Su-Bin asked. I shook my head, and she grinned. "Alright. Room 1301, correct? I'll be up after I grab my pre-calc book."

The three of us chatted for a while until Su-Bin got off. When Bianca and I got to my room and I opened the door, her eyes widened. "Wow, this is way better than my place! You've got a whole living room! And a separate bedroom? I got my own room, but not like *this*. Do you have rooftop access?" She started checking random handles, and I cringed as she tried to turn the maintenance door.

"Locked? Bummer." She glanced into my bedroom before tossing herself down onto the couch. "So, *The Importance of Being Earnest*?"

"Yeah. Carl said the first scene and then any scene of our choice." I grabbed my laptop. "We could watch a video, but I have a better idea."

"What?"

"You'll see," I said.

The door buzzer buzzed, and I let Su-Bin in. Then we had to go through the whole "what a fabulous room" routine again before she finally sat down on the carpet, legs crossed, and set a massive math book and a giant plastic cup of soda in front of her. "Thanks, Annie. I do a lot better with some background noise, to be honest. Oh, what are you doing Friday night?"

"I have plans," Bianca said quickly, then covered her mouth. "You . . . weren't talking to me, were you? Sorry, sorry, sorry."

I laughed, even though Su-Bin would be disappointed with my answer. "I also have plans. What are you doing, though? And can I get either of you some water?"

"Nah, I'm good," Bianca said.

Su-Bin clicked a mechanical pencil against her lips. "No thanks. Some of the other girls in the 1232 suite and I are going to see a movie. *I Dance in Fading Starlight*—it's a silly rom-com, but it looks fun to make fun of. I told them I'd go, but I wanted to see if a couple of friends could join, but I'm going anyway. Veronica's not coming, thank god, and I want to avoid her."

I pouted a little and stared at my computer screen. Some regular stuff like that sounded relaxing. "I wonder if I could cancel my plans. We could try them sometime next week. Lemme send a text real quick." I grabbed my phone and tucked it in close so Bianca and Su-Bin couldn't see the screen. Then I quickly typed out a message.

<Hey Peter. Let's go for Sunday night instead. Things came up - Annie 4:08>
<Alright. ty for heads up - Peter 4:09>

I looked back over to the script and stared at Su-Bin, trying to keep my face straight. "Bianca, we're going to do a script reading the way I used to in high school. Pay close attention. You might learn something. I'll be Lane. You be Algernon."

"Alright." Bianca gulped and started her line. "Did you hear what I was playing, Lane?" Then she looked at me expectantly.

I scrunched up my nose, stretched my lips, and said, "I didn't think it polite to listen, sir," in the most high-pitched, nasally voice I could manage.

Su-Bin snorted into her math book. Bianca stared for a second, wide-eyed, before she cracked up. As I watched her break down and roll on the couch, I started laughing, too, and for a minute, the three of us sat and giggled in my apartment's living room.

Once we'd recovered, Bianca glared at me mischievously, then continued, reading her lines in the deepest voice she could muster. And so we plowed through the first scene in *The Importance of Being Earnest*—with an occasional pause to break down laughing and once for Su-Bin to clean her math book when she spewed soda onto the page.

Finally, Bianca finished with, "Literary Criticism is not your forte, my dear fellow. Don't try it," and stopped to catch her breath.

"Is that . . . is that far enough?"

"I think so," I said.

"I *hope* so," Su-Bin added, grinning. "I haven't gotten a single damn problem done. You two are outrageous."

"I try," I said. "In fact, I try really hard. This is a lot harder with a play like *Romeo and Juliet*, where every line has a rhythm and beat, but some of Shakespeare's stuff is funny enough that it holds up through silly accents."

Su-Bin stood up. "Where's your bathroom?"

"Next to the bedroom, to the left. The right's just a maintenance room. I can't get it open." I pointed to the correct door, and Su-Bin disappeared.

"So," Bianca said, grinning and turning to face me. She had surprisingly blue eyes for how black her hair was. "Are all drama geeks this funny?"

"Yeah, actually. Some of us are even more funny than this," I said.

"Tell me more?" She stretched and yawned.

"I learned silly-voice readings from the older kids at Riverside High and taught them to the younger kids once I was older. I didn't play any sports, but acting was okay."

Rocko had recommended theater clubs and classes the first time we'd met and ensured there would be no Episodes while we were in them. I'd gotten so into theater that I would have done it even without Rocko's encouragement. Peter hadn't stuck with it past sophomore year, though. He had important science stuff to get to instead.

"Yeah, we had silly rituals on the soccer team, too," Bianca said. I waited for her to elaborate, but she didn't. After a minute, she turned around and sprawled over the couch's back, staring into my bedroom. "What is that? Some kind of drone? Cool! I always loved the idea of flying!"

Oh god, I'd left the damn Lil Pal sitting on my nightstand. I flushed a little and pulled the door shut. If she got a good look at it, she'd figure out that it wasn't just a drone but a *Genius-designed* drone.

"It's a gift from my boyfriend. I haven't built it yet, though."

"Alright, it's been fun, but I need to get going," Su-Bin said. She packed up her math book and smiled. "See you Friday night, okay? I bet it'll be a great time."

I nodded and showed Su-Bin to the door. The whole time, I felt Bianca just *radiating* frustration. I waited until Su-Bin had left, then sat on the couch. "What's wrong, Bianca?"

"I just . . ." She wouldn't look at me. Instead, she shifted from one foot to the other and spun a lock of hair in her fingers. "I had so much fun with the play reading, and I wanna keep hanging out, but I'm not sure what to do now, and I need to go back to my place. I have a morning class and stuff."

I stopped her. "Deep breaths, Bianca. I had a lot of fun too. You're welcome to come by anytime, and if you want to stay a while, we can find something to watch. I don't have much food in the place, though."

We sat on the couch and talked while I tracked down some old minor-league reruns for background noise. Bianca started getting restless about halfway through an early *The Agent* Episode. She kept sneaking glances at me, her mouth open like she wanted to say something and then thinking better of it.

Before *The Agent* could even empower a temp hero, she stood up and cleared her throat, fidgeting. "I think I need to go. I'm sorry."

I stared at her. We'd been having fun, right? And the Episode wasn't over. It didn't make sense for her to leave. "You okay?" I asked.

"Yeah. I just . . . I have a lot to do tonight."

"Alright. I'll see you in class."

"See you then."

I still had a scene to pick from *The Importance of Being Earnest.* I sat back down and started looking through the script for something fun to read. A pinging sound dragged my attention to my email.

Subject: Episode
Scared?

Nah, I'm kidding, Snack. Next Sunday night works if you're not worried about being up early Monday morning. Nine days. It'll be a late night for us all.
Roth Arena. 10:45
Bring Wombat with you. They need the exercise.

I had a second email waiting as well.

Subject: TUSSA/SSS Joint Superpowered Job Fair
Greetings, Powered Student,
We hope you'll attend the first-ever joint event between TUSSA and the SSS: our Superpowered Job Fair.
When?: October 4, All Day Long!
Where?: Roth Arena
What?: A chance to network with the majors and minors who keep our city safe, sign up for internships, and potentially earn work-study pay
Who'll be There?: Tele-Portal, McHammer, The Agent, Drs. Jackson and Mays, representatives from 3V1L, and many more supers
Ikenga
Prescient President, TUSSA
Monologue
President, SSS

I ignored them both for now. I was too excited about the weekend's fun. It'd been a long time since I'd been a movie-watcher, not a popcorn girl.

27

Not a Popcorn Girl

FRIDAY, SEPTEMBER 5

Hey Peter, how's work been? - Annie 6:45>

I'll be honest. I was exhausted. Thursday's classes hadn't gone well. Algebra was proving just as confusing as ever; I needed Su-Bin to tutor me or something. Maybe I could pay her or have her over more often. She couldn't enjoy living with four other girls—and sharing a room with one sounded miserable.

Being an only child rocked sometimes.

But no, algebra hadn't been good, and unfortunately, Professor Quailman's second lesson hadn't been better than his first. I'd spent most of the time idly wondering if I could convince Rocko to show up for a day. Sure, the treaties all said the Ilneats needed to stay in special districts, and he'd be miserably cold, but it might be worth it to see my Ilneat Relations professor's face.

<It's been boring. I wish you were here so much, Annie. - Peter 6:47>
<Classes have been pretty good. Got a couple nemeses, but they're not as cool as you - Annie 6:48>

That was probably a lie. I hadn't seen Gourmet in action, but she seemed way more powerful than Peter. And Jumper was . . . Jumper, but her Short was so different from Peter's evil plots that it'd almost been refreshing. Other than the van, I mean.

Today had been way better. Teaching Assistant Smith clearly cared a lot about post–Lauch Day history, and we'd almost—almost—gotten a third tenant on our codes for Superpower Ethics. Dr. Jackson intervened for the first time when tempers flared between Punch and the Bread Cape villain, who called himself The Crumb.

Yeah. Jumper wasn't the lamest villain in Tokyexico City.

Bianca and I had even survived talking about *The Importance of Being Earnest* in class. Well, she'd survived. I'd loved it, even if Earnest wasn't *really* a drama. We'd talked on the Doyle Building couch for a bit, which was becoming a habit, and then returned to our dorms.

I pulled up a floor plan for Roth Arena and perused it while waiting for Peter to text back. If Gourmet wanted an Episode there, something there would give her an advantage. But I couldn't see what. The maps just looked like another indoor sports arena: a weight room, a few classrooms for the sports and recreation students, but nothing out of the ordinary.

My phone buzzed, and I mindlessly opened it and read the message. Then I reread it.

<It's your BFF! Hi hi! - Bianca 6:50>

I rolled my eyes. We'd only hung out once or twice, so now we were best friends? Well, if she wanted to play that game, I had a dumb nickname in mind!

<Hi Bee, what's up? Finish the drama homework? - Annie 6:51>
<Har har. Yeah, I did. Without help this time. Are you going to the movies w/ Su-Bin? - Bianca 6:51>
<I hope none of them replace me. But if they do, at least I'll still be #1 in your heart - Peter 6:51>

I started texting Bianca back since I had her messages open already.

<Yep! Should be a lot of fun - Annie 6:52>

She started typing—I could see the little dots—then stopped. And then started. And then stopped again.

<I don't think anyone's replacing you, hun. We've been through a lot together. I'm just having an off night tonight - Annie 6:52>
<Alright, Annie. So, who are the nemeses? - Peter 6:53>
<Gourmet gains powers from food, I guess? I have no idea what Theseus does. And Jumper . . . jumps around and runs away. I could be getting a sidekick role in the minor leagues, though! - Annie 6:54>
<That's really great. Work sucks. When are you coming home? - Peter 6:53>
<Not for a while. Things are busy, the megafauna's picking up around here, and I'd need to figure out a ride share. Probably a month :(- Annie 6:54>
<Can I come? - Bianca 6:54>

I shrugged and shut my computer. The map told me nothing; whatever Gourmet was planning, it was more abstract. It actually made a lot of sense for Bianca to come. She was a friend—maybe not a "BFF," but pretty cool—and according to her, she needed to get out more.

<Sure. My place, 7:30 - Annie 6:55>
<Great I'll be there I'm so excited eeeeee - Bianca 6:56>
<Too much? Sorry - Bianca 6:56>
<Nah, see you in half an hour - Annie 6:57>

I laughed and sashayed into my secret base. My bathroom had a pretty lovely mirror, but the green room's lighting just couldn't be beaten for a night out. I started working on a quick, easy makeup job. But Peter's texts made it hard to focus.

<I see. - Peter 6:57>
<If you change your mind, let me know. - Peter 6:58>
<Ive got a great Episode in mind for you - Peter 6:59>
<Spoiler Alert! Giant Freaking Robot - Peter 6:59>
<It's not up to me, Peter. Its a long drive and I just got up here Sunday. - Annie 7:00>
<If you wanna come over, I've got plenty of room. This beds gigantic ;) - Annie 7:00>
<Seriously, though. First 3-day weekend I get, unless you get time off first - Annie 7:01>

I put the phone down and put on my lipstick, waiting for a response. Nothing came for a while, and I stretched out on the couch and waited for *someone* to text me, whether it was Peter, Bianca, or Su-Bin.

Shit.

I still hadn't given Su-Bin my phone number. What kind of friend was I?

<K - Peter 7:10>
<No days off for a while, but maybe I can swing something w/ dad - Peter 7:11>
<This distance sucks - Peter 7:11>
<Yeah it does. Sorry, babe - Annie 7:12
<I gotta go. Seeing a movie w/ friends soon - Annie 7:12
<That's fine. TTLY - Peter 7:13>
<TTYL - Annie 7:13>

I stared at the ceiling and groaned. I'd worried about Peter after how he'd handled himself before the "Payout Plan" Episode. But his late-night messaging had stopped, and Professor Panic hadn't texted me once except jokingly. He'd done a good job on my needs, and I hadn't followed through on his. Sure, he had a good time during our video call. But I hadn't even looked at the Lil Pal.

"Screw it," I mumbled as I headed to the bedroom and dumped the robot out again. The eye stared at me, so I flipped it over and started looking through the directions. Then I sighed. "Tails, this is a job for Lab Assistant Panic later on."

<I suggest you try. It'll meow-n a lot to Peter if you make progress,> Tails said from the bed.

I nodded. "I know, I know," I said and started tinkering with Step One. The tiny tools and parts turned out to be more frustrating than I expected, though, and I'd only made it to Step Three by the time my phone buzzed.

<Hey, let me iiiiin! - Bianca 7:27>
<Wait, I'm coming down - Annie 7:27>

I tossed the box in front of the parts pile and hurried downstairs to meet my friends.

"Annie, are you okay?"

"Yeah, I'm fine."

The ADR theater complex didn't hold a candle to the Superpower Ethics classroom. The chairs here were . . . fine. I'd gotten comfy eventually in an end chair next to Bianca. But it definitely wasn't a La-Z-Boy. And it wasn't as clean either—no surprise. They'd already shown a matinee and an early evening showing of *I Dance in Fading Starlight,* and the stale popcorn and spilled soda made my stomach roil. I'd cleaned up too much of it working in Riverside's movie theater, and I didn't envy the high-school kids working here in a few hours.

I hadn't been able to shake the aftereffects from my text conversation earlier, either. I felt like a terrible girlfriend; now that I looked, I saw a dozen ways I could have helped the relationship this week. Honestly, it was hard not to feel for him. He still had his parents nearby, but he couldn't *really* talk to them. I'd been the only one who got him, and now he'd lost me, physically at least.

I wouldn't tell him about all my Episodes and superhero stuff unless he asked anymore. That'd help. Hopefully.

The speakers blared, and the theater's lights dimmed. A preview popped up on the screen, which I ignored as best I could. It was just another Stella-Lunar film, though this one had an exciting team-up with Mister Felsic. I frowned. I thought he'd retired, but the villain—whoever it was, must've needed a special touch, or Mister Felsic countered them. Maybe it was Mindstorm. She'd been his rival.

"You don't seem fine," Bianca said. She glanced over at me. "You're gonna have marks from your nails."

I unclenched my fists. Sure enough, my nails had dug into my palms, leaving painful gouges in my skin. I winced. "I guess I'm not fine."

"Do you want to talk about it?" Bianca asked.

"No. It's just boyfriend stuff." I shrugged and made a show of watching the screen. Bianca didn't look away from me, though. She just stared. I fidgeted, then looked at her and started whispering. "Okay, Peter's a good guy, but he's really stupid about a lot of stuff. He had a hard time with me leaving for college because . . . well, I was the only person he could talk to about some stuff. So things got bad between us and . . . uh . . . we had a fight."

Yeah. A fight. If "Professor Panic's Payout Plan" was just a lover's spat, I'd hate to see what'd happen if the relationship fell apart.

"Oh, what—"

I'd started now, though, and I couldn't stop. I kept whispering, "It's not all his fault, though. I left him there, and he doesn't have anyone else who gets him. And I've been focused on my classes and making friends here instead of our relationship."

"Hold on—"

"And he . . . never mind." I'd been about to tell Bianca about how he'd been my rival, and now he had to settle for a thirteen-year-old, but I couldn't do that.

Bianca reached out and patted my shoulder. Somehow, the incredibly awkward touch helped ground me just a little. "Sorry you're, uh, dealing with that. Do you need a hug, or do you need help?"

"What?"

"It's something I learned in a psych class in high school. People who are venting either need advice or a hug. But if you guess and get it wrong, it feels terrible for the venter. So, hug or help? Or neither. Neither is fine too."

"Hug. Definitely hug."

She side-hugged me across the armrest—just a quick squeeze—and then let go.

"You're my friend, Annie, and it hurts seeing you bummed out, and I don't like feeling like that." She smiled at me. "Let's enjoy the movie, okay?"

The lights darkened the rest of the way, and *I Dance in Fading Starlight* started playing. I let my mind wander, not paying much attention to the movie or anything else. Bianca slurped on her extra-large soda and munched popcorn the whole time, getting more and more fidgety until, by the end, her knee kept bumping into mine.

As the credits rolled, Su-Bin yawned. "Alright, let's get going."

"Oooh! Shotgun!" Bianca yelled and jogged for the exit.

Su-Bin rolled her eyes. Once Bianca had run out of earshot, she said, "So, Annie, you gonna let her crash on your couch?"

I shrugged. "I don't know. Should I?"

"Yeah. Otherwise, she has to walk all the way across campus, right? It's dark. The least you could do is ask. I'd invite her to my place, but Veronica snores. A lot. And there's not much space either."

I needed sleep, and Bianca had half a gallon of sugar and caffeine in her. If she said yes, it was going to be a long night. But maybe we could watch TV or something until she burned off her caffeine overdose. Or I could toss a blanket her way and ignore her. Either way, it beat having her cross Tokyexico University at night. Who knew what kind of villains were waiting to start an Episode out there?

I climbed into Su-Bin's back seat and folded the seat back up for Bianca. Once we'd buckled in, I cleared my throat. "Hey, Bianca, it's pretty dark. If you wanna crash on my couch tonight, I'd be okay with—"

"Slumber party! I accept!"

I sighed as she practically bounced in her chair. I'd been right; it was going to be a long, long night.

PART FOUR

28

Sportsball

SUNDAY, SEPTEMBER 14

[**Starwave Sail**]!" I threw myself off Walnut Tower's roof and zipped through the air. Roth Arena's gigantic white dome loomed in the distance. I was early, but I'd agreed to meet Fursona there to catch the Episode right at the start. If Gourmet started on time, that is.

I snorted. Supervillains starting when they said they would? Impossible. They'd be early to get a jump on us or late to throw us off.

I'd stayed up most of Friday night with Bianca, making fun of first-gen superhero Episodes together. The first couple of seasons right after Launch Day had been crazy. There hadn't been leagues, and some of the power mismatches were . . . painful. In one Episode, Mister Felsic went up against Cinder-Ella. The poor villain had almost exactly his power set, only weaker in every way, and the Episode was only fun to watch after Felsic rolled her up in the first act and then spent most of the second giving her pointers while she tried desperately to fight back.

And then we watched the Man vs. Nature shows. They still made those, but most of the megafauna and flora just . . . weren't a threat anymore. The walls around cities helped keep them out, but The Huntsman had to get out there for a scythetooth pack every so often, and full Man vs. Nature events needed most hands on deck. But back then, Man vs. Nature was every super, heroes and villains both, against the wilds, with humanity's survival at stake. I shuddered. Of all the Episodes I'd watched, Man vs. Natures scared me the most.

Then, when she'd finally gone to sleep on the couch and I retreated to my room, I learned a terrible truth about Bianca. She snored like a freight train. We'd had such a good time, though, that I didn't mind.

Saturday was refreshing, especially for my relationship with Peter. I got time to tinker with the Lil Pal but only got to Step Seven. Peter was happy, though. We watched an action flick from before Launch Day with a disillusioned soldier angry at the military complex. Peter said there were like thirteen more movies in the series, but we didn't have time to watch them all. Probably. It felt nice, though.

Since then, it'd been endless classes and homework all week. It kept piling on; I'd never had to deal with so much. And Peter had overtime at the drill shop. Something about upgrading the code, he said. So we'd only been texting. And to be honest, we were running out of stuff important enough to text about. *Someone* needed an Episode.

And now, I had one. I landed next to Fursona and waved.

[Show-off! +1 Flamboyance Point]

[Casting Call]
[Episode: Short: Whey Too Few Leg Days - PG]
[Role: Heroine! Do you accept the role? (Yes/No)]
[Role Focus: Flamboyance+Grit]

"Why are we here again?" Fursona asked. They shifted from paw to paw, staring at Roth Arena's gigantic white dome and glass walls. The arena sat dark this late at night. I hadn't had a chance to check it out since I never got a tour, but I'd seen the map. Concessions, trophy cases, and a basketball/volleyball court. Just like Riverside High's, but bigger. Way, way bigger.

"Because Gorgonzola said to be," I said. I accepted the role and walked toward a hole in the wall. A shiny camera drone followed me; now that the Episode had started, Rocko was definitely watching.

The concrete seemed to have been eaten away. I shuddered. I'd wondered what, exactly, Gourmet's power did before. I'd find out soon enough.

[Whey Too Few Leg Days: Act One in Progress]

"Yeah, but what's she gonna do?"

I shrugged. "Does it matter? There's villains in there, so she's probably not selling cookies."

Fursona nodded, their kangaroo snout shaking up and down. "I wonder how many cookies she can eat in a sitting." The Marsupial of Justice stepped into the toothmark-covered hole in the stadium's wall into a locker room. "Hey, Understudy, I don't think you're allowed in here."

"Fursona, I've seen it all before," I said, following them into the dark locker room. My wand's pale pink glow barely lit up my feet, and I wrinkled my nose against the stale BO smell. "They really can't make it *smell* better in here, huh?"

"Nah, locker rooms are all bad. Back in school, ours stunk too." Fursona hop-ran toward a door, poked their head out, then pulled it back in. "At least college athletes are mostly over that body spray. Some of them, anyway. That **[Beep!]** downright offensive. Oop!"

"Yeah, you can't swear in a little-league Episode." I laughed.

"Got it, got it!" Fursona said. "Alright, that door's the way to the arena. The lights were on over the court, so either something's up or . . ."

"Or they keep it lit all the time," I finished.

"Yeah. Either way, let's check it out."

I followed Fursona onto the basketball court, half expecting Gourmet's voice to echo from the PA system like Peter's had at Riverside High. The lights over the court cast long shadows into the bleachers; the high-appetite supervillain could be hiding anywhere. We stood on the Rams logo at center court, peering into the darkness.

[Inkling] pointed behind the basketball hoop, so I went there first. Something stood up from a seat—or someone.

[Good Thinking! +1 Cunning Point]

"Well done, heroes. You've fallen into my trap!" Gourmet took a bite from a baseball glove. "Chewy! Yeah, that's right, the **[Maniacal Reveal]**!"

I groaned. "Does every villain have that power?"

"Only the *good* ones. Now, Snack, listen carefully. While you and the Wombat were tracking me down, my partner in crime was finishing up an . . . arms deal, shall we say? An arms deal upstairs in the workout rooms. You're too late to stop him—not that you'll beat me to get there! Ahahahaha!"

"Is this the part where we fight her?" Fursona asked.

"Yeah, this is the part where we fight her. **[Stellar Ray]**!" The light beam punched toward Gourmet, who took it square in the chest.

[Dramatic Damage! +1 Drama Point]

She shrugged it off, finished off the baseball glove, and grinned. "It's like jerky, but with a drier texture! And if that's the best you can do, it's time to play ball!" She whirled her arm like a softball pitcher, and even though she'd had nothing in her hand, a ball whipped toward me. It caught me on the shoulder, spinning me around and knocking me onto the hardwood floor.

[HP 5/6]

I popped back onto my feet—superhero damage helped shrug off hits like that, but Gourmet's arm packed every bit of punch Peter's **[Hypercompression Cannon]** had. I had just enough time to regret not having **[Hometown Heroine]** before the next baseball ricocheted off the floor next to me.

[Gritty Recovery! +1 Grit Point]

"It's time to strike you out, Understudy," Gourmet said as she wound up for another pitch. She brought up her leg and snapped her arm for—

"Hey, Gourmet, that's a bean ball! Ejected!" Fursona leapt through the air and slammed into the larger supervillain, who toppled over a bleacher and hit the ground hard. Fursona leaped onto her, and they rolled down the steps and bleachers in a tangle of limbs, tail, and plush.

I dashed up the steps toward them, but as I got there, Gourmet took a bite from Fursona's shoulder and chewed the plush. She swallowed, reeled her feet back, and kicked Fursona in the stomach with brand-new marsupial-like legs.

Fursona flew through the air and landed on a bleacher. It bent a touch under the impact, and they lay there, dazed. The camera drone that had been following them turned in my direction.

Which meant it was all on me.

"[**Spotlight Strike**]!" I said, dashing toward Gourmet and spinning in the air. My kick followed the light pink spotlight into her stomach, knocking her back as she got to her feet.

[**Stylish Combat! +1 Flamboyance Point**]

I tried to follow up, but before I could, Gourmet rolled away, kicking at me and forcing me to keep my distance. It wasn't fair! She had a better power-stealing power than [**Adaptive Armoire**]! I started chasing her, but she pulled something out of a large pocket before I could close in and started eating it.

As I got closer, my stomach rolled. I could see the arm and neck holes in the bright red . . . wrestling singlet . . . hanging out of her mouth. She slurped it down and grinned. "What?"

"You . . . eugh, that was clean, right?"

Gourmet shrugged. "I dunno. Who cares? Come get some, Snack!"

"That's disgusting, Gourmet," I said. Then I leaped toward her, fist back for a big haymaker. "[**Spotlight Strike**]!"

The spotlight zipped up toward her face, and so did my fist. It landed with a satisfying crunch, knocking her head back. I started dancing back out of range to plan my next attack.

[**Stylish Strike! +1 Flamboyance Point**]

Or at least, I tried.

She moved so quickly I couldn't piece together what'd happened. One moment I stood out of reach. The next, she'd slammed me facedown against the concrete steps, arms pinned painfully behind me. "Understudy is down for the count! One!"

[**HP 4/6**]

"Two!"

[HP 3/6]

Something slammed into Gourmet, knocking her off me and spinning me into a bleacher face-first. I picked myself up as Gourmet and Fursona wrestled and grappled, rolling until they hit the basketball court before the marsupial kicked themselves free.

Gourmet backpedaled to half-court. Her face glistened with sweat, and I could hear her panting breaths all the way from below the hoop. "Alright . . . you two . . . you win this round. But I'll be back!"

I fired off another [**Stellar Ray**] as she ran toward the locker room tunnel, but it crashed into the glowing green exit sign in a blaze of sparks. She ducked down the passageway and disappeared.

Fursona breathed heavily enough I could hear it through the voice modulator. They put their paws on their knees. "Wow. That was *way* harder than fighting Jumper."

"Yeah. Jumper's not a fighter, but that was worse than Professor Parsley, too. Or his bots. Did you catch what she said about an arms deal?"

"Yeah. Upstairs, then? Maybe we can catch her partner. Think it's Theseus?" Fursona started climbing the steps up to the upper levels.

"[**Starlight Sail**]!" I zipped past them and waited at the door. "Probably. Unless she's got henchmen. The SSS pamphlet said they had a Rent-a-Hench program, so we could be fighting classmates from our regular classes. Be ready for anything."

We burst through the door and into a long, arcing hallway. Pictures of student athletes, all larger than life, covered the walls: basketball stars, runners, and weight-lifters. As we followed the signs to the weight room, I couldn't help but notice that one athlete's arms didn't match his body. Under the mismatched weightlifter was a plaque. "Andre Kolowitz, Three-Time Post–Launch Day Unpowered Weightlifting Champion," I read.

The weightlifter's arms were about three shades darker than the man himself and far too skinny to support the plate-covered bar he'd lifted over his head. And something else felt off. I got closer. Were the arms . . . three-dimensional? And—I touched one—slightly warm?

"We never figured out what Theseus's power was, did we?" I asked Fursona, a lump forming in my throat.

"Nope."

"Alright. It's got something to do with arms, though. Clearly."

The arms creeped me out, and I hurried down the hall toward the weight room door.

Fursona put their hand on my shoulder. "Maybe you should let me go first. The suit takes some of the damage for me—I only took one point that whole time."

I nodded. It made sense since I had a ranged power and Fursona didn't. I took a deep breath and counted down on my fingers so they could see. Jerking the door open, I yelled, "Now!"

Fursona ran in.

A bar with a half dozen plates on the end swung into them.

Crash!

They flew into a weight machine, which fell on top of them.

"What, did you think I'd just *let* you in?" Theseus asked as he stepped between us. He dropped the bar he'd been holding in his . . . arms.

I barely heard the weights and bar clattering on the rubbery floor as I stared. Theseus flexed his—no, those were definitely the Andre Kolowitz poster's—biceps. "I told you girls I was minor league. Now it's time to prove it."

"Uh, Understudy," Fursona said shakily, untangling themselves from the weight machine's rubble. "I think we're in trouble."

29

We're in Trouble

[Stellar Ray]!" I aimed my wand at Theseus as the paper-armed villain reached for a pair of dumbbells. The beam hit him, knocking him away from them; he might've been minor league, but he wasn't as physically tough as Gourmet. I pegged him as more of a Badass villain to her Grit.

[Dramatic Damage! +1 Drama Point]

Even so, the beam hadn't done enough. It felt like shooting at LABRAT but without the success. He picked up a weight and slung it at me, paper arm flapping in the wind. The weight crashed into the wall, punching a hole the size of my head through the drywall.

I froze and blinked, staring at it. Rocko's words from when they shot down my interest in the minor leagues flooded back to me: "Minor leaguers are loose cannons." Theseus wasn't fighting to perform. He was fighting to *win*.

Theseus snapped up another weight and launched it toward Fursona. It slammed into them, driving them into a rack of medicine balls. "I'm *armed*, I'm dangerous, and I'm head and shoulders ahead of either of you," he boasted.

"How do we—oof!" The wind flew out of Fursona's lungs as another weight slammed into them. I winced. Even through their superhero damage, that looked painful. "How do we fight him?"

How *could* we fight him? We ducked and dodged around weights—and medicine balls when he ran out. I'd had the same dilemma with Professor Panic's FEAR 2.4 power armor. Except this time, I could just **[Stellar Ray]** him down.

But unlike Peter, he could close the gap, and I couldn't disarm him like I had the suit. Or could I?

"Heh," I snorted. "Disarm."

"What?" Fursona asked.

"Just a sec! Distract him!" I sprinted away from Theseus as he picked up a barbell and tossed it toward Fursona, where it shattered a mirror. Then I pulled out Peter's goggles.

"THESEUS MAY BE ARMED, HOSTILE, AND DANGEROUS,
BUT LAB ASSISTANT PANIC'S HERE TO OBTAIN JUSTICE!"
Green flash. Spin/jump/hands. And there I was, in the Lab Assistant Panic Costume, ready to fight . . . with science!

[Rejuvenation Activated: HP 6/6]

"Understudy, that rhyme was awful!" Fursona said.
"54% to villainous breakdown!" TA-1LZ yelled.
"Shut up, minion! Professor Panic had a whole rap group write his lyrics. I'm doing them on the fly!" I would have said more, but a barbell caught me on the shoulder and spun me around.

[HP 5/6]

"Ahahahaha! It's time to **[Maniacal Reveal]** your weakness, Theseus!" I shouted, letting the dark side flow through me. Going Dark Girl would be so much fun; I could do this all the time! "If we *disarm* you, I bet that super-strength goes away just like that! And those arms look strong, but I bet they're not *tough*! **[Stellar Ray]**!"
Nothing happened.
"Whoops." I charged up the **[Hypercompression Cannon]** instead.
BANG!

[Dramatic Damage! +1 Drama Point]

Theseus's—no, Andre's—arm rippled and waved as the air blast rushed past it. He dropped the barbell he'd been swinging like a club, but the arm didn't rip like I'd hoped. "Get the arms, minion!"
"I'm not your minion. I'm your sidekick!" Fursona launched themselves at Theseus, who parried with the *other* barbell he'd been holding. They went back and forth, with Fursona's suit looking more and more ragged as Theseus pushed the magnificent marsupial around the room. I fired another **[Hypercompression Cannon]** shot just as Fursona grabbed the arm in their paws and pulled.
BANG!
RIP!

[Dramatic Damage: +1 Drama Point]
[Team-Up Combo!: +1 Drama and Badass Points]

With only one arm, I expected Theseus to give up. That would have been critical damage to the FEAR suit. But he just . . . laughed.
"Hahahaha! Alright, you got me there. Hold on a second. I want to explain someth—"

BANG!

[Dramatic Damage: +1 Drama Point]

"Ow! I said hold on a second! If you replace all the parts of the Body of Theseus, I assure you I'm still the same villain!" He reached his torn and shredded bicep toward a workout machine. "**[Surrogate Limb]**!"

A moment later, Theseus flexed—bowflexed, even—his new arm. One made from steel, rubber, and foam. Andre's tattered arm hung from the workout machine while the workout machine's "arm" whipped back and forth like a flail.

I backed up as he ran toward me. "Yep, we're in trouble! Protect me, minion!" Then the metal arm thrashed against my back and knocked me toward the door.

[HP 4/6]

I picked myself up and fired my **[Hypercompression Cannon]** again. The air blast hit Theseus and bought me a second, but I couldn't compete with him. Not up close. I turned and dashed toward the door.

[Gritty Recovery: +1 Grit Point]
[Dramatic Damage: +1 Drama Point]

Right into a wall of flesh and wrestling singlet!

"Miss me, Snack?" Gourmet asked, wrapping me up in a wrestling hold. I tried to find something—anything—to fight back with, but I couldn't hack her, and she'd pinned the cannon away from her. I tried to turn my head.

"Don't worry about her. Just finish off the Wombat," I heard Gourmet say behind me just before she slammed me into a bench press station.

[HP 3/6]

"Who's in charge here, anyway?" Theseus asked, but he nodded and started toward Fursona. Within a few seconds, his metal arm had taken them out of commission; they lay unmoving on the floor.

Then he swaggered over toward me. "You know, you and Fursona are an inconvenience. Those were the strongest arms on campus. Now one of them's trash. But that's okay because I got the chance to beat you. I'll see you in class tomorrow. Gourmet? Finish her."

"With pleasure," Gourmet said. "Nightie-night, Snack!"

I tried. I really did. I flailed, kicked, and even tried to bite Gourmet, but her hold was too tight. When she started slamming me into the floor over and over, all I could do was wiggle feebly and watch my HP fall as a camera drone hovered over my head.

[HP 2/6]
[HP 1/6]
[HP 0/6]

Just before my face slammed into the rubber floor with no superhero protection, I got a new System message. One I'd seen before and that I hated.

[Episode Finished!]
[Episode: Whey Too Few Leg Days! - PG]
[Penalties: N/A]
[Short Finished! +3 of each Style Point]
[The Agony of Defeat! +1 of each Style Point]
[Role Focus: Flamboyance+Grit - Goal Unmet!]
[Alias - Understudy] [Archetype - Magical Girl] [Community Rank - 475/523]
[HP 0/6]
[Styles and Skills]
▶ Archetype Skill - Transformation Sequence
▶ Badass (29)
▶ Cunning (11)
▶ Inkling 1
▶ Drama (20)
▶ Stellar Ray 1
▶ Flamboyance (13)
▶ Signature Skill - Adaptive Armoire 1
▶ Stored Costumes: (Lab Assistant Panic)
▶ Starwave Sail 1
▶ Spotlight Strike 1
▶ Grit (39)
▶ Rejuvenation 1

"Wake up, Understudy."

Alarms blared in the Roth Arena's weight room. I winced against them. Then I screwed my eyes shut tighter as Fursona's paws shook me. "Fivemoreminutes . . ."

"Nope. You have to get up. We need to get moving. It's gotta be midnight, and we both have classes in the morning." Fursona's voice had an edge I hadn't heard before, even through the modulator. It sounded raw, like they'd been crying. I opened my eyes slowly and grabbed their extended bed paw.

"Owww," I winced. I'd have a black eye tomorrow, and had I shifted back to Understudy when Gourmet knocked me out? I growled at the ceiling tiles. "Losing sucks so much! Especially like this. When I lost to Professor Panache, he just did whatever he was doing. He didn't knock me out like that."

"So . . . we definitely lost?" Fursona asked. Their shoulders slumped, and I realized they'd been holding out hope for a turnaround.

"Yep, Fursona, we lost. Episode's over, there's no comeback coming. We didn't get outmaneuvered until the end, and they didn't get lucky. We just got outmatched." As I said it, I realized that even though I'd meant it as a lie to comfort Fursona, I'd told the truth. We weren't ready for the minor leagues. *I* wasn't ready for the minor leagues. Hell, we'd been thrashed by a minor leaguer and a little leaguer, and it honestly hadn't been that close.

"We'll go to my place," I said as we jogged down the stairs into Roth Arena's basement. "We need to talk through this."

"Alright . . ." Fursona mumbled.

We snuck through the tunnels. I had no idea how long it'd been since Gourmet and Theseus had made their escape, but I didn't want to run into them down here, so we took our time. Fursona didn't want to talk, and I was trying to mentally frame this crushing defeat as a victory or . . . anything but what it was.

I'd never gotten my ass kicked so thoroughly.

The silence had skipped past awkward, blown through uncomfortable, and was orbiting oppressive when the elevator finally dinged. Fursona went right for their chaise lounge and flopped onto it dejectedly. They blew a frustrated breath out. Then another.

I twiddled my thumbs—metaphorically—and waited for them to finish.

After another painfully awkward minute, they rolled over to look at me. The goofy cartoon eyes locked on mine surprisingly intensely. "What the hell happened, Understudy? We *had* Gourmet. We could have beaten her if she hadn't gotten away. We should have hunted her down before we checked out the weight room!"

<I can't run accurate numbers in this form, but I'd say you two beating Gourmet would have been a toss-up,> Tails said, stretching out on the floor and kneading the rug. **<She's rated 325th. Well, 322nd now, with that win. She's on the edge of the minor leagues—in fact, she'd be there if she had the motivation to ask her producer for a promotion.>**

"Right. We bit off more than we can chew, and that's on me. I hadn't checked with Tails to see if the match-up would be close. I thought we could force a draw at the worst, not that they'd both be powerhouses." I sighed and rubbed my eyes, then stopped as the shiner on my left one sparked with pain. "I wasn't ready for them, and neither were you. In fact, you did really well, Marsupial of Justice."

"But we lost. It doesn't matter how well we did if we lost."

"You said you were on a sports team in school, right?"

Fursona nodded grudgingly. "Yeah."

"Did you ever have a loss you couldn't improve on?" They shook their head. "How about a bad practice where you didn't learn something or get better?"

"No," Fursona pouted. "But this is different."

"How?"

"This *hurt*!"

I laughed. They were right, there. It *had* hurt. Peter had only pushed me that far once, and he'd had to call the Episode right after since his FEAR 1.8 suit showed critical damage and he was out of Panic Pals. "Yeah, it did. Is your suit okay?"

"Yeah. It seems like it regenerates damage overnight . . . or overday, in this case."

"Then we have a problem. Theseus probably got a big power increase from that Episode, Gourmet's going to be insufferable tomorrow in class, and we absolutely *cannot* get into an Episode they're involved with right now. The last thing we need is for Rocko or their producers to decide we'd be a good set of rivals for each other."

Fursona shuddered theatrically and stood up. They started pacing, clearly thinking. Then they stopped. "If they're not our rivals, who is?"

"I have no idea. As your partner and friend, you should go back to your place and get some sleep. Tomorrow comes early," I said. I held out a hand to help Fursona up. They moved stiffly, like they'd been in a fight and lost. Superhero damage didn't prevent everything, and Theseus hadn't been gentle on them.

"Thanks, Understudy," Fursona said reluctantly. They walked over to the elevator and pushed the button. The door opened, and they stepped in.

As the door shut, though, they suddenly stood up straight. "Wait, Understudy! What about tryouts with Sara-N-Dipity?"

I lunged for the door, and so did they, but it clicked shut before we could stop it. I waited for the elevator to return, but it never did. Eventually, I got an email from them.

Subject: Tryouts
Hey Understudy
It's going to be okay, Understudy. We'll think of something to get you through your tryouts with Sara. Worst case scenario, we'll check around town for a good little-league Episode. There's gotta be one somewhere, right?
Fursona

I sighed. I had three days. Three days to figure out an Episode for Sara-N-Dipity. Gourmet and Theseus had really screwed me over with their victory. And worse, I couldn't be sure our loss wouldn't have other repercussions.

30

Repercussions

As soon as Post–Launch Day North American History ended, I declined another offer of coffee from Avan and headed to the SUB for breakfast instead.

I thought about last night as I munched on my cereal and played around on my phone. I'd had to really cake the makeup on to hide my black eye, but more importantly, I had no idea where I'd be able to find an Episode for Sara-N-Dipity, and I only had a couple of days. I typed "Superhero Online Episode Dating" into my phone, just in case someone had built a "dating app" for supers to fight each other through, but if anyone had, a quick search couldn't find it.

"Damn. That would have been really convenient," I mumbled to myself.

"What?" Su-Bin slid into a seat across from me and set a plate full of syrup-drowned waffles on the table.

"Oh," I started, locking my phone, "I'm just, uh, mulling over an algebra problem for tomorrow."

It was the wrong lie. Su-Bin perked up. "Oh yeah? I tutored middle and high schoolers back before college. I could probably teach you some tricks." She cut into her waffle, took a gigantic bite, then struggled to chew while I snorted at her.

"That'd . . . that'd be great," I said between laughs. It really would be, too. I'd been meaning to ask her once everyone fell into a routine. "You can come over to my place sometime. You help me, and it'll get you out of your dorm room for a while."

"Oh, thank fucking god!" Su-Bin exclaimed. "Veronica has a boyfriend, and she keeps having him over. I think they're grosser than normal to get me to leave. The problem is that it's *working*."

I rolled my eyes. "Ugh, boys, right?"

"Honestly, I don't mind him. But *she's* driving me insane!"

I listened to Su-Bin vent about her shared space for a while, while I ate. Then, when she wound down, I cleared my throat. "Are your classes really empty today?"

"I mean, yeah, it's Monday. No one goes to early classes on Monday if they've been partying. And, from your eye, you had a rough weekend. Let me guess. Ran into a lamppost? Got hit by a frisbee? Those things are menaces! Maybe a rogue scooter ran into you?"

"No." I laughed. "Even for Monday, though, it feels weird for *half* my Post–Launch Day History class to be missing."

"Half on the second week? That seems like a lot," Su-Bin said. She ate another gigantic bite of waffles.

"Yeah. I mean, we're just talking about stuff everyone knows, so maybe they figure they don't need to be there for it?" I hadn't read the syllabus all the way through, but the class seemed laid out by unit. The first unit was the nuclear launches, Ilneat intervention, and heroic negotiation by the prime minister of New Zealand, whose country had disappeared from the map while she watched from space.

"Teaching Assistant Smith cares so much about history, but we've all heard it before," I said. "I want to get to the good stuff we only skimmed or learned from early major-league reruns. We've all seen the Man vs. Nature Episodes—"

"I haven't."

"Really? Mega-Tom vs. the Bees? Soldier of Fortune vs. Grizzly Number Seven? Father Thyme vs. Kudzu-Zilla?" That last one had been *wild*.

"Nah. I don't really like superheroes," Su-Bin said. "They don't really help anyone. But go on."

I blinked. She'd slapped me. Not, like, across the table, but with her words. How could she not like *superheroes*? "Okay. Most of us have seen the Man vs. Nature Episodes or the Power War Saga, but my high school classes just covered up to Launch Day. They said everything after that was either 'current events' or 'Ilneat relations,' and *god*, that class is boring. So I don't get why people aren't interested in what happened after Launch Day."

"Your high school teachers were right," Su-Bin said around her waffle. "Everyone *lived* through post–Launch Day. Teaching Assistant Whatshername is probably the oldest person to think of Man vs. Nature or the Power Wars as history. I mean, I *lived* through the Second Power Wars in Tokyexico City. I was just a toddler, but I was there."

I raised an eyebrow and pondered. If I'd been born in Tokyexico or one of the big cities, I'd have grown up watching the Power Wars from my bedroom window, not seeing them on TV. It really was current events, and suddenly, the class's emptiness made much more sense. I told Su-Bin that, and she nodded.

We chatted for a while about her classes and set up a time tomorrow after Ilneat Relations to tutor me in algebra, but soon enough, she needed to get going for her pre-calculus class. I finished my soggy cereal and returned to the week's most important task: finding an Episode.

I could try a pick-up Episode like Fursona had said. If I just traveled nearby, surely some little leaguers would be starting *something*. But that ran some risks. What if I ran into *Playpen Patrol* or one of the little kids' stars doing an Episode? I couldn't beat toddlers on my way to the minor leagues . . . could I?

Nope. If I got into that, I'd have to lose, even if they were villains.

I thought about solutions the whole way back to my place to get transformed. And there just . . . weren't any safe ones. I *really* needed an Episode app. Or maybe TUSSA had some resources I could use.

Dr. Jackson paused the Episode with Tapdance midmove, a collapsing skyscraper behind him. He'd been dancing up a storm, and the Yorkston city center looked terrible. The tremors grew every time his feet hit the ground until the city started tearing apart.

"Today's lesson is on collateral property damage since that's something *some of us* seem interested in causing," Dr. Jackson said sternly once we'd found our seats. I looked down, embarrassed, but Theseus and Gourmet just grinned. "And on how heroes and villains can use their codes of ethics to minimize it. Tapdance is a good example of why heroes need codes of ethics as much as villains. Now, let's watch the villain in this scene—because, believe it or not, Tapdance is the hero here."

She pressed play.

The villain catapulted in on a ridiculously oversized dirt bike. "Tapdance, stop!" As the rider skidded to a stop, asphalt and dirt shot everywhere. The bike's tires seemed to shred everything they touched.

"No! You'll tear this city apart, Outrider! I have to stop you!"

"Look around you! The city's gone! You ruined everything! You ruined my *home*!" Outrider shouted. She revved her engine and shot straight toward Tapdance. As she flew past, she grabbed the hero and pulled him off his feet.

"Stop! Breaking! Yorkston!"

Tapdance tried to get to his feet, but Outrider turned her dirt bike every time and flipped him away from the ground. She drove between half-ruined buildings, carefully avoiding whatever undamaged bits of the city she could.

Dr. Jackson pushed pause.

"Tapdance had no code of ethics. With a power like his, one that's a city-leveler, he desperately needed one. Conversely, Outrider had always been a minor leaguer. But her code of conduct forced her to limit collateral damage—an important thing when her power shreds whatever she rides over. Why did she include that in her code?"

"Because she didn't wanna win," Theseus said, kicking back in his armchair. "Duh."

"Theseus, you're being a Theseu-ass," Fursona said. Gourmet snorted key-lime yogurt out her nose.

Dr. Jackson stared at Theseus and Fursona until they both had the courtesy to at least *look* ashamed. Then she cleared her throat. "Anyone else?"

"Wasn't Outrider a local villain? A minor leaguer in the Yorkston area?" Punch asked.

"Yeah, she would have had an incentive to keep her hometown as intact as possible. I mean, she couldn't rule over a shattered wasteland, could she?" The Crumb added. "If I were in a position to take over Tokyexico, I wouldn't want it burned down."

"Correct. In comparison, Tapdance didn't have a home. He was a wandering hero, one of the Ronin heroes after Launch Day whose homes weren't salvageable—or at least weren't salvaged. Still, if he'd had a code of conduct and followed it here, both his path and Outrider's would have been much different. They switched sides after this Episode. Outrider's actions prevented billions in damage, and Tapdance had proven he was willing to go too far.

"Now, consider property in your codes of conduct—but remember, if you can save a life or you can save an empty building, always choose the life. Break."

We all dragged the La-Z-Boys into a circle. "Anyone else get the feeling this lesson's aimed at you, Theseus?" Fursona asked.

"Shut up," Theseus said. "Alright, by right of conquest, I declare myself president of this group. And my first decree is we're actually working on this assignment this time."

"Whatever, Theseu-ass," Gourmet said. "That was brilliant, by the way. You may have been a pushover during the Episode, Wombat, but at least you've got banter down."

"Enough," President Theseus said. He crossed his arms. "You two heroes. What do you think?"

"Uh, don't . . . break stuff?" Fursona asked. When we laughed, they crossed their paws over their pouch and pouted.

"No, that won't work," I replied. "Look at Theseus. Based on last night, he *has* to break stuff to use his power. And I broke a lot of stuff in my Episodes with Professor Pent-up, so even heroes need some flexibility."

"Don't forget I eat stuff," Gourmet said.

"Yeah, and Gourmet eats stuff. I hope that wrestling doublet gave you a stomachache!" I said.

"Didn't feel a thing. I have guts of iron!"

"Ladies, marsupials, can we please focus?" Theseus asked, scowling.

"Okay, okay, what if we put in somewhere that we avoided nonessential property damage and tried to save structures when we could?" I asked. "That'd give us flexibility."

"But then we're right back to the Mister Felsic problem," Theseus said.

I groaned. We were four class periods into Superpower Ethics, and our code of conduct was going nowhere!

Code of Conduct: September 15
We will not ~~endanger harm threaten~~ endanger ~~civilians~~ Extras ~~needlessly~~
Destruction of ~~non-government residential~~ non-corporate/non-government property is ~~to be kept to a minimum not necessary~~ not okay

Medical Extras are off limits. Healing heroes ~~should only be targeted if involved in the fighting are a low priority target~~ *are not a target unless they directly engage*

Property damage must ~~have a point be for a purpose~~ *be directly related to the Episode's goals*

Fursona sprawled across the chaise lounge in my secret base/dressing room, tossing a bouncy ball up in the air and catching it with both paws over and over. "So, are we finding an Episode? There's gotta be a Short out there with our name on it."

"I think we need to find Honeycomb," I said.

"What? But she's gotta be the weakest hero in Tokyexico!"

<Magical Girl Honeycomb is currently five hundred and second out of five hundred twenty-three. She outranks you by three places right meow, Fursona,> Tails said. I repeated it so Fursona could hear.

"Really? That's some bullshit!" Fursona stood up. "How does she outrank me?"

<She's been superheroing for almost three years. Her growth rate is slower than yours, Understudy, but without the small-town excuse.>

"That hurts, Tails," I said jokingly. Then I shook my head. "No, we don't need her for her strength. We need to help her find and beat Jumper, and we need to do it in the next two and a half days. Otherwise, we're out of time."

"So, we find Honeycomb, she helps us find Jumper, and we beat the snot out of her the next time she tries an Episode?" Fursona nodded slowly and moved their neck like they were cracking it. The sound they made came from the modulator, though. What a goober!

"I'm in. Let's go find Honeycomb."

31

Let's Go Find Honeycomb

'I'm in. Let's go find Honeycomb,' I said. 'It'll be easy,' I said," Fursona grumbled as they looked in their pouch. "I shoulda packed some snacks in here."

"How would you even eat them?" I asked. "That thing's stuck to your head."

"I'd find a way!"

We'd searched around the art gallery for hours, looking for any sign of Magical Girl Honeycomb. They'd cleaned up the alley; someone had taken the painting's frame, and a new dumpster stood without a me-shaped dent. But no Magical Girl Honeycomb.

Tokyexico's University District was shockingly upscale. Movies and TV shows seemed to think college students were all broke, so I couldn't figure out why jewelry shops and art galleries would be nearby. Most of the nearby apartment buildings seemed to house older students or college staff, and my professors were probably well-off, but not *that* well-off. Except for Dr. Mindstorm. Everyone knew she had *billions* piled away somewhere from her supervillain career.

Honeycomb had to live around here somewhere. She felt like a local heroine. We'd checked the local businesses, but no one could point us toward the bee-themed Magical Girl. The cashier at a convenience store did snort into her register when we asked, though. "Yeah, she's some *hero*, alright. *Really* helped out when Jumper cleaned me out a month ago." Clearly, Honeycomb wasn't doing a great job as a friendly neighborhood bee.

We'd found plenty of Episodes, though.

Most were minor league, with a few major-league ones thrown in for good measure. But even the few little-league ones we *thought* we could handle had problems. Like the roles available. A lot of sidekick roles, but none for a team of two.

"One more loop, Marsupial of Justice?" I asked. This would be our fifth time around—we'd gone a little bigger every single time—and both of us were beat. "I have homework to do, too. Plus, I have to try to get this math done so my tutor can at least tell me what I'm doing wrong."

"I need to eat *something*, Understudy. But . . . yeah, one more loop."

We hadn't gone two blocks when we passed a daycare sign—a car on a long pole with block letters under it. *Tottergarten*, the sign read. Even this late, the lights inside were still on, and movement inside showed a handful of toddlers inside.

[Casting Call]
[Episode: Short: Playpen Peril with Jungle Jim - G]
[Role: Day-Saver! Do you accept the role? (Yes/No)]
[Role Focus: Silly+Strong]

Fursona stopped in their tracks. "Do we accept this one?"

"You never saw *Playpen Patrol* as a kid? Absolutely not." I kept walking, even though my feet ached in my boots. "We'll end up coming in and teaching the kids about kangaroos or something. What do you know about kangaroos?"

"I know I'm one and that they're marsupials," they said. "Other than that, nothing."

"Well, don't accept any G-rated Episodes unless you're willing to teach toddlers about your Costume, and maybe get beaten up by them," I said. We kept walking through the University District, but Magical Girl Honeycomb had vanished.

Worse, even though I kept seeing white vans, the people driving them certainly weren't S, or at least they weren't wearing a mask. It wasn't even the same person behind the wheel every time. I stayed on my toes, though. One of the drivers could go hostile at any point, and I was *not* getting vanned again!

It took almost an hour to walk our last loop. Fursona kept reaching down to massage their oversized feet, though what they could accomplish through the rubber pads and thick plush, I couldn't tell. If they were making an impact on them, though, I was jealous. My feet *hurt*!

But eventually, we saw the Mister Felsic statue in the distance. I groaned. "Honestly, I'm tempted to try again."

"Oh, hell no," Fursona said. "Understudy, I've been walking for hours, and this suit doesn't have Pataki's upgrades yet. And I'm starving. I'm sorry, but I'm done for the night."

Fursona had a point. It had to be close to seven, and I had homework. "Alright. Email me. We'll set up a time to look for Honeycomb tomorrow."

"Deal!" Fursona waved and started slowly hopping away toward their dorm tower.

"**[Starwave Sail]**!" If I wasn't still searching with Fursona, I sure wasn't walking anymore. The sooner I made it to Walnut Tower, the better.

Plus, my phone was buzzing.

I landed, slipped inside, and untransformed. Then I opened my phone.

<Hey, I saved the company 30000 monthly today. How r classes? - Peter 6:58>
<Hanging in there, hun. Stuffs busy. Lots of homework - Annie 6:59>

I wasn't lying. I opened my algebra book and tried a few problems while I waited for Peter. "5x squared times 32x minus 14 equals -7?" Math had never, ever been my strong suit. I supposed I could try Lab Assistant Panic; TA-1LZ had math skills, and I could act like I didn't care about cheating.

<Oh? Whatcha working on? - Peter 7:01>
<Just algebra. Hows supervillain stuff? - Annie 7:01>
<Tremble, Riversiders, therell be no pity! My bots are taking over the city! - Professor Panic - 7:02>
<Are you in the middle of an Episode? - Annie 7:02>
<Maybe . . .yep! - Peter 7:03>

"Aaaauugh!" I slammed my math book shut and jammed my palms into my face. It was so frustrating! Everyone was doing Episodes except for Fursona and me! And Peter was *texting* me during one. His stupid Genius powers let him just chill and earn Style Points as his stupid bots did their stupid thing!

<That's great. Fursona and I searched for a good Episode tonight - Annie 7:04>
<Didn't find one - Annie 7:04>
<We got our asses kicked yesterday, though. Did I tell you about that? - Annie 7:05>
<No. Collidus is coming. Tell me, will read later - Peter 7:06>

I sighed and started texting. I told him about Gourmet and Theseus, how I'd needed the win to make it to the minor leagues as a sidekick, and how we'd gotten clobbered by the villains in the weight room and they'd gotten away with one of the weightlifting champ's arms. He didn't respond. My messages just stayed on "Read," and my math problems weren't solving themselves.

More importantly, I wasn't solving them either.

After an hour of staring at the phone and math book, I gave up. I couldn't stop thinking about Honeycomb. Where *was* she? I needed something to distract me, so I grabbed some pillows and flopped down next to the Lil Pal parts on my bedstand. If I couldn't do the math, and Peter was busy, I'd occupy myself with building his gift instead.

Tuesday, September 16

He didn't text me back until after Ilneat Relations the next day.

<Hey. Sorry, the Episode went long. Way past Collidus's bedtime - Peter 3:15>
<It's fine. - Annie 3:16>

I headed back toward Walnut Tower. It was fine, honestly. I'd told him not to text during class, so he'd waited. He shouldn't be texting at work, but that was a Peter problem, not an Annie one. I hadn't meant to lose it with myself, either, and I felt guilty about that. I'd been frustrated all day, but that wasn't his fault.

<So, we're on for a video call tonight, right? - Peter 3:18>
<Yeah. 6:30 is good, right? - Annie 3:19>
<See you then! - Peter 3:20>

That'd give me a few hours to relax and eat, work on homework, and eat dinner. I rode the elevator up, stepped inside, and kicked off my shoes. I hadn't even been inside for a minute before the elevator intercom buzzed at me. I pressed its button.

<Hey, MOJ here. You wouldn't believe what I found online. Let me up, and I'll show you>

I started my **[Transformation Sequence]**. As the room filled with light and sound, I wondered what Fursona had found. Whatever it was, they were excited enough to stand in the tunnels and push the intercom button over and over for almost half an hour. I rolled my eyes.

The last bow finally tied itself into my hair, and my feet touched the ground again. As soon as I let her go, Tails stretched out on the couch, plushie back arched.

<Are we searching again? Right meow? I was settling down for a nap.>

"Nah. Fursona's coming over." I pushed the button to open the elevator below and headed into my secret base. Sure enough, it wasn't hot pink anymore. Instead, Fang Swee's power had toned it down to a lovely light pastel rose. The couches and the chaise lounge seemed less overstuffed, and a few spots on the back wall beside the stairs had TVs running. Both were set to different Tokyexico City news shows.

"How long have you been waiting down there?" I asked when the doors opened.

"Twenty-five minutes."

"Fursona, just send me an email next time. Even better, I'll give you my number."

"Forget the number. Get me a laptop!"

"Hold up. New Costume? Pataki's been busy!" The Ilneat tailor had switched out Fursona's sweatshirt and pants for something more formfitting. The orange-and-blue color scheme stayed, with racing stripes and a zipper for their pouch instead of baggy sweats. The kangaroo looked more like a proper superhero now. For some reason, though, they wore a little cat collar around their neck. They couldn't stop fidgeting with the metal paw charm.

"Yeah. Pataki said it'd fit better with the Speedster theme, even if I'm not a traditional one. Rocko says I'm probably more of a hybrid Bruiser/Speedster. They braced up the feet a whole bunch, though, so it won't hurt when I kick something or have to hop for a while, and they had a Genius work on the tail. It's controllable now, so hopefully I'll get some powers for it soon. Now will you please get me a computer?"

I laughed. "Alright, one second." Then I dipped through the "maintenance" door and grabbed my laptop.

We opened it up, and Fursona started typing—with their paws on, they had to chicken-peck at the keyboard. "So, I searched 'Magical Girl Honeycomb Episodes.' Did you know she's been in like fifty?"

I hadn't known that. Of course, I hadn't looked for her. Still, it was odd I'd never heard of her if she had that kind of reach . . . unless . . .

"No. There's no way."

Fursona pressed Enter.

"Of course she would," I muttered. Every result was the same. "Playpen Pals and Magical Girl Honeycomb Save Christmas!" or "Playpen Pals and the Jealousy Triplets, Guest Starring Magical Girl Honeycomb." Honeycomb was a G-rated heroine!

We'd been so close. She'd probably been inside Tottergarten when we declined the Episode, and we hadn't even bothered to check it out. "God dammit."

"Yep." Fursona flopped back onto the chaise lounge. "We messed up on that one for real. So, what are we gonna do?"

Just then, my doorbell rang.

"Shit!" That *had* to be Su-Bin. I hopped up from my comfy couch, popped open the door, and sprinted into my apartment. "Just a minute! Getting straightened up."

Then I dashed back to Fursona. "Okay, you can't be here. I'll email you when I'm done with my tutoring. Thanks for the tip. We'll come up with a plan soon!"

I practically shoved the protesting kangaroo superhero into the elevator. As soon as it started down, I untransformed, took three deep breaths, and grabbed my math book and a pillow.

I was *not* ready for algebra tutoring. I'd only solved a few problems from the previous class's homework, and I certainly hadn't touched today's. Worse, I couldn't even say I *wanted* Su-Bin's help right now. My brain was totally on Tottergarten and Magical Girl Honeycomb. But I couldn't do anything about that tonight—not if I had tutoring and Peter's video call.

I opened the door.

Su-Bin stood there, armed with her phone, a gigantic fast-food cup, and an even bigger smile. I struggled not to shudder. It didn't feel like a friendly smile.

Her smile meant math.

32

Her Smile Meant Math

You want to bring the $12x$ to the other side by subtracting $12x$ from both sides. That'll make it negative, but it'll let you get all your x values on one side and your actual numbers on the other. Then you can figure out what x is worth," Su-Bin said. She wrote on her notepad, creating a map I could follow.

Then she sipped on her soda and turned to her own math book. I sighed quietly and got to work. The x's on the right. The numbers on the left. Divide the whole thing out. It took way longer than it should have. We'd been working for a couple of hours, and I still had more to do. And I was starting to hate Su-Bin. She wouldn't let me just quit. But I thought I had it this time. Maybe. I hadn't had it in high school.

She checked my fifth problem and nodded.

I'd been right! Su-Bin was the meanest friend I'd ever made. But thanks to her patience, I knew how to balance equations. "Thanks so much, Su-Bin."

"No problem. I can stick around for a few more problems if you want to make sure you have it," she said.

"I can't." I shut the math book with the paper inside to mark my page and set it on my Tuesday/Thursday pile. "I have a video date with Peter in half an hour. But let me see your phone. I'll give you my number so we can hang out sometime."

"Sure."

We exchanged numbers, *finally*, and Su-Bin left. As soon as she did, I pulled open my computer and sent a quick email.

To: Fursona.SH@tokyexicouniversity.student.edu.
Subject: G-Rated Honeycomb
Let's check Tottergarten after classes tomorrow. 4:00 work for you?
Understudy

We'd find Honeycomb tomorrow, and if anyone could lead us to Jumper, it was her. I flicked over to the video call app, opened a chatroom, and hurried off to make sure my hair and makeup looked okay after a full day's wear and superhero stuff, too.

I hadn't really put that kind of effort in back in Riverside, but we'd seen each other at school every day. And we'd done weekly *actual* dates, which I'd *actually* dolled myself up for a little. But something felt off in our dynamic, and if a little extra effort on my part could fix it, then a little extra effort it was. Not that I wanted to wear the nightie. It qualified as pajamas at this point; I'd worn it to bed every night since I unwrapped it. Instead, I grabbed a black T-shirt with a stylized skull on it. I didn't want to look like I was putting *too* much effort in.

"Hey, Annie, you there?" Peter's voice echoed from my computer speakers. He was early.

I breathed, adjusted the shirt so it sat comfortably, and slid onto my couch. "Hey, Peter. Just figuring out some things. How's work been?" I tried not to cringe. The question felt so . . . Mom and Dad. So . . . adult.

"It's been pretty good. I saved the company a ton of money, so Dad thinks I earned a day off next month. I'll have Friday off, the eleventh of October, if you still want me to come up."

"Yeah, I'd like that. I'll make sure the place is ready for that weekend."

Something about my tone must've been off, because suddenly Peter backtracked. "If you've got plans already, that's totally fine. I can start something down here instead."

Oh, right. Peter'd had that Episode against Collidus. "How's PP holding up?"

"That madman's taken over half the town," Peter said, winking at me. He was in his bedroom at his parents' place. Even though he was making the big bucks, he hadn't moved out yet and had to be a little subtle about his secret identity. "Today at work, I heard a rumor that he'd successfully drained the rec center's pool, then pumped it into an underground storage tank. But why would someone do something like that?"

"I don't know." The conversation was routine. We'd had it dozens of times in the cafeteria, usually both exhausted from a night of supering. I could walk through it in my sleep. "What do you think, Peter?"

"I think he's gotta be planning a new weapon. He used that air cannon for so long, but it doesn't seem as effective against Collidus as it was against Understudy. Maybe he thinks water will slow the Destruction Derbyist down, but—"

"Hold on. He's calling himself that?" I burst into laughter.

Peter scowled. "Yeah, he is. Anyways, he might think water will slow the kid down or make him slip. That way, Prof P's bots can actually do something against the New Protector of Riverside."

I rolled my eyes. Collidus was just being too much. I missed fighting Professor Panic with the kiddo. Even if he'd been kind of stupid, his power just let him be. In fact, it seemed to reward dumb decisions. One time, during the season finale of my junior year, he'd thrown himself off Riverside Elementary's flagpole to ambush LABRAT. As far as I knew, the crater was still there, but Collidus hadn't even taken superhero damage.

I wondered if I could get that power from Collidus. Or what Fursona's hops would be like with no collision damage. They'd be an absolute wrecking ball because Collidus couldn't hold his own unless he moved. Fursona was—well, would be—a powerhouse as a Speedster/Bruiser combo. If they were indestructible, too—

"Annie, are you paying attention?"

"Yes." I was not. I kicked myself, metaphorically.

"Alright. You zoned out there for a second. Anyway, work's been great. I went through the drill-creation software and removed about five hundred lines of unnecessary code. The number of redundant checks and needed human inputs per step is down by 8%, and without any difference in safety on the line—I know when businesses talk safety, people get antsy. I quadruple-checked. The new program is more efficient, faster, and just as safe."

"You're giving a sales pitch, Peter."

Peter stopped like I'd physically put a hand over his mouth. Then he closed his eyes. "Sorry. Look, work's been a lot the last couple of weeks. Last night was the first time Professor Panic's really done much of anything since Understudy went to school, and he should have waited a few days. Why don't you tell me about your day?"

I sighed and fiddled with a loose strand of hair while I stared at the ceiling. What *had* I done today? "I went to algebra, realized I was horribly out of my depth—again—and spent most of that class fiddling with a project I'm working on with a friend. We're trying to track down a real superhero."

"Oh? Which one?" Peter was starting to drift a little. Did his eyes seem less dilated?

"Her name's Magical Girl Honeycomb. She saved our butts last week, and we needed to talk to her after. Anyways, then I went to Ilneat Relations. The professor's Doug Quailman—"

"Isn't that an Ilneat name?"

"You'd think that, wouldn't you? No, he's just a boring old dude. He insists on talking about Ilneats like they're totally alien, as if we couldn't visit some in the Hot Zone—or . . . other ways. I'm almost tempted to see if I can find one to come to class one day to watch Dr. Quailman lose it. But anyway, we're learning about Ilneat world systems. There are nursery worlds and studio worlds, like Earth is now. But there's gotta be a dozen different kinds of Ilneat planets, and I *do not care* about most of them."

Yep, his eyes had fully undilated. He was deep in Genius mode, nodding along while I talked but not really listening. He'd probably had some idea for a Professor Panic gizmo or weapon, and he was working on it as we—yep. A camera drone hovered nearby, filming as he sketched out his plan on a sheet of notebook paper.

I sighed again. "I'll talk to you later, Peter."

He half nodded. "Later."

I shut the computer. Peter did that sometimes. Even on our dates, he'd drift into Genius mode. It was so much easier to deal with it when we were in person.

I stopped.

Actually, when we were in person, it was so much easier, full stop. Easier to deal with Peter's Genius stuff. Easier to manage our superpowered secret lives. And so much easier to feel a connection. This video call hadn't been a disaster, but . . .

I just didn't care about Peter's work. It wasn't even that it was boring. It just . . . didn't matter to me. And he didn't seem to care about my classes. So that left . . . Episodes? And what else?

<Hey, Peter. You're zoned, but when you get this . . . things felt weird - Annie 6:43>

<I don't think we're doing long-distance right. A lot of this sucks - Annie 6:44>

I struggled with the next message. How was I supposed to word what I felt? My tease last week hadn't felt good, and Peter wasn't . . . no, *neither* of us was engaged tonight. Not like we needed to be. I flopped onto my bed and groaned at the half-finished Lil Pal on my bedstand.

<I'm going to take a little time to think about how to make this work. I'll text you tomorrow. Thursday at the latest. I'm still committed here, but we're messing it up somewhere. You have to feel it too. If you come up with ideas, we'll text then - Annie 6:51>

<I <3 you, Peter. Just gotta figure this out - Annie 6:54>

I set the phone aside and hopped in the shower. The scalding water ran down my face, mixing with makeup and tears, then into the drain. I wanted to make it work. Peter had been there for me, just like I'd been there for him. We'd figured out the superpowered thing together. We'd even hidden it from our parents together: excuses about where we were on nights we were out, lies about sports injuries and hiking trips, and helping each other recover from the nasty beatdowns we'd inflicted.

If we could figure *that* out, we could figure this out, too.

When I'd finished showering, wrapped my hair in a towel like Mom taught me, and pulled on the nightie, I checked my phone. I had three new messages. And none were from Peter.

<Hey, Annie! Whatcha doin for lunch tomorrow? Wanna grab a bite @SUB? - Bianca 7:16>

<If not, that's cool. Just thought we could hang out and stuff! - Bianca 7:23>

<If nothing else, we end up talking about Pygmalion or something - Bianca 7:28>

I smiled for the first time since shutting my computer. Did I want to have lunch with Bianca? Sure. Would it devolve into a conversation about the most recent play we were looking at in Intro to Drama? Maybe. Was it a trick to get me to do her homework for her? Almost certainly. But I didn't care. I needed a friend to talk to for a bit.

<Hi Bee - Annie 7:38>
<I'd love to! - Annie 7:39>

It was early, so I texted back and forth with Bianca for a while about . . . honestly, whatever. It didn't really matter what. It was just nice to talk to someone who wasn't Peter for a bit, and who wasn't wrapped up in superpowered stuff. Eventually, it got late, and my morning class started getting too close for comfort, so I said goodnight.

Tomorrow would be a good day. I'd meet Bianca for lunch, then go to Intro to Drama with her. Fursona and I could hunt Honeycomb after. It'd be easy; we knew she'd be at Tottergarten.

33

Tottergarten

WEDNESDAY, SEPTEMBER 17

I left Walnut Tower just after noon. Bianca's text said to meet at 12:15, so I had plenty of time to walk to the Student Union Building. After Superpower Ethics, I needed a little downtime with some unpowered friends.

We could *not* agree on whether a super needed to stick to Episode themes.

But oddly enough, Fursona was with Gourmet on this one, and I'd lined up with Theseus; the theme was important. If you could fill your [**Role Focus**], that'd go a long way toward making an Episode a hit. The Style System assigned [**Role Focuses**] for a reason, after all. We all needed to stay focused together.

Gourmet had disagreed. Strenuously. And Fursona had joined her. Gourmet said getting the win beat everything else, and Fursona was just as determined to stop the villains from winning, no matter the cost. I couldn't help but hear some frustration from the "Leg Days" Episode in their voice.

Every other team was *getting* somewhere on their code of ethics, and we couldn't agree on anything. At this point, we'd have to work outside of class to catch up. Or worse, let Theseus steer the ship and just row for him, and I didn't want that.

No one wanted that.

So, anyway, the team had fought, and Dr. Jackson had to get involved. So now I was mad at Fursona. Hopefully, I'd be over that before our trip to the daycare later.

<I'm in line at the pizza booth - Bianca 12:18>
<Cafeteria, not shops - Bianca 12:18>

I hurried inside and headed to the cafeteria side of the building. Just like my first full day on campus, the lines looped back and forth through queues to maximize space. Bianca stood near the middle of the pizza line with a tray and her gigantic backpack. She waved the whole tray at me, then turned to the frat bro behind her and apologized for almost hitting him.

I snorted, grabbed a tray, and ducked the rope to stand beside her. "Hey, Bee."

"Hi, Annie! How were your classes today?" Bianca looked flushed. I couldn't tell if it was embarrassment at almost taking out that guy or the class she'd been in before lunch.

"Fine. It's Biology, so nothing new there compared to high school." My lie was getting smoother. Soon I'd be an expert. "Little red, there, huh?"

"I'm in, um, fencing. So it's kinda a workout." She lifted her arm and gave her pit a quick sniff. "Nope, we're good!"

"Is the pizza line the best place for that?" I asked.

"Uh, I guess not. Sorry, that was probably kind of gross, huh? At least I smell okay, I guess."

That was true. Bianca smelled fine—or if she did stink, it wasn't noticeable over the smells of pizza, burritos, and burgers—and something faintly green-apple-scented. We scooted toward the line's front, where I grabbed a slice of cheese pizza and Bianca debated between the sausage and barbecue chicken before settling on one of each.

Then we found a spot to sit. Bianca tore into her first slice while I questioned her. "So, fencing, then? Why that?"

"Need a PE credit to graduate," she said between bites. Then she chewed on another bite, barbecue sauce smeared across her face. "I didn't want something tough, like weights, and hiking burns weekends until mid-October, so I went with fencing instead. I'm not very good at it, but it's definitely teaching me how to move."

"I see." I'd have to consider fencing for my credit. Or maybe a martial arts class. I needed to figure out how to move better, too. I took a bite of my cheese pizza. It tasted like grease and the Freshman Fifteen pounds they'd warned me I'd gain. I loved it.

"Yeah. Alright, you seemed pretty down last night. You can always tell me what's up." Bianca wiped her mouth on a paper napkin and balled it up in a fist. "More boyfriend problems?"

"And other things." I'd thought I was being clever by *not* talking about Peter, but I guess not. I wasn't going to start now, though. I ate another bite. Then another.

Bianca waited. When I went for my third bite, she frowned. "Alright. Subject change. Why do you call me Bee?"

"It's easier to type than Bianca, and I like nicknames." I'd given nicknames to Peter, Collidus, Fursona, and S, plus a bunch of my high school friends back home. It made sense to give one to Bianca, too. "Plus, it's kinda cute."

"Well, I think it's cute, too. I'll be your Bee." She froze midway through a bite. "Was that weird? Yeah, that was weird sorry sorry."

I laughed into my soda. It was a little weird but nothing out of the ordinary for Bianca. She spent the next minute eating sausage pizza and avoiding eye contact until I finished composing myself. "It's fine, Bee. It really is."

We finished our pizza slices—I was shocked at how quickly she inhaled hers—and talked about our classes for a while. She wanted to check out the Broadway Mall this weekend. It'd be a multiday trip to see the whole thing, of course, and the

Broadway Mall often had major-league Episodes running, but it sounded fun. I told her I'd think about it.

Then it was off to Intro to Drama for us.

I kept whistling to myself while we walked to Tottergarten, and it was driving Fursona *up the wall.*

"What's got you in such a good mood?" they asked, turning back and staring at me with their cartoon eyes. "Class was a disaster, and we don't know if this is gonna work."

"Oh, it's going to work. I have 100% confidence in your research skills. And I forgive you for being wrong in class." Bianca and I had talked on the couch outside of Intro to Drama until we both had to go. She had a tutoring thing, and I had . . . well, I *told* her it was a club meeting, but I was lying. Was lying to my friends wrong? Yep! Did I do it anyway, all the time? Uh-huh. Anything for the secret identity!

Fursona was right about one thing, though. Hanging out with Bianca did wonders for my mood. I couldn't stop smiling, and we hadn't even done anything. I was going to have to invite her over for . . . I stopped. What did college girls invite each other over for? Drinks? Board games?

Tottergarten's car sign loomed over us. I could see shapes moving through the translucent windows, a few adults and some smaller figures that would *not* stop running around. More importantly, I got a **[Casting Call]** as we got closer!

[Casting Call]
[Episode: Short: The Playpen Pals and Honeycomb Save the Bees! - G]
[Role: Bug Collector! Do you accept the role? (Yes/No)]
[Role Focus: Silly+Sad]

"Yes! She's in there!" I shouted. I accepted the **[Bug Collector]** role and ran toward the door. I opened it up and ran straight into a woman in a tweed jacket. Her curly hair and hoop earrings belied a sense of confidence and power. She looked down at her clipboard, then at us.

"The two **[Bug Collectors]** approached the daycare politely," she said, and snapped her fingers at me.

I walked toward the door and then stared right at the camera drone that had suddenly appeared next to me. "I think Honeycomb's in there, but we should be polite. It's super-important to be polite, especially at a business!" It was weird; it felt similar to when Dr. Mindstorm took over my body because I had no control over what I did or said. That woman, whoever she was, must've been a really, *really* powerful super.

I reached out, opened the door, and said, "Hello! I'm Magical Girl Understudy, and this is my sidekick, Fursona. We're here about the bees." As soon as I said my line, I felt the pressure on my mind relax—a lot.

The tweed-suited woman smiled at me. "Of course. The **[Beekeeper]** is just inside. Before you go in, I need to explain something. *Playpen Patrol* is *my* life's work. And I've done *so much* good with it. So, if you act out of line for a G-rated show, I'll narrate you out of the Episode. Understood?" The threat didn't seem villainous, and there wasn't a single sign of a **[Maniacal Reveal]**. Just a raw reveal of power, like a mother bear rearing up to protect her young.

I nodded. So did Fursona.

"And the two **[Bug Collectors]** headed inside, where the children and Magical Girl Honeycomb awaited them."

We headed inside, propelled by the woman's power, whatever it was. Inside, sitting in a circle, were four children in super-suits—and one confused-looking Honeycomb. "And, Patrollers, we . . . uh . . . we have to remember to, um. Just a second. What are you two doing here?"

"We're here to save the bees!" Fursona said an instant before the entirety of Playpen Patrol swarmed them.

The first one hit them at the knees. I winced as the very confused kangaroo catapulted into the ground; the kid was way stronger than the pint-sized powerhouse had any right to be. But instead of pressing the attack, he screamed, "I wanna pet the mouse!" at the top of his lungs.

"Uh, Patrollers, they're not a mouse. They're a kangaroo. Look over here!" Honeycomb said, trying desperately to bring their attention back to the model insect in her hand.

"Yeah, I'm a kangaroo. They're marsupials, and they live in Australia," Fursona said from under the pile of kids. "Can you get them off me?"

Despite his strength, the tiny-tot super-soldier was surprisingly easy to pick up. Once he was off the ground, I carried him back to Honeycomb. Then I looked at Fursona and sighed. The one with the crackly blue light around her would be easy, but the fast one and the one zipping around the ceiling looked like a total pain in the ass to wrangle.

I had an **[Inkling]**. "Hey, lady, can we get some help here?"

[Good Thinking! +1 Smarts Point]

I groaned. The G rating had even infected the Style Point updates! "Luckily, Honeycomb had told the Playpen Patrol about their incoming guests."

We headed inside. There, Magical Girl Honeycomb sat in a circle with four super-suit-wearing children. They struggled to contain their excitement when they saw Fursona, but all of them stayed seated, though one stayed sitting four feet in the air.

"These are my friends I told you about, Patrollers. Magical Girl Understudy is a Magical Girl like me, and my other friend is a kangaroo. No, not a mouse, Milkbar. Let's take a couple of minutes here. Why don't you four go see if you can find out what Pranky Jones is up to while I talk to Understudy?"

"Awww, please!"

"No! I wanna pet the mouse!"

"Comeoncomeoncomeon! Please please please please please!"

Fursona laughed and flopped onto the floor. "It's fine. Send 'em over."

"Your fur is so soft!" The fast girl skidded to a halt in a splash of orange, way too close to Fursona's face. Her hands were already wrist-deep in plush before Fursona had even finished speaking.

"Yeah, it is. Okay, first things first, I'm a kangaroo. That's a kind of marsupial. Can you say that word?"

Honeycomb stood up. With the cameras off of us, she flushed a little. "How'd you find out?"

"About your kids' show?" I asked. She nodded, and I shrugged. "We found an Episode here two nights ago. But we didn't get it until last night, and then we had classes. Listen, we need your help. Where's Jumper?"

She looked like she'd burst into tears at any second. "I don't know."

"Marsupials all live in Australia," Fursona said behind us. "I think."

"Oooooh!"

"Wow!"

"How do you know so much?"

Not all marsupials lived in Australia. I'd talk to Fursona about it later, though. I'd come so far, and neither Fursona nor the kids could distract me now. "Come on, Honey-bunches. You have to know more than that. Or could you at least text us the next time she starts something?"

"My producer already hates both of us, and if you just roll up and crush her, that'll look terrible for me. You've gotta give me something in return if I help you track her down." She smiled just slightly through the near tears.

"What?" My stomach got ready to plunge. I had a guess already, but I hoped it wouldn't come to that.

"I need help taking down Jumper. Not you doing it for me. Just help."

I nodded. I could do that.

"There's more," Honeycomb said to me. Her face screamed nervousness, and she chewed on her lip for a second.

"I need help with the kids, too. I need you to guest star."

34

Guest Star

Guest star? Did she expect me to fight some ridiculous G-rated villain for her? Or do some babysitting? I raised my brow in confusion. "What do you mean, guest star?"

"Shhhh!" Honeycomb shushed me. She leaned in close and whispered. "Look, these Episodes are all prebuilt for the kids. We have to check on the three beehives around the building because Pranky Jones keeps messing with them. They're sealed off with plexiglass, so we don't have to worry about getting stung or anything. Just take one of the Playpen Patrol with you."

"If I help you babysit, you'll help me find Jumper as soon as we're done?"

"Yeah. Of course. I'll get your number and text you as soon as I hear anything, I promise," Honeycomb nodded. She stuck out her hand. "You in?"

"Yeah, we're in." I shook the bee-girl's hand.

"Awesome. I saw you on that sailboard. You can fly, so you can have The Cloud. You can collect him before he floats away if he drifts off. Fursona can have Outlet since their suit *might* be insulated, and I'll take . . . Milkbar and Kid Zoomies, I guess."

"Does that happen often? The flying kid?"

"Yeah." Honeycomb rolled her eyes. "If you weren't here, the Narrator would have to keep an eye on him. Either that or . . . I've used a ribbon before and dragged him around like a balloon sometimes."

Alright. Okay. This was all fine and wasn't a total waste of time. "Let's get this going," I said.

Honeycomb spent the next minute herding the Playpen Patrol into place by their respective guest stars. "Okay. Mrs. N, we're ready!"

The woman in the tweed jacket looked up from her clipboard and pushed her curly black hair away from her glasses. "And then Pranky Jones struck!"

A tall, purple-haired man popped out of the daycare's ball pit, and I found myself face-to-face with a childhood nightmare.

I'd sneaked into the living room one night when I was nine. I couldn't sleep, and TV sounded like a great idea. Even before I became Understudy, I was really into superheroes. But the Episode I'd watched was a major-league one. My *first* major-league one. One I wasn't ready for—one featuring Mister Twister. I'd had nightmares about his clown makeup for weeks, and I'd never told *anyone* about it, not even when Rocko contracted me. The odds I'd run into Mister Twister were near zero, especially since he retired when I was in tenth grade.

When he appeared in front of me, I lost it. I was nine again, and instead of menacing Tokyexico, the villain was menacing *me!* I didn't know what chance I had against a top-fifty major leaguer, but I wasn't a nine-year-old Extra anymore. I had powers, and I could fight back!

Mister Twister started laughing. "Ahahaha! Playpen Patrol, it's time to feel the *sting* of loss! Wait, no—"

"[**Stellar Ray**]!" I waved my wand and gave Mister Twister a faceful of light beam.

[**You Hurt Someone! +1 Sad Point**]

"Hold up, hold up!" Mister Twister yelled. He held up his hands, revealing a sinister-looking device in one hand. I started waving my wand again, and he fled through a door into another room. "[**Shrink-Wrap Surprise**]!"

As I chased him through the door, my face bounced into something I hadn't seen, and a second later, I slammed down on my back, driving the air out of my lungs. "Oooof!"

[**HP 5/6**]

I picked myself up and started chasing after Mister Twister. But before I could, I heard the tweed-suited woman's voice. "Understudy, Fursona, Honeycomb, Pranky Jones, and The Narrator sat down to talk calmly while the Playpen Patrol played in the ball pit."

[**Tough Girl! +1 Tough Point**]

We'd sat down in a circle around a low table. The soft-cornered plastic furniture seemed like it shouldn't support Fursona or Mister Twister, but it somehow held up. The woman—I assumed she was The Narrator by Honeycomb's earlier explanation—cleared a few kid drawings off the table and coughed once. "Alright, Understudy, what was *that*?"

As soon as she said it, I felt her control slip, and I was me again.

My jaw dropped. How was this *my* fault? "That's Mister Twister! He blew up a bus on TV! I had nightmares for years!"

"Heh, yep! Good times," the purple-haired supervillain said. Then he smiled. The smile was genuine . . . almost warm. "Kid, I *retired* years ago. The whole Anti-Naptime League did. Mister Twister disappeared. He's gone. Nowadays, I'm . . . Pranky Jones!"

Pranky Jones. They were letting a known supervillain—one with no moral code who'd spent years in Almhurst—do kids' Episodes? My jaw dropped.

"It's totally safe," The Narrator said. "None of the villains here want to hurt these kiddos. They're just here to have a good time while we make fun, educational television. And if they did, I could narrate it all away in a heartbeat."

"Alright." My head was spinning. I was three feet away from my childhood nightmare, with nothing but a plastic table separating us, and no one seemed concerned. I made a mental note to look up The Narrator's power, but if it worked on "Pranky" like it did on Fursona and me, the kids were probably fine. Probably.

I hoped.

"So, what do we do, then?"

Pranky Jones looked at me. "First, I apologize for scaring you, and you apologize for blasting me in the face. Sorry."

"Sorry," I said. This was all so ridiculous! The camera drones lurked nearby, and everything we did felt like a kids' show.

"Alright, now, you're gonna grab The Cloud, and I'm gonna run. I'm gonna set five or six traps. Make sure The Cloud only hits a couple, but do it sneaky if you can. You can take four or five shots at me, however you want to. I've got a lot of superhero damage to burn. Then I'll disappear into a play structure and vanish or something. After that, let The Cloud lead. Got it, kid?" Pranky Jones stared at me.

"Got it." I took a deep breath.

"Oh, and, uh, sorry about scaring you when you were little, too." Pranky Jones cracked his knuckles. "Alright, Narrator's got our backs. Remember, it's a kid's show, so make it cheesy! And go!"

"Suddenly, the Playpen Patrol noticed Pranky Jones!" The Narrator said.

The villain dashed past the ball pit, and Milkbar pointed at him. "There he is! Let's get him!"

"[**Newspaper Nightmare**]! [**Stacked Cup Smackdown**]!" Pranky Jones yelled. He ran through a door, which slammed shut behind him.

A second later, Honeycomb called out over the chaos. "Milkbar, Zoomies, you can come with me! We *have* to check the beehives in case Pranky Jones is pranking the poor insects. Outlet, show the kangaroo where the second beehive is, and Cloud, you can—"

"The Cloud! I'm The Cloud!" The boy started tearing up, and I heard a faint peal of thunder.

"*The* Cloud, then. You're with Magical Girl Understudy. Show her the third beehive." Honeycomb clapped once. "Alright, Playpen Patrol, go!"

"Playpen Patrol, go!" the pint-sized superheroes shouted, and off we went.

The Cloud took off toward the door Pranky'd been through. Literally. He left the floor, drifted toward the ceiling, and paused at the door. "Uh, miss? Help!"

I sighed. The kid couldn't reach the doorknob while floating near the air vents and ceiling tiles. I grabbed his foot and pulled him back toward the floor. As soon as his feet touched the ground, his hand wrapped around the door handle. He jerked it open and ran in.

I heard a terribly loud tearing sound. Then the sound of a hundred Solo cups clattering across the linoleum flooring. And then a sob.

When I tore through the wreckage of the newspapers that'd been taped to the doorframes, I found The Cloud hovering over a mound of red cups, tears dripping onto the floor. He held his knee, so I quickly looked while a camera drone hovered nearby. He was fine. Totally fine. "Looks like you got a little rug burn when you fell. Do you think you can be very, very careful from now on, The Cloud?"

The tiny-tot superhero nodded, unkempt red hair flopping everywhere, and sniffled. "Y-yes, Miss Understuffy. I'll . . . I'll try."

While I worried over The Cloud's slightly skinned knee, part of me was frustrated. This was taking way too *long*. If the toddler kept rushing off, he'd actually get hurt, or it'd slow us down too much. Then, I got an idea. I helped the kid up, then pointed at Tails. "This is my best friend, Tails. She's a scaredy-cat—"

<Am not! But I see what you're trying to do, nya!>

"—and she needs your help to get to the beehive. Can you stay with her so she doesn't get scared?"

[Good Thinking! +1 Smarts Point]

"Yeah, I can!" He wrapped a fist around Tails's collar. She fidgeted, tail swishing, but didn't hiss or pull away. Much.

Back on track. We'd only spent a minute caught by Pranky Jones's first traps. We weren't too far behind. I gestured toward a long, wide room at the end of the hall. "What's back there?"

"Oh, that's where we keep the first beehive! It's shut right now, though. It's so much *fun*! The bees walk down a tube, and then they fly away."

"That sounds neat. Can you show me?"

As we got close, I realized I didn't need The Cloud to show me the gigantic beehive behind plexiglass walls. It covered the whole back wall; there had to be a million bees. Maybe more, even. They swarmed down a long, clear tube and flew off outside, and the whole room smelled like honey—so much that it stank. I watched, fascinated. "I bet Honeycomb loves it here."

"That she does, kid," a voice behind me said. "I figured *she'd* come here, but I'll settle for bee-ting you!"

"Buzz off, Pranky Jones," I said, twirling so my wand pointed at him.

[Silly Joke! +1 Silly Point]

So, bee puns earned Style Points here? Huh. I could use that. I opened my mouth to engage in a silly pun war, but Pranky Jones started laughing before I could. "You think you can joke with me? Don't make me laugh! It's time for my [**Maniacal Reveal**]! I'm a clown, Miss Understudy. [**Joke Joust**]! Why was the bee's hair always sticky?"

I groaned in advance, but The Cloud looked at the villain as he started hovering again. "I dunno. Why?"

"Because it used a honeycomb!"

[HP 4/6]

Had his pun . . . hurt so bad I took damage? This was so much *worse* than the Panic Pals' rap songs. I groaned a second time, but The Cloud took one look at Pranky Jones and burst out laughing and squealing. "That's Miss Honeycomb's name!"

"What do you call a beehive with no exits?" Pranky Jones yelled.

"I have no idea. [**Stellar Ray**]!" My wand swished. A light ray zipped into his stomach, drawing an overly dramatic grunt.

[You Hurt Someone! +1 Sad Point]

Then he turned and ran again. Was he ever going to stand and fight? He pointed toward the door again. "Un-bee-lievable! [**Shrink-Wrap Suprise**]!"

"When Pranky Jones ran away, The Cloud and Magical Girl Understudy decided to check out the giant beehive," The Narrator said over the loudspeakers.

The Cloud looked at me, eyes watery. "Are you okay, Miss Understuffy? Pranky Jones didn't hurt you with his jokes, right?"

"I'm fine. Let's check out the beehive. He was in here, so he might have messed with it somehow." I strode over to the plexiglass barrier. Inside, I could see a little door with dozens of wooden frames. Each had honey on them, but the ones nearest to us seemed . . . empty. "Cloud, could you—"

"The Cloud!"

"—Yeah, The Cloud. Sorry. Do you remember if these all had honey?"

"Yeah, they did. The bees need some for winter. That's what Miss Honeycomb said. We can only take a little bit at a time because if we take it all, the bees won't be happy over the winter." The Cloud floated over to the window.

I already had my suspicions about how this Episode was going to go. But before I could voice them, The Narrator's voice boomed over the loudspeakers again.

"And that was when The Cloud realized that Pranky Jones wanted to steal all the honey!"

35

Steal ALL the Honey

The Cloud gasped. "Miss Understuffy! Pranky Jones wants to steal *all* the honey!"

Seriously? I tried not to roll my eyes at the kid. His eyes were so big, so worried. But every single Professor Panic plot felt more dangerous than this ridiculousness. Rated-G Episodes were so painfully . . . wholesome. "I know, The Cloud. What do you think we should do?"

There I was, asking a four-year-old for advice on camera.

On the other hand, The Cloud had experience with Pranky Jones, or at least with other Anti-Naptime League members.

"Let's go get him!" The Cloud took off, floating down the hall.

Well, *that* wasn't going to work. I grabbed his foot, pulling him down to the ground. "Watch out for, um, pranks, okay? Jones might have left them around." I tapped on the near-invisible [**Shrink-Wrap Surprise**] in the door. It bounced back and forth, slapping into my hand.

[**HP 3/6**]

"Ow! Really?" Shaking my hand helped with the sting, but why would Pranky Jones make something hurt so much? He was playing a role with kids!

"Are you okay, Miss Understuffy?" When I nodded, The Cloud ducked under the [**Shrink-Wrap Surprise**] and waved for me to follow. Beyond the doorframe, the hallway seemed empty of traps, but I opened the door to the main area carefully all the same. It was a good thing I did because even more red Solo cups clattered to the ground. I shut the door and waited for the sounds to stop.

"I like stopping Jungle Jim more," The Cloud said suddenly. "He's not sneaky. Just big."

"Yeah. My old rival was sneaky, and he liked robots a lot." The cups stopped falling. A second later, the door opened from the other side.

Fursona's head poked through. "Hey, Understudy. Was your beehive missing honey frames too?"

"Yeah." The Cloud spoke up first. "He's gonna steal all the honey, and then the bees will get hungry this winter, just like Miss Honeycomb says. Someone has to help!"

Honeycomb waved from her circle spot by the ball pit. "We will. But first, let's go over what we learned about bees today. Have a seat, Playpen Patrol!"

"Playpen Patrol, go!" The Cloud joined his friends and ran to the circle. I wandered behind him, watching as he threw himself onto the rubber-tiled floor and sat on the blue square. Milkbar got red, Outlet yellow, and Kid Zoomies orange. They stared at Honeycomb.

The bee girl cleared her throat. "Okay, Patrollers! How do bees make honey?"

Fursona sidled up to me, tail swishing agitatedly. "We need to talk away from the kids."

I followed them back toward the front. The Narrator sat there, drinking a coffee and reading a newspaper. She looked at us, shook her head, and returned to the article. The top headline read "Megafauna Sightings on the Rise: Analysts Say Man vs. Nature Five Soon."

I hadn't been powerful enough for Man vs. Nature Four. I'd just gotten my powers, and Riverside was out of the way enough that even with a Man vs. Nature happening, a couple of Ronin had been sufficient to keep us safe. Rocko had forbidden us from Episodes for the duration, though, and I'd been thankful for the break—and the Ronin protection. I was looking forward to finally being able to protect myself, even if it was only a little bit.

"I asked Outlet a few questions when she wasn't trying to stick her tongue into electric plugs. That girl's a nightmare to babysit. But yeah, questions," Fursona said. "I guess the beehives aren't new or anything. Tottergarten's had them as long as she can remember. And, according to her, Honeycomb's *always* here. I don't know for sure, but this screams 'lair' to me. Or 'secret base' or something."

"There's more, though." The kangaroo fidgeted with their paws and bounced on the balls of their feet. "Outlet said Honeycomb hasn't missed an evening in like two weeks. She's not getting out there and fighting Jumper. She's just staying here and doing kids' Episodes over and over."

"Is she trying to train?" I asked. "Sure, she could earn some Style Points, but it doesn't seem very efficient."

"Ahem." The Narrator cleared her throat and looked over the top of her newspaper. "You two need to get back in there. I won't make you . . . yet . . . but Honeycomb should finish her lesson in the next minute. Small brains need small bites of knowledge."

"We'll figure this out after," I said. But something felt . . . off. I'd almost returned to the circle when it hit me; if Honeycomb wasn't looking for Jumper, she couldn't follow through on our deal! I scowled a little. We were going to have words later.

"And if the bees don't have honey, they get sick over the winter. Bees need food to grow strong just like people do," Honeycomb said. "So we have to help the bees. Right, Understudy?"

". . . Right." I unballed my fists. I hadn't realized how angry I felt. I'd run out of time, and I needed Honeycomb to help me out here, but I couldn't ignore the current Episode, either. "What do we do here?"

"We go outside!"

"Yeah, outside! Pranky Jones always hides outside!"

"It's playground time!"

The kids sprinted to the door, popped it open, and started screaming as a bucket of water on a string upended itself on them.

"Be careful," Honeycomb admonished them. "Pranky Jones has all sorts of mean pranks!"

Milkbar nodded thoughtfully and made a show of tiptoeing out the door. I tried hard not to facepalm as the camera drone followed him toward a gigantic play structure with slides and ramps. A handful of red tricycles sat parked everywhere, and half-buried action figures dotted the sandbox.

More importantly, a wooden bucket filled with golden liquid sat on the concrete, and a ridiculous-looking car idled near the fence's gate. It honked its horn, piercing the evening quiet with its duck quack, and a hulking figure got out of the back. "Jones, you finished here?"

"Yeah, no, boss. I've just gotten started. Do you know how much honey a regular-sized beehive makes in a year? Forty-five pounds of the stuff. And this place ain't average. Is Teacher's Pet coming with the truck? We're gonna need it!"

"No, you're not, Pranky Jones! Playpen Pals, go!" Milkbar yelled.

"Playpen Pals, go!"

Pranky Jones found himself under adorable attack from all four pint-sized heroes. The camera drone followed their fight as electricity arced through the air, and a bright orange streak ran around, cleaning up pranks and traps almost as fast as Pranky Jones could cast them. Almost.

But I had bigger problems—much, much bigger ones.

Another pair of villains exited the car. Though smaller than the massive one, they towered over the toddlers fighting Jones, and both they and the massive one started running toward the fight.

"And so the adult superheroes distracted Jungle Jim, Trike Mike, and Felicia Fire!"

I dashed toward the three villains. Unfortunately for me, the big one headed straight to me. It looked like it'd be a solo melee fight against . . .

"Are you . . . Brick House?"

"Shut up, kid. I used to be, but now I'm Jungle Jim!" The gigantic, red-haired clown's makeup didn't do much to conceal who he'd been—a midtier major leaguer famous for being indestructible. I thanked The Narrator mentally for making sure this fight was rigged.

A massive fist flew my way, whizzing through the air as Jungle Jim grunted. I ducked under it, then jumped the kick that followed. Jungle Jim may have been massive, but I was much faster than him.

I let one more punch sail past my head. Then it was time to earn some points. I needed Silly and Sad points—Flamboyance and Drama, maybe? "[**Spotlight Strike**]!"

The spotlight zipped up to Jim's shoulder, so I punched there. The big villain grunted, then rolled his eyes. "Gonna have to do better, Magic Gal!" Not much better, though. I'd made contact, and Jim had felt it.

[Funny Damage! +1 Silly Point]

He roared and rushed toward me, fists swinging, so I ducked and dodged while trying to get some distance. One hit, spinning me in a circle. My skirt flared as I dropped to a knee and put a hand on the ground to stabilize myself.

[HP 2/6]

Huh. For a Rated-G Episode, I'd taken a lot of damage. And I had a feeling that going Lab Assistant Panic was out. The Narrator would reset me; if she didn't, the villains might not appreciate me stepping on their toes. They had a good thing going here, after all.

"Jungle Jim, huh? More like Junk-el Jim!"

I waited for the pun damage to set in.

"That only works on Pranky, Magic Gal! His [**Joke Joust**] makes him vulnerable to them. But sticks and stones won't break my bones, and words can *never* hurt me!"

He kept swinging, and I activated [**Spotlight Strike**] and hit back. The Style System went nuts.

[Funny Damage! +1 Silly Point]
[Funny Damage! +1 Silly Point]
[HP 1/6]
[Tough Girl! +1 Tough Point]
[Funny Damage! +1 Silly Point]
[HP 0/6]
[Tough Girl! +1 Tough Point]
[Funny Damage! +1 Silly Point]

I disengaged, panting for breath. Jungle Jim barely looked winded, though, and I'd taken a beating. After all, he'd been a major leaguer, and his Grit had to be through the roof. Even if the gigantic man wasn't more than a punching bag, I couldn't afford to stay in close.

So I dashed for the play structure, spinning and firing off a [**Stellar Ray**] as I ran. It hit Jungle Jim, doing about as much good as my fists and feet had, but at least he couldn't hit back.

[**You Hurt Someone! +1 Sad Point**]

With a second to catch my breath, I took stock. Fursona and Honeycomb were both losing, but not badly. More importantly, Pranky Jones lay on the ground, swarmed down by the kids. He tried dramatically to lift his arms, but Milkbar had them pinned. Then he said the most important words of the night.

"Stop! I give up! I'll give the honey back!"

Jungle Jim stopped picking up a tricycle to throw at me. "Alright, Playpen Patrol, you've won this round! But the Anti-Naptime League will be back! Mike, Felicia, we're leaving!" He jogged back toward his car. Felicia slid into the passenger seat, Mike into the driver's, and they took off.

Leaving Pranky Jones behind.

"What do we do with him?" Fursona asked. I wasn't sure. Usually, the winning side would wait for the cops to show up. But in toddler Episodes, did we need the police? Everything had been so scripted. Even my fight with Jungle Jim hadn't felt out of control. I wasn't sure he'd even used a power during it.

"Finally, Pranky Jones and the Anti-Naptime League had been defeated. The Playpen Patrol and its heroes gathered for one last lesson."

We'd all assembled by the ball pit. A handful of parents waited nearby, and the toddler heroes couldn't stop yawning. Luckily for them, the camera drone seemed entirely focused on Honeycomb and Pranky Jones.

". . . and I'm sorry for trying to steal the bees' honey. Now that I know they need most of it, I'll leave them alone and come to you when it's harvest time instead," Jones said. He smiled sadly at the camera. "I'll be back, though! You'll see!"

"I'm sure you will, Pranky Jones. But until that happens, think about what you've done, and remember that sticky fingers aren't sweet!"

We all laughed, the Episode ended, and I felt myself in control again.

[**Episode Finished!**]
[**Episode: Short: The Playpen Pals and Honeycomb Save the Bees! - G**]
[**Penalties: N/A**]
[**Short Finished! +3 of each Style Point**]
[**Winner Winner! +2 of each Style Point**]
[**Role Focus: Silly+Sad - Goal met! +20 Focused Style Points**]
[**Alias - Understudy**] [**Archetype - Magical Girl**] [**Community Rank - 473/523**]
[**HP 0/6**]

[Styles and Skills]
▶Archetype Skill - Transformation Sequence
▶Badass (34)
▶Cunning (18)
▶Inkling 1
▶Drama (28)
▶Stellar Ray 1
▶Flamboyance (44)
▶Signature Skill - Adaptive Armoire 1
▶Stored Costumes: (Lab Assistant Panic)
▶Starwave Sail 1
▶Spotlight Strike 1
▶Grit (47)
▶Rejuvenation 1

Well, I hadn't earned any rolls, and that was disappointing, but at least I had a win. Maybe it'd be enough for Sara-N-Dipity.

The Playpen Patrol's parents (say that ten times fast!) took their kids, and Honeycomb, Fursona, and I stood alone by the ball pit. None of us said anything for a moment. Then I cleared my throat and scowled.

"Do you know where Jumper is?"

Honeycomb looked miserable. She couldn't even look me in the eye; instead, she just stared at her feet. All my annoyance at her vanished, especially when she started talking.

"Um . . . about that . . ."

36

Um...About That

What do you mean, 'about that'?" I asked. My stomach dropped. Honeycomb didn't have a clue where Jumper was, and I was running out of time. But she looked so miserable. She was almost crying.

"We can't talk about it here," she said, heading down the hall and ducking under Pranky Jones's leftover [**Shrink-Wrap Surprise**]. "Follow me to the Honey Hive."

"The Honey Hive?" Fursona snorted through their modulator.

"Shut up!"

The Honey Hive turned out to be Magical Girl Honeycomb's secret base, and, of course, it was inside the beehive. Honeycomb fiddled with a few controls, and a whole section filled with smoke. Then we just . . . strolled through the acrid gray fog and ludicrously sweet-smelling air. She opened the back wall, flicked on a fan to blow away the few unsmoked bees, and ushered us inside.

"Welcome to the Honey Hive," Honeycomb muttered. She stared at the floor, face flushing red—the color contrasted poorly with her yellow dress. She gestured to some chairs. "Have a seat. I'll explain."

I didn't really want an explanation. I was out of time, and I needed a serious Episode *now*. Otherwise, I'd be giving Sara-N-Dipity "The Playpen Pals and Honeycomb Save the Bees!", and as funny as that'd be, she'd pick Punch and Grapple for sure. It had to be after six already. Maybe even closer to seven.

But Honeycomb had already started talking. "I want to show you something." She clicked play on a wall-mounted TV surrounded by stylized honeycomb patterning. A highlight reel started playing. Or, more accurately, a *lowlight* reel. Honeycomb falling on her face while chasing Jumper. Jumper tricking Honeycomb into her own honey puddle. Even Honeycomb getting flattened by a familiar-looking van—I couldn't help but feel a twinge of jealousy for a second since S hadn't hit her intentionally. Or at least he hadn't backed up and hit her again.

As I watched Jumper run across a wall and avoid a jet of bees, Honeycomb sighed. "I can't beat her. She won't *stay still*. And my flight power can't make the corners she can, so I can't chase her down. Ed's losing their mind. 'It's one thing to have a loss or two, kid, but the hero's gotta *win*!' 'If you can't win, you'll never make the minors!'" As she imitated her Ilneat producer, she got more frustrated. Her hands waved in the air as she made air quotes.

"But Jumper won't play fair. She keeps leaving whenever I show up. And she's funny. I'm just funny-looking." She pointed at her Costume. I had to agree there. Whoever her Pataki was hadn't done her any favors. "Ed's about to give the show to Jumper and try making her an antihero—like Robin Hood or something."

"Or that archer in the movie after everyone disappears and he gets a sword?" I asked. It was a pre-Launch Day movie, one the Ilneats really enjoyed. They called it *The End of an Era*, dismissing the rest of that series.

"Yeah, like him. Ed says I have three more chances—two, because I got involved in your Episode a couple of weeks ago—and if I can't beat Jumper, the show's hers. So I've been hiding from Jumper Episodes here since you two caught S. My mom thinks I'm volunteering with the kiddos, but I'm trying to train."

"Train?" Fursona asked. Then they stood up from their seat. "Wait. You can just do G-rated Episodes until you're strong? Why aren't we doing that?"

"It doesn't work well." Honeycomb shook her head slowly and wiped her eyes. "The first Episode did. But after that, the Style Point penalties for G-ratings started stacking. I earned three points for that last Episode. Total."

"So what do you want from us, then?" I asked.

"Can you help me take down Jumper?"

I facepalmed. I actually did. Then I tried to recover as she burst into tears. God damn, this girl was sensitive. "You know, if you'd helped me out tonight, we could have tried to track her down. We could have beaten Jumper, I could have gotten my minor-league sidekick role, and we'd both be happy right now."

"I know, but . . . the kids really love having me around. The Anti-Naptime League is—"

"What's with those guys, anyway?" Fursona asked.

"They're ex-supervillains. Or, I guess, retired supervillains. Pranky Jones has at least three hundred million in the bank, and Jungle Jim fought in the First Power Wars and Man vs. Nature One and Two. They're here for fun and to hang out with the kids. And The Narrator is a meta-powered hero. She can rewrite Episodes. The Ilneats hate her because she was a kid therapist before Launch Day, and she refused to change careers. Eventually, Yakko convinced her to do educational TV though. So now she runs Tottergarten."

"Hang on, let's talk business here," I interrupted. I wanted to know all about Tottergarten. The place seemed . . . weird . . . for a daycare, although The Narrator's presence alone probably made it the safest place in Tokyexico City. But I didn't have time. "I need an Episode tonight. Can you find Jumper?"

"No." Honeycomb looked away. "My . . . my mom's picking me up soon. I have trigonometry homework and an essay due in Ancient World History."

"Wait, how old are you?" I asked.

"Fifteen."

Honeycomb was fifteen? A sophomore in high school. And if she spent her free time doing trigonometry homework or hanging out at the daycare, she probably didn't have a ton of friends. I rubbed my temples. "Alright. Listen, I have to go. I've got to find that Episode. Fursona, are you coming with me?"

"No, I've got homework too."

"Alright. I'll go it alone again," I said. "Keep in touch, Honeycomb. You hear anything about Jumper, you give me a text."

"You got it," she said.

I hurried outside. The sunset came early behind the looming wall, and long shadows covered Tokyexico University's streets. A single car sat outside Tottergarten; two parents carried a struggling super-toddler toward it. The kiddo struggled gamely to get airborne, but his mom and dad knew how to handle him. I waved at The Cloud, and he started squirming even more.

The streetlights hadn't come on yet. I still had time. There had to be a little-league Episode popping off somewhere. "[**Starwave Sail**]!" I shouted.

The sailboard popped under my feet, and I took off, skimming slowly under the parking lot lights.

"Miss Understuffy, wait! I love you!" The Cloud managed to squirm free from his parents' grip just long enough to get over their reaches. If I could get moving fast enough, though, he wouldn't be able to cut me off, and he'd have to go home.

I started getting up to speed when suddenly—

Bonk!

I looked down. The Cloud hung off my board's nose, waving with one hand that held a ripped-up bit of cloth. Was it . . .

It was. The floaty toddler had shredded his cape on something, and he held it out to me after clambering onto my now-hovering sailboard. "Miss Understuffy, you were the superest teacher ever!" He hugged my leg with his free hand.

"Uh, thanks, but Honeycomb is pretty great, too," I said. The poor girl was here every day with these kids. She deserved their love. Although . . . if they were typical toddlers, they probably loved everyone. "Tell me about your cape."

"It makes me fly, and it rains when I get sad. I can't do it now because I'm so happy, though!" He gave me another hug.

"Alright, thank you so much for the gift!" I ruffled his hair, and he glared at me. "Head back to your parents, okay? I have to go."

His parents stood about twenty feet below with expressions that wavered between worried, bored, and annoyed. Mom hovered under my board while Dad tapped his foot near their car. He held one of those kid-walker leashes they advertised on late-night TV sometimes. Usually, that seemed tacky, but it made a lot of sense with The Cloud. A kid balloon on a string worked better than a kid balloon three hundred feet up.

The Cloud didn't seem to mind being far up. "Bye, Miss Understuffy. Bring my cape with you when you come back!" He jumped off my sailboard and drifted down to his mom's waiting arms. She grabbed him, his dad clipped the leash harness around his chest, and they got in the car.

I waved. Then I zipped off into the evening sky, The Cloud's cape waving in my fist as I flew one-handed. Time had run out. This was the last chance. The last, last chance. I didn't have to go far to find one—only to Bleaker Avenue.

[Casting Call]
[Episode: What 3V1L May Bring - R]
[Role: Hapless Sidekick! Do you accept the role? (Yes/No)]
[Role Focus: Drama+Grit]

If it had been a minor-league Episode, I'd have accepted the [Casting Call] right away. Even as it stood, I thought about it. The role name made it sound like I wouldn't have to *do* much. But a major-league loss wasn't what I needed right now.

I hadn't heard of 3V1L before, but it sounded like one of those cartoon villain organizations with an acronym that spelled out Every Villain Is Loony or something. That Episode was either crawling with henchmen or a group of villains working together. Either way, I'd probably end up fighting someone above my rank or a bunch of people way below it, and neither option sounded great.

I left "What 3V1L May Bring" behind. There had to be something else.

But, somehow, the "Hapless Sidekick" role was the best thing I found all night. I wasn't ready to lead-role a minor-league Episode, and all the other major-league ones had way more pressure on the sidekick role. I circled back to Beaker Avenue as the sun finally disappeared.

"What 3V1L May Bring" had ended. I didn't even know who won. And Beaker Avenue looked like it hadn't changed at all. Whatever 3V1L had planned, it had either worked, or they'd gotten stomped worse than when Theseus and Gourmet crushed Fursona and me.

Which left me with nothing for the night unless you counted "The Playpen Pals and Honeycomb Save the Bees!". I sighed. My algebra homework would have to wait.

One more search. This time, into the skyscraper canyons. Nothing popped up. Nothing, that was, except major-league Episodes. What was *with* this city? Didn't it have anything for a *starting* hero?

Nope. It sure didn't. At least, not after dark. I turned my sailboard toward Tokyexico University and Walnut Tower, Room 1301, suppressing a yawn. There was too much to do before bed; I couldn't afford to get tired now.

I flipped open my laptop and typed in "Superpower Pickup Episodes." Nothing. "Superhero Episode sign-ups" got a similar result. So did "Superheroes for Hire" and "Looking for Episodes." At least, none of them gave me what I needed. There didn't seem to be an Episode sign-up service or one that'd tell me where Episodes were happening so I could go there myself.

I made a note. I was *going* to ask someone about an app for that tomorrow. Or at least soonish.

My email dinged.

Subject: Luck?
Hey Understudy,
Any luck? If not, your best bet is the kiddie Episode. It'd be better to show you work well with others since we got wrecked by Theseus and Gourmet in ours. I think if you approach it right in your email, it could be convincing. Springlock also said that Sara needed a combat specialist, and you could do that if you built right. You stood up to Brick House. That's worth something.
Either way, let me know how it goes.
Justice-Roo

I sighed. Then I flopped onto my back. Fursona was right. I didn't have much choice if I wanted to look serious at all.

To: LuckyGirl777.SH@tstudent.tokyexicouniversity.edu
Subject: Episode
Hello, Sara-N-Dipity
I'm waiting on an Episode I guest-starred in. It's a G-rated Episode, but it showcases my combat skills and ability to work with others. In it, I worked with several other heroes, including Fursona (my sidekick), Magical Girl Honeycomb, The Narrator, and members of the Playpen Patrol.
I also fought against Mister Twister and Brick House, both formerly major-league villains. While I couldn't defeat either, the heroes I worked with took care of Mister Twister, and I forced Brick House to retreat.
I hope this Episode shows that I'm a viable choice for a minor-league sidekick role.
Either way, thank you.
Magical Girl Understudy

I sent it to Sara-N-Dipity. Then I shut my laptop and groaned. My stomach felt tight, and I had a little ache between my eyes, which I kept rubbing. As I lay down for what promised to be a restless night, I couldn't shake a bad feeling. Then my phone buzzed.

<Hi hi! Busy tomorrow? If not, your place, Man vs. Nature, 4:00? - Bianca 10:47>
<Sure. I'll be here. Already got an Episode picked out! - Annie 10:48>

Brick House vs. The Florida Man-Eater. I'd wanted to watch that villain get his ass kicked for a while. At least I'd have some fun tomorrow while I waited for my Episode to air so I could actually show Sara. If she was willing to wait to see it herself, that was.

<Yay! I'm bringing something to drinky-drink - Bianca 10:49>

37

Something to Drinky-Drink

THURSDAY, SEPTEMBER 18

DuPont! Come on in, come on in!" Rocko yelled. "Find a seat, find a bottle, and let's get talking!"

I held The Cloud's cape scrap in one hand and reached for bottled water with the other. As soon as I sat down, Rocko was up in my grill. "What happened, Annie? You get clobbered by Theseus and Gourmet, and since they both outrank you, the studio only gets 40% of the cut. And then a G Episode? A *G*? And one with *Ed's* hero?"

They started crying. I struggled not to roll my eyes, though. Ilneats didn't cry. Rocko was faking it for me—they'd probably put eye drops in. They glanced at me, then stopped the crocodile tears. "DuPont, just tell me we're still on the same team."

"Yeah, we're on the same team, Rocko. I'm trying to move up, though, and I wanted a minor-league sidekick guest role." I sighed. I wasn't going to get the role, and I knew it. There was no way. But Fursona and I had a plan; the job fair Ikenga had told us about. It was time to get serious. "Look, can I talk to you and Pataki? I got another Costume piece for Adaptive Armoire."

"Sure, sure," the suit-wearing producer said. They knuckle-walked over to the machine, where Pataki sat. "Hey, Pataki, she's finally here about the toddler's cape!"

Pataki glanced at me. "Hey, you know you can only equip one Costume right now, right?"

She was right. **[Adaptive Armoire]** only had one Costume slot. But all the same, I wanted the Costume. "I think I can put the Costume in the System and take out the Lab Assistant Panic one, though." I couldn't help but roll my eyes as I said, "Lab Assistant Panic," and Rocko caught it.

"Oh, having some troubles? Don't really wanna deal with Peter right now? I get it, believe me. My ex and I never talked the last few months." They clapped their squeezing hands before I could say he wasn't my ex. "Give Pataki the cape scrap and hop in the machine!"

I did, determinedly not staring at my nude model or saying anything. Rocko sat down at their desk while Pataki walked me through the process. "Hands here, head still, blah, blah, blah. You're getting better at this, DuPont," they rasped.

When they finally finished, Rocko started talking. "Alright, you got a good one, DuPont! That's a possible major leaguer's Costume right there! We're talking flight, electric powers, maybe water stuff, and a real neat Grit skill. So let's see. Start with the standard magical girl setup. The tot's original Costume was blue and red. Let's lighten up the red to pink—"

"That's the same as my colors," I complained.

"They look good on you, and think about the branding for all the merch we'll be making! We'll shorten the skirt, do full leggings—make those blue—and add a cape."

"Nope," Pataki rasped. "No capes."

"That movie was fiction, Pataki! Fiction! No hero's been sucked into an airplane because of their cape in fifteen years, and Sky Pilot had a million other things go wrong! Gimme a blue cape with cloud patterning. Now, Annie, you had some personality stuff with Lab Assistant Panic, eh?"

"Yeah. When I'm Lab Assistant Panic, I'm a villain," I said. "I'm still me, but it's bringing out my villainous side, which, apparently, exists."

"Well, it makes for hilarious TV, especially against Professor Panic. Reviews are finally in on 'Professor Panic's Payout Plan,' and the fans love that dynamic. Whatever happens in your relationship with Peter, it'd be a shame if you two didn't do Episodes together."

I hadn't considered that before. Peter and I could just . . . stop. It could be over, and I wouldn't have to put up with his lack of effort the last few weeks anymore. It'd be so much easier on me. I'd been making most of the contacts. I'd been scheduling video calls. I'd been coming up with ideas for long-distance dates. But I'd put so much effort into it already; we'd been together so long. I shook my head. "I don't know what's up with him, but we're not breaking up. We can get through this."

"That's good to hear, DuPont!" For a second, Rocko looked almost genuine. Then they shook their head and shoved an unlit cigar in their mouth. "It'd be a nightmare to lose one of you now when you're both moving on up. Financially devastating."

He pointed at the door. "If there's nothing else, go check out your Magical Girl Rainy Day Costume. I think you'll like its powers! But also, be aware that it might come with some changes too. Get outta here!"

I nodded, smiling, and left. For all his faults, Rocko cared a little. Or at least, he cared about the cash *Small-Town Super* and *Heroics 101* brought in. And that was the same thing, wasn't it?

Back in my pastel-pink secret base, I clapped my hands twice and grabbed Tails. My transformation to Magical Girl Understudy felt so slow—I knew it was excitement over the new Costume, but all the same.

"The itsy-bitsy spider went up the waterspout!" I said, going through the silly hand motions. "Down came the rain and washed the spider out! Up came the sun and dried up all the rain, and the itsy-bitsy spider went up the spout again!"

Thunder crashed. The smell of fresh rain filled the room. And in a flash of lightning, I transformed. Before I could adequately take my new Costume in, though, a System Message filled my vision.

[Costume - Magical Girl Rainy Day]
[HP 6/6]
[Styles and Skills]
▶ Archetype Skill - Transformation Sequence
▶ Strong
▶ Smart
▶ Sad
▶ Light as Vapor 0
▶ Hometown Heroine 1
▶ Silly
▶ Signature Skill - Adaptive Armoire 1
▶ Stored Costumes: (Understudy)
▶ Ride the Lightning 0
▶ Tough
▶ Rejuvenation 1
▶ Cloudy Disposition 0

"Whoa. I wonder what [**Ride the Lightning**] does," I said, then covered my mouth. My voice sounded strange. Higher pitched. More . . . kid-like. Something had gone horribly wrong, and I ran to the makeup mirror. When I got there, I stared in horror. A pimply, childish, early middle-schooler's face stared back at me.

I ignored the cloudy, poofy sleeves and the lightning patterns on the full tights. I even ignored Misty Kitty, the cat-shaped cloud I knew was Tails. I recognized the girl in the mirror.

She was me. Me from sixth grade.

The doorbell rang at precisely four o'clock.

To be honest, I wasn't up for this. My conversation with Peter . . . had been bad. It didn't ease any of my worries about us. And Ilneat Relations was never *not* going to be a bummer. I couldn't imagine a world where I'd need to know about their digestive tract. It wasn't like I planned to have Rocko over at the dorm room.

The doorbell rang again. I shook my head and breathed deeply. Now wasn't the time for Rocko *or* Peter—even if fixing our mess was priority one for me. It was time to hang out with a friend. I opened the door.

Bianca pounced as soon as I did. Between the giant backpack and her nervous energy, the quick hug nearly knocked me over. Then she'd dashed off to the couch in front of the enormous TV. "Hey, I got something to make this a real party. No peeking, though!"

I turned around, letting her unzip the backpack. She pulled out something that clinked, then rezipped the pack and set the clinking something on the table. "Okay, turn around!"

A bottle of vodka and a pair of tiny shot glasses sat on the table. I raised an eyebrow. "Where did you get that?"

"Fake ID. I've been doing it since my sophomore year. Gotta know where to buy, but there's always somewhere that'll sell to a pretty girl."

Bianca certainly was pretty. Her wavy black hair framed her green eyes nicely, and she had an athlete's build. She'd played soccer, though, so that made sense. I shook my head and sat down. "Alright, today's Episode is 'Brick House vs. The Florida Man-Eater.'"

"Why Brick House?" Bianca asked curiously, flopping on the couch next to me.

"Uh, I don't like him much," I lied. Well, I sort of lied. Jungle Jim had seemed like a reasonable guy, but Brick House? He'd been a *problem* for the superheroes in the First Power War. "And he gets his ass kicked most of the Episode."

"Oh really?" Bianca asked, a twinkle in her eye. "How about this? Every time Brick House gets clobbered, we take a shot?"

I'd drunk a little with Peter at Flat Top, and once or twice at house parties— enough to know that Bianca's game was trouble. I'd seen Brick House vs. The Florida Man-Eater a few times before. We'd be lucky if we didn't die before the Man-Eater did. "I've seen the Episode, Bee. How about just a sip every time Brick House gets hurt?"

"Deal!" Bianca poured two shot glasses full and handed one to me. She held one up and grinned. "Cheers!"

I bonked my glass into hers, tried to drink as much of it as I could, and pressed play. The booze was already hitting my brain before Brick House waded into the mangroves for the first time.

"So, anyways, she wanted to go party, and I said sure, why not? Because, uh, I'd never been to a party," Bianca slurred. Loudly. We'd been drinking for two hours, and we were finally on "Brick House vs. The Florida Maneater IV: Get Housed!" And boy, was Bianca housed! "I'm not much of a party girl. But she says her friends'll be there, the liar. There's, um, no one there we know, and everyone else is a senior. But we get red Solo cups with something—"

The sound of a snapping pier mixed with a completely unedited curse as Brick House, bleeding from a dozen bites but somehow still in one piece, ran from the Florida Man-Eater. The gator must've been forty feet long; its teeth were the size of my arm, and it'd been using its size against Brick House most of the series. But the villain had landed a good blow to the monster gator's back leg at the end of Part III, and now the tide was turning.

"—and she gets super, *super* drunk. Kinda like me right now. And I'm drinking too because there's nothing else to do at this party. But, uh . . ."

"Yeah?"

She was wasted. I wasn't doing a lot better. I'd forgotten how many times Brick House got tossed around in these four Episodes. He looked a lot like I imagined we had against Theseus, except he had *so much Grit*. I couldn't help but feel jealous of how tough he was. He'd probably taken fifty or sixty points of superhero damage altogether. And he just kept *going*.

Bianca was leaning on me. Or was I leaning on Bianca? It was hard to tell, but she looked so happy with my head on her shoulder. "I wish I had snacks," I said.

"Me too! We should order snacks! We can do that, you know? So, anyways, uh, she's super drunk. Totally wasted. And we get up to leave, but she kinda falls on me, and we crash into the wall. The *entire* fucking party's looking at us, and she . . ." Bianca trailed off, face reddening. She started staring at the TV intently. "Never mind."

"She what?" I asked.

Brick House had turned it around. The Florida Man-Eater's back leg dragged uselessly, and a chunk of scale and skin bled where one eye used to be. Brick House wasn't doing much damage per hit, but the slow, unwieldy megafauna wasn't long for this world. It tried grabbing Brick House in its mouth and death-rolling, but the villain's arms held its jaws shut while he kicked its skull repeatedly.

Bianca shook her head. Then she turned to me, grinning, and asked, "You really wanna know?"

I nodded. "Yeah, you've got me *so* curious!"

"She drags me outside, just around the corner, and we're both stumbling around. The goddamn party music is still bumping. And suddenly, she's kissing me."

Huh. I leaned in a little, the megagator's death roar ignored. "What was that like?"

"Oh, it was great! I kissed her back. We were together until . . . just before college. Uh, distance wasn't gonna work for us." Bee looked at the floor for a bit. "I . . . I should get back to my place."

I looked at the TV screen. It was asking if we wanted another Episode of Man vs. Nature. I pressed Yes on the remote. "Nah, stick around for a while. It's not dark yet, and I've got questions!" My phone buzzed, but I ignored it. "Brainiac vs. The Forest That Walks" was up, but I ignored that too. "Tell me more," I said. "Did you know you were into girls before her?"

"Uh, yeah, she was my first girlfriend, but I'd kinda known for a while. It just sorta felt right. How'd you know you liked boys?"

Oh, yeah, that made sense. It *was* just like that, huh? "Peter and I sort of clicked. We . . . had similar interests. Kinda like—"

"Hey, that tree's gonna grab Brainiac! Why'd they send him to fight a *forest*, anyway?" Bee interrupted. Sure enough, the tree grabbed the Genius and tossed him across a clearing. I glanced at Bee, who nodded. We both took another sip.

"Ha, this was a Man vs. Nature I Episode. They did the best they could." Honestly, Bee's interruption didn't bother me at all. Because I'd been about to say something I couldn't resolve with my relationship with Peter. I'd been about to say, "Kinda like us."

PART FIVE

38

The Agent

WEDNESDAY, OCTOBER 1

Bianca flashed a smile as I let her push me onto the couch. "Ever kissed a girl?"

"No." I smiled back, heart thumping. "No." It was happening, but what would it be like? Was she going to take control, or would I need to?

Her lips touched mine, and my brain stopped. She moved them slightly, kissing the corner of my mouth, then my chin. They were so soft—softer than Peter's, the only other person I'd kissed. When she pulled away momentarily, I tasted something lemony on my lips that hadn't been there before.

I wanted more.

I tried to sit up, but Bee pushed me back down. She leaned over me for another kiss and—

"Hey, Underoos, you in there?" Gourmet asked. "Class is starting."

I shook the fantasy away, face hot and flushed. The last two weeks had been rough. I'd been a theater kid, so I'd changed Costumes with the other girls in school, and I'd noticed some other actresses were gorgeous. Didn't everyone do that?

Everyone did that, right?

Anyway, everyone did that. So it wasn't a big deal. It was a lot like checking out Punch and Grapple. Even if I was still dating Peter, I couldn't help but notice both were ripped. I bet they lifted with Avan or something. Or maybe with Milo, but I doubted it.

But Bianca felt different than all that.

I headed in and made myself comfortable in a black La-Z-Boy before that train of thought could leave the station.

"Today's lesson is on Extras and whether they should be involved in Episodes. And if they *are* involved, how to do so safely and respectfully. We'll be focused on The Agent today." Dr. Jackson sniffed, looking down her nose and narrowing her eyes. "The Agent, for those who don't know, has two unique powers. One of them lets heroes and villains license their powers to him. The second allows him to assign those powers to volunteer Extras temporarily."

I replaced my stupid-looking fantasizing grin with an eager one. The Agent Episodes were always chaotic as hell and so much fun to watch.

"This one is from the Second Power Wars, the first point The Agent showed up in Episodes. In it, he's up against Getaway Driver, whose plan revolves around a turbo-powered bus. We'll jump right into the action."

The TV flicked on, and the Kill Bus took off. Getaway Driver had covered the whole thing with spikes for this one, and as we watched, it backed out of the side of a bank. Unlike that ancient superhero flick, it didn't try to blend in with other buses. It took off down the street, accelerating with a roar.

The screen flicked to a brown-haired man in a three-piece suit ambling down a residential street. He opened a picket fence, knocked on the door, and waited. A middle-aged woman opened it. She blinked. "We don't accept traveling salesmen. I didn't know they still *did* that."

"I'm not a salesman. How would you like to be . . . a hero?"

"Y-y-you're . . . the . . ." the woman began, eyes wide.

"The Agent, yes. Listen, people's lives are at risk, and there's a 20% royalty in it for you. So, what do you say?"

"My son'll never let me live it down if I say no. I'm in."

"Wonderful. Now, fill out these forms. Sign here, here, and initial here, here, and here. This is a liability waiver. Sign here." The Style System popped up next to the woman, rolling until it stopped. "Wonderful. Whey Tee Lif's power. So, what I need you to do is . . ."

Dr. Jackson paused it and fast-forwarded while talking. "The Agent asks Sarah here to stop the bus since Whey Tee Lif could have handled that job. Then he knocks on the next door and recruits another Extra as a temp hero. Let's watch Sarah handle the bus."

Sarah got flattened by the bus.

"She lived. But she was in and out of Los Tacoma Hospital for the next year. The Agent covered all her bills, put her kids through college, and ensured she didn't have to work. But more importantly, he changed his code of ethics after what happened to Sarah. So, as we break into teams for the day, whose fault was Sarah's injury? Hers? The Agent's? Or Getaway Driver's? I had one team two years ago argue that it was Whey Tee Lif's fault. Once you assign responsibility, discuss how your codes can prevent this from happening to you."

We circled the chairs and got ready to discuss.

"Alright, on three, say who you think is to blame," Theseus said. "One . . . two . . . three! Sarah!"

"The Agent!"

"The Agent!"

"Sarah!"

I looked around, but the battle lines were drawn. Fursona and Gourmet high-fived while I glared at Theseus. We both agreed it was Sarah's fault she'd been hurt. So, like it or not, we were on the same side.

For now.

Gourmet cleared her throat. "Guys, The Agent is responsible here. He knew what Sarah was getting into. He could have done what he started to do later: swarm tactics with dozens of temp heroes."

"Why do you think he started doing that?" I asked.

"Yeah, Understudy's right on this one," Theseus said. "The Agent had a liability form. He was legally protected from responsibility. And he waited for her to read it. She chose not to. Besides, this was the first time The Agent hurt a temp this badly. He had no way of knowing what could happen."

"Nah," Fursona said. "New Power Boldness Syndrome was well understood by the Second Power War. The Ilneats even said it'd happen, and it kicked off the first war."

"Aren't you a newbie hero?" I asked, annoyed. "How do you know so much about superpowered stuff?"

"I've done a lot of research since signing with Rocko," they said smugly.

"Okay, back on topic. We all agree that it's Sarah's fault, right?" Theseus asked.

"What! No!"

"Oh, come on!"

"Holy shit, guys, we've gotta agree on *something* here!"

Code of Conduct: October 1

We will not ~~endanger harm threaten~~ endanger ~~civilians~~ Extras ~~needlessly~~

When Extras must be involved, ~~every effort must be taken to make them aware of danger~~ they must be clearly informed of danger

~~What about Henchmen?~~

WHO CARES ABOUT HENCHMEN?

I care about henchmen!

Destruction of ~~non-government residential~~ non-corporate/non-government property is ~~to be kept to a minimum not necessary~~ not okay

I can't agree to this, guys. I need to eat!

Bring your own snacks. I bring my own! And quit making fun of me!

You ate a wrestling singlet!

Medical Extras are off limits. Healing heroes ~~should only be targeted if involved in the fighting are a low priority target~~ are not a target unless they directly engage

Property damage must ~~have a point be for a purpose~~ be directly related to the Episode's goals

Thursday, October 2

I woke up the following day to bright, bright sunlight. The alarm clock read 10:30. Algebra started at ten. I must've really needed my sleep, because I slept clean through the alarm.

I groaned. Why couldn't I have slept through Ilneat Relations? I actually *needed* algebra classes. Su-Bin could only help me so much; if I wasn't in class, I'd miss *something* important. I'd have to email the professor and ask if he'd send me the slides for today's lesson.

I opened up my computer to a pair of emails.

Subject: RE: Episode
Hello, MGU
Lol. K.
Ill wait for your Episode. The boys havent gotten theirs screened yet, either. I hope yours is more fun than it sounds.
Sara

Alright. That one wasn't so bad, other than the beginning and how little effort she'd put into it. But the other one was worse. Much, much worse.

Subject: Megafauna Rising and Wall Closure Information
To All Students
The Huntsman's reports from the Rockies and Great Plains point toward increased megafauna activity. Experts in Tokyexico City and elsewhere believe the world is on the verge of the seventh Man vs. Nature event.

As per Tokyexico City policy, nonessential travel into and out of the city will be restricted leading up to and during Man vs. Nature Seven. This applies to trips home as well as visits from family and friends. For those students without a reliable way to video call with loved ones out of town, Tokyexico University offers free use of video call tools in the ballroom at the Student Union Building.

*This is a reminder to our powered students. Heroes and villains in the major and minor leagues should report to The Huntsman or the Tokyexico Council of Heroes for the [**Man vs. Nature Casting Call**]. Join The Huntsman for fighting in the Great Plains and Mountains or the TCH for city defense. Signing up for the [**Man vs. Nature Casting Call**] is mandatory for major-league heroes and villains and strongly encouraged for minor leaguers.*

Little leaguers and unpowered students are required to avoid the wall and Man vs. Nature Episodes at all costs, though they may defend themselves as necessary.

All powered students are requested to avoid Episodes that could require major-league intervention during this trying time.
Thank you for your cooperation,
Helen Barber
Vice President of Student Services
Tokyexico University

If all the minor leaguers and up were busy, what'd that mean for Sara-N-Dipity's recruitment drive? She hadn't emailed anything about that, so it probably didn't affect her plans too much. Or maybe she'd just put us on hold or tell me I'd won the sidekick spot and then wait until after the Man vs. Nature. Peter and I couldn't do Episodes during MvN Six because . . .

Shit. Peter.

I needed to talk to him. Or at least text him. The Episode-hunting and classes had kept me busy, and I'd forgotten to text him back. And . . . I didn't know what I wanted to do about that, either. I didn't want things to be over—they just needed to feel better. I headed to the bedroom and dumped the Lil Pal on my nightstand.

<Hey, Peter. I've been thinking a lot. We need to fix some things - Annie 10:43>

The tiny repulsors wouldn't fire, so I kept checking and rechecking my wiring while I waited for Peter to respond. He probably wouldn't. He was probably at work. He'd text back when he—

My phone buzzed. Then it buzzed again.

<Hi. I'm sorry. I don't know what I did, but I did something. - Peter 10:48>
<We can't see each other on the 11th. - Annie 10:48>
<City's locked down. MvN 7 - Annie 10:48
<Oh - Peter 10:49>

I waited. Then I waited some more, throat tight. He didn't respond beyond that "Oh." I started typing a text and hit send. My phone buzzed less than a second later as his reply finally came.

<How do we fix this if all you can say is 'Oh?' - Annie 10:52>
<Okay, on break at work. Gotta eat and stuff too - Peter 10:52>
<Im at work, Annie. Gimme some slack? - Peter 10:53>
<Okay. Sorry. Just . . . this all feels wrong the last few weeks - Annie 10:53>
<It's k. Chill - Peter 10:53>

Had he *really* just told me to chill? Didn't he realize what was at stake? I almost stopped replying. Hell, I *did* stop responding. I rubbed my temples and glared at the Lil Pal.

<I could get over there safely. I've got a lot of Panic Pals - Peter 10:53>
<And two LABRATS now - Peter 10:53>
<They'd get me there safely - Peter 10:53>

I screamed into a pillow for a second, then rage-worked on the Lil Pal. He didn't see the problem! It didn't matter if he visited because most of the time, we'd be apart! The left repulsor popped on with a hum, and the Lil Pal flung itself off the side table. I grabbed it, flicked it off, and went for my phone.

<We have bigger problems - Annie 10:54>
<Oh yeah? Like what? - Peter - 10:55>
<Like focusing on US when it's US time! We don't do that well - Annie 10:56>

The damn Lil Pal wasn't working right. Its right repulsor wouldn't go. Every time I flipped the On switch, it hummed Professor Panic's theme song and the left repulsor flipped it off the table. I shoved it into its bag again.

<Okay. I want to come up, though. I'll stage an emergency or something - Peter 10:59>

You know what Peter's problem was? He thought if we could see each other, it'd solve everything. But that wasn't the issue. That wasn't the issue at all.

<No, you won't. It's not worth running into megafauna - Annie 10:57>
<Just . . . stay home - Annie 10:57>
<And pay attention when we video chat! It hurt when you went Genius - Annie 10:58>
<K - Peter 10:59>
<Break's over. <3 you - Peter 10:59>
<<3 - Annie 11:00>

I rolled over on the bed and screamed again. I wished I were home, with my parents. Nothing had been solved. Nothing had been talked about. And I wasn't sure if he'd ignored what I said because of time issues or if he just . . . didn't care.

What were we going to do?

39

What Were We Going to Do?

FRIDAY, OCTOBER 3

Peter. Was. *Late.*

I stared at my laptop's screen, at the black box where he was supposed to be. My throat was tight, and my stomach rolled. The little clock read 8:49, which meant he was twenty minutes late. *I'd* texted him to make sure he'd be here. *I'd* done my makeup, curled my hair, and even put on the nightie he'd bought me. *I'd* spent an hour getting ready.

And *he* wasn't here. Not to enjoy it, and not for me to enjoy . . . us.

So I lay there on my giant bed, mind wandering. Man vs. Nature Seven had started with a buffalo herd the size of Yorkston Island heading right for us. I'd seen some videos of Yellowstone pre-Launch Day; buffalo were scary enough before you tripled their size and made their fur as tough as steel wool.

They were coming from the plains. The mountains to our west would break them up; the big herds never made it to Riverside. I wondered if the heroes and villains who'd signed up for the job fair were fighting already.

I couldn't do that, and everything I'd tried for weeks had failed. The fight against Gourmet and Theseus. The fruitless searches for Episodes, both before and after the Tottergarten run. Tottergarten itself. Everything. And my relationship teetered on the edge, too.

"What if I were dating someone here?" I muttered at my ceiling. At Tails. At the Lil Pal, whose repulsor still wouldn't fire, sitting on my end table. None of them responded. But I knew the answer. Someone closer—someone *here*—wouldn't leave me waiting in front of my computer. Punch, Grapple, or Avan wouldn't leave me waiting in front of my computer.

Bianca wouldn't leave me waiting in front of my computer.

Actually, let's pursue that, I thought. Why *did* Bianca keep popping up in my daydreams? And why could I taste lemon on her lips in those fantasies? I'd never seen her put on lipstick, chapstick, lip gloss, or anything. And we'd only hugged a couple of times. I didn't *know* what it'd be like to go on a date with her. But I had a guess it'd be awesome.

I hadn't crushed on someone like this in . . . huh. *Had* I crushed on someone like this?

Before I could follow *that* line of thought, Peter popped up on my screen. He pulled goggles off his dirt-covered face. I'd rarely seen the inside of his lair, but I recognized a workbench with a mostly assembled LABRAT lying on it behind him. The welds in its armor looked fresh. He looked tired . . . and a touch annoyed, maybe. "Sorry I'm late. I lost track of time."

He sure had. It'd been—I checked the clock—thirty minutes since we'd scheduled this. And he hadn't texted me all day. Not even to respond when I'd messaged him to confirm the time. I felt my lips press together thinly and sighed. Could I tell him it was fine again? Could I keep doing this? Relaxing my lips and sighing again, I decided to try.

"What are you working on, Peter?"

"LABRAT upgrades!" His exhausted face shone with excitement all of a sudden. "This is the 1.4 model over here. Its battery is good for five to six hours of active use and twelve to fifteen of idling. I need more. So 1.5 and 1.6 ditch their nonessential armor for additional battery cells and light solar arrays. The 1.5 is the combat model, and the 1.6 is a walking Panic Pal recharger. It only gets a light [**Hypercompression Cannon**], but it can run support for six Pals."

"Peter, don't come. It's too dangerous. They shut down the wall today. There's a three-million-strong herd of turbo-buffalo on the way. You won't be able to fight through them, and the herd's too much to fly over."

"Oh, I'm coming, Annie. At this point, it's a challenge, and Professor Panic doesn't back down from a challenge. Besides, the LABRATs and Panic Pals need upgrades anyway. Collidus is *really* stepping up, and I won't take over the town without upgrades. How are classes?"

Before I could even open my mouth, the LABRAT popped at one of its weld seams, sending sparks across the room. Peter threw himself down on the floor with a scream. The LABRAT's chest burst into flame, and he scrambled for a fire extinguisher. He shouted toward the screen, his words rapid-fire. "It might be a while sorry gotta put this out!"

"That's . . . fine," I said, standing up as he started fighting the fire. I should have been worried about him. I should have watched and cheered him on. "I need to go to the bathroom."

I fled the bedroom. The sound of the fire extinguisher faded as I shut the bathroom door and sat on the toilet lid. The tears started, and I couldn't stop them.

It was over.

"God dammit!" I screamed—quietly—at my towel. My throat hurt, and my palms wouldn't stop sweating. But I wasn't Peter's priority, and try as I might, he wasn't mine anymore. I waited, letting my tears stop slowly, then looked at myself in the mirror.

I snorted at the smeared, runny mascara that'd plowed through my makeup. I didn't look like Anika DuPont. I looked like Tearjerker in her Costume. And speaking of the villainous goth . . . Peter wasn't going to be happy. And, little leaguer or not, he was a supervillain. I'd have to be careful and let him down easy.

I cleaned up some of my makeup mess and returned to the video chat. Peter couldn't get the fire out. Every time he stopped spraying, it flickered back to life. Eventually, he unplugged the LABRAT. "Shit. That's twelve hours of work down the drain. Do you know how expensive Ilneat ionic capacitors are? I'm going to have to *actually* rob the bank this time."

"Peter."

"And that's to say nothing of the wiring that just burned or the pop-out solar paneling that needs, at the very least, cleaning. I wonder if 1.4 can do some of that. Hey! 1.4! Get over here. Strip down the 1.6 here. Any part with more than 90% structural integrity, clean. Anything with more than 60%, pile here. Anything less, scrap. Don't mess it up this time, or I'll have you scrap *yourself* too."

"At once, Professor!" the robot monotoned and got to work.

"Peter!" I said more insistently.

"Alright, at least the blueprint is digital. I wonder why it didn't show up in the simulations. It's so obvious." Peter was full-on Genius-mode. I could see his eyes flicking across his computer screen. The asshole didn't even have me focused. He was probably staring at LABRAT's schematics right now!

"PETER! This. Isn't. Working. I'm done."

Fuck. Fuck! I froze, watching Peter's face as his eyes undilated, and he came up from Genius mode. I wanted to facepalm myself. I wanted to hide. This wasn't letting someone down easy.

"What?" His voice was emotionless. Monotone. Like one of his LABRAT bots, but without the humanity.

"Thank you for finally listening." I couldn't stop myself. The words just kept coming. "I've been trying for weeks, Peter. I've scheduled phone calls and video chats. I've tried to come up with stuff for us to do together. And it feels like the gap between us keeps getting wider and wider. I'm out of ideas, and you've been busy building robots or whatever."

"I'm doing this for you," Peter said. His voice was still monotone, but I could see his face reddening. His following sentence was almost a whisper. "I'm doing this all for you."

"I don't want it, Peter. I appreciate it, but I don't want it anymore." I chewed the inside of my lip. It did *not* taste like lemons. "I just want to be done."

"Fine," Peter said. His fists balled, and he shifted to the fast, manic voice of Professor Panic. "Fine, then. We're done. Magical Girl Understudy. I'm an honorable villain, so there's no need to hide. I swear I won't seek revenge on your family in Riverside."

Before I could say anything else, his screen went black.

I sniffed the air. I reeked of stress and sweat; the kind of sweat that stank when you were scared. The foul stink filled my room, and I felt soaked and disgusting. Pulling off Peter's—no, *my*—nightie, I started the shower and let the warm water run down my back. My body shivered and shook, and I couldn't stop crying as I tried to scrub off my blush and foundation.

Had I done the right thing? Or had everything just pressed down on me too hard? Was this a reaction to Peter or to the distance? To the failure? To . . . to . . .

No, I'd done the right thing. I knew I had. Peter hadn't been all-in on the relationship, and I had. Except for once or twice, but that wasn't my fault. Everyone slipped. But a voice still asked me, "What did you do?"

I didn't bother washing my hair or scrubbing myself clean. Even toweling myself dry felt like too much effort. So I crawled into my soft, warm bed, dripping wet. I'd deal with the consequences tomorrow. I needed to be alone.

No.

I needed to talk to someone.

I flipped through my contacts on my phone and pressed Call. The phone rang. Then it rang again.

"Hey, Dot. What's going on?" Dad asked.

I burst into sobs again. Dad waited patiently at first. But when I didn't stop, he took a guess. "Professor Panic broke things off, right?"

"N-no. I did it just now. He'd b-been so busy, and he'd been ignor—" I stopped and froze under the blankets. Shit. Dad *knew*. "How long—"

"Anika, we've known since you were thirteen. You're not *that* sneaky, Miss Magical Girl," he said. Shit, shit, shit. "About the third time your transformation went off in your room, we bought earplugs. We weren't about to stop you from being a superhero—Mom wanted to, but I talked her out of it—but you were screwing with our sleep, and we both had to work."

Oh.

"So what happened, Dot?" Dad asked.

For the first time in five years, I told him everything. Our problems leading up to "Professor Panic's Payout Plan"—how he'd gotten obnoxious as college grew closer for me. How we'd tried to hold it together and even made a plan but both been busy with our own lives. Our little break. And then after it, when it felt like I was doing all the work, and our breakup. I was mostly coherent. I hoped.

"Alright, Annie."

I breathed out a shuddery breath as he continued. The tears wouldn't stop.

"Mom and I love you. She's at work. You know how the diner is. But give her a call tomorrow. She's got the day off."

"It hurts, Dad. We were together for so long."

"Yeah, you were. Look, Dot, I'm not gonna pretend it doesn't hurt. But you're a tough cookie. Tomorrow's Saturday, so you're gonna have a couple of days to mope as needed. But on Monday, you need to get your butt back in those lecture halls and keep learning. That's what the scholarship is for, right?"

"Right, Dad," I said. I tried to pull myself together. Fresh tears kept running, but the sobs and shakes stopped. "Thanks. Love you."

I paused. Should I tell them about Peter's—no, Professor Panic's—promise not to attack them? My brow scrunched. Then I shook my head. No. He'd keep his word on that, at least.

"Love you too."

He hung up, and I stared at the black screen on my computer for a bit. As I went to shut it down, it dinged at me. I had a new email. I unlocked the screen, closed the video call window, and opened my email.

Subject: First Annual Superpowered Job Fair Tomorrow: You're Super-Suited for This Job!

40

You're Super-Suited for This Job

SATURDAY, OCTOBER 4

I awoke to a horrid buzzing and a slightly sour scent in my bedroom. My head pounded like it had after drinking with Bianca, and the buzzing wouldn't stop even when I slapped at my phone.

Which meant it was one of the intercoms. My phone said . . . 9:43? I'd barely slept. Every time I shut my eyes, I saw the burning bank. Only instead of a bank, it was my parents' double-wide. I'd wake up in my damp sheets, sweating and breathing fast. So sleep had been rough. Who'd bug me on a Saturday? I staggered to the speaker. "Hello?"

<Hey, Understudy! It's Fursona. It's job fair time! You didn't pick up your phone. Lemme up>

Sure enough, half a dozen messages covered my phone screen. I ran to the bathroom. The face staring back at me in the mirror looked terrible, but I didn't have time for a good cleanup, so I pulled yesterday's jeans and sweater on, grabbed Tails, and pushed the button for the elevator.

I held Tails up to start my oath and transform. Then I stopped. Most of it didn't make sense anymore. I wasn't in Riverside, and if I never fought Professor Panic again, I'd be thrilled. I'd have to fix it later with Rocko and Tails. There wasn't time right now.

"I swear on my family, who I love very much, that I'll stand up against Professor Pan . . . Panic, his minions, and evil all over Riverside! I'll fight for justice, peace, and hope! And I'll never stop 'til evil does first!"

By the time I'd finished transforming, I could hear Fursona in my secret base. I took one last look at the girl in the mirror. She still looked miserable. Her bloodshot eyes had bags under them. But the outfit was on point. It'd be fine for a job fair. Most likely, no one would even notice, and we were just getting info on superheroing opportunities, right?

When I opened the door, the first thing I got was a gigantic kangaroo hug. The second was a gigantic, dramatic kangaroo retching sound. "Eugh, Understudy, how're you surviving in there? My eyes are burning inside this suit. Dammit! I can't even rub them!"

"Sorry. I broke up with my boyfriend last night. It's been . . . rough." That was an understatement. Slipping through the door, I pulled it shut and headed for the elevator. "Let's just go."

I could see that Fursona wanted to say something. They fidgeted in their fursuit, and once on the way down, they reached out to touch a shoulder, only to pause. When the elevator dinged, they said, "I'm sorry. If you need anything, let me know anytime, okay?"

"Sure. Thanks. Let's get moving."

"What's the plan here, anyways?" Fursona asked.

"Well," I started. I didn't breathe a sigh of relief, but only barely. I needed to focus on something that wasn't Peter. "The way I see it, I'm probably not getting that sidekick role with Sara-N-Dipity. So we need to find another way to get some minor-league or assisted major-league experience. And there's going to be some big guns here. We need to get signed up with Tele-Portal or The Mutual Assistance League. Or *anyone* but The In-You-Endos."

"Not them?"

Fursona—and their fursuit—would honestly fit in with them with a personality tweak or two, but I'd never recommend them to anyone. Not after watching their "Dame Thirst Takes Them All" Episode on late-night TV when I was fifteen. I shuddered. "No. Not them."

Other super students wandered down the tunnel—I had questions about how we'd keep our lair and base elevators secret, but no one seemed to pay much attention to the doors. In fact, as our numbers swelled, I realized I hadn't noticed a single person coming out of an elevator yet. I thought I saw Gourmet for a minute, but most of the heroes and villains in the tunnel were new to me. Were there really so many vigilantes at Tokyexico University? Or . . . were most of these villains?

"So, what happened, Understudy?" Fursona asked.

Ugh. This again. I told them what I could—obviously, no names or mention that he was a villain. But the general story.

"So, he just didn't care anymore?"

"Yeah. I tried to hold it together, but he worked on other stuff last night during our video chat. He couldn't focus on me. On us. Distance is hard."

"I see," Fursona said. They wanted to say something. But before they could, we reached the stairs. Springlock and Milo stood at the top on our side, with Tearjerker on the other.

Of course, we got Tearjerker's side. She didn't recognize me, but one look at my red eyes, and she grinned. "You don't even *need* me! Alright, let's get some names."

"Fursona."

"Magical Girl Understudy."

"Perfect, you're on the list. Ikenga's worried some Extra's gonna try to sneak over to the powered side, so I have to be a bouncer with these two dweebs." She pointed at Springlock and Milo, then down the hall. "Accept the **[Casting Call]** and come on in. And *don't* start anything. If I catch you fighting in there, it'll be *Where the Red Fern Grows* for you. If you're lucky, and I catch you before Mays and Jackson, that is."

[Casting Call]
[Episode: You're Super-Suited for This Job! - PG]
[Role: Job-Hunter of Justice! Do you accept the role? (Yes/No)]
[Role Focus: Flamboyance+Cunning]

I accepted the role. "You got **[Job-Hunter of Justice]** too, right?"

"Yeah," Fursona said. "I wonder what the villains got."

"**[Minion-in-the-Making]**," Gourmet said. She rolled her eyes from where she leaned against the wall, finishing off a banana. Surprisingly, her skin wasn't yellow or peeling. "Good luck in there, Snack and Wombat."

"It's *still* Fursona! And why are you here? You could be in the minor league by now and earning points in the Man vs. Nature," Fursona said, bouncing on their feet.

"I could be. I've got the ranking. But I don't care." Gourmet tossed the peel into her mouth and chewed vigorously. "My powers aren't headliner powers in the minor league. I could help out with Man vs. Nature, and then what? Lieutenant for Theseus some more? Find a minion gig? I'm not built like a headliner, kids. Anyways, I'm out. Just hanging out to scope stuff out and eat free food."

"Can you tell what powers you'd get from something you eat?" Fursona asked.

"Maybe."

I grabbed Fursona's paw. "Let's go." The career fair awaited, so I dragged them through the door.

[You're Super-Suited for This Job!: Act One in Progress]

The basketball court was covered in tables and booths. Big signs hung over them, flashing neon. 3V1L had a booth with a tent; I was really curious about them, especially when I saw a dozen devil-masked henchmen, complete with horns and plastic goatees, working the booth. The Mutual Assistance League's minor leaguers glared at them from their table across the makeshift hall at the free-throw line.

And near center court, a handful of A-list major-league heroes and villains held court. Tele-Portal, who I'd seen in action, lay on a hammock tied to itself between two of her portals. I was her biggest fan growing up; I'd even had her poster, and I kicked myself for not bringing it along to get signed. McHammer, in his flowing plaid parachute pants, talked with a trio of supervillain students, including Theseus. And Drs. Jackson and Mays were having a heated discussion with a familiar-looking, business-suit-wearing man.

The Agent.

Whatever they were talking about, Mays looked pissed. Not angry, but way beyond it. I hurried to get closer and caught The Agent finishing up his sentence. ". . . filled out the paperwork correctly, and both student organizations gave me permission, so I'm afraid I'm doing nothing legally wrong here. In any case, a longer laundry list of powers helps Tokyexico, and since you two are exempt from the draft, the least you can do is help me help the city."

Mays started to talk, but Jackson nodded grudgingly. "Fine. You can run your collections drive, but pay a reasonable price here. And nothing meta, as usual. We don't need more of us running around."

"Agreed." The Agent stuck out his hand and shook Jackson's, then waited a moment in case Mays wanted to shake, too. He didn't, so The Agent turned toward the nearest students. Us.

"Hello, super students. How would you like to make a hero?" He held out his clipboard toward Fursona and me. "I'm offering to license your [**Signature Skills**] for my [**Hire a Temp**] power. I can pay in cash, property, or . . . Style Points."

"Style Points?"

I could almost hear the kangaroo's mouth start watering. Other super students heard The Agent, too, and a crowd began to form.

"One at a time, form an orderly line," Dr. Jackson called.

"I told you he'd do this. He *always* does this," Mays grumbled.

"Yes, Style Points. [**Power Broker**] allows me to pay my own Style Points to you young up-and-comers in exchange for licensing your powers. I'll offer five Style Points in whatever Style your skill is, plus two in the other Styles." He looked at me. "Do we have a deal?"

"I want eight and three," I said. "My power's going to be a major-league one with some work, and if the licensed version keeps its upgrades, you're getting a lot of power."

The Agent's eyes glazed over for a second. I could see him digging through System messages. Then he nodded slowly. "I can do seven, three to two other Styles, and two to the other two. And everyone, I *do* negotiate, but don't start too high."

"Deal. Three to Drama and, um, Grit." We shook, and I got a bunch of messages.

[**Bold Negotiator! +2 Badass Points**]
[**Know Your Worth! +2 Cunning Points**]
[**Dramatic Haggler! +3 Drama Points**]
[**Flashy Sale! +7 Flamboyance Points**]
[**Hard Bargain! +3 Grit Points**]

As the style points rolled in, a boy in a white hoodie and plaid scarf walked past.

Fursona also licensed their power, though they didn't get quite as good a deal. As we left, I heard a kid ask for twenty of each point. The Agent flatly said, "No," and refused to negotiate at all. He ended up getting the 5 to one, 2 to the others split.

Then Dr. Mays started an advertisement for Trelach Oil at half-court. As he froze everyone, Dr. Jackson grabbed Monologue's and Ikenga's hands. Silver bubbles covered their bodies, and they started moving again.

"Hello, supers, and welcome to the First Annual TUSSA/SSS Job Fair. We don't have long before Mays finishes his ad," Ikenga said, "and I know there won't be a Monologue speech today, *right?*"

Monologue said nothing, glaring at Ikenga. There was *something* there that wasn't just hero/villain hatred. "So, a couple of things to know. First, our recruiters are on the court. There are a few rooms downstairs for testing powers. If a recruiter wants to check out your moves, you can do so in relatively safe environments—away from your rivals. No powers on the main floor, please. A full-on fighting Episode with all of us here wouldn't end well for us or the university."

Yeah, that made sense. I saw a few vigilante heroes and villains power down weapons around us. They didn't put them away, but they relaxed . . . for now.

"Second, we're *not* here to fight our rivals. That means you, Iron Fist. Stay *away* from Milo and Springlock." Ikenga glared at the power-glove-wearing brawler. "Remember, the goal here is networking. I know a few of you are going to start things. I'm not going to try to stop you. But Flare, Dark Girl Anima, and Kairo, Dr. Mays has his eye on you specifically, so be ready to get stopped."

A few villains and one hero fidgeted nervously and avoided the professor's eye. Dark Girl Anima, wearing a bloodred skirt, fishnets, and a top that showed far too much cleavage, flounced toward the stairs, rolling her eyes. "Whatever, Ikenga."

Monologue cleared his throat. "Well, Dr. Mays probably can't make up much more about Trelach Oil, so let's move to our last point. Let's all have a good time and find some internships!"

41

Let's Find Some Internships!

We dove into the maze of booths on the court. I could practically feel all the powers around us; it was like a tickle on my skin or the ozone smell of lightning in my nose. I could tell Fursona felt it, too. They seemed twitchy inside their suit, and their head kept looking from one booth to another.

The excitement and energy in the air felt fantastic. It almost pushed the pain in my heart away. It almost made me forget about Peter for a bit.

Almost.

I needed an internship, and that did a better job of focusing me than anything else.

We found ourselves deep in the "Teams, Squads, and Organizations" half of the room, and it was crawling with people. Oddly, they were mostly Extras. I stared at the arena door and saw a pair of supervillains. They guarded the entrance, passing out helmets to the Extras labeled "Temporary Hench: Do Not Attack."

"The SSS must be using this as a henchman recruiting drive," Fursona said. They pointed at the SSS table next to the much larger 3V1L booth. Both were doing brisk business. The Student Supervillain Society's booth included a trio of tablets and a stack of blank cardboard boxes a touch bigger than my head. Every time an Extra student signed the form, they received a box and pamphlet, and a booth worker (there were six, and they all wore helmets with little decorative spikes on top) guided them toward a door near the away team bleachers.

3V1L, by contrast, had set up a tent right in the gym. They didn't have papers to sign. Instead, "temporary henches" went in, something happened inside, and devil-masked henchmen came out. The black walls of the tent seemed soundproofed, since I couldn't hear anything near them.

"That's where we want to be," I said, pointing at the third booth in the "Teams, Squads, and Organizations" section. There, a handful of heroes sat, looking businesslike.

As we approached, an angelic-looking woman cleared her throat. "Welcome to the Mutual Assistance League's booth. We're a small but up-and-coming superhero organization working our way into real major-league representation. Right now, we mostly work to counter 3V1L's presence in the east and northeast Poudre districts of

Tokyexico City, but as part of our growth plan, we're looking at expanding into the University District. Are you interested in fighting for the cause of peace and justice?"

"I, um, already do," Fursona said. "I'm the Justice-Roo."

"Yeah, I've been fighting for peace, love, and justice since I was thirteen," I said. A nearby camera drone approached us, and I waved into it. "Hello, *Small-Town Super* fans! Remember to look out for each other and trust in your friends!"

I could feel Fursona roll their eyes behind me, but I didn't care. They didn't have to face the cameras directly yet, and I knew what my fans wanted. I cleared my throat as the drone got distracted by whatever was happening at 3V1L's booth. "But yeah, we'll take a brochure. We're looking for some internship opportunities. We'll be back after we tour the rest of the booths."

"Wonderful," the angel said, passing me a pamphlet, which I handed to Fursona. They tucked it into their pouch with a modulated snort. "I'm Tranquility. I'll be here for the next couple of hours. Then War Bear is taking over."

I nodded, shook her hand, and walked into the thick of things. It'd been crowded by the "Teams, Squads, and Organizations" area. By comparison, the main booth area felt almost empty. As I got closer, I realized why. Our peers had swarmed one man standing at center court and two booths near him.

The first was The Agent. How he was staying on top of negotiating with three super students at a time, I couldn't see. But he managed. He must've had hundreds of Style Points to spend—maybe thousands. I ignored him. We'd already gotten what we needed from him.

McHammer's booth was packed with villains, and Tele-Portal wasn't in her hammock anymore. She couldn't be. Too many heroes were talking to her. It seemed like every hero wanted to work with her. I had an **[Inkling]** that I could figure out why.

I ducked toward the booth and squeezed past Punch and Grapple. "Just want a brochure."

"Bro, sure," Punch replied automatically. He snorted at his own joke. Then he looked at me. "Hey, Underoos, you heard anything from Sara yet?"

"No." I slithered through and grabbed a pamphlet. "You'll get it, though. Trying to find a decent Episode was a disaster."

"Well, good luck finding something else here," Grapple said. "If we get an internship with Tele-Portal or something, we'll back out on Sara, and maybe she'll take you then."

"Thanks." I slipped back through the crowd and rejoined Fursona. Then, together, we read Tele-Portal's bio.

Tele-Portal is a premier major-league sidekick and support, currently working with Lightbeam and The Underdelver. Her powers are well documented in the team's Episodes and during her minor-to-major push during Man vs. Nature Six. With her ability to link two surfaces and move matter and light through the resulting portal, Tele-Portal's powers help give her team a tactical advantage in every Episode.

While Tele-Portal works as a support and sidekick in the major leagues, she encourages interested recruits from Bruiser and Tank to Elementalist and Genius to try out for an internship. If selected, you'll be required to perform at least two patrols with Tele-Portal each month, during which time you'll learn the ropes of midtier superhero work.

"She's a dedicated support and sidekick, so she'll make even her interns look awesome. That's why everyone's here. They're looking for a fast route from the little leagues to the minors or majors. Those jerks!"

[Good Thinking! +1 Cunning Point]

"Aren't you trying to do the same thing?" Fursona asked.

"It's different. It's *really* different." It wasn't different at all.

"We need to get in line," Fursona said. "We've got a good shot. We bring a lot to the table."

"Did that really say Elementalists?" I asked. I was an Elementalist now. Or, at least, I thought I was. That seemed right based on the power set I'd gotten from The Cloud's cape. **[Light as Vapor]**, **[Ride the Lightning]**, and **[Cloudy Disposition]** all felt like Elementalist powers. The fact that the archetype had been called out specifically gave me hope.

On the other hand, the line to actually *talk* to Tele-Portal looked brutal. There had to be twenty heroes there, maybe more. The heroine waved a man in a black suit and sunglasses over, then pointed at one of the aspiring intern heroes. He joined her, and they were gone, whisked away through a portal. The man started talking to the crowd, organizing and taking notes on them.

I sighed. Waiting in line wasn't going to buy us much. "Let's go check out the rest of the job fair," I said.

We spent the next hour wandering the B-list major-league heroes' booths. Most of them were working on their own. A couple had people in suits to help, but most were solo. We talked with Aimbot, a representative for Revengeance Incorporated, who'd filled out the form wrong, and a dozen minor leaguers looking to break into the majors with some community support. They all offered internships—Aimbot didn't even ask for a tryout. He was just happy to talk to someone, but he wasn't what I *wanted*.

I kept looking for people I knew, but I couldn't find anyone other than Springlock and Milo, who waved on their patrol. The only people talking to the B-list heroes and villains, or the minor leaguers at the court's edge, were other little leaguers like us who wanted to take smaller steps.

Most everyone was swarming McHammer and Tele-Portal, so that made sense, but I couldn't shake a funny feeling. Someone was missing.

I hadn't seen Tearjerker anywhere. Not since we walked in, at least. Actually, I hadn't seen some of the villains who'd kidnapped me during the Orientation Episode.

Iron Fist was here. So was Monologue. But most of the others had . . . left when Ikenga called out Dark Girl Anima and Flare? Could that be right?

"Hey, where are all the villains? They can't all be at McHammer's table," I asked and handed Fursona yet another pamphlet—this one to work with a Genius whose Artificial Intelligence Magical Girl did all the fighting for him. That one was probably a no.

"I dunno. I haven't seen Gourmet since we got here. Theseus was at McHammer's table, but that one weird villain on Punch and Grapple's team is missing. So's the goth chick who checked us in. And Monologue."

"No, Monologue's here." I pointed at the bleachers, where Ikenga and Monologue sat at their own table. The hero and villain wouldn't even look at each other, though both tried to bring heroes and villains over to sign them up for their clubs. They occasionally fought over table space for their signs and pamphlets.

I ducked past a heroine in a yellow super-suit with wings stitched onto it— maybe a Speedster or dedicated flier—and stopped at their table. Ikenga nodded in greeting, but I didn't go to him. Instead, I put my hands on the table right in front of Monologue and leaned in. "Where are your people?"

"The Student Supervillain Society?" Monologue laughed. "I assure you we have every intention of treating this event with the respect it deserves. We've gained over a dozen Rent-a-Hench henchmen, and I've signed three villains up for the SSS. How many do you have, Kingy?"

"Two. I told you not to call me that anymore, Monologue." Ikenga looked irritated. He turned to me, rolling his eyes. "As part of the agreement we hashed out, neither of us can use our powers. Otherwise, Mays and Jackson get involved. It was a way to keep *Logs* over here from starting something, but right now, it's just annoying the hell out of me."

"So, you have no idea where Tearjerker, Lockless, or Iron Fist are?"

"Nope. I'd imagine they're helping out somewhere. Tears and Iron Fist are on patrol," Monologue said. "Lockless only shows up for the first meeting and the SSS parties. She's hardly a *real* member."

"Yeah, that doesn't match what I'm seeing," I started to say.

"Understudy, we're not going to start trouble here, okay? There are a dozen major-league heroes, plus the doctors and The Agent. And we have a Neutral Field running. Monologue would have to be an idiot to try an actual Episode here." Ikenga cleared his throat, glaring. "More of an idiot than he already is, I mean."

"Get over it, Kingy. It was years ago."

Ikenga rolled his eyes and kept talking. "I can't stop you from digging around, but I believe we're secure here. The SSS never tries anything without their aces in the hole, Monologue and Tearjerker, and I've got Monologue wrapped up here."

"But where's Tearjerker?"

"Oh, that's easy," Monologue said. "She must've taken a break to try out with McHammer."

"Fine. Thanks for your time, you two." I stomped off, Fursona following me. Then I grabbed their arm and dragged them into an alley between two tent-covered booths. Why they needed a tent inside the gym, I didn't know, but it gave me a quiet place to talk to Fursona.

"We need to find Tearjerker and Lady Lockless," I whispered. "The SSS has to be up to something, and if they've got Ikenga and the rest of TUSSA locked down, it's up to us to stop them."

"Well, Tearjerker just came out of the trial rooms with McHammer. She doesn't look happy, but she's here."

"She never looks happy," I said but looked anyway.

Sure enough, Tearjerker stood there with even more mascara running down her face than usual. She was actively crying. A nearby villain started to say something, but she pointed at him and said, "You. I warned you. *Red Fern*, now!"

The boy burst into racking sobs, and she stomped over to Monologue. They started shouting at each other while I leaned in toward Fursona. "We still need to find Lady Lockless. Where's the farthest place away from Roth Arena?"

They shrugged. "I've only been on campus a month or so, and I've never explored past Ash Hall. There's no reason to."

"Okay. Let's just—"

Suddenly, I had an **[Inkling]**. This Episode had just gotten a lot more complicated. With the camera drone circling, I turned to Fursona. "We need to go if we want to find Lady Lockless and the villains who left. She's up to something for sure, and it'll happen soon."

[**Good Thinking: +1 Cunning Point**]
[**End of Act One! Act Two in Five Minutes! Skill Rolls Activated!**]
[**Alias - Understudy**] [**Archetype - Magical Girl**] [**Community Rank - 473/523**]
[**HP 6/6**]
[**Styles and Skills**]
▶ **Archetype Skill - Transformation Sequence**
▶ **Badass (36)**
▶ **Cunning (22)**
▶ **Inkling 1**
▶ **Drama (31)**
▶ **Stellar Ray 1**
▶ **Flamboyance (51) (Skill Roll Available)**
▶ **Signature Skill - Adaptive Armoire 1**
▶ **Stored Costumes: (Rainy Day)**
▶ **Starwave Sail 1**
▶ **Spotlight Strike 1**
▶ **Grit (50) (Skill Roll Available)**
▶ **Rejuvenation 1**

I cheered and looked at Tails as we headed for the doors. "Roll the Skills!"

[50 Flamboyance Credits Used. Rolling Skill!]
[50 Grit Credits Used. Rolling Skill!]
[New Skill! Flickerform 1! Flicker to another Costume momentarily, using a power before shifting back. Does not trigger triggered powers. 2/Act]
[New Skill! I-Frame Transform 1! A moment of invulnerability with each completed transformation. 2/Act]

42

Roll the Skills!

Flickerform] looked neat. It seemed powerful, especially when I got more Costumes. I could see flickering over for a **[Speed Hack]** and then to another for a big follow-up attack on a weakened Genius or using **[Cloudy Disposition]** to survive a hit while . . . not being a preteen again. At least not for very long. And even if I didn't get another rank of it, it'd keep scaling with my other powers.

I wasn't so sure about **[I-Frame Transform]**. Usually, I didn't switch Costumes while I fought. I'd change if I got a lull, but not when Peter's FEAR armor was in my face or when I was fighting Jungle Jim. I didn't see how two moments during an act where I couldn't take damage outcompeted **[Rejuvenation]**.

I equipped **[Flickerform]** in place of **[Starwave Sail]**. Losing the mobility hurt, but the flexibility felt more important than a noncombat movement power. **[I-Frame Transform]** needed some thinking, so I dumped it in **[Skill Storage]**. I'd refine my build later, back in my secret base, when I had time to think about it properly.

[You're Super-Suited for This Job!: Act Two Beginning]

I still wasn't sure where to go, though. But as I watched a group of students in spiked helmets jog toward the Beaumont Administrative Building, I had the easiest **[Inkling]** of my career. Whatever the SSS was planning, it'd happen there. There had to be a dozen of them, maybe more, but they were all henches.

We could take them.

"Go get 'em, Fursona," I said. "But be gentle. They're basically Extras."

"Yeah, like the one that hit you with a van?"

"Right. I changed my mind. Do what you have to do." I cleared my throat and shouted across campus. "Looking for me, henches?"

The henches started murmuring to themselves. After a few seconds, one said the line I'd been waiting for. "There's fifteen of us and only two of them. Let's get 'em!"

[Good Thinking! +1 Cunning Point]

I grinned. I'd never fought henches unless you counted S, but I'd watched enough Episodes to know they'd be predictable. "Come on then, villains. Let's do this!"

They ran at us, and Fursona and I ran at them.

And I learned right away just how many advantages a super has against a pile of mooks. This wasn't a fair fight. First, we had powers. Obviously. But Fursona and I were also faster, stronger, and tougher—superhero damage gave us a massive advantage against unarmed henchmen. Not a single hench had brought a weapon, either.

Three henchmen rushed me, fists swinging. I blocked the blows to the side with one arm, used **[Spotlight Strike]**, and punched one in the gut. He went flying. More fists pounded on me, and while I blocked a few, one snuck through and caught me on the cheek. I spun with it. Luckily, the spin turned into something graceful, and I used it to retreat from the sea of henches even as Fursona waded *into* them.

[Stylish Strike! +1 Flamboyance Point]
[HP 6/7]
[Gritty Recovery! +1 Grit Point]

Armed with a bit of breathing room, I launched a **[Stellar Ray]** into the pile of henchmen and was rewarded by one falling to the ground and holding her stomach. Fursona smashed about with their tail and feet, laying henches out. We were giving a good show, but somehow, the number of henches wasn't going *down*.

[Dramatic Damage! +1 Drama Point]

Something had to give. I **[Flickerformed]** into **[Ride the Lightning]**. My body jerked up as a blue-yellow lightning bolt sliced into the warehouse floor below me. An electric tendril reached out and touched minion after minion. The shock threw henchmen through the air and across the sidewalk. After what seemed like an eternity but was about three seconds, my lightning stopped. I fell to the ground, all four-feet-eight inches of me—I remembered how tall I'd been in sixth grade.

[Stylish Switch! +1 Flamboyance Point]
[Electric Lightshow! +2 Flamboyance Points]

A handful of the shocked minions got up. Most didn't; they lay around, writhing on the ground. But that still left six or seven that wanted to fight. One rushed me, swinging his fists. They slammed into my stomach a moment before I yelled, **[Stellar Ray]** and blasted him in the face.

[Dramatic Damage! +1 Drama Point]
[HP 5/7]

The next thirty seconds passed like a blur; I ducked a fist, caught one to the back of my head that didn't knock off HP, and fired a pair of **[Stellar Rays]** into the thinning tide of minions. Another caught me, dragging me to the ground, and her friend kicked me in the ribs before I could get away. That one got another **[Stellar Ray]** as Fursona landed on the one who'd tackled me.

[Dramatic Damage! +1 Drama Point]
[Dramatic Damage! +1 Drama Point]
[Dramatic Assist! +1 Drama Point]
[HP 4/7]

I spun to my feet in a whirl of skirts, only to be clobbered by something much, much bigger than a minion. As I tumbled into the browning grass, I caught a glimpse of a white van—this one with the SSS logo painted on its side—speeding away. I pushed myself onto a knee, took aim, and fired one last **[Stellar Ray]** toward the open driver's window. Against all odds, it hit, and the van jerked to a stop.

[HP 3/7]
[Dramatic Damage! +1 Drama Point]

"What the **[Beep!]**" I shouted, looking for another henchman to take my sudden anger out on. What was *with* henchmen and vans? But not a single henchman still stood. There weren't even any students nearby; they'd all run for cover when the super-fight started.

The quad outside the Beaumont Administrative Building was, for the first time since I'd arrived on campus, empty.

Except for over a dozen minions in various states of injury, that is. And, of course, for two annoyed superheroes.

I stared at the groaning minions. "When will you learn that crime doesn't pay?"

A henchman snorted. "It pays really well, actually. We only have to hench twice a semester to pay for room and board. Three times if you heroes interfere like—ow!" He rubbed his helmet where his co-worker had smacked him.

"Fine. Crime pays. But it's not *good!*" I sighed, stretching. "Stay here and wait for the cops. If I see any of you on campus tonight, I'll assume you're hostile, and I won't be merciful. The itsy-bitsy spider went up the waterspout . . ."

Fursona turned around and stared as I kept going. "What are you doing, Understudy?"

". . . and washed the spider out . . ."

Henchmen were laughing. I couldn't blame them.

"No, seriously, that's ridiculous!"

". . . and the itsy-bitsy spider went up the spout again!"

[**Rejuvenation Activated: HP 6/7**]

I dropped a foot as I finished transforming into Magical Girl Rainy Day. Fursona stood there, silent, for a moment. Then they started laughing.

"Holy [**Beep**], Understudy! When did you get that? Ahahahahaha!"

"Shut up!" I flushed red in embarrassment, but the deed was done. My sidekick knew about my little secret. "This is the Magical Girl Rainy Day Costume. It'll be better inside."

"Haha! I'm gonna call you Squirt!"

"No!" I stomped a foot before realizing it made me look even *more* my "age." I ducked a paw that was going for a hair ruffle, stepped inside, and headed straight for the secretary's desk.

"Can I help you, miss?" the secretary asked, looking at me with a puzzled expression. I opened my mouth to say something, but Fursona got there first.

"Superhero business, sir. Please stay calm. Which floor is the Speech and Debate department?"

"Uh, floor seven," he said, unable to tear his eyes off the kangaroo. Fursona thanked him, and we headed for an open elevator.

"What do you think she's doing here, anyway?" Fursona asked.

"At the Speech and Debate department? I dunno." I closed my eyes as the elevator took us up. What would she need there? Didn't she have Monologue for all the speech stuff? Wait. Was Monologue covering for a heist or something? But that still didn't explain *what* Lady Lockless wanted to steal. Or what there *was* to steal there.

The elevator door dinged and opened. I took a look around at a familiar-looking hallway. I'd been here before. So had Fursona—the Department of Superhero Studies' offices were to the left, and the sign that said *Speech and Debate* was to the right. No one should be in the building on a Saturday. I doubted the secretary would have let us up if we hadn't been superheroes.

I turned the corner.

"Boss, someone's here. Yeah, I'll take care of them. You keep doing what you're doing," a voice said.

I looked, expecting a henchman.

It wasn't a henchman. A student in a black Costume with orange racing stripes stepped into the hall in front of us. Red-orange sparks danced across his knuckles as he popped them, and he grinned. "So, heroes, you caught on to our plans and found Lady Lockless's [**Calling Card**] and note. Wonderful! You did so well. But your story ends here. I can't let you get to the boss before she finishes up in there, so it's time for you to burn."

"Who are you again?" I asked. I didn't care, but I needed him out of the way so we could get back to job-hunting.

"I'm Flare." He got on the radio again. "Boss, one of them's a little girl. You're sure I need to fight them?"

"Oh. I thought you were Monologue for a second there," I interrupted.

"Never mind, boss. I'm gonna kick their [**Beep**]!"

Flare sprinted at us, sparks ripping across his super-suit as he dashed down the hall. He leaped into the air and swung his fist back. I tried to dodge, but he was so *fast*! I flinched back as the fist headed straight for my face. It made contact with the bridge of my nose. I *felt* it hit. I *felt* the almost instant explosion as his sparks detonated.

[Cloudy Disposition Triggered. Damage Negated. Cooldown: 0:30]
[Stood Your Ground! +1 Tough Point]

From behind me, Flare growled in anger. "That shoulda fried you!" He'd traveled *through* me instead of hitting me, sparing me the damage. At least the physical damage. A tear ran down my face, and an intrusive thought filled my head. He'd attacked me because he didn't like me. He thought I was annoying. I *was* annoying!

I tried to push it down, but it came out as a sob. "Why do you *hate* me?"

Fursona jumped into action, [**Double Kicking**] Flare and sending him crashing into a water fountain. They waited a beat too long for their quip, though. "Time to *cool* down, Flare!"

"Ugh!"

"What, Squirt? Didn't like that pun?" Fursona asked. They looked at me just in time to take a spark-filled punch from Flare. Their fursuit took some of the flare-up. The explosion still hit, though, and they staggered from it.

Clearly, we couldn't mess around with Flare. He wasn't as powerful as Theseus or as flexible as Gourmet, but his gimmick hit *hard*! Luckily, I had something that hit hard now, too.

Still sniffling, I jumped into the air, letting [**Light as Vapor**] carry me toward him. I bounced off the ceiling tiles and into a wall, but I got there. "It's time to [**Ride the Lightning**], Flare!" I shouted.

He didn't have anywhere to go. Or he couldn't get moving quickly enough.

Either way, the blue-yellow lightning tendrils caught him, coursing across his skin. He flashed three times, looking like a cartoon character getting shocked, and then the electricity stopped. He twitched, then shook it off.

[Electric Lightshow! +1 Flamboyance Point]

It hadn't stopped him—superhero damage had gotten in the way—but he turned to me. "Fine. You're next."

His explodey fist slammed into my chin. This time, [**Cloudy Disposition**] didn't activate. The explosion threw my small body across the hall and into a door labeled *"Professor Alan East, Chiropterology."*

[HP 5/7]
[HP 4/7]

My jaw *burned.* I wanted to cry some more, not from **[Cloudy Disposition]** but from the embers burning against my cheeks. He'd hit a *kid*? For *two* points of damage? I wondered how many **[Ride the Lightning]** did.

Apparently, enough. Flare stepped back, away from Fursona and me. His shoulder muscle twitched, and his suit had holes fried through it where the lightning had touched it. "I'll rise **[From the Ashes]**, and we'll fight again," he said. Flames licked across his outfit, repairing my lightning storm's damage. He ran down the hall, gathering speed and skidding on the tile as he rounded the corner.

A fire sprinkler went off, and an alarm howled for a minute before something overrode both. Fursona and I followed Flare. If we were lucky, he'd lead us straight toward his boss, Lady Lockless!

43

Lady Lockless

Was this place designed by architecture students?" Fursona complained as we wandered the halls after Flare. I couldn't help but agree with them. The halls weren't even straight lines. Instead, they seemed to weave around office spaces, zigzagging nonsensically around the building. Luckily, the place was signed well—otherwise, I could see the professors getting lost on the way to their offices.

We stopped outside Office Suite 765. Fursona fidgeted on their paws, hand inches from the door handle. "So, Squirt, what's the plan?"

"Stop it, Wombat." I transformed back into my Understudy Costume. Rainy Day's [**Ride the Lightning's**] damage was higher than [**Stellar Ray**] or [**Spotlight Strike**]. I still didn't know if it hit for two or three superhero damage—I'd guess two since it didn't kill the henchman I'd fried—but it only had two uses per act. And I'd used them, which left me with only Understudy's powers. They'd been enough for years against . . . Peter. Professor Panic.

I swallowed painfully. They'd be enough now.

"You okay, Understudy?" Fursona asked. I heard a touch of concern through the modulator. It was quite a shift from their teasing when I'd been Rainy Day. They knew I'd . . . broken up with—I couldn't think "dumped"—Peter. They were just checking up on me.

"Yeah, I'm fine." That was a lie, but I shoved that thought to the back of my head. I was fine, and we had a job to do. "Okay, game plan. We have to get in there and pressure Flare until he gives up or goes down. Hopefully, we'll catch Lady Lockless in there, too, and we can take them both down."

"Alright. As long as you're fine."

"I'm good."

"We don't have to do this, you know? We can call it if you're not ready."

"No. We're doing this. We'll get up close with Flare and give him too much to think about. He's a little-league villain, I think. Right, Tails?"

<Nyah! He's currently ranked 413/523 in the city. Lady Lockless is 213/523 and a meowner-league villain, but she recently lost against a rank 450ish hero in a straight fight. She's not a combat villain, so don't worry about her.>

"Thanks. Tails says he's little league. We can probably fluster him and get him off-balance, so we'll fight him in close. Just don't let him get moving, or he'll probably escape. He seems like a Speedster with one gimmick attack. You're a Speedster/Bruiser hybrid. Neither of us is catching him if he runs."

Fursona nodded and got ready to jump into the room. I grabbed the door handle, narrowing my eyes. We were going to win. We had to. *I* had to. Fursona nodded, and I opened the door. Fursona leaped into the room feet-first.

"Boss, they're he—oof!" Flare started to shout just before he caught Fursona's paws. Both of them. To the chest. He stepped back a single pace, coughing. "I can't let you in. Lady Lockless will fire me. This is my one chance, and I'm not letting you take it from me!"

I opened my mouth to warn Fursona, but it was too late. Flare's fist sparked as he drove it into the kangaroo's stomach, just above our brochures! The cardboard burst into flame, and they patted their stomach desperately to put themselves out.

"**[Stellar Ray]**!" The pale blue light surged from my wand, catching Flare on the shoulder.

[Dramatic Damage! +1 Drama Point]

He jerked back like he'd been punched and slid back into a defensive posture. I swished my wand again as Fursona circled, but before I could find a window, Flare shouted, "Is it getting hot in here?" A flickering red flame manifested over one arm, heat pouring from it in waves.

Fursona backed off, shielding their face from the inferno. I screamed in frustration. If we couldn't keep up the pressure, he could move however he wanted. Every instinct said to cover the door against his escape.

[Inkling] said to pressure. That there wasn't time to be defensive.

I didn't want to guard the door anyway, so I followed the battle plan I'd set out. **[Spotlight Strike]** marked his extended arm. The one that was on fire. The dumbest possible place to attack.

I hesitated. But I needed a win. I hadn't succeeded at anything since I got here. We'd tied against Jumper, lost to Gourmet and Theseus, and scraped out a scripted win at Tottergarten. Classes weren't great. And Peter . . .

I dashed toward him. Flare turned, and the heat almost physically shoved at me. But I got a hit in, slamming my fist against his elbow. He flinched, waving his arm in pain, and the fire went out with a pop that scorched my skin. "It's time to cool down, Flare!"

[Good Thinking! +1 Cunning Point]
[Stylish Strike! +1 Flamboyance Point]
[HP 3/7]
[True Grit! +1 Grit Point]

With the flame aura gone, Flare dashed for the open door, but Fursona got there first. He ran into the kangaroo hero, and they crashed to the ground, kicking, punching, and headbutting each other. I started toward them.

A door creaked open behind me. I turned on a heel, skirt swishing, to face the new challenger. Lady Lockless.

"Stop at once! Coppers, unhand my lieutenant!" She was wiry—built like a twig, even, but tall. The striped black-and-white ballgown she wore brushed the floor, and she held a walking stick in her hand. No. A cane.

A very, *very* stylish cane with a key on its end and a glass cube that hung from the handle by a chain.

She pointed it at the door, which clicked shut. Fursona had the upper hand against Flare. At least, I thought they did. So I squared off against the minor-league villain. A camera drone hovered between us, and I wished I had [**Maniacal Reveal**] ready.

"I assure you, Miss Magical Girl, that you don't wish to fight me," Lockless said. "So many other villains are doing worse things than I ever could. I'm practically a Robin Hood by comparison."

<She's stolen from at least six banks and a credit union in the last year. It's even in Episodes,> Tails interjected. **<No orphanages or charities saw any of it, either.>**

"Sorry, Lockless. I can't let you go. I need this win."

"Shame." Lockless swung the cane at me, but I'd just been fighting Flare, and she was slow by comparison. I stepped back, and the key slipped past my nose with a hiss.

I countered with a punch—not a [**Spotlight Strike**], but a punch to the face. She awkwardly spun away from the blow and smashed her cane handle into my stomach. I felt it, but . . . my HP didn't drop.

"The [**Key to Lockpicking**] is knowing how to exploit weaknesses," Lady Lockless said, and her cane glowed. I knew her next hit was going to hurt.

Unless she didn't get another hit. "I know how to find weaknesses too! [**Spotlight Strike**]!" For the first time, the spotlight couldn't pick a spot. I stared as it spun wildly across Lady Lockless's dress and arms. Was her whole body a weak spot?

I charged in and swung. My fist crashed into her chest, and she went flying. Her cane clattered to the floor beside her, and she groaned in pain.

[Stylish Strike! +1 Flamboyance Point]
[Double Damage! +1 Badass Point]

Double damage? Not a critical hit. Not a villain with a known weakness, like Icee-Freez and heat attacks. Just raw double damage. How weak was Lady Lockless anyway?

She scrambled to her feet and clutched her fancy cane, wheezing. "Enough . . . of this. Let's see how you handle . . . the [**Escape Room**]!"

"The what?" I asked. But before I could get an answer, my vision collapsed into a pinprick—just like when Rocko brought me to the studio. I could hear Fursona asking a similar question and Flare shouting something at Lady Lockless, but his voice slowed down more and more as my vision faded until it was just a loud, deep drone in the background.

When my vision cleared, Fursona and I stood in a room with a glass ceiling and walls. I could see gigantic, blurry figures slowly moving above us. One wore black-and-white stripes, while the other wore black with a hint of orange. Flare's droning voice wouldn't stop. It just went on and on, buzzing in the back of my head like a swarm of bees. What was with all the bees, anyway? Magical Girl Honeycomb, and the droning voice, and Bianca. Bianca was pretty cool. And cute.

"Understudy, what's going on? What is this?" Fursona sounded confused. They kept glancing up at the enormous figures above them.

I didn't blame them. I felt my breaths coming faster and faster as the combat adrenaline burned off, and I realized we'd probably lost. Whatever Lady Lockless had done, I'd never experienced anything like it. I sat down on the floor. "I don't know. She called the power [**Escape Room**]. I think we're trapped in her cane."

"Oh! That's it?" Fursona laughed and started looking around the room. "I've heard of those. They were a big thing when my parents were kids. So, we're gonna need to solve the puzzles to leave. There's usually a 'first hint' somewhere obvious if Lady Lockless follows the rules. And sometimes there's a time limit."

I took a deep, shaky breath. "We don't have time for this, Fursona. They're getting away. We're going to lose!"

"Don't worry about that." They pointed up. The two gigantic villains hadn't moved, and the droning hadn't changed much. They seemed to be in slow motion. "I think we have plenty of time."

Standing up, I sucked in another breath. This one felt better, especially when I saw the camera drone with us inside the [**Escape Room**]. Whatever Lady Lockless had done, the Episode wasn't over. It hadn't even gone to Act Three, which made sense. The Episode was "You're Super-Suited For This Job," not "Lady Lockless Steals a Speech" or something.

"What's the first clue, then?"

"Let's look around."

There wasn't much to see. It took only a few seconds to glance over everything. Colorful crates covered half of the room; Fursona sat on one, staring at a bookshelf filled with brightly bound hardcovers with no labels. A kitchen counter lined an entire glass wall, set up to make . . . a salad? And on the fourth wall was nothing except a sign saying *Do Not Break*.

I decided to take that one seriously.

Fursona pulled a rope hanging from the ceiling, and words lit up on the floor.

First color first, then second last,
Fifth third, third fifth, fourth stands steadfast,
Seventh comes after its mother and before its father,
And sixth is second to last still, the first and fifth's daughter.

"It's a color riddle, Fursona said. They pointed at the bookshelf, where seven books sat on the shelf. "Red, orange, yellow, green, blue, indigo, and violet."

"So, first is red." I grabbed the red book and pulled on it. It didn't come off the shelf. Instead, something clicked.

"Then fourth, because it talks about it being second?" Fursona pulled the green book, and both slid back into their spots. The glass ceiling made a slight cracking sound. "I guess there's no time limit, but we only get so many attempts. It's like playing Hangman or something."

"Okay. Okay, Understudy, you can do this. I need an **[Inkling]**." But the power wouldn't activate. Both my **[Inklings]** for Act Two had already triggered. It was just Fursona and me against the **[Escape Room]**.

44

The [Escape Room]

"Red is first, then violet because blue and red make violet and violet's their kid," I said. We'd been puzzling for a while—I'd have killed for a paper and pen—but we almost had it. "Blue is next because fifth is third. Green stays at fourth, then yellow is fifth. Sixth stays sixth, and orange, the second, is last. So, red. Violet. Blue. Green. Yellow. Indigo. Orange."

[Good Thinking! +1 Cunning Point]

As I listed the colors, Fursona pulled on the books. When they'd finished, a black book popped out of the wall. I let out a long-held breath. Neither of us knew how many times we could fail before the ceiling cracked or what would happen if it did. "You're Super-Suited" was a little-league Episode, so it couldn't be death—could it?

Fursona picked up the book and opened it quickly, but they didn't have time to read anything before the bookshelf rose off the floor. "A secret passage! This is just like the videos my parents showed me," they said.

The secret passage didn't lead out. Not even close. Instead, it led to another room. One wall was covered in clocks with different times; Tokyexico's clock was clearly labeled, and so were Yorkston's and San London's. The fourth had no label; below it was written *The Clocks Hold the Key* in red ink.

"What does that mean?" I asked. I rolled a strand of hair between my finger and thumb. No matter what I did, I couldn't stand still; the massive figures of Flare and Lady Lockless had started to move, and Flare's droning voice had been replaced with a slightly higher buzz. They were leaving. We had to hurry.

"It means we need to take a deep breath," Fursona said. "There's a solution to every escape room. It's got something to do with these clocks—and this book."

We glanced at the clock again; unlike the others, two brass knobs stuck out of the side. When I twisted one, the clock's hour hand changed. The other obviously had to control the minute hand, which meant figuring out what time to put in was the answer. So we just had to figure out what the correct time was.

"Check the book?" Fursona asked.

"Yeah."

"Alright." They fiddled with the black-covered book. "Most of the pages are glued together. There's only one we can open to, and there's an empty cut-out like it was supposed to hide something."

That couldn't be right. "Did escape rooms try to hide the answer somewhere the players wouldn't look? Like, the colored boxes or the kitchen counter?"

"Yes, but not in a situation like this. We might have to go back for those, or they might be different routes through the puzzle, but we *should* have everything we need."

I puzzled for a while as the gigantic figures looming over us kept moving. "How about the page numbers? Could they be times?"

"2:28 and 2:29."

I tried them both. Neither worked, and the ceiling cracked just a little more each time. "**[Beep]**! Fursona, we can't let them get away!" I started to slam my hand into the wall, but the camera drone was watching. Magical Girl Understudy didn't lose control. She couldn't; too much was at stake. I sucked in another breath.

[Rating Warning #2! Episode Rating - PG! Censor in Effect]

"Relax, Understudy. We're going with them, aren't we?" Fursona said. Sure enough, the glass rooms kept pace with the enormous supervillains. Fursona shrugged. "Why don't we try adding them together? That'd be 4:57."

I put the number in, and all four clocks started spinning. When all the hands were on the six, another door opened in the glass wall. This one led to a gorgeous, luxurious dining room with three tables. Each had a menu at the center.

[Good Thinking! +1 Cunning Point]

"See!" Fursona practically bounced, they were so excited. "I told you we'd need to go back. Let's see . . . this one wants a Cobb salad."

"And this one's ordered a Ceasar. One of us is the chef, and one's the waiter, huh?"

"Oh, I call waitressing!" Fursona said. They dashed to the last table. "This one's a standard house salad. Get to work, Chef Understudy."

"Gourmet would love this crap, I bet," I grumbled as the camera drone followed me back through the clock room and over to the kitchen counter. "I'm making *salads* in an Episode. What has my career come to?"

The Ceasar was easy; pile up the lettuce, toss on cheese, dressing, and croutons, and wait for the Justice-Roo to take it away. The house took a little more effort. I'd never been much for slicing tomatoes. They squished under the knife every time, and finishing it took a frustratingly long time. Fursona tapped their paw on the ground the whole time, and the two supervillains kept moving.

And as for the Cobb, it took so long that Fursona started plating it as I cut. I could only imagine what'd happen if we messed it up, and it had so many stupidly unneeded ingredients. But at last, Fursona bounded off with it. I groaned and followed them; how many more stupid games would we have to do?

Fursona bounded back toward me before I even got to the dining room. They held a sheet of greenish paper in their hand. "I got a tip!"

[Good Thinking! +1 Cunning Point]

"You got paid? This is ridiculous! There wasn't even anyone at the tables!"

"No, a *tip*. I mean, it's on a dollar bill, but it's a *clue*. We need to check out the purple box. It's got the next puzzle or something." They showed me the dollar bill with a purple key drawn on it. "Let's go!"

"Hopefully this is the last one," I grumbled.

Fursona tried to open the purple box as soon as we arrived, but it wouldn't budge. "Try the key," I said, pointing at a tiny, drawn-on lock on the box's lid.

"Oh. The drawing?" Fursona asked.

I shrugged. Everything else about this place was just a weird delay tactic. Why not the lock, too?

They set the dollar bill next to the lock, then tried again. The box popped open, revealing a can of 4th Wall B-Gone. I grabbed it. "I guess we spray it on the empty wall? And then what? This keeps going forever?"

"I hope not," Fursona said, shuddering. "Most escape rooms lasted an hour, but this one's probably much faster."

"Alright, here goes nothing." I sprayed the can onto the wall, then stepped out of the hole it made, feeling a lot like Livestream doing the same with frames in the comic books. As I did, my vision contracted again, collapsing into a pinprick.

[Good Thinking! +1 Cunning Point]

My vision cleared. Lady Lockless stared at me, speechless, just two feet away. I could literally reach out and touch her. Flare stood next to her, and Fursona cracked their knuckles behind him. Not one but two camera drones hovered inches away from us.

And one very, *very* unhappy teaching assistant stood by the buttons on the elevator, fidgeting and eying the emergency stop.

"Who's going first?" Fursona asked.

"I'd like to get out," Lady Lockless replied.

The teaching assistant cleared his throat and adjusted his tie. "Me too."

I didn't say anything for a second. I just grinned. This Episode ended here. Unless Flare had a lot of juice left, we'd won. "Let's get started. **[Spotlight Strike]**!"

Everyone moved at once. Flare jerked backward, slamming his head into Fursona's face. They kicked out and caught him in the back of the knee. I punched Lockless, who reeled back but trapped my arm with her cane. And the teaching assistant ducked and covered his head.

[Stylish Strike! +1 Flamboyance Point]
[Double Damage! +1 Badass Point]

I yanked on my arm, but Lockless had it pinned. The key on her cane's tip glowed as she poked it into my bicep. The pain ripped up my arm and into my shoulder. I bit my tongue from the sensation—like fire and ice simultaneously—and jerked and flailed until I knocked the cane away.

[HP 2/7]

Lady Lockless stumbled back into the elevator's corner. I needed to pressure her, but the glowing key was a *threat*. I shook my head. She was a minor-league villain; even if she was a pushover compared to her peers, she was still dangerous to me. I wanted to **[Flickerform]**. One **[Ride the Lightning]** would end the fight against Lady Lockless and give Fursona the edge on their brawl.

If I could use **[Ride the Lightning]** again, I would have by now. But Rainy Day wasn't an option.

The elevator jerked to a stop. Flare and Fursona careened through the center into the doors. A moment later, they popped open. The teaching assistant ducked out as an alarm went off; he'd gotten a hold of the emergency stop button.

Lockless tried to follow him, but a drone got a full shot of my sidekick's tail tripping her. I waved my wand for a **[Stellar Ray]**. It caught her as she went to stand up, slamming her back into the carpeted floor.

[Dramatic Damage! +1 Drama Point]

[Stellar Ray] didn't do double damage, but even without it, Lady Lockless looked exhausted. She couldn't have many more points of superhero damage left.

She got to her feet and started running down the hall. I looked back at Fursona. "You okay?"

The kangaroo grunted and punched Flare. "Just go!" They rolled. Flare got free from the Justice-Roo's paws and hands for a second. He made it three steps—not enough time to get moving. Then Fursona tackled him again.

They had Flare under control. I took off after Lady Lockless. The teaching assistant had ducked into an office. He poked his head out, pointed quickly at the stairwell, and slammed the door shut.

"Thanks!" I yelled. I ran faster and slammed the door open.

Lady Lockless picked her way down the stairs, her ballgown skirts hiked up with one hand while the other held on to her cane. I threw myself off the landing and landed in front of her. "Surrender, Lady Lockless. You can still make up for what you've done here!"

"What *do* you think I've done here?" Lady Lockless laughed, but she didn't move to run away. Instead, she dropped her cane and sat down on the stairwell.

"I don't know. You must've had *some* reason to break into the Speech and Debate department's offices."

"Promise you won't tell? It'd destroy someone's reputation." Lady Lockless grinned wickedly.

"Of course."

She leaned forward. "Monologue's failing Intro to Speech. Again."

"No way!"

"Yeah. He can't get through his 'About Me' speech without **[Monologue]** stunning the audience, which means his professor can't grade it. It'd also out him as a supervillain, and that'd be bad news for everyone. And he refuses to let the Superpower Studies professors talk to Dr. Harding. He hired me to hack—he said 'unlock'—the professor's grade sheet and fix that grade for him. If he fails Speech again, it'll ruin him."

"That's it?" All of this had been . . . because of *that?* I shook my head as Fursona dragged a thoroughly beaten-up Flare down the stairwell.

"You can't tell anyone!" Lady Lockless told me. "No one else knows, and Monologue will know it's me if you talk."

"Not a word, but you need to learn that crime doesn't unlock doors of opportunity!" I waited for the Episode to end. The camera drone hovered in my face, catching my victorious pose.

The Episode didn't end.

"Uh, Understudy? It's not 'Lady Lockless Breaks into Beaumont,' it's 'You're Super-Suited,'" Fursona said.

"Right," I said, clearing my throat. Maybe Rocko could edit it into a stand-alone Short or something. "You two, come with us. I still need an internship!"

[End of Act Two! Act Three in Five Minutes!]
[Alias - Understudy] [Archetype - Magical Girl] [Community Rank - 473/523]
[HP 2/7]
[Styles and Skills]
▶ Archetype Skill - Transformation Sequence
▶ Badass (38)
▶ Cunning (28)
▶ Inkling 1
▶ Drama (39)
▶ Stellar Ray 1
▶ Flamboyance (9)
▶ Signature Skill - Adaptive Armoire 1
▶ Stored Costumes: (Rainy Day)
▶ Flickerform 1
▶ Spotlight Strike 1
▶ Grit (3)
▶ Rejuvenation 1

45

I Still Need an Internship

I'd never, *ever*, been so glad to see the police.

When the officers cuffed both villains and shoved them into a cruiser's back seat, I breathed a sigh of relief. The lawyers were probably already on their way to bail them out, but at least they weren't our problem anymore.

No, my problem was bigger. Much, much bigger.

"Come on!" I said, dragging Fursona toward Roth Arena. It wasn't too late. Now that we'd stopped Lady Lockless and Monologue's plan, we could slip back into the job fair and try out for internship positions. I didn't have much faith in trying out for the real prize—working with Tele-Portal would be fantastic for my career, but everyone else was trying too. But surely I could land a B-list major-league internship?

And dammit, I was going to try for the big one!

[You're Super-Suited For This Job!: Act Three Beginning]

Fursona and I dashed back into the gym and waved at Springlock and Milo at the door. They were keeping a line of Extras moving toward the "Teams, Squads, and Organizations" area. We ducked down the stairs and onto the basketball court.

And promptly ran straight into a furious-looking Monologue.

"How dare you interfere with my work and the work of my great organization, the Student Supervillain Society? Do you know what you two's meddling has cost me today? Everything!"

I found myself unable to move, but inside, I beamed. Then the inside smiling stopped suddenly. Peter had ranted and raved like this. Once, after I stopped him from taking over the farmer's market for the finale of Season Three, he'd launched into a tirade that didn't stop even when the police put him in a cruiser and drove off. I'd been scared to talk to him about it for weeks.

It felt like a weight lowering onto my shoulders. I should have been at home, in bed, with a cheesy movie on my phone and a box of pizza getting grease on my sheets. Instead, I was here. Pushing myself even harder than I had been. It wasn't fair.

"I'm going to lose everything because of you! My speech scholarship? Gone. My work-study running this club? In jeopardy! But I won't be going down alone!"

Dr. Jackson walked serenely up to the [**Monologuing**] student supervillain, shook her head, and asked, "You could have asked for help any time. We even offered it. You refused. Are you finished yet?"

"You'll both rue the day you crossed the SSS! I'll see both your reputations as heroes ruined and your careers in tatters! As soon as I get Lady Lockless back from lockup, you'll see! You'll all—sorry," Monologue said, looking at Dr. Jackson. "I got a little carried away there. I get so frustrated when things don't go my way, and ever since Ikenga and I—"

"You're still doing it, M," Dr. Jackson said.

"Yeah, you're right." He stopped talking for a moment, and I felt the pressure fade. I could move again. I could *think* again.

"I can't believe you betrayed our deal!" Ikenga said. "I saw your future, and at no point did you leave the job fair. You never even left my sight. But to use a lieutenant to carry out your dirty work? That is unbelievable."

"Is it?" Monologue spat, fists balled and glaring at Ikenga. "It's no worse than your betrayal! When you took over, you said TUSSA would be open to supers of all ethical persuasions. You promised me being president wouldn't change . . . us. Then, two months later, you kicked me out of the club and dumped me!"

"Okay, boys, now's *not* the time for this. That was years ago. Deal with your relationship baggage on your own time. Monologue, as the job fair's faculty co-sponsor, I'm ejecting you for compromising the Neutral Field you both agreed on. Ikenga, not a word about it, or you'll be right behind him."

"One word, please, Dr. Jackson?" Ikenga asked. "It's not about our personal lives. It's about our club statuses."

"Oh, alright. Make it fast, though. People are staring."

Sure enough, as I looked around, I could see B-list major-league heroes and villains staring. None of them wanted to go up against Dr. Jackson, but I could see one villain looking restless—McHammer rubbed his hammer's handle like he wanted to swing at Jackson or Mays. Tele-Portal, by contrast, was nowhere to be seen.

"Monologue, for this betrayal of the Neutral Field agreement, I swear this is the last time TUSSA will work with the SSS as long as I run it. Further, the TUSSA stands against you, and we'll pursue you and your accomplices in crime to the ends of campus to stop your heinous plans."

"Hey, now, Monologue's *my* name," Monologue said. He started heading for the door, then looked over his shoulder and stared at me. "I'll be seeing you soon, Miss Understudy."

I waved, trying to show his threats didn't bother me. Peter had threatened me like that, but he was my nemesis. It was expected there. "Are we done here?" I asked.

"I don't believe we need to address anything else." Dr. Jackson shrugged as Dr. Mays walked toward her with a fast-food Styrofoam cup in each hand. "I'm going to take a break. Ikenga, let me know if anything suspicious is going to happen. The Neutral Field no longer applies, and you can use your powers."

"Great," I said. "In that case, I'm off to Tele-Portal's table. No risk, no reward, right?"

As Fursona and I dove back into the crowd of super students, I couldn't help but look back at Ikenga's hurt expression. He'd broken it off with a supervillain *years* ago, and Monologue still hadn't forgiven him.

Did the same fate await me?

When we arrived at Tele-Portal's booth, the crowd had thinned dramatically. We walked over to the suit, who cleared his throat. "Hello, and welcome to Tele-Portal's booth. Tele-Portal is taking care of some important hero work, but she'll be happy to see you after I vet you first."

"She's sleeping," Fursona said. Sure enough, the woman's curved and bladed stilts sat on the ground next to her hammock, along with her cannon, and . . . was she snoring? I watched for a minute. She was!

"Yes, she is," the suit said. "She's on her rest day. During a Man vs. Nature, heroes are contractually required to serve three days, then take one day off to prevent burnout and mistakes. This is her day off, and yesterday, The Triad fought near the Flatirons. It was quite intense. Tele-Portal already committed to being here, and she couldn't back down if McHammer didn't. Someone has to be here in case he goes rogue."

I glanced meaningfully at Mays and Jackson, who'd taken seats on the bleachers and were drinking fast-food coffees. With the Ikengalogue drama over for now, both super professors looked much more relaxed.

"Of course, they're more than capable of handling McHammer. But Tele-Portal can't think like that. So she's here, she's recruiting, and most importantly, she's sleeping. It's in her contract for being here, signed and notarized, that she can rest as needed. And her Man vs. Nature role as a rescue and redeployment specialist is tiring work indeed."

"Oh." I suddenly realized just who this guy must be, and I shuddered. "So, you're . . . her . . ."

"Lawyer, yes. E. Braningham, esquire. She keeps me on retainer for things like this; the legalities of internships, sidekick work, and liability. If she needs my assistance at the front desk, far be it from me to argue. Now, alias, archetype, and **[Signature Skill]**, please?" He produced a fancy, gold-plated pen from his jacket pocket and wrote down my information. Then he asked a few clarifying questions about *precisely* what **[Adaptive Armoire]** did.

"Allows you to acquire different supers' powers, you say? That's potentially interesting. Tele-Portal asked me to wake her for interesting heroes, but before I do . . ." He cocked his head at Fursona. "Alias, archetype, and **[Signature Skill]**, please?"

"Oh, no thanks," Fursona said. "I'm much too new for this. I'm just here to support Understudy."

I grinned stupidly at them.

They punched me on the shoulder lightly. "Go on, Understudy. You've got this!"

God, it felt good to know people had my back. First my parents; they'd kept the charade that I was just an ordinary girl for five years, never hinting to anyone who I really was. And now, Fursona. They had to be going out of their way to pick me up after Peter. No one turned down an offer to try out with a major-league hero otherwise. I wanted to hug them. But this wasn't the time.

"Very well. Miss Understudy, this way, please."

I followed the lawyer behind the booth to the hammock. He barely touched Tele-Portal's shoulder before she sprung up, reaching for her massive cannon. She froze, narrowing her eyes at me, and I winced. Not a great first impression. "Who's this, Edgar?"

"This is Magical Girl Understudy. She has an interesting power. Interesting in that it's very flexible and in that it might be . . ." He leaned forward to whisper something in her ear.

Her eyes widened just a fraction of an inch. If I hadn't been watching her, I wouldn't have noticed. Then she nodded and rolled gracefully off the hammock and onto her stilt legs. "Alright, Miss Understudy, you're up. Through the portal, please. It'll take you to our practice gauntlet. I've got it set for late little-league difficulty unless you need something different."

I shook my head. This was it. A chance to prove myself and maybe, just maybe, get to the minor leagues on a speed track—and with a childhood idol! I wasn't going to mess this up. I *couldn't* mess this up. So I stepped through the portal into a wide, tall-ceilinged room filled with rectangular pillars and boxes.

"Welcome to the Triad's training room," Tele-Portal's voice boomed out from a loudspeaker. I looked up, but I couldn't see her. The room felt like a paintball arena or something built for laser tag. Some sections were dark, and some shone in the fluorescent lights overhead. "This is meant to simulate Episodes. I've loaded up the setup from the 'Missile Man and the Helmettes Take Over Mission Control' Episode. In it, Missile Man—"

"Used his henchmen to stall out minor-league Stella-Lunar until Golden Goose showed up and took over the Episode," I finished.

"Right. You've done your homework. I'll be playing the role of Golden Goose in this exercise, which means I'll jump in when the timer hits five minutes. I've reduced the number and damage of the henchmen to match little-league standards. Now, Edgar says your power lets you switch forms to mimic other superheroes and villains. That's interesting. Show me another form," Tele-Portal's voice said.

"Okay, but all I have is the Magical Girl Rainy Day Costume. It's based on a rated-G hero, but my producer thinks it's got major-league powers."

"If it's based on a *Tottergarten* kid, it might. Have you tried it out yet?"

"I did during Act Two, but I haven't built it up yet. It's a weather-based Elementalist build with a high-damage all-in-style move, weak flight, and a unique-feeling defensive ability. I think it's meant to be a combo caster if I can unlock a few more skills." She didn't respond over the intercom, so I took a deep breath. Then, I started my transformation to Magical Girl Rainy Day.

"The itsy-bitsy spider went up the waterspout!"

46

Up the Waterspout

"... went up the spout again!" I popped into my Rainy Day Costume and nodded at the ceiling. "Ready!"

[Rejuvenation Activated: HP 5/7]

In the few seconds before the tryout started, as the pillars and boxes started shimmering from holographic overlays and the room turned into a mock-up of Mission Control, I devised a plan. I had a massive advantage over other would-be interns; I'd *seen* "Missile Man and the Helmettes Take Over Mission Control." Twice. In the last year.

And I thought I had a way to beat the scenario in the first two minutes—well before the five-minute timer where Golden Goose intervened.

One: Get upstairs and avoid the henchmen. I could fly, so I could skip most of the fighting. Missile Man waited upstairs for the rocket launch, so if I went up, I'd cut off time. Stella-Lunar couldn't get there because of his minions and her move-set. She'd been running Moon Form and didn't have her Star Form mobility for the first three minutes of the Episode until her switch cycle happened. I didn't have that limitation.

Two: Fight through the hall. Missile Man had a couple of guards. I didn't hit as hard as Star Form Stella-Lunar, but I bet I could take them down quickly enough.

Three: Beat Missile Man. Close range, with his code of ethics? Shouldn't be an issue. He wouldn't hurt the civilians directly under his watch, so most of his weapons were offline.

I could already see the training room's layout. The administrator's office was on the third floor; I looked to be starting next to the rocket itself, right where Stella had.

The set finished projecting, a half dozen mooks with guns and opaque fishbowl helmets appeared in front of me, and Tele-Portal's voice filled the training room. "Begin!"

"Hey, freeze!"

"Magical Girl sighted! Boss, it's not Stella!"

"Hands up, or we'll shoot!"

The digital henchmen expected Stella-Lunar, not a preteen. Their guns wavered for a moment. Clearly, they weren't interested in shooting a kid. I grinned and activated **[Light as Vapor]**. Then, as I took off, I started counting. If they were the standard-issue henches from the Second Power Wars, I'd have about three seconds before one of them opened fire.

One. A henchman dashed toward me and jumped; I felt her fingers graze my boot, but I was too high for her to grasp. Instead, the bump spun me in a spiral I struggled to slow.

Two. The first shot rang out. I winced. I'd been wrong about the henches' reaction time. Two other henches started screaming at the trigger-happy one.

Three. Another gunman opened fire. Bullets pounded into me. The first triggered **[Cloudy Disposition]**, but the second hit, shoving my lighter-than-air body into the main building's wall. I screamed—superhero damage or not, bullets *hurt*! Then I punched the glass and threw myself inside, deactivating **[Light as Vapor]**.

[HP 4/7]
[Stood Your Ground! +1 Grit Point]
[Clever Plan! +1 Cunning Point]
[Dramatic Escape! +1 Drama Point]
[System Warning: 50% reduction in Style Points for the first monthly training exercise]

"Huh," I said as I picked myself up off the floor and poked at the red welt in my thigh where I'd been shot. Did training come with Style Point reductions? Interesting. I could still earn them, though, just not as fast. I'd have to figure out a way to train properly with Fursona.

I'd have to figure out a lot of things.

I poked my head out the window and immediately came under fire. The mooks had split up. Three kept firing at the window while three others—including Trigger-Happy—rushed the building. And there were probably more inside. If they had comms, and those helmets almost certainly did, they'd spread all over the building. **[Ride the Lightning]** needed a big priority target, or maybe a bunch of clumped ones. I transformed back to Magical Girl Understudy and opened the door.

[Inkling]. Duck.

A mook with an electric baton swung at me. I ducked under it, feeling it crackle and spark inches above my head. "You're in my limelight!" I shouted as I used **[Spotlight Strike]**. Then I punched her right in the center of her silver body armor. The armor cracked and caved in, pushing into her sternum. She screamed and crashed to the carpet. One down.

[Good Thinking! +1 Cunning Point]
[Stylish Strike! +1 Flamboyance Point]

Two more henches charged me with batons. "[Stellar Ray]!" punched one in the fishbowl, but the other swung at me before I could stop her. We traded blows for a moment before I got a [Spotlight Strike] off and dropped her, too.

[Dramatic Damage! +1 Drama Point]
[Stylish Strike! +1 Flamboyance Point]
[HP 3/7]

Alright. This wasn't working. If I fought every henchman I came across, I'd never get to Missile Man before Golden Goose arrived and the spotlight and drones shifted to her, and the best way to impress Tele-Portal was to make it to Missile Man in . . . the next two minutes.

Shit.

I started running. I *definitely* didn't have time to fight the gun-wielding mooks beginning to pour into the hallway. Their gunshots were deafening—their helmets probably reduced the noise, so they didn't care, those jerks.

Or maybe they were just projections and didn't care. Right. Training simulation.

I avoided their shots and sprinted up the stairs toward the administrator's office. If I remembered correctly, it was on the fifth floor facing the massive Saturn rocket just finishing fueling outside. Missile Man would be there, watching the rocket take off.

I crashed through the doors to the fifth floor. A long hall stretched in front of me; at the far end stood a trio of mooks. There wasn't any cover, and I didn't have time for anything fancy. I'd have to close the gap somehow. So I started running as they opened fire.

[HP 2/7]

The first bullet hit me in the stomach, leaving a welt through the superhero damage, but I kept going. My wand pointed at the first gunman. "[Stellar Ray]!" The blue light beam blasted into her, knocking her to the floor. She held up her hands and dropped the gun.

[Dramatic Damage! +1 Drama Point]

The mook holding a shock baton charged me. We'd meet halfway, so just before we hit, I used [Flickerform] with [Ride the Lightning]. We hit each other at the same time. I got zapped, but she got knocked cold by my lightning tendrils.

[Stylish Switch! +1 Flamboyance Point]
[Electric Lightshow! +1 Flamboyance Point]

Then it was just the last henchman. Another gunman. More bullets slammed into the walls around me as I charged. Another hit me.

[HP 1/7]

Then, just before I got to the henchman, a booming voice rang out over the speakers. "Attention, evildoers! Your goose is cooked, and mine's golden! Now, throw down those guns and surrender, or you'll be on my highlight reel—and in the hospital watching it!"

The holograms over the training course flickered, then stopped, and I groaned. With Golden Goose on the battlefield, the simulation was over. Which meant I'd failed. Again.

Sure enough, Tele-Portal joined me on the training ground floor, popping in through a green portal. "Why did you rush Missile Man?" she asked, yawning.

"I'd seen the Episode. I knew the henchmen were expecting a grounded Stella-Lunar. I figured I could skip some of the mooks and get to Missile Man quickly. He's a Genius, not a Bruiser, and in the administrator's office, I could beat him since he couldn't use his . . . well . . . missiles."

"But why take the risk?" The major-league support heroine's face wasn't giving me any hints. Was she pissed, thrilled, or confused?

"Because Missile Man needed to be—" I stopped. She wasn't asking about the scenario. She wanted to know why I thought it'd look good as a tryout. "I figured with your powers, you were used to thinking outside the box. Stella's solution was to hole up and fight mooks until Golden Goose won the fight. But I wanted to make a splash and try out my Rainy Day powers."

"Good answer. We'll be in touch. Here's my card." Tele-Portal handed me a business card with an incredibly cute anime version of herself giving a thumbs-up while holding the giant cannon. Then she opened a portal, which we stepped through.

[Episode Finished!]
[Episode: You're Super-Suited for This Job! - PG]
[Penalties: 2x Rating Warnings - No Penalty]
[Episode Finished! +5 of each Style Point]
[Winner Winner! +2 of each Style Point]
[Role Focus: Flamboyance+Cunning - Goal Partially Met! +10 Flamboyance Points]
[Alias - Understudy] [Archetype - Magical Girl] [Community Rank - 449/523]
[HP 1/7]
[Styles and Skills]
▶ Archetype Skill - Transformation Sequence
▶ Badass (45)
▶ Cunning (37)

▶ Inkling 1
▶ Drama (49)
▶ Stellar Ray 1
▶ Flamboyance (30)
▶ Signature Skill - Adaptive Armoire 1
▶ Stored Costumes: (Rainy Day)
▶ Flickerform 1
▶ Spotlight Strike 1
▶ Grit (11)
▶ Rejuvenation 1

I was so close! So close to getting my first Badass power and another Drama one too. I'd never had a Badass power before; [**Spotlight Strike**] almost filled the role, but not quite. I needed to sit down and focus on a build.

Something bothered me, though . . .

"How are you going to get in touch with me?" I asked Tele-Portal. "I don't have a card to give out."

"Oh, I'll talk to Cathy. Hey, Cathy, I'm gonna email you a couple of names. Can you get me their contact info later?" Tele-Portal asked Dr. Jackson.

"Sure."

"Great. See, Understudy? Easy enough. Now, in full confidence, I'm going to be emailing you. You got the third-least henchman takedowns, but you were also the hero that got closest to Missile Man. I like that initiative, even if that wasn't the objective. I'll be seeing you."

"Holy shit," I said as Fursona bounded up to me. "Holy shit."

"You okay?" Fursona asked.

"Yeah." I couldn't breathe; every time I tried, they came in useless, shallow waves that wouldn't fill my lungs. Eventually, I got enough air to continue. "I think I just got a Tele-Portal internship. What do I do?"

Fursona hopped up and down and cheered. "Good job, Understudy! Now, back on my team, we always trained hard and then dropped the training off just before a big game. I'll see if I can put together a workout program for you, and we can start tomorrow. We'll definitely need to hit the gym, running, and stuff. I feel a lot slower as a superhero since I stopped working out as a regular person."

The job fair had ended while I fought the henchmen. Minor-league heroes and villains packed up their booths and tables, while 3V1L's swarm of henchmen had collapsed the tent. Several TUSSA heroes and one or two SSS villains with morals picked up stray pamphlets and snack wrappers. I was too dazed to care about what was inside 3V1L's tent or to help with the cleanup. I just let Fursona guide me toward the tunnel back home. I'd . . . won. Or at least I thought I had. And god had I needed the win! Things were turning around—and not a minute too soon.

It was only four in the afternoon when I stepped out of the elevator, transformed into my dirty jeans and sweater, and collapsed on my bed. I thought about texting Peter for a second, and my mood almost slipped.

Almost.

But I was too tired to think about him. The adrenaline had burned off, and I felt like I hadn't slept in days. I was too tired to think about classes, how tough superheroing was in Tokyexico, or even how excited I was to get an internship—maybe. I fell asleep before I could even brush my teeth or change into my nightie—the funky smell from my bedding be damned!

47

Neutral Fields

FRIDAY, OCTOBER 24

Today's lesson is a little different. Traditionally, we'd save Neutral Fields for later in the semester—"

"Wait, this isn't a year-long course?" Gourmet blurted, standing up from her La-Z-Boy as Dr. Jackson stopped to stare at her.

"Just a semester. Normally, Neutral Fields would be later, but after the TUSSA/SSS incident at the job fair three weeks ago, the other professors and I agreed to move it up. Neutral Fields are critical for hero/villain dynamics to work properly and to prevent unnecessary violence. And in moderation, they look great in Episodes. They give a chance for both sides to talk about their goals, grandstand, and monologue. One of the most famous is in 'The Final Battle,' when the three remaining heroes talk with the villain before the big, climactic . . ."

I'd gotten emails from Sara-N-Dipity and Tele-Portal on the same day. Sara's was a rejection—she needed more firepower than I had, and Punch and Grapple filled that role. Disappointing, obviously, but Tele-Portal's message more than made up for it. She wanted to find a Short for us when she had time. Something minor league, or at least late little. It'd have to wait; Man vs. Nature Seven was in full force. A pack of dire wolverines had followed the turbo-buffalo herd. They'd decided thirty-foot buffalo were less tasty than Tokyexico's residents, and they circled the walls day and night, looking for a way in. So the major-league heroes were even busier.

Fursona had me working out five days a week. I was on my way to becoming a gym rat like Avan, Punch, or Grapple. My bench press max was up by fifteen pounds, my squats by twenty-five, and my muscles didn't ache on my off days anymore. Fursona wouldn't work out *with* me, though. Something about secret identity protection, which I understood. They kept me disciplined when it came to exercise, but it was still lonely in Roth Arena's weight room sometimes. I needed someone to work out with.

Maybe Bianca. She'd be an entertaining workout partner, and I bet she looked great in a tank top.

Peter hadn't contacted me since the breakup. I'd figured he would, so when he hadn't sent so much as a text in three weeks, I breathed a sigh of relief. Maybe he was over it. Maybe he'd be more mature than Monologue, and I wouldn't be dealing with him later. Maybe—

"Pay attention!" Fursona elbowed me, then poked at Theseus. The supervillain kept drifting off. He'd missed a few classes—if I had to guess, he'd been in at least a few Man vs. Nature Episodes in the last week.

"From a practical standpoint, Neutral Fields are the most misunderstood aspect of superhero Episodes. They're often seen as a way for a powerful side to bring the less powerful side to the table or to negotiate a peaceful end to an otherwise dangerous Episode. But, as Lord Destructo demonstrates in 'Destroying the Golden Idol,' the Neutral Field can be an opportunity to win an otherwise unwinnable fight. This is unedited, and it didn't air."

The movie screen flipped on. I practically bounced in my seat; I hadn't seen "Destroying the Golden Idol" before.

Lord Destructo stood in the middle of a soccer field, the only clean, unbroken space in view. His Full Metal Sportcoat armor had craters and cracks all across it. He breathed heavily, leaning on his warhammer. Across from him stood a curvy, almost uninjured heroine in a green-and-gold skintight bodysuit. A few other heroes, including The Underdelver, Stella-Lunar, and Liege Lord, stood behind her, glancing nervously at her.

"Golden Goose," Lord Destructo said, spitting something from his mouth. "I'd say you honor me, but we both know you don't have any."

"Shut up, Derrick. I'm here to bring you in since no one else can." Golden Goose smiled, twirling a strand of blonde hair, and shot a glance over her shoulder at Stella-Lunar. Stella-Lunar flinched under her gaze. I shivered, and so did a few other super students. There wasn't a hint of sincerity in Golden Goose's eyes as she casually outed Lord Destructo on film—just malice, frustration, and boredom.

"Your producer really tightened your leash, didn't they? Are you allowed out in public anymore outside your role?"

Her eyes flashed in the camera drone. Another camera panned over Stella-Lunar and Liege Lord, who shot each other looks like they knew something terrible was going to happen. Stella leaned over and whispered, "Cleanup team on the way?"

Liege Lord nodded slowly, paling noticeably.

"I mean, honestly, Goose, there's a fine line between working with the producers, working *for* the producers, and being the producers' bitch, and you passed that line when you signed on with Snowball. I doubt there's anything left in that head but what they want you to be. Right, Jenny?"

Dr. Jackson fast-forwarded. "Lord Destructo had no chance at winning in a straight fight. Even alone against Golden Goose, his odds were too low for anything but a miracle. But with all four heroes here, he needed a different strategy, so he asked for Neutral Ground, and Golden Goose agreed. She couldn't lose, after all. Lord Destructo kept up the insults and jabs until *this* happened."

"This is your last Episode, Derrick!" Golden Goose charged Lord Destructo, who swung his hammer to keep the ridiculously powerful superheroine at bay. She threw a soccer goal at him, then followed it up with an entire section of bleachers. The field erupted in light a moment later as Stella-Lunar and Liege Lord attacked. But they didn't go after Lord Destructo.

"You can't, Goose! He's got protection!"

Golden Goose found herself under attack by three heroes. Punches, light beams that dwarfed [**Stellar Ray**], and a gigantic drill all flew, and Lord Destructo had vanished by the time the fight abated for a moment. Goose screamed in rage. "You fuckups! You cost me a win," she said, and barreled toward Stella-Lunar, who fled before Golden Goose's laser vision and flight.

"So what happened?" Dr. Jackson asked after she paused the screen on Golden Goose's furious, vein-popped face.

I opened my mouth to say something, but The Crumb cleared his throat before I could. "Three heroes respected the Neutral Field. Golden Goose never intended to, from how she outed Lord Destructo immediately. And Destructo used Goose's emotions to force her to break the Neutral Field first, and in a way that'd get the heroes to intervene."

"Good analysis. You're getting better at this. Golden Goose agreed to the Neutral Field, so by breaking it, she temporarily became the Episode's villain, similar to in *War of the Brothers*, a pre-Launch Day flick. Destructo also respected the letter of the Neutral Field but not the intent. The heroes knew that, though. So, the goal for the next week is to figure out what place neutrality has in your code of conduct."

The team was already arguing before we even got circled up. Well, *most* of the team. Theseus was asleep again. I woke him up once, but he just glared at me. "*You* try a six-hour fight against D-wolvers in the sewer and see how much you care about this fucking class," he muttered.

That was a shift from "I'm in charge," but I guess I'd be exhausted, too. So it was all on me to lead the team. I took a deep breath. "Gourmet, Fursona, I think neutrality should always be respected. There's too much at stake not to."

"Nope. Self-serving heroes always use it to worm for advantages."

"Bullshit. I've seen Episodes where villains use Neutral Fields to stall out the heroes while their henchmen or lieutenants finish robbing a bank or uploading computer viruses."

"Come on, you two! We need to focus. We're falling behind, and arguing won't finish this code of conduct!"

Code of Conduct: October 24

We will not ~~endanger harm threaten~~ endanger ~~civilians~~ Extras ~~needlessly~~

When Extras must be involved, ~~every effort must be taken to make them aware of danger~~ they must be clearly informed of danger

~~What about Henchmen?~~

WHO CARES ABOUT HENCHMEN?

I care about henchmen!

Destruction of ~~non-government residential~~ non-corporate/non-government property is ~~to be kept to a minimum not necessary~~ not okay

I can't agree with this, guys. I need to eat!

Bring your own snacks. I bring my own! And quit making fun of me!

You ate a wrestling singlet!

Medical Extras are off-limits. Healing heroes ~~should only be targeted if involved in the fighting are a low priority target~~ are not a target unless they directly engage

Why? Good tactics are to take out the healers first so the rest of the team actually takes damage.

Property damage must ~~have a point be for a purpose~~ be directly related to the Episode's goals

Neutrality will be respected

When it's convenient for heroes?

Eat a sandwich, Gourmet. It'll make you feel better

I walked back into Walnut Tower and pressed the thirteenth-floor button on the closest elevator. We'd just finished Intro to Drama. Carl had explained how it was going to work. We'd meet outside, by the fountain, and head in together. He had fifth-row seats for the whole class. I was pretty excited; Episodes were great, but seeing *Macbeth* live was on another level for me. Bianca, though?

Bianca had been acting . . . weird . . . the last few weeks. We still talked in class, but she hadn't texted me much since Peter and I broke up, and the quick lunches were a thing of the past. To say nothing of having her over for a drink and an Episode or two. So I didn't know if she was excited about *Macbeth* or not.

That didn't stop me from thinking about her, though. Not. At. All. I kept dreaming about snuggling up against her and letting her wrap her arms around me. I'd be in my nightie, and she could wear whatever she wanted. I'd roll over every once in a while, and it'd be Peter in my imagination. But mostly, it was just Bianca.

The elevator stopped, and another student got on. I did a double take. "Avan? I didn't realize you lived in Walnut."

"Ha, nope. I'm not so lucky. I've got a place on floor 3 of Ash, but my friends live here, so I come over to play games. What are you doing tonight?"

I shrugged. "I have to watch a play for Intro to Drama."

"On video?"

"Nope. The class is meeting at the Doyle Auditorium in a few hours."

"Oh. Maybe dinner some other time?" Avan pressed the 1st floor button, then winced as the elevator rose instead of dropping.

"Maybe?" I said, a question in my voice.

We rode the rest of the way up in awkward silence, and he nodded when I got off. "Let me know how the play was on Monday."

"Will you be in class?"

"Will *you* be in class?" he asked, and I winced. I hadn't been ditching consistently, but apparently, it'd been enough to be noticeable.

I shrugged. "Probably," I said. The elevator door mercifully closed, and I unlocked my apartment door. As soon as I was inside, my phone buzzed.

I stared at it. Without Peter, my phone buzzing was rare enough to be unusual. I waited for it to buzz again. Surely it was a spam call?

It wasn't. I unlocked the screen.

<Hey, Annie. Whatcha wearing to the play? - Bianca 3:15>
<Hi Bee! I've got a semi-formal dress - Annie 3:15>
<From homecoming - Annie 3:16
<Color? - Bianca 3:16>
<Light blue - Annie 3:16>

I turned on the shower and pulled off my scarf and jacket. The late-October chills had settled over Tokyexico. Fog and snow flurries mixed with the D-wolvers' growling, snarling calls outside the wall, creating an eerie atmosphere even in the afternoon. More annoyingly, the wet chill struck deep, and I shivered as I climbed into the shower.

While I shampooed, soaped, and enjoyed the hot, billowing steam and eucalyptus smell, I pondered Bianca's sudden interest in texting me. Not that I minded. It'd been weird having her so distant, especially when I was crushing hard.

And I was definitely crushing.

The last soap suds washed between my feet and swirled around the drain, but I stood in the almost-scalding water for a while. Bee wasn't even the first girl I'd been into, now that I thought about it. Maria had been in my math classes in high school for a while. But even though we'd been close, I'd been dating Peter, so I'd never thought seriously about her.

Bianca, on the other hand? I wanted what I'd had with Peter, but with her.

No.

My whole relationship with Peter had been built on our superpowers. With space, I could see that now. I wanted to just be myself with someone, and Bee seemed like the perfect someone to snuggle on the couch and watch an Episode with. With more of that vodka if she had it.

I toweled myself dry and checked my phone.

<Great! I'm going with white. It contrasts my hair. Plus some fake jewelry - Bianca 3:17>
<You should look fantastic. Just make sure it's warm enough - Annie 3:32>
<Got a nice long puff jacket - Bianca 3:32>

As I got dressed and put on my makeup, my mind kept wandering to Bee in a white dress. She really would look amazing. Her athletic build looked good in anything, though. I typed that into my phone. Then I deleted it. I was going to ask her out. But what to say? "Hey, I like you a bunch" felt too childish. "Wanna date?" was too up front. Eventually, I sent something before I could overthink it.

<You're sitting with me tonight, right? - Annie 4:13>

48

You're Sitting With Me Tonight, Right?

I got my first chance to play a lead character during my senior year at Riverside High—Hermia in *A Midsummer Night's Dream*. I practiced my lines for hours at home until Mom and Tails both begged me to stop. I'd go out on Episodes and run through the words silently. And on opening night, I couldn't eat anything, even though I knew it'd mess with my energy. I paced the green room behind the auditorium's stage, back and forth, back and forth. Then . . . I threw up. And after, I felt better.

I felt almost as nervous tonight. Almost.

Did I know Bee? Yes. Did I think she liked me? Yes. Did I have any experience dating—or even pursuing—*anyone* who wasn't Peter? Nope. Nuh-uh. Zero. So I could be reading the situation all wrong. This might not be a date thingie. But she'd replied almost instantly to my text.

<Of course ;) - Bianca 4:13>

So instead of pacing in the green room, I froze my butt off by the fountain outside Doyle Auditorium. And instead of throwing up, I swallowed down my insecurity. Bee was running late; it was 4:40, and the theater opened in five minutes. Where *was* she?

<On my way. Three minutes! - Bianca 4:41>

"Alllllllright, Intro to Drama students, we're heading inside in four!" Carl shouted. "We're row five. Stay together with your study buddies, have a great time, and think about the elements of drama while you're watching."

Bee was cutting it a little too close. I kept fidgeting with Tails's tails. I'd jammed her into a handbag with my wallet and phone, though that was in my hand.

Then, there she was. Her white dress went to midthigh—a touch short for an audience member at a play, but it was college, so that could be forgiven. I could see its lacy hemline peeking out from under her gigantic puffer coat and covering black tights. And she'd curled her already wavy hair, so it rolled like waves off her head. She'd gone to great lengths to look gorgeous, and her glasses didn't ruin the effect at all.

It *was* ruined a little by the gigantic backpack she always carried around.

I gave her a quick hug before I'd even thought about whether that was appropriate for a pseudo-date, but she hugged me back. "Told you I was on my way," she whispered, grinning impishly.

"What took you so long?"

"Alright, Intro to Drama, weeeeeeee're going in!" Carl shouted.

"I had to pick up a few things," she said. "Let's go. They're all for later."

"What are you going to do with that coat? It won't fit in your backpack."

"It's fine. I'll just tuck it by my feet."

Outside of my apartment, the auditorium was the first place I'd found on campus that truly felt like home. Sure, the comedy and tragedy masks were much bigger and more ornate than Riverside's. And yeah, the velvet chairs felt much better than the worn and patched seats back home. And it could hold a few hundred more people, but so what? It was a theater!

Bee sat down at the end, and I sat beside her. As the theater filled up, we made small talk; I figured out what the weather was like in winter here, and she told me it was her first time at a play. We took off our coats, and I caught her taking a peek at me and my dress, which was fine. I was doing the same thing.

This close, her perfume was strong but not overpowering—a green-apple scent, crisp and sweet and teasing. It touched on something light in my mind.

"When shall we three meet again?

In thunder, lightning, or in rain?"

Macbeth started. The curtains lifted as the First Witch began to speak. The lights faded off a moment later, throwing us into darkness lit only by the stage lighting. I heard a few classmates groan, and someone zipped a notebook back into their pack.

"I guess we're not taking notes?" Bee asked.

"Guess not."

"Pity." She smiled. I could barely see it in the darkness, but her eyes still weren't on the stage. She bumped an arm into mine, and I jumped for a moment before relaxing. We had to share the armrest somehow, after all.

"Fair is foul, and foul is fair:

Hover through the fog and filthy air."

We couldn't do much talking. Carl cleared his throat from a few seats over if we said too much. But it didn't matter, because I loved the show. By the time Macbeth performed the dagger monologue, I was grinning, and so was Bianca. Whoever the Macbeth actor was, he gave a *hell* of a speech.

And when the witches said their most famous lines—

"Double, double toil and trouble;

Fire burn and cauldron bubble."

—I thought I saw Bee's lips moving with them. Had she been studying *Macbeth*, or were those words just that famous?

I looked down. Bee's hand was in mine. How long had *that* been there? "Uh . . ." I started.

"Shhh. It's fine." Bianca winked at me. And you know what? It was fine. We meshed fingers at the end of the armrest. She'd squeeze my hand and I'd squeeze hers back as the actors said their lines, like a quiet version of reading lines from *Earnest*.

"As I did stand my watch upon the hill

I looked toward Birnam and anon, methought,

The wood began to move."

The messenger said his line. The trees were coming, and the end was nigh. Macbeth was losing, and worse, the witches' prophecy—that he need not fear anyone born of a woman—had a loophole. Macduff was going to kill him, and there was nothing anyone could do about it. Somehow, Bee's hand had gotten outside of mine. She squeezed it the whole final scene right up until the end.

"So, thanks to all at once and to each one,

Whom we invite to see us crowned at Scone."

"We're gonna fail this assignment," Bee said as we left the Doyle building. She was right. We hadn't really paid attention to the craft side of the performance—I'd been distracted and just let it entertain me instead. Honestly, I was shocked I'd paid as much attention as I had.

I was glowing vicariously. The witches, especially, had really broken a leg up there, and it showed. I'd had performances like that, where I was just *on*. It always made me feel unstoppable, and I could see that feeling in the cast as they came out for their final bows. Some of the soldier actors even bowed with their trees on. That energy was infectious, and I couldn't stop smiling.

Or maybe it was Bianca.

We were still holding hands. We'd been doing that for a while now, and I couldn't escape. I didn't think she'd let my hand go anytime soon. More importantly, she was steering us toward Walnut Tower.

"So, I was thinking that since it's only like nine and tomorrow's a Saturday, I could come over to your place. I've got something to drinky-drink in my pack, and you have a really, really nice TV and couch. We'll watch a couple of Episodes and chill. Unless you're busy tonight?" Bianca asked.

"Sure." Why not? It *was* a Saturday tomorrow, and Bee *had* packed a drinky-drin—a bottle of booze. Dammit, I was an adult. I could call it vodka, not a "drinky-drink." "Let's watch a Golden Goose Episode."

"That bitch? Really?" Bianca asked.

"Yeah. Love her or hate her, she's the best."

"Uh-huh. She's a loose cannon."

"She gets the job done."

"She's a danger to everyone around her," Bianca said.

"That's true." We rode the elevator up, still arguing about Golden Goose's pros and cons. As the elevator dinged at the top, Bianca finally gave up. "Fine, I'll watch one Golden Goose Episode. You get one chance to prove she's not a wildcard who'll do anything for the limelight. Better make it a good one."

"Oh yeah?" I snarked, pulling my hand away to fiddle with the door keys. "Or what?"

She ran straight to the couch and dug through her backpack until she found her bottle. "A sip every time Golden Goose commits a war crime? If she commits less than four, you walk me home."

"Deal." That bet was as good as won.

"Holy shit, Annie, she just *killed* Deathclock!"

"I know! Drink!"

We were fifty minutes into "Metal Machines IV," and I'd solidly won the bet. I hadn't picked this one because I'd seen it. I'd picked it because it was a rare Episode that featured Golden Goose from the beginning. She didn't take part in minor-league Episodes; she was just too strong. And too ruthless.

Deathclock hadn't had any business being in an Episode with Goose. He hadn't had her strength, flight, lasers, or ridiculous super-suit. A healer hero was working on him, but it didn't look good for the villain. He'd probably never walk again, and his days of crime were *over*.

Golden Goose stared at the camera, a glare plastered on her face, along with a slight mist of blood. She tossed a car over the drone. Someone screamed when it landed. "Villains, cowls, and henches, I'm coming for you. This is *my* world, and I'm the goddamned heroine. And as for the rest of you, remember who protects you. Remember who drops everything to exterminate every little rat that scares you in the darkness. When you're scared and the villains close in, remember that they're *more* scared of me than you are of them. Golden Goose, out!"

She jumped into the air, a cloud of dust whooshing behind her in a shockwave, disappearing as the credits rolled. The healer hero had stabilized Deathclock. Either that, or he'd given up; he headed for some of the henchmen Golden Goose had annihilated, and the screen went black and asked if I wanted to watch another Episode of Golden Goose.

"See! She's worse than the villains," Bianca said. She pushed me off her gently and stood up, wobbling a bit. We'd both been drinking too much. "I counted eight war crimes."

"The bus stop wasn't a war crime. Bullet Time evacuated it before she hit. It was seven."

"Oh hell." Bianca drank a shot, shivered, and flopped back onto the couch. "But what about the office building explosion? Why'd that happen anyways?"

"Deathclock had a time bomb inside. When Golden Goose tried to laser him, the beam clipped the bomb, and it detonated early. I'm not sure if that counts as a war crime, but let's do it. Drink."

"Hey, aren't you supposed to be arguing for less war crimes?"

"Not if I don't want you to leave." The words slipped out before I could stop myself. I sat down and drank another shot.

"You don't, huh?" Bianca smiled.

I laughed. She was trying too hard to be cute or sultry or something, but she'd drunk too much to pull it off. She pulled me against her and wrapped an arm around me.

My mind froze. I'd been thinking about this—fantasizing about it—for almost a month. And now it was happening. I didn't even hear what she was saying. I was too caught up trying not to squeal, cheer, or both.

"It's quiet in here," Bianca said. She kissed my cheek quickly, and I felt my face growing warm. "Start the next Episode. I'll stick around."

PART SIX

49

Build Me Up

SATURDAY, OCTOBER 25

Bianca was hot.

After we went to bed, I'd spent too much time scooching away from her under the blankets. That girl was a furnace! But eventually, she'd cornered me. With nowhere to go, I'd fallen asleep perched precariously on the edge of the bed, her arm around me.

Which was also how I woke up, much more sober than the night before.

"Shit," I whispered. We'd finished the bottle after the next Episode—a minor-league one from the Second Power War because we both needed a palate cleanser after Golden Goose. That was why my head hurt. Then . . . we'd crashed. Well, Bee had crashed. And she'd tried to use me as a cuddle pillow.

Succeeded at using me as a cuddle pillow, actually.

"Shit," I said again and started to get up.

"Noooooo. Staaaaaay," Bee's sleepy voice whined while her arm tightened around me, dragging me back down.

I tried to resist for a moment. Then I gave up. It was Saturday, the room was chilly, and she was warm. I closed my eyes to go back to sleep.

My phone buzzed.

"Shit," I muttered for the third time. This time, I escaped Bianca's grasp before she could tighten it and pulled the blanket off both of us. She still smelled faintly of green apple perfume from the night before. We both still wore our theater dresses; we'd been too drunk to change. Not that Bee had anything to change *into*, but she could have borrowed something of mine. Shorts and a T-shirt, maybe?

I sat on the bed's edge and checked my phone while Bee wrapped her arms around me again. It wasn't a text, though. It was an email from anonymous.tp@tokyexicocity.gov. I turned my phone off, hoping Bianca hadn't seen anything.

"What was that? I've never gotten anonymous emails. Not like that, at least," Bianca said. I tried not to facepalm. She'd been *all* in my business when I left the Lil

Pal on my end table, and she was in it now, too. Huh. I hadn't seen that damn thing in a couple of weeks. I'd gotten rid of most of my Peter stuff, but not the nightie—and not the little robot. Not yet, at least. If I *found* it, that'd change.

"Nothing. I'm starting up an internship with the city, and they're getting me some dates and times."

"Oh, that sounds cool." Bee tried to pull me back down onto the bed, but I stood up through her grip. She pouted dramatically, and I laughed.

"Yeah, it'll be pretty neat. It's a great opportunity for me to get some on-the-job experience and start building a reputation for after college. That's really important in the career I want."

"What career do you want?"

Uh . . .

"You know, uh, superhero law's what my parents want for me, and . . . um . . . it's probably the best job for my future, so that's . . . that's what I'm leaning toward."

"That's surprisingly noncommittal for a girl who thinks an internship is a 'great opportunity' to 'build a reputation for after college,'" Bee teased.

She poked me in the side, and I squirmed away from her. "Hey!"

"Sorry! Are you ticklish?"

"No," I lied. I crossed my arms over my chest, covering my armpits in case she got any ideas. "Let's go get breakfast. I'm starving, and my head hurts."

Bee was out of bed before I'd finished talking. She grabbed my hand and dragged me to the door. "Okay, but you're buying!"

Bee stood on tippy-toes to kiss me goodbye outside of the Student Union Building. I returned the kiss, a little flustered. She grinned at me. "Good luck with your work stuff, Annie!"

"Thanks! See you later!"

As I walked the long, wide pathway from the SUB to Walnut Tower, *still* wearing my theater dress from the night before, I pulled out my phone to *finally* read Tele-Portal's email.

Subject: Patrol Duty

Hello, Magical Girl Understudy. I've finally got a day off on a weekend. The D-wolvers keep pushing, but we'll hold them off until the herd moves on, and they have to follow or starve. It's happened before. We just have to give them time to get hungry.

I'm patrolling Mid-Town tomorrow from 9:30 until 11:30. It's usually a pretty safe district since most of the major-league studios have offices there. Meet me at Baliman and Croft Financial. I'll teach you about public relations, patrol duties, and maybe even run a Short or two with you unless you have other obligations.

If you haven't already, I strongly recommend you solidify your power set before we run. I work best with a damage-output hero or an investigator, so if you can fill one of those roles, that'd be wonderful.

When: 9:30
Where: Baliman and Croft Financial, Mid-Town
What: Patrol
Tele-Portal

I hadn't settled on any builds for my powers yet. Magical Girl Understudy had always been an all-arounder, and I didn't really want to mess with that identity. But Rainy Day . . . had the potential to be something special. The little girl Costume did *way* more burst damage than Understudy could.

<Hey Fursona. Got a patrol with Tele-Portal tomorrow morning - Understudy 11:15>
<Wanna help me with my builds for it? - Understudy 11:15>

They didn't reply until I'd made it to my room and transformed into Understudy.

<Sure! I'll be over in a few. Working out. What are you thinking? - Fursona 11:28>
<Pure ranged Elementalist for Rainy Day - Understudy 11:29>
<Possible melee generalist for US - Understudy - 11:30>
<Sounds good. What about Lab Assistant Panic? - Fursona 11:31>

I froze halfway into my secret base. What *about* Lab Assistant Panic? I didn't *want* to use Professor Panic's powers right now. But the Costume might be a powerful option as . . . an investigator or full Genius to complement my other builds.

I grabbed the goggles from my bedroom—I'd thrown them into a nightstand drawer where I wouldn't have to look at them—then searched for the Lil Pal. I tore the room apart, smelling an occasional whiff of green apples, but the tiny bot was nowhere to be found. It hadn't been finished and wouldn't even take off, so it couldn't have left on its own power . . . could it?

I started checking the living room couch cushions, but Fursona buzzed on the elevator before I could dig too deeply. I shrugged and let them up. I'd figure out the Lil Pal problem later.

"Alright, so you're trying to build a melee build?" Fursona asked. "I happen to be a melee specialist Speedster/Bruiser hybrid, so you're in luck. I'm an expert!"

"Everything you know you learned from me," I quipped back.

"Har har. Pataki gave me some advice too, and they built the Costume. Sort of. Uncle Jeremy did some too. If you're going to specialize in melee fighting, you'll want a gap-closer. Otherwise, ranged specialists with a movement buff can—"

"Run rings around me. I know. I've done it to melee-centric villains before." Only one, actually. Just Professor Panic. "Let's go with **[Hometown Heroine]**. We'll trade out **[Stellar Ray]** for it." I gulped a little. I'd *never* run without

[Stellar Ray] before, but I'd soon be slapping that into the Rainy Day powerset if I had room.

"Idea. Can you run powers from your other Costumes on Understudy? That Grit power you used a couple of times in 'You're Super-Suited' would be amazing for a melee hero."

"I've never tried it, but it's worth a shot." I tried to trade out [Rejuvenation] for [Cloudy Disposition], but it wouldn't take. "I know I can run Understudy powers on my Costumes, but it doesn't go both ways."

Fursona snorted.

"What's so funny?"

"Nothing. So, no cool Grit power, then."

We worked on Understudy and Rainy Day until I was happy with both builds. Understudy turned out to be pretty much the same build I'd expected, with [Flickerform] giving it a ton of surprise firepower as needed. Other than that, I'd fight like I had in the training simulation, but with more speed and less range.

[Styles and Skills]
►Archetype Skill - Transformation Sequence
►Badass (45)
►Cunning (37)
►Inkling 1
►Drama (49)
►Hometown Heroine 1
►Flamboyance (30)
►Signature Skill - Adaptive Armoire 1
►Stored Costumes: (Rainy Day)
►Flickerform 1
►Spotlight Strike 1
►Grit (11)
►Rejuvenation 1

Rainy Day was more complicated. I *wanted* to make the Costume a pure ranged specialist, but I immediately ran into problems. [Ride the Lightning] had a short range, and [Stellar Ray] was really the build's only consistent damage. Despite everything I could throw at it, Rainy Day had too many powers that felt like filler.

I *was* due for some new skills in Badass and Drama, so maybe that'd help patch those holes. But what I *really* needed was the Flamboyance points for another roll or two. If I could level up [Adaptive Armoire] enough to run a third Costume, I could specialize Understudy into a melee fighter even more, or into an investigator if the other Costume wasn't LAP. I crossed my fingers for anything new so I wouldn't have to use it.

[Styles and Skills]
▶ Archetype Skill - Transformation Sequence
▶ Badass
▶ Cunning
▶ Drama
▶ Light as Vapor 0
▶ Stellar Ray
▶ Flamboyance
▶ Signature Skill - Adaptive Armoire 1
▶ Stored Costumes: (Understudy)
▶ Ride the Lightning 0
▶ Flickerform 1
▶ Grit
▶ Cloudy Disposition 0

"Alright, you've got two builds figured out, Squirt." Fursona stared at me, and I moved like I wanted to punch them, but they held their hand on my forehead until I shifted back to Understudy. "How about Lab Assistant Panic?"

"What about her?" I started playing with my hair.

"Well, you told Sara-N-Dipity she had some pretty unique powers. You should definitely take advantage of those if you can. What's she got?"

"[**Maniacal Reveal**], [**Hypercompression Cannon**], and [**Speed-Hacker**]."

"What do they do?" Fursona asked.

I slapped my hand down on the makeup table. "I don't *want* to talk about Lab Assistant Panic! I don't want to think about the Costume, or him, or anything! I want to find Lil Pal, throw it away, and pretend he didn't exist!"

Fursona held up their paws placatingly. "Okay, whoa. I'm sorry—I just thought we should be thorough with your power sets since you get so many of them. Do you . . . want some help with the Lil Pal problem?"

"No. I'll find it myself." I wasn't crying. Fursona was crying. Not me. Nuh-uh.

"Alright. I'll catch you later," Fursona said. They stood awkwardly for a minute, then headed for the elevator, which closed behind them. I didn't say anything. I just stared.

Then I shook out the tension. Fuck it. Fursona was right. It was too much power to throw away. I grabbed the goggles and started a rap.

"LAB ASSISTANT PANIC'S HERE TO SAY . . ."

But I couldn't finish; I couldn't shift into the Lab Assistant Panic Costume. It wasn't like Peter had taken back the Costume. I just couldn't do it right now.

<Hey, Fursona. I'm sorry I snapped. Lots of bad emotions still - Understudy 1:15>

I untransformed and headed back into my apartment. I had all afternoon to work on homework and get ready for my patrol with Tele-Portal.

50

Tele-Portal

SUNDAY, OCTOBER 26

I felt like I was flying.

The monorail from TU to Mid-Town snaked between, around, and even *through* buildings packed in so tightly they made the canyon-like streets Mom had driven the station wagon through seem open and airy. The train cars seemed to ride on air; I'd hardly felt them accelerate, and buildings flashed by with barely a bump.

<Hey, Understudy. Idea. - Fursona 9:15>
<We've been trying to win Episodes. We should focus on our style more - Fursona 9:15>
<That's a change from 'win at all costs' Fursona - Understudy 9:16>
<Yeah, well, long-term it's more wins, and bigger ones - Fursona 9:16>

The train started braking. I could barely feel it, but everyone rocked slightly as it began to pull into the station near the Baliman and Croft Financial Building. A few people looked at me funny—I was in full Costume, after all—but most shrugged and ignored the superhero in their midst. They had more important things to do, and as long as I wasn't panicking or running, no one here cared.

<Uh-huh. That's what I was saying in class - Understudy 9:18>
<So what do you think? - Understudy 9:19>
<We throw a fight and just use styles close to leveling up - Fursona 9:20>
<Oh, and see if the growth outweighs the victory bonus? - Understudy 9:20>

The train stopped, and I joined the crowd exiting. I followed a swarm of men in black suits down a flight of stairs and across the street to the Baliman building. Tele-Portal hadn't mentioned whether or not she'd be inside, but she wasn't waiting by the glass revolving doors, so I pushed my way through them and found an armchair to sit in.

<Could work. At B and C. Waiting for Tele to show. TTYL - Understudy 9:24>

I'd barely tucked my phone away when Tele-Portal pushed through the door, giant portal cannon slung over her shoulder and stilts strapped to her back. She yawned and waved. "Glad you're here, Understudy. The D-wolvers won't leave the wall alone, and I've been pretty busy, but we'll do a quick patrol and show you the ropes. Any experience with public relations beyond the normal cheesy lines in Episodes?"

"Yeah." I told her about speeches with Mayor Albright, especially the most recent one, just before I left.

"So, we're doing a little of that, a little autograph signing, and a little schmoozing with the Extras. We'll head over to Broadway Mall. That's still in Mid-Town, but it's more casual, so the Extras will be more interested in chatting."

"Are we going to portal over?" I asked. If not, I hadn't equipped any good movement powers. It'd be a long walk.

"Nope." I tried not to look crestfallen as she continued. "Part of patrolling is being visible, and using a power to skip the sidewalks wouldn't fit with that."

"Right. And visibility reassures the public that we're here."

"More than that, having heroes walking the street makes the villains second-guess the nastier Episodes." We pushed through the revolving doors and stepped out onto the busy sidewalk. People in business suits bustled every which way, while the more casually dressed seemed to flow mostly in one direction. "If The Equalizer knows I'm around, he's less likely to start a bank heist Episode. I hard-counter him, and I know today's his day off Man vs. Nature and that he wanted to hit First Launch Bank, so being nearby helps mitigate that."

That made sense. Peter . . . Professor Panic . . . never started things near me unless he wanted a fight. In our final Episode, he hadn't even made an appearance at either of the first two battlefields.

Tele-Portal waved to the crowds and said corny lines the whole way to Broadway Mall—"Don't worry, I'm just a portal away!" and "I love you too, kiddo!" and "My sidekick Understudy and I are here. Everything's totally safe." She'd practiced this for a long time, while I'd mainly tried to stay out of the public eye except for Episodes and speeches. Everyone knew each other in small towns.

We made it to Broadway Mall. It was a wide, sprawling glass-and-stucco building taking up most of the space between the skyscrapers in front of us. I'd wanted to come here since Mom and Dad dropped me off at Walnut Tower, but it hadn't worked out. And now, here I was, but I couldn't really *shop*.

The kids swarmed me as soon as we walked into the food court. Their noisy shouts and the smell of cinnamon buns, pizza, and grease were almost overwhelming.

"Hey, you're Understudy, right?"

"I saw your season finale against Professor Pancreas!"

"Are you going to fight him again?"

I looked toward Tele-Portal, who grinned at me. "My grandpa taught me to swim by throwing me in Bear Creek Lake until I figured it out. Go swim, Understudy."

Alright, some teacher *she* was. I took a deep breath. "Yep, I'm Magical Girl Understudy, here to make sure no villains are messing with you. I'm . . . not sure I'll ever fight Professor Panic again." I didn't use one of the stupid nicknames I had for Peter; it didn't seem right anymore. I swallowed.

"I'm here in Tokyexico City, and he's in a small town still. Neither of us can get to the other, so he's going to have to get used to fighting Collidus instead."

"Aww, man. Collidus isn't as fun as you. All he does is run into stuff and win."

The girl looked disappointed, and I knelt and put my hand on her shoulder. "I'm still fighting crime, kiddo. I'm just not fighting Professor Panic right now. I haven't given up on you, and I'm still out there, so don't give up on me, okay?"

"Okay." The kid swarm chatted with me for a while about their favorite Episodes. I cringed every time one of them said "Panic Prof and the Beastly Boys." Why *did* kids like nineties hip-hop so much anyway? And I ended up signing two books—neither about me, superheroes, or anything relevant—and a shirt sleeve.

When I'd finished, and the kids had left, Tele-Portal raised an eyebrow at me. "How do you think you did?"

"Alright. They all seemed happy at the end."

"Uh-huh. And did you notice McHammer?"

"Wait, what?" I whipped my head around.

"He went toward Rick's Sporting Goods just after you signed the T-shirt sleeve. You should probably tail him, huh?" Tele-Portal asked, winking.

"Ye—" Wait. She wasn't serious. I pondered for a moment. "Nope. He saw us, right?"

"Right. He knows we're here. He parted the crowd like a hot knife through butter, but he wouldn't start anything right now if he was after something serious. Not when I can bring the whole Triad into an Episode in five seconds. The only way he'd start anything is if he were working for someone else, and McHammer only works for himself—and occasionally, for Lord Destructo, but they split the payoffs 50/50."

"Alright. So he's not a threat?"

"We'll check back at the food court later," Tele-Portal said. We patrolled past one of the big department stores. I made a mental note to come back to it later; the signs outside screamed about a sale.

A man's voice interrupted my gaze, and Tele-Portal and I turned to look at an angry man with an early-teenage son behind him. The kid wouldn't stop looking at his phone. "Hey, 'heroes'! When's Bridgefield Middle opening? The Triad leveled it two months ago, and Andrew's driving me crazy."

"I've got this one," Tele-Portal whispered, then turned to the man. "Hi, sir. 'Haze-Matt's Escape from Almhurst!' wasn't the Triad's fault. We got lucky to herd him into the school building before classes started, but his chemical attack made the building a total loss."

"Well, when's it getting finished?"

"Let me check." Tele-Portal sighed and pulled out a phone. I watched as she typed "When is Bridgefield Middle School in Tokyexico construction supposed to be finished?" into the search bar. Then she sighed again. "Sir, it's on schedule to reopen for next semester. Rogers Construction pulled out all the stops to get it leveled and rebuilt as quickly as it has, but it needs a couple more months."

"This is bullshit," he grumbled. The kid rolled his eyes at me as his dad went off. I rolled mine back at him. Mom got like this sometimes.

Tele-Portal let the dad's tirade roll off her, then smiled. "I know the Triad paid for alternative school arrangements for every kid at Bridgefield Middle and equipment for remote learning as needed. If your current arrangments aren't working out, TCSD said they accepted transfers in the cases of Episode damage, Man vs. Nature issues, and Power War refugee status. This counts as Episode damage."

The man tried to argue for a while, but eventually, I spotted McHammer stomping back from the sporting goods store with his giant hammer in one hand and a bag of golf clubs in the other. "Uh, Tele-Portal, should we . . ."

"Yes. Sorry, sir, but I've done all I can for you. We've got superhero work to get to." Tele-Portal started walking away, and I followed, leaving the dad sputtering and the teenage phone-starer rolling his eyes again.

We followed McHammer back to the food court, where he got in line at a burger joint. He turned, glared briefly at Tele-Portal and me, then nodded slowly. Tele-Portal nodded back. "He didn't have to route past us. He could have left us with that angry Extra," she said.

"Why didn't he?"

"Professional courtesy. We defended the same stretch of the wall last week, and he's probably as tired as I am." She yawned again. "I'd bail him out if he were in the same boat. But he wouldn't be. Not many Extras approach villains unless they're looking for henching work."

My phone buzzed in my pocket, but I ignored it. "Why do you call them Extras? We're not in an Episode right now."

"Bad habit. I've been doing this for a while, Understudy. After eight or nine years, you realize an Episode could start anytime, so it's easier to think like one's always happening."

"That doesn't seem healthy." My phone buzzed again. A text? An email wouldn't be this persistent.

"No, probably not. Especially because Extras only get System protection during Episodes. Some heroes forget they're fragile most of the time. The Triad tries not to, but it's easy to slip up." Tele-Portal looked embarrassed. When my phone buzzed for a third time, she cleared her throat. "Why don't you check up on that?"

<Understudy, TUSSA's putting out a call to arms against the SSS - Fursona 11:05>
<All hands on deck, set for 1:00 - Fursona 11:07>
<You there? Ikenga said everyone in the email - Fursona 11:08>

"One second." She nodded and sat at an empty table near the end of the food court. I sat next to her, phone on the table. The email came first, then a response to Fursona.

Subject: Response to the SSS

Attention, TUSSA Members,

Monologue and the SSS have proven their untrustworthiness after their duplicitous actions at the job fair. Unfortunately, their "antics" are not over.

Sara-N-Dipity and the UFC Brothers have discovered that Iron Fist and Tearjerker are planning something. They've been secretive enough that Sara and her team haven't been able to find out more.

*I am declaring an [**Investigative Casting Call**] at 1:00 PM at the TUSSA Cave. All Tokyexico University Student Superhero Association members not currently involved in Man vs. Nature Seven should attend for the good of the association.*

Ikenga

Prescient President, TUSSA

"Looks pretty serious. Do you need to get going?" Tele-Portal asked from next to me. I nodded, but before I could say anything, my phone buzzed *again*.

<You there? Ikenga said everyone in the email - Fursona 11:08>
<Yeah, one sec. Meet me at 1301 in 45? - Understudy 11:08>

I shut the screen down and stood up. "Sorry, Tele-Portal. It's a—"

"College club drama. I get it. I'm exhausted anyways, so I'm going to say hi to McHammer and make sure nothing's going down today, then I'm going home."

I nodded. "Email me the next time you're doing a patrol. We'll find that Episode and see how we fight together."

She nodded, stood up with a groan, and walked over to McHammer. I didn't stick around for the conversation; I was already sprinting for the train station back to Tokyexico University. My phone buzzed again on the way.

<Yeah. Noon. Your place. What's an [Investigative Casting Call]? - Fursona 11:15>

51

[Investigative Casting Call]

Investigative Episodes are usually how superheroes start Episodes. Most of the time, the villain is the one starting stuff."

"Yeah, that makes sense." Fursona sprawled across the chaise lounge, and I thanked Fang Swee's power for giving me *that* particular piece of furniture in my secret base. "But not always."

"Right, not always. Sometimes, heroes need to act proactively. So heroes can start up Investigative Episodes. They're usually Shorts that lead into full-blown Episodes, and unless a hero starts fighting or does something obvious, the villains don't get a **[Casting Call]**," I said. I'd used Investigative Episodes against Peter when I'd tried to hunt down his lair. Honestly, they were a pain in the ass; I didn't have the powers to do them right, so they ended up being frustrating.

"So if Sara-N-Dipity and the boys can't get to the bottom of it, why involve TUSSA in the hunt?"

I finished adjusting my build *again* to make sure I had **[Inkling]** equipped. Surely I wouldn't need **[Flickerform]** for an Investigative Episode, right? Then I shrugged. "We'll have to find out. Ikenga's powers should be enough for any investigation, and Sara's built for it exclusively. Remember what Springlock and Milo said at the barbecue?"

"Yeah." With a stretch, Fursona picked themselves up off the lounge. "It's 12:15. You done?"

"Almost. What do you think Iron Fist and Tearjerker could be up to?" For a moment, **[Card Curio]** stood out as a power I'd like to have. It'd be an excellent backup to **[Inkling]**, or something more active to help us figure things out. But I didn't *have* a Tarot deck, so I couldn't do any readings. And there wasn't time to buy one before the meeting.

"No idea," Fursona said. "Knowing Monologue, it's probably something stupid like getting his grades changed again."

"Or poisoning all the pizza in the cafeteria so people get stuck in the bathroom for their afternoon classes."

"Hey, that sounds serious, not stupid!"

"It sounds like something my ex would do." I grabbed Tails and flopped her onto my shoulder. "Let's go."

"Thank you all for coming," Ikenga said from the slightly larger seat at the head of the oval conference table. "As I said in the email, the SSS is up to something."

"The SSS is always up to something," Milo said, watching Springlock's hands. "They're supervillains without frontal lobes. All they *do* is get up to something."

The TUSSA Cave was under the Perkins School of History—in fact, its entrance was right next door to where I had Post–Launch Day History. The main room had all the bells and whistles—and smell—of a good bar: a pool table, a few ancient-looking arcade machines, and a jukebox that was, sadly, silent. A few taps sat behind a counter, unused, and a massive fridge was filled with drinks. We weren't here to celebrate anything, though.

We were here to listen to Ikenga.

"Yes, yes, they're always up to something. Monologue always has a little plan he's working on," Ikenga said. He furrowed his brow, glaring. "But this one's different. He doesn't seem to be involved, at least not directly. I'll let Sara take it from here."

Sara-N-Dipity stood up in her suit and pulled out a clicker. She flicked it, and a slideshow started on a big TV. I groaned. So did half the other heroes, but she ignored us. "Me and the boys were out on a Short near Almond Street when I got a [**Hunch**]. It said with 78% certainty that something was going down two blocks over. So I left the boys to finish the Episode—Dark Girl Anima was about done anyways—and I went to check it out."

"Iron Fist and Tearjerker were talking about 'the plan' when I got there, but I calculated only an 8% chance of them spilling the beans, so I followed until they split up, then I headed back to the boys." She pointed at a map on the screen. "Almond Street is up in the Poudre District, which is Mutual Assistance League and 3V1L territory, so the SSS shouldn't have been up there at all."

She clicked her button. "The boys had mopped up Anima, but she didn't know much or wasn't talking. So we're out of leads since we can't just catch Lady Lockless and make her squeal."

"Why not?" Fursona asked. "Lady Lockless is a talker. She'd probably tell you everything."

"That's villain shit, Roo. We don't kidnap and interrogate," Sara said, staring. Fursona didn't look embarrassed, but then again, they *were* a fursuit kangaroo.

"Thanks, Sara," Ikenga said. He waited until she sat down. "It was lucky that—"

"It's not . . . sorry."

"Let me rephrase. Sara, Punch, and Grapple did us a great service by uncovering this 'plan' of the SSS's. Now we need to figure out what, exactly, it is. To that end, I'm starting an Investigative Episode effective immediately. Please accept if you can help."

[Investigative Casting Call]
[Investigative Episode: What's the Plan, Man? - PG]
[Role: Amateur Sleuth! Do you accept the role? (Yes/No)]
[Role Focus: Cunning+Drama]

I nodded at Fursona and accepted the [Investigative Casting Call]. I'd hated these so much against Peter, but with this many heroes, *someone* would probably solve it before us, and we'd be on the shortlist for the follow-up Episode. Hero-started Episodes almost always ended up as hero wins.

[What's the Plan, Man?: Act One in Progress]

"The first team is Hephaestus, Springlock, Milo, and myself. We'll cover where we think the SSS has its most recent lair, near the football field. Sara and the boys are on off-campus duty because they're the most likely to get lucky." Ikenga ignored Sara's glare and kept talking. He assigned two more teams before finally getting to Fursona and me.

"You'll be on campus patrol. Most of the time, the SSS villains don't run around in Costume, but you have villains in Superpower Ethics. They're mostly little leaguers, so someone might let something slip accidentally, especially if they've been brought in as a lieutenant for the first time. Sometimes braggarts are the best informants."

The teams asked questions about their areas of responsibility, the odds of finding something—Sara helped answer most of those—and how to report their findings back to TUSSA. Ikenga got everyone's number and started a group chat. And then the meeting was over.

Fursona walked to the TUSSA Cave's rec room and stood in front of a *Ms. Pac-Man* machine. The ghosts started wabble-wabbling around the maze as they moved the joystick back and forth. "Mom used to play these games. I had them on my laptop, but the actual machines are really neat. So, how are we gonna bust up the SSS's plan?"

"Well, it's Sunday in the middle of the afternoon." I watched Fursona eat a blinking blue ghost, then run from its friends as they turned back to normal. "I think we go to whatever classes we have before Superpower Ethics and keep our ears open. Maybe we'll hear something. We'll see if Gourmet or Theseus spill anything in class. Ikenga and Sara should have it wrapped up when class ends."

"Hmmmm." Fursona went silent and maneuvered their Ms. Pac-Man away from the incoming ghosts. When they finally cornered and ate her, they turned to me. "You're putting a lot of faith in Ikenga and Sara-N-Dipity, but they need us or they wouldn't have asked for help, right?"

"Right."

"So we need to do our best."

"Look, I don't know what else we *can* do. I searched for Professor Panic's lair for months, even with an Investigative Episode, and I couldn't find it. If the minor-league heroes haven't figured it out by noon tomorrow, we'll make another plan, okay?"

"Okay." Fursona pushed away from the machine with a sigh. "I don't have the skills for it either, but we need to try, that's all. I'll see you tomorrow, Understudy."

"Hey, Dad. Hey, Mom. Has anything weird happened in Riverside?" I asked. After Peter . . . after the breakup . . . I'd started video-chatting with Mom and Dad every Sunday night before showering. It was a nice new tradition, at least when Mom had the day off. I'd lie on my bed and talk, and they sat around the kitchen table.

Mom wrinkled her brow, thinking. "No, Anika. It's been quiet. A few Ronin heroes showed up and fought a scythetooth, but other than that, nothing much. I had a couple of days off in a row this week, which was relaxing." She took a drag from her cigarette.

"Now that you mention it, Claire, Professor Panic hasn't done anything obvious in two . . . no, three . . . weeks."

"He's probably up to something big. He's done this before," I said. "Like when he was working on—"

"That set of power armor, huh?" Dad asked.

"Uh, yeah." My parents knew *everything* about what I'd done as Magical Girl Understudy. They knew things Peter didn't know. Hell, they probably knew things *Rocko* didn't know. And I still hadn't figured out *how* they'd learned so much about me.

"How are classes, Anika?" Mom asked. "Are you going to history again?"

"Yes, Mom, I am *going* to Post–Launch Day North American History again." I rolled my eyes. "They're going well except for math. I'm meeting with Su-Bin tomorrow after history and before biology to go over multi-variable equations again, but I didn't get them in high school, and I won't get them now."

"Sure you will, Dot. I'm shocked Peter didn't teach you how to do it, though," Dad said.

"Oh, he tried. He *tried*. We had a Short about it, so he never tried to teach me after that. How's he been?"

"Haven't seen him," Dad said. "I think he's avoiding me. Can't imagine why?"

"Har har."

Mom and Dad talked a lot about Christmas break and their plans. If the Man vs. Nature ended, they'd pick me up just after my "Biology" final on Friday. I still hadn't told them I wasn't in Biology. If not, we'd video call and stuff. They urged me to make a plan; after all, Christmas was only a month and a half away, and I wouldn't want to be alone. They were right, but Bianca's parents didn't live in town either. Maybe I could have Christmas at Su-Bin's place? Were we close enough to ask?

When we finally said our goodbyes and I closed the video chat window, it was close to ten, and I hadn't touched my Post–Launch Day reading for tomorrow. I rolled out of bed and threw myself onto the couch, where my textbook sat.

Chapter Thirteen: Implications of the First Power War for the Yorkston-Columbia Megapolitan Area

After the First Power War ended, the Yorkston-Columbia Megapolis was in jeopardy. Liege Lord's battle with Doombringer had leveled much of Manhattan Island's infrastructure, Tapdance's rampage had left vast swaths of the city damaged, and though the Ilneat studios each offered to pay for the rebuild, the Ilnean government chose not to intervene as they had after Launch Day.

The city may have been in jeopardy, but I was drifting off. Professor Ellen Suarez, whoever she was, was not a very interesting writer.

With near-infinite funding but no silver-bullet solution, the Yorkston and Columbia governments embarked on the largest construction project in human history; a complete rebuild of Manhattan Island from the seafloor up, along with a complete rebuild of the crippled road systems in North Yorkston. Properly funded by the Ilneat studios and with both powered and unpowered labor in abundance, the project started on . . .

I yawned. The clock said 10:26. I'd been reading this page for thirty minutes, over and over, without realizing it.

Nope.

I took off my clothes and hopped in the shower. Teaching Assistant Smith could teach me the importance of the Yorkston-Columbia Megaplex's construction project. The steam and the industrially clean soap bar smell filled the bathroom as I mentally ran through Gourmet, Theseus, Flare, The Crumb, and all of tomorrow's potential informants.

52

Potential Informants

MONDAY, OCTOBER 27

The rebuild process in Yorkston received a huge boost from Longshore Construction's ongoing feud with Brightwing Industries. Both companies went into hiring frenzies for the Manhattan Proj—whoops, the Manhattan Island Restabilization Act's Construction-Led Enterprise, or MIRACLE. At one point, almost a tenth of the megapolis's population was hired by the two companies or their subcontractors . . ."

A yawn escaped before I could stop it, but no one noticed. Avan was sound asleep next to me, and over half the auditorium had dozed off or were playing on their laptops or phones. A few doodled mindlessly. Teaching Assistant Smith looked annoyed, but she kept soldiering on with her slideshow and notes. Only a few students heard what she said, and I doubted more than five or six paid any attention.

I wasn't one of them today.

I couldn't stop playing with my hair or tapping my pencil. Instead, I'd been trying to get a good look at other students' computer screens in case one of them was in the SSS and they were communicating by email. No dice. The students next to me didn't have anything juicy on their screens.

"So, why do we care?" Teaching Assistant Smith asked. When no one answered, she cleared her throat and waited some more.

"Because . . . because the MIRACLE model worked?" One student in the front row asked half-heartedly.

"Hell yeah, it worked. MIRACLE finished two months ahead of schedule. Yorkston's been one of the easiest cities to get around since then, and it solidified its importance as *the* financial hub of North America and *the* place for major-league supers to go. There's almost always something world-ending centered on Yorkston; alien portal invasions, dark god attacks, and rogue inventions, to name a few recent crises. With great powers comes great opportunity for everyone else, as long as you're willing to take a risk.

"More importantly, though, other cities adopted the MIRACLE model for rebuilding after a disaster." Smith kept the lecture going, but I . . .

I . . . I didn't care. I'd spent the night tossing and turning. Sure, Ikenga and Sara-N-Dipity would almost certainly have "What's the Plan, Man?" solved by noon—one at the latest—but a small, nagging voice in my head kept asking, *What if you got there first? What if you found the critical clue? Wouldn't that be something?* By three in the morning, I'd decided to solve this Investigative Episode—or at least give it my all. I'd texted Fursona but hadn't heard back.

"By Wednesday, you need to have *Chapter 14: The Battle of Blast Ridge* read. We're shifting focus to the Silicon Valley crisis to our west and the emergence of AI-driven machines between California and southern Alaska. Be ready to *discuss* this time," Teaching Assistant Smith said sadly. "Please. It's a fascinating topic, and the Pacific's post-Launch problems are so different than ours that it's like studying a different world. I'll see you then."

I had an hour before Superhero Ethics, where I'd be more focused on spying than on whatever the lesson was. But if I were smart, I'd be able to learn something during breakfast.

Plainclothes detective work had its risks. I could get caught out untransformed like I had during the Orientation Episode. Most supers didn't have that problem; they could still access their powers since they weren't tied to their Costumes. Magical Girls—and Fursona—were an exception. Without my Costume, I was just an ordinary girl.

But despite that risk, it also gave me some anonymity.

I hurried to the cafeteria. Ten minutes to get there, twenty to eat, ten to Walnut Tower, and ten to the Mister Felsic statue and class; that gave me ten minutes of wiggle room. I slipped into the pizza line. It was only ten, but pizza was still delicious even if I'd probably eaten too much of it, and with how Fursona's workout plan was going, it wasn't like the calories would be an issue.

I kept my ears open. It would have been nice to have an **[Inkling]** of what to do, but I doubted a villain would willingly give anything to a uniformed super. They'd have to be pretty stupid, especially if the SSS was counting on them for something.

So I was listening but not expecting anything. And I wasn't disappointed. A few students nearby talked about the Man vs. Nature outside. The D-wolvers kept finding ways through the wall; there'd been an outbreak in the Poudre District last night, and The Triad had to get involved. I imagined Tele-Portal was pissed. It was supposed to be her day off. The turbo-buffalo herd was leaving, so that was good. But something funky was happening in the mountains, with the plants, and that might push them back to Tokyexico. Father Thyme was on the way from Tortuga West.

I grabbed my pizza: two slices this time, both pepperoni and olives.

"Hey! Annie!"

I turned as Su-Bin walked toward me, giant soda in hand. "Hey, I was going to text you later today. I've got . . . math problems."

"I'm not just your math tutor, Annie," Su-Bin said, laughing good-naturedly. "If you're going to complain about math to me, I get to complain to you."

"Deal!" We grabbed a table, and I explained my problems with multi-variable equations between bites.

"So to solve those, you need to get one variable on one side and the other on the other. Then you can figure out how many $x = 1y$ is, or whatever your numbers are," Su-Bin said as she wiped her mouth after a big gulp of soda. "That's the first step. Then once it's on one side—"

"Hold on, I'm not going to remember *any* of this when I get back to my math book," I interrupted. If I could get her to talk, I could listen to the conversations around us. "And my pizza's getting cold. Can you walk me through it sometime later?"

"Sure. Tomorrow?"

"Sounds great. How's Veronica? That's what you want to complain about, right?"

"Well"—Su-Bin paused—"not great. I'm actually spending every weekend with my parents again to get away from her boyfriend bullshit."

"Sounds rough." I took a bite of pizza and tried to talk around it. "Awe dey stiww bein' gross?"

"Yeah. They put a sheet up, so I don't see, but that makes the sounds *worse*. She makes the most horrible sounds—like a pig or something. And I think she's hamming it up on purpose." She sipped from her drink again. "Honestly? I hate her so much. She's the worst person on campus."

"I bet." She wasn't. Su-Bin's roommate was *not* the worst person on campus. That title belonged to Dr. Mindstorm, literal supervillain supreme.

"That's why I'm with my parents a lot, though," Su-Bin finished.

"Uh-huh. Hey, what are your Christmas plans?" I asked, then hurried with an explanation. "I know it's early, and it's super-rude to invite myself to your place, but if the Man vs. Nature keeps going . . ."

"You won't be able to get home. I'll ask my parents. It won't be much, but it'd be better than being alone in the dorms. How are your other classes?"

"I'm bored with Post–Launch History, but my parents figured out I was skipping, so that's a no-go. Even though I'm on a scholarship, they still tell me what to do." I shrugged, looking around. No one sat near us. This was the worst detective work ever! "It's just . . . I only care so much about what Yorkston was up to. It's not even focused on Tokyexico."

"Well, duh, it's North American history, not Mountain Belt history."

"Yeah." I shoved the last of my pizza into my mouth, swallowed, and washed it down with some soda. "Gotta go. My next class awaits!"

I did not care about dogpiling either.

But I saw how it made for tough TV to watch, and I could imagine being on the wrong side. Right now, Big Fish was fighting Cinder-Ella, Battle Bro, Dark Girl

Steel Will, Cannonball, and a dozen henchmen. "Fighting." Yeah, right. Big Fish kept trying to activate his power, [**It Was This Big!**]. If he could convince a couple of his enemies to believe his bragging, he'd be able to start snowballing as boasts became reality. He could handle any of these villains one-on-one *without* his power.

But he'd been lured into a trap. Against all four, plus the henchmen, he couldn't finish his boasts to get his power going.

Dr. Jackson paused the screen as three henchmen broke bats and pipes on Big Fish's shoulders and Cannonball rocketed toward his face. "Did they break any ethics rules by dogpiling? If so, what did they do wrong, ethically speaking? If not, why don't more heroes and villains dogpile? Break!"

Theseus cleared his throat. "I'm back, babes! I put my foot down—"

"Enough body-part jokes. We get that your power's cool, okay?" Gourmet said.

"I've got my finger on the pulse of what's in, and it's bad puns. Anyways," Theseus said as Gourmet groaned, "I put my foot down and said I needed more time for classes. As a minor-league villain, the Tokyexico Council of Heroes couldn't mandate that I fight, so they offered me weekend duty with an eye toward fairness. I can finally rest between D-wolver patrols and classes now!"

"That's great. What do you think?" I asked.

"Well, I don't see a problem with dogpiling," Theseus said, smirking. "It's just good business, like when Gourmet and I wrecked you in the weight room, only with numbers instead of quality. This lesson feels like a trick question."

I half-assed my part in the conversation, letting Gourmet and Theseus dictate what our code of ethics would say since Fursona couldn't out-argue them by themselves. I'd have to get my points in during any revision we did.

But I was much more interested in Flare and The Crumb today.

They'd always seemed engaged, especially The Crumb, even if his whole schtick seemed to be "burn it all down." No wonder he and Flare were getting along so well. Their team—with Punch and Grapple—was so far ahead on their code of ethics that it was more unbelievable than a Pranky Jones joke.

But today, only Punch and Grapple were working on their codes. The villains were missing.

[**Inkling**]. They knew the SSS's plan. I needed to follow them.

"I'll be back. Bathroom." I slipped away as Gourmet and Theseus jotted something in my team's notebook. Honestly, dogpiling seemed fine. It was a great way to handle an enemy you couldn't manage alone. I didn't see another way to beat someone like Golden Goose or Magical Girl Stella-Lunar.

Outside the movie room, I heard whispered voices farther down the hall. I crept closer. It was definitely The Crumb—he talked so much in class that I'd recognize his voice anywhere—and Flare.

"I don't know why we're even talking about this," Flare said. "The plan's simple. We just have to help move parts in. If we do that, the dealer will take care of the rest."

[Good Thinking! +1 Cunning Point]

A dealer! Was the SSS involved in the drug trade on campus? Or had they already been doing that? Did . . . did drugs have parts? I cursed that my class required me to be relatively good. I knew so little about *actual* criminal conspiracies.

"But *where*?" The Crumb asked. "They wouldn't tell me *where*."

"That's because they don't trust you. You're their weakest, newest lieutenant. If you wanna be trusted like me, you need to prove yourself."

I tiptoed closer. There should be a couch around the corner. Were they sitting on it? Or were they farther down the hall? I had to check. I poked my head around the corner. Sure enough, The Crumb was pacing agitatedly while Flare sat on the couch and smirked.

"Look," Flare sighed. "Neither of us is on Monologue's 'nice' list right now. If I tell you, you're not telling anyone. Right? Good. Grant School of Engineering."

[Clever Girl! +1 Cunning Point]
[Dramatic Spywork! +1 Drama Point]

Was that enough information? I wasn't sure, but I'd run out of time. The faux-leather couch creaked as someone stood, and I hurried back to class and our discussion about dogpiling. As I pushed open the door, I could hear the two villains hurrying to catch up behind me.

53

Behind Me

I sat next to Fursona with a sigh of relief. It'd been close, but I didn't think Flare and The Crumb saw me sneaking away from their conversation. I settled into my armchair. "What'd I miss?"

"None of us hate dogpiling," Theseus said.

Fursona nodded. "Yep. Fair tactic. The reason most heroes and villains don't use it must be growth related. If it takes Stella-Lunar six attacks to take someone out, she gets at least six Style Points. If she, Liege Lord, Golden Goose, Tele-Portal, Big Fish, and Flyboy all fight the same enemy, they get one each at best."

"It's also not good TV, if you're worried about that sort of thing," Gourmet added. "Unless the villain is super-unpopular, most people like some tension."

Fursona glanced at me. I couldn't see their face, but I imagined a raised eyebrow and an unspoken question: "Did you get it?" I wanted to answer, but Flare and The Crumb returned before I could. They both glared daggers at me, and I gulped.

Maybe I hadn't gotten away with it after all.

As they returned to their La-Z-Boys, I tried to think of a way to signal Fursona that wouldn't give away anything to Theseus and Gourmet. The villains wouldn't start something here—not when Dr. Jackson was around, but tipping off Gourmet or Theseus was a guaranteed loss. The conversation shifted from whether dogpiling was ethical to how we wanted to refer to it in our code, and I took up the pen.

Code of Conduct: October 27

We will not ~~endanger harm threaten~~ endanger ~~civilians~~ Extras ~~needlessly~~

When Extras must be involved, ~~every effort must be taken to make them aware of danger~~ they must be clearly informed of danger

~~What about Henchmen?~~

WHO CARES ABOUT HENCHMEN?

I care about henchmen!

Destruction of ~~non-government residential~~ non-corporate/non-government property is ~~to be kept to a minimum not necessary~~ not okay

I can't agree with this, guys. I need to eat!

Bring your own snacks. I bring my own! And quit making fun of me!
You ate a wrestling singlet!
Medical Extras are off-limits. Healing heroes ~~should only be targeted if involved in the fighting are a low priority target~~ *are not a target unless they directly engage*
Why? Good tactics are to take out the healers first so the rest of the team actually takes damage.
Property damage must ~~have a point be for a purpose~~ *be directly related to the Episode's goals*
Neutrality will be respected
When it's convenient for heroes?
Eat a sandwich, Gourmet. It'll make you feel better
Dogpiling is acceptable under ~~all most all~~ *almost all circumstances.*
Are you sure that's the wording we want? We could go with most instead. <u>*Got it?*</u>
Yeah, I got it, Fursona.
I support 'all'
Almost all or bust

When class finally ended, I bolted for the door, Fursona right behind me. Class policy, strictly enforced, meant that no one had their phones or computers. It'd be too easy to spill a secret identity that way, so we left them at home, which was great for privacy and focus.

But when you had an important message to get to Ikenga, and the closest phone was in Walnut Tower, *and* you'd left your movement power unequipped, *and super-villains were right behind you trying to stop you from saying anything?*

It wasn't so great then.

The only good news was that Flare was . . . well, not a pushover, but we'd beaten him before. And The Crumb wasn't exactly Lord Destructo or Tapdance—Punch and Grapple didn't have much respect for him. Plus, they probably wouldn't say anything to Theseus or Gourmet. It'd look bad for them if the SSS found out.

The two supervillains were only a few steps behind us when we dashed up the ramp to the Mister Felsic statue. Looking over my shoulder at The Crumb's makeup-covered face glaring at me, I knew we wouldn't get away with it. Flare was too fast to run from. We just had to hope the other villains were taking the tunnels today.

A few Extras stood up as Fursona and I skidded to a stop. "Get out of here! I'm a [**Hometown Heroine**]! Run, and I'll keep you safe," I shouted.

"Stop her! She hasn't told the kangaroo yet," The Crumb yelled. He held his hands out, bread cape rising around him, and *blew*. A torrent of flour rushed toward us, and I braced for impact.

The powder covered us and hung in the air, but it didn't do any damage. I started laughing. "That's the best you've—"

Flare rushed up the ramp a moment later. He activated his flame arm and sprinted toward me.

Hell broke loose under the Mister Felsic statue.
WHOOOOOM!

[HP 4/7]

"What the **[Beep!]**" A massive fireball had thrown me all the way to the grass. I coughed, picking myself up. My Costume smoldered and smoked, and the jerks had singed my bows! "Fursona, don't let them do that again!"

[Rating Warning #1! Episode Rating - PG! Censor in Effect]
[Gritty Recovery! +1 Grit Point]

"You . . . you got it, boss." Fursona's suit had fared more poorly than me. Flames roared from their pouch and tail as they hopped back toward the two villains. I took a deep breath, coughed, and hurried after them.

Fursona barreled straight toward a totally unscathed Flare, leading with their feet in a two-legged kick. They caught the Speedster in the chest and sent him flying past one of the enormous granite pillars. The Justice-Roo tried to close the gap and keep the pressure on, but Flare started running.

The Crumb coughed. "I *hate* that combo so much, but it's just so strong!" His ugly jacket smoked; the explosion had clearly hurt him, too. Maybe Flare had **[Fire Resistance]**.

Either way, I had to keep the pressure up. **[Hometown Heroine]** ticked down, but it got me in range of the bread-themed villain—who came up with these power sets, anyway?

I aimed a **[Spotlight Strike]**-guided fist right at The Crumb's face, but he swung a baguette like a sword and parried my punch. A moment later, the baguette flashed out, drawing a line of crumbs across my chest. The crumbs melted into an oily mess, staining my Costume, but they didn't do any damage.

[Hometown Heroine] faded instantly, though.

I backed off. Was The Crumb a support villain? He'd ripped my buff right off with his stupid . . . bread stains. And it'd explain why Flare said neither was on Monologue's "nice" list; he'd lost against us during "Super-Suited," and The Crumb wouldn't ever be more than a lieutenant.

It also meant I needed to recalculate. The fight wasn't about beating the villains. It was about getting my findings to Ikenga. The only way to do that was to get to Walnut Tower, though, and I couldn't just burst through the door. But . . .

I could use the tunnels if I could regroup with Fursona. If they held the two villains off at the entrance, I could run to the Walnut elevator. This wasn't a fight for me; it was a chase scene.

"Fursona, back to the Mister Felsic ramp!" I yelled.

The kangaroo hero nodded and leaped back toward the stone-gloved granite statue. As they arrived, I blurted everything at them. "They said something about the engineering college and a dealer. We need to tell Ikenga. Can you hold them off while I run?"

Fursona nodded. "You got it, Understudy. Go!" They dropped into a stance I'd never seen before, with one paw behind the other and one hand outstretched. It looked like it'd be uncomfortable for a 'roo, but not for a person in a fursuit.

Flare zipped through the stone pillars a moment later. His sparking fist flickered toward Fursona, but they stepped back and redirected the blow against the tunnel's wall. "Go!" Fursona yelled again.

I started running. The sounds of combat faded as I ran past the theater room, then turned a corner and dodged the couch. Another explosion echoed down the hall, and the sounds grew louder again.

I almost turned around. Fursona was a newbie hero, and I was an asshole for leaving them to fight not one but *two* villains. But the fighting sounds didn't stop. They'd stayed up after the explosion, and I doubted Flare could spam his trigger ability for the combo. The camera drone following me kept looping ahead to look over my shoulder instead, watching whatever action was behind me, so Fursona was probably getting crazy amounts of Style Points.

So I kept running. I turned one corner, then another. The tunnels below TU weren't straight and easy to follow—they weaved back and forth, swerving and branching to connect with each building's elevator, or a maintenance door, or even a classroom that never had any classes. I relaxed a little. They couldn't possibly follow me through here.

[Good Thinking! +1 Cunning Point]

The Walnut Tower elevator sat nearby. I stepped into it, pushed the button, and slid my key card. When the elevator finally dinged open, I dashed through my secret base and into my living room. I opened my computer and typed out a quick email.

Subject: Info
Ikenga,
Grant Engineering School. Fursona fighting in Mr. Felsic tunnels. Send help. Going back in.
Understudy

Then I turned and rode the elevator back down. I'd won. When Ikenga opened the email, the Episode would be over. But that didn't mean I'd let Fursona fight by themselves. I tried activating **[Hometown Heroine]** as soon as the doors opened, but it wouldn't go. Whatever The Crumb had done, I'd need a dry-cleaner or a Costume change to fix it.

The sounds of fighting grew louder. Then, as I rounded the corner, I received a System message.

[Episode Finished!]

[Investigative Episode: What's the Plan, Man? - PG]

[Penalties: 1x Rating Warnings - No Penalty]

[Episode Finished! +3 of each Style Point]

[Winner Winner! +1 of each Style Point]

[Role Focus: Cunning+Drama - Goal Partially Met! +5 Cunning Points]

[Alias - Understudy] [Archetype - Magical Girl] [Community Rank - 449/523]

[HP 4/7]

[Styles and Skills]

▶ Archetype Skill - Transformation Sequence

▶ Badass (49)

▶ Cunning (49)

▶ Inkling 1

▶ Drama (54) (Skill Roll Available)

▶ Stellar Ray 1

▶ Flamboyance (34)

▶ Signature Skill - Adaptive Armoire 1

▶ Stored Costumes: (Rainy Day)

▶ Flickerform 1

▶ Spotlight Strike 1

▶ Grit (16)

▶ Rejuvenation 1

I rolled the skill while I ran. The villains probably wouldn't stop fighting just because the Episode was over.

[50 Drama Credits Used. Rolling Skill!]

[New Skill! Bit-Part Barrage 1: An aerial assault against an enemy with high damage but high risk. A miss leaves you vulnerable to counterattack.]

I didn't have time to deal with a new ability or what it might actually do. Fursona needed me. The second System message popped up just as I rounded the corner and saw the fursuit-wearing hero backing up against both villains' assaults. I was too busy to read more than the first line.

54

Grant Building Dogpile

[Casting Call]
[Episode: Grant Building Dogpile - PG-13]
[Role: Dog in the Fight! Do you accept the role? (Yes/No)]
[Role Focus: Cunning+Drama]
[Grant Building Dogpile!: Act One in Progress]

I assumed the whole Student Superhero Association had gotten the [**Casting Call**]. I didn't mind. I definitely couldn't solo a minor-league Episode—although it *was* strange that the System had decided to rate it that high.

I didn't have time to think about it, though.

Around the next corner, I heard the sound of fighting and saw a puff of flour. My heart leaped to my throat; was Fursona about to receive a gigantic flour fireball? And if they did, would they be able to tank it? They were tough, but they'd also been fighting solo for—

Another cloud of flour poofed out into the hall. A moment later, I skidded around the corner. "Don't fear, Fursona. Understudy is . . . oh."

Milo, the toga-clad TUSSA hero, had his arms wrapped around The Crumb's waist. Every time the baking-themed villain struggled, the wrestler squeezed, and more flour filled the air. His arms tightened around The Crumb, tighter and tighter, and I drooled at all the Badass points he was earning. Fursona battled with Flare just down the hall. They seemed evenly matched for now.

"Hey, kid, Springlock's on her way with Sara and the boys! Surrender, villain!" Milo picked The Crumb up, ignoring his flailing fists and feet. When he didn't surrender, Milo shrugged and threw him into a wall.

I squeezed past the massive, red-tinted Greek wrestler as he closed in to finish The Crumb. Fursona's suit was singed and scorched, and I could see a black long-sleeve shirtsleeve through one arm. They needed my help. [**Spotlight Strike**] highlighted a spot between Flare's shoulder blades. A moment later, my fist hit that spot at full speed.

[Stylish Strike! +1 Flamboyance Point]

Flare stumbled. Then he got his balance and started running.

I took off after him, but the couch I'd run past flew down the hall. We both dodged the faux-leather three-seater as it slammed into a wall. Splinters and springs flew everywhere. I **[Flickerformed]** into **[Ride the Lightning]** and filled the hallway with thunder and arcing electricity. Flare got caught in the worst of it.

[Electric Lightshow! +1 Flamboyance Point]

A moment later, Grapple jumped—no, Grapple was *dragged* by his shoes—into Flare. The villain tried to get away, but Punch and Springlock came around the corner, and he quickly surrendered.

Milo tossed The Crumb onto the floor a moment later. "God *damn,* dogpiling the little leaguers is fun!"

Springlock walked up to him, fingers flying. He cleared his throat. "Ikenga's having the rest of the TUSSA team meet in Weber Quad. It's just outside of the Grant School of Engineering. Leave these two here. They're not going anywhere. *Right?*"

The two villains shook their heads. "You gonna tell the cops where we are?" The Crumb asked.

"Of course," Milo said, still staring at Springlock, who looked at the villains and signed, "Stay here, or we'll be back."

I looked at Fursona's suit as we jogged up the ramp toward the Mister Felsic statue. It looked even worse this close than I'd thought in the tunnel. They'd been through hell. "Thanks. You gave us the win." I gave them a quick side hug.

"Yeah, but my suit's pretty much toast. I couldn't stop all the big fireballs, and Flare's straight-up dangerous with The Crumb. That bastard locked me out of **[Double-Kick]** *and* my fursuit's Grit defensive power." Fursona stopped. I could practically see their grin. "Hey, I can swear!"

"*Don't you dare use an F-bomb!*" Milo interrupted. "If you give it to Springlock, she and I both get one, since I'm just interpreting. It's a nice way around the censor."

"Fine, whatever." Fursona shrugged. Then they stopped running. "I don't think I can do this next Episode. I'm at one superhero damage left, and my suit and powers are in bad shape. I'll meet you at your place, alright?"

"Alright. Take my extra key card for the elevator." I handed the Justice-Roo a key card and waved goodbye.

The Grant School of Engineering was one of TU's biggest selling points. From nanobots to heat-shielding to small-scale teleportation research, the program advertised itself as being at the forefront of Ilneat-human technological integration. That sounded like a bunch of buzzwords to me, but I wasn't on that track for my education.

What I did know was that the Grant Building sprawled out just north of Weber Quad. I'd passed it a few times, but most of my classes weren't near its chrome-and-glass exterior, so I hadn't paid much attention to it. With the TUSSA team assembling outside of it, that was about to change.

"Alright, team. Once inside, we've got to spread out and check every lab. Stay in earshot, but be efficient," Ikenga was saying. "They won't be on the first floor, but there could be surprises for us, so take it slow and steady. We should have numbers on the villains, but they may have henchmen. I haven't *seen* any, but my focus has been on Iron Fist and Tearjerker. Both are inside."

"So, are we operating in teams?" Sara asked.

"Yes. You and the boys will check the aerospace wing. I predict no one will be there, but as I said, my focus has been elsewhere. Hephaestus and I"—Ikenga pointed at a man in a steel exoskeleton carrying a pair of forging hammers—"will go center and get the stairs secured, along with the rest of our little-league heroes. Springlock and Milo will go into engineering and fabrication. They'll have an advantage there if the machines are running."

"We're taking Understudy too," Springlock signed.

"Fine. That evens out our numbers. Stay with your teams. Stay in touch with Heph and me. Be safe, and we'll push into the basement labs after the upstairs is secure." Ikenga nodded, then pointed at the front door. "Go."

The door was locked. Punch found a window next to it and shattered it. The howling alarm rang out five times before Hephaestus plugged into the wall inside and turned it off. "I hate noise."

"You run a forge," Milo said incredulously as he ran by.

"Doesn't mean I like noise. Get going. You've got a job to do," Hephaestus replied. Milo turned, bowed sarcastically, and ran toward the building's east side. I followed.

The labs were empty. That was . . . odd . . . for a school day. Not only that, but they were clean. Computers and drafting tables were packed into some, while others housed shiny drills and laser-guided metal cutters. I had an **[Inkling]** and pushed through one of the machine shop's doors. Sure enough, the room hummed with the sounds of running tools. It sounded familiar, and my throat tightened.

A small steel box sat on the floor. It was the size of a midsized dog, with clasps and a very secure locking mechanism. I'd never been inside a lab like this—the closest I'd been to one was a semester of woodshop at Riverside High and in Peter's lair a couple of times when he'd "kidnapped" me—but a box like this felt like it *should* have been in a student's locker or on one of the shelves. It definitely shouldn't have been in the middle of the machine shop's floor. It weighed a *ton*, and all I could do was drag it across the rubber-matted floor to the door. "Hey, Milo! I found something!"

[Good Thinking! +1 Cunning Point]

"Alright, we're on our way!" Milo shouted back. He arrived a moment later, carrying a box just like mine. "You thought these were weird, too, huh?"

"Yeah. Machine shops probably need to be kept clean for the other students, right? Leaving crates the perfect size for tripping next to power tools seems stupid."

"Yep. Dr. Richardson wouldn't be pleased," Milo confirmed.

"Let's get these back to Ikenga and wait for Sara. She'll get them open in no time," Springlock said. We left the engineering labs. Springlock and I carried one, while Milo hoisted his over his shoulder.

"What do you think they are?" I asked.

"Some kind of villain tech?" Milo said. He shrugged, the shiny crate reflecting the lights. "Let's talk it over with the others."

Ikenga nodded in greeting as we stacked our two crates with the one Punch, Grapple, and Sara-N-Dipity had found. Against all odds, they'd gone straight to it and come right back, and Sara tapped numbers into its control panel seemingly at random. It beeped red once, and she swore. Then, five button-pushes later, it popped open.

"Shit, third try. Getting rusty," she said. "That's a robot."

It was, indeed, a robot. Was this Professor Panic's work? Was he *here*? I knew I could beat him; I'd done it a dozen times before. But I didn't know if I could *fight* him, and I couldn't use Lab Assistant Panic. There was no way.

I stared at its gold-chrome finish and four legs, though, and relaxed. Professor Panic used green lighting and steel bodies, and these weapon systems looked different than the **[Hypercompression Cannons]**, teeth, and limbs that LABRAT and the Panic Pals relied on.

"Heph, what do you see here?" Ikenga asked. I watched as he drifted off, looking into the robot's future or something.

"It looks like it's got a stun Gatling cannon and a vibrating blade. Heh. If you ditched the blade, you'd have a good Captain Vibration weapon," Heph said. He winked. "Frequency is about right for a good time."

I rolled my eyes. Captain Vibration was the In-You-Endos' leader—at least, as much as that team *had* a leader. The rest of them claimed they all followed A Cat Who Can Talk, but *someone* had to be making the decisions, and listening to a cat for advice? That was just crazy!

"It runs on four legs like—"

"Get away from it, Hephaestus!" Ikenga shouted.

Heph stood up, letting his exoskeleton take his weight, and backed away, not finishing his sentence.

The TUSSA team backed off, hurrying to the room's far side.

The robot's servos started spinning a moment later. Its legs forced their way out of the box, its vibrating blade revving and its cannon tracking Hephaestus. The other boxes also sprung open, revealing more of the gold-chrome bots, which stood almost three feet tall fully extended.

The stun cannons fired, and Hephaestus crashed to the ground, twitching. A metal foot—thankfully, not one with blades—slammed into the Genius's head over and over, quickly taking him out of the fight.

Two villains ran up the stairs. Tearjerker pointed at Milo. "You! The scene in *Remember the Titans* in the hospital!" Milo burst into tears, knocked out of the fight.

The other villain, Iron Fist, grinned. He revved his mechanical boxing gloves. "Welcome to the Grant Building, heroes. Sorry our dealer missed you, but my fists won't!"

Two of TUSSA's minor-league heroes were down, and the fight hadn't even started. I had no idea what to do.

55

What to Do?

The situation reminded me of my second battle with LABRAT. I hadn't had a good counter for machines then, either. Hell, I hadn't had a good counter for LABRAT until after LABRAT wasn't an issue anymore. The robot pushed and bullied me until I hit a knee joint and slowed it down. With this many bots, fishing for crits wouldn't work.

No one moved. That was weird. The villains must have been getting ready to gloat, but Springlock wasn't even facing them. She held out one hand flat, staring at me, and put her other pointer finger between two flat fingers. She pointed it toward the Grant Building's main door. Then she did it again.

The hallway erupted into chaos as Punch and Grapple charged Tearjerker. The goth villainess took Grapple out of the fight with a well-placed question about the boy's goldfish, but Punch kept the pressure up until a stun shot caught him in the back. Springlock took off toward the engineering wing while Sara ran in the other direction. Iron Fist hesitated, then turned the corner after Springlock.

Well, everyone else was running. I'd do the same.

I headed for the doors, a four-legged bot right behind me. It glowed just like LABRAT and the Panic Pals, but red, and its gold armor glistened in the fluorescent lights. I dodged a stun shot and kept running.

The Weber Quad was packed with students as I pushed the main doors open. "Move! We've got a problem!" I yelled.

No one moved.

"I said we've got a problem! Run!" I tried again. Nothing.

A second later, the golden robot crashed *through* the door behind me. As I whirled to face it, people started screaming all around me. The camera drone *had* to be loving this.

The bot sprinted toward me. **[Inkling]** said to dodge right, so I ducked under its vibrating blade. But I still couldn't use **[Hometown Heroine]**, and this bot made LABRAT look *slow*.

[Good Thinking! +1 Cunning Point]

I tried a [**Spotlight Strike**]. The light whipped around its body before settling on a tiny joint on its front leg. I groaned and punched for it.

[**Stylish Strike! +1 Flamboyance Point**]

I tried to dance away from the bot, but it followed quickly. It fired its stun shot, and a moment later, my chest twitched and burned as tasers started impacting. Individually, one would have been fine, but together, they were too much. My muscles spasmed and I fell to the ground.

[**HP 3/7**]

As the machine closed in and its knife revved, the stun-shot's pain eased, then stopped. I picked myself up and started running.

[**Gritty Recovery! +1 Grit Point**]

The machine breathed down my neck. Metaphorically, I mean. It didn't breathe, obviously. It would either be a long run to the Mister Felsic statue . . . or a short one. It didn't have turning issues like LABRAT did while flying. It didn't have a speed issue like the FEAR Power Armor. And my [**Spotlight Strike**] hadn't accomplished much.

What the hell was it doing with a vibrating knife, anyway? Didn't they know this wasn't *serious?*

No. This *was* serious. This was a minor-league Episode, and a vibrating knife was the *least* I'd deal with in those. The henchmen had guns, the villains aimed to kill, and the stakes were higher. One mistake and the whole city could—

The robot's footsteps stopped.

I looked back over my shoulder, threw myself over a concrete bench, and hit the ground on the other side with a thud. A split second later, the Gatling taser whirred and popped. The tasers clattered against the concrete bench, buzzing.

Then, as quickly as the cannon had fired, it stopped.

I started running again as soon as I heard its feet thudding on flagstones. It closed in, then stopped. I looked for cover as the Gatling gun began to whir.

I dove into a tangle of branches and twigs, half swimming into it. A taser hit me, then another, but most ricocheted or tangled in the bush's branches. It *hurt*, but I didn't spasm out.

[**HP 2/7**]

I had to take cover twice more before I finally got to the Mister Felsic statue—once behind a giant stone ball near the quad's edge and once behind the pillars at the statue itself. As the tasers stopped hissing and spitting, I dashed down the ramp.

The double doors slammed shut behind me. I kept running, expecting the machine to bash through the door any second. But it didn't. It just stood at the top of the ramp, unmoving. Its red glow had faded, too. I took a deep breath and cracked the door, expecting it to move or fire its Gatling tasers or rev its vibrating blade or . . . anything, really.

It did nothing.

I took three panting breaths, hands on my knees and eyes on the robot. I had no idea why it had stopped, but I didn't have time to investigate. The rest of the TUSSA team needed help, and I knew it was up to me to save the day. That's what heroes did. So, once I'd caught my breath, I started jogging down the tunnel.

[End of Act One! Act Two in Five Minutes! No Skill Rolls Available!]
[Alias - Understudy] [Archetype - Magical Girl] [Community Rank - 449/523]
[HP 2/7]
[Styles and Skills]
▶ Archetype Skill - Transformation Sequence
▶ Badass (49)
▶ Cunning (51)
▶ Inkling 1
▶ Drama (54)
▶ Stellar Ray 1
▶ Flamboyance (37)
▶ Signature Skill - Adaptive Armoire 1
▶ Stored Costumes: (Rainy Day)
▶ Flickerform 1
▶ Spotlight Strike 1
▶ Grit (17)
▶ Rejuvenation 1

[Grant Building Dogpile: Act Two Beginning]

Fursona lay on my chaise lounge. They looked up at me. "Did you win already? I knew it was a dogpile, but that's *fast!*"

"No. It was a trap. They . . ." I paused and took a deep, shaky breath. "They had robots and minor-league villains waiting for us. I don't know how they knew we were coming or if they just reacted when we went inside, but they took out Milo and Hephaestus and Grapple before I ran and—"

"Slow down," Fursona said. They stood up and started pacing. "Which villains?"

"Tearjerker and Iron Fist. Iron Fist chased Springlock, and Tearjerker and some of the robots were beating up the others. The TUSSA team's front line got wiped out, and no one could handle the bots. This is bad. It's really bad." I explained about the bots, too, and how lethal they seemed.

Fursona nodded. "Yeah, it's not good. Is the Episode still running?"

I checked. "Yeah. We're in Act Two now."

"Then it's not over yet. Someone's still fighting back."

"Probably Springlock."

"We need a plan," Fursona said. "We can't just burst in there and start fighting."

"You're right." I breathed again and sat down. "Alright, they have Iron Fist. He's a Badass-stacking Bruiser—like Theseus, but with more experience—so we can't fight him one-on-one. And Tearjerker. She's a one-trick-pony Drama villain, but we can't counter her. Wait. Springlock countered her during the Orientation Episode. That must be why Iron Fist went after her. And they have the dog bots with the tasers and blades."

"Yep. You could counter those with Lab Assistant—"

"No. I can't. And even if I could, I don't have it equipped." I groaned. "Look, there should be two bots left unless the one chasing me started up again. Two isn't so bad."

"Two with supervillain backup, Understudy." Fursona stood up, tail swishing agitatedly, and I looked at Tails. Her tails were doing the same thing.

"What?"

<I think you're wrong. There's a way to get the Lab Assistant Panic Costume, and you're ready to use it meow.>

I groaned. But whatever the villains were up to, it wasn't good for Tokyexico University. Heck, a minor-league Episode could easily hurt the whole city. That was bigger than me not wanting to think about Peter.

"Fine. Tails thinks she can get me the Lab Assistant Panic Costume. How?"

<Follow meow!> Tails took off for the door to Rocko's studio, and I groaned again. But I grabbed the goggles and followed as her plushie body slid across the floor and bumped into the door.

[Welcome to Rocko's studio. System Disabled. Now arriving Backstage.]

I winced, anticipating Rocko's shouted greeting. But it didn't come. Instead, the Ilneat producer stared at us from behind their desk. "Understudy, what are you doing here?"

I started to explain, but they cut me off before I could, blowing cigar smoke from their nose. "I know *why* you're here. Let's start over. Aaaaaayyy! Understudy! What do you want? You're in the middle of an Episode. I've been watching, and you've gotta do better than *that*!" His tone was *not* encouraging. Frustration boiled off of them just like it rolled off me.

"I know."

"I mean, you wanna be a minor leaguer? This is what it's like, kiddo." Rocko shook their head frustratedly and put their cigar out on their desk. "The only *good* news is that this disaster's not on us. Phil and Lil get this flop."

"Tails thinks we can turn it around. We just—"

"*How* are you going to turn this around?"

"I don't *know*!" I shouted, slumping into a chair. "Tails thinks we can, but we need your help! I need Lab Assistant Panic, but you can't switch powers mid-Episode!"

"You need my help? Well, that's all you had to say," Rocko said, rolling their eyes. "So here's the deal. I'll make some phone calls, pull some strings, and get the System to cooperate. You've got a great reconciliation storyline coming to terms with the breakup, which counts for a lot with the Style System—lots of Drama. If you *did* turn this around, it'd be great for Phil and Lil, but that's not bad for us. They don't compete in the little leagues, so a solid guest star appearance in the minors helps us."

The Ilneat sat down. "Pataki! Get Fursona's suit back in shape! Fursona, you're out of the fight for Act Two, but the damage is mostly from an Episode that's over, so we can fix you up. Understudy, go . . . watch the Episode or something. I'm busy."

"Fine. Thanks, Rocko," I said, pushing my anger down. My hands were balled into fists; Rocko could be so *frustrating*, and everything was about money with them.

The TV in the corner played a feed from the "Grant Building Dogpile" Episode, unedited and raw. The drone followed Iron Fist, who looked a little worse for wear, as he searched for Springlock in the machine shops. He poked his head around the corner, then pulled back as a drill bit rocketed toward him.

So, at least one hero was still fighting. If Rocko could pull off whatever movie studio mumbo-jumbo they were working on, and I could get Lab Assistant Panic back . . .

. . . well . . .

. . . I had an inkling of a plan.

56

An Inkling of a Plan

Do you want the good news or the bad news first, Understudy?" Rocko asked.

"Good news, please." I tore my eyes from the TV. Sara-N-Dipity was still up, too. As Milo had said, she couldn't fight her way out of a wet paper bag, but she kept predicting the pursuing bot's every move. She'd hidden in a wind tunnel lab in the Applied Sciences wing.

"You can swap out Rainy Day for Lab Assistant Panic, but you're gonna miss all of Act Two. Between the time to figure that out and Fursona's fursuit repairs, the heroes could escape or the vils could wipe them out before you get there."

They handed me a bottle of water—my third—and I opened it and downed it gratefully. I'd *never* spent this long in Rocko's studio before. Sweat dripped down my forehead, and I resisted the urge to check my armpits. Bee might've gone for it in the pizza line, but Magical Girl Understudy had to be dignified.

"Great. Can we get going, then?"

"Yeah, yeah." Rocko escorted me to the door, where we met Pataki and a much-less-singed Fursona. The Ilneat film executive nodded at us. "Hey, if you *do* get a win here, make sure you say something about *Heroics 101*. It'll be good advertising."

I gave him a thumbs-up and smiled. It felt fake and weak. We had everything we needed—or at least everything we could *use*—to win the Episode. But as we stepped through the door, I kept staring at the goggles.

[System Enabled]

"What's the plan, Understudy?" Fursona asked.

I hesitated. Then I took a deep breath. "I need to be Lab Assistant Panic. But I don't know if I can hold it."

"What do you mean?"

"I usually start a ways toward a full-on villainous breakdown, so I don't stay in the LAP Costume for long. But I'm going to have to *be* Lab Assistant Panic. And I'm . . . probably closer to a breakdown than I was before Professor Panic and I broke up, so it'll be hard." I took another, even deeper breath. "I'm going to need you to be ready to fight me."

Fursona looked as hesitant as a kangaroo fursuit could. "Have you ever had a breakdown before?" they asked.

"Yes, just after I got the Costume. I kind of destroyed Riverside's downtown." I *really* didn't want to do this. "Just . . . be ready."

"You got it, Understudy."

I sighed, took a deep breath, and shut my eyes. Then I pulled the goggles on. "EVERYONE STOP! THE LAB ASSISTANT'S BACK!
TIME FOR THE GENIUS TO START HER ATTACK!"

I spun, the lab coat whipping against my legs. As the transformation finished, my stomach clenched. I hadn't *really* focused on using the LAP Costume before our breakup, and now that we weren't together anymore, it'd probably be that much harder to use.

[Rejuvenation Activated: HP 5/7]

Shockingly, though, I felt pretty much in control. I opened my eyes. Fursona was staring at me. So was TA-1LZ. But other than my stomach rolling at the thought of *wearing* Peter's goggles, things felt mostly stable.

"Ahahahaha! Sorry. TA-1LZ. Breakdown check?" Mostly.

"37%. It's shockingly low, considering your previous performances. However, I predict that using your—"

"Good enough! Let's roll," I interrupted. "We've got a campus to conq—er, save."

"Understudy, are you sure you can do this?" Fursona asked. The modulator wobbled with concern.

"I'm fine! Better than fine. I'm *alive*, and the campus is my oyster. Just remember the plan, okay?"

"Yeah, uh-huh. Fight you if you go crazy until you transform out. Understudy, I'm not so sure about this. I don't know if I can beat you, and I don't know if you can stay in control, and honestly? What's the worst that happens if we lose this Episode? It's just one Episode."

[End of Act Two! Act Three in Five Minutes! No Skill Rolls Available!]

"It's not just one Episode. It's what we've been waiting for! A chance to prove we belong in the minor leagues, and we are *not* missing it just because you're nervous," I said. "Now, let's get going. I have a shiny new power set to play with!"

Fursona kept glancing at me as we rode the elevator down to the tunnels. I didn't see why. I felt *great*. My stomach wouldn't stop churning, and I wanted to take Peter's goggles off, but aside from those minor inconveniences, I was ready to make my mark on campus.

"TA-1LZ. Odds of victory?"

"Calculating." The robot cat hummed as we started jogging down the tunnel. "Odds of victory are 13%. If your plan works, that percentage will jump to 27%, increasing if Springlock and Sara-N-Dipity are willing to follow the plan and decreasing to less than 1% if they think you're a villain. I calculate a draw at 25%, 42%, and less than 1%, respectively."

[Grant Building Dogpile: Act Three Beginning]

"Showtime!" I burst out of the tunnel and stared at the unmoving dog-bot. Its cannon didn't even track me as I walked around it. I shook my head pityingly. Whoever designed these hadn't fixed the limited range control problem. Peter had solved it with the Panic Pal 1.1 model. "Oh well. More dog-bot for me!"

[Speed Hack] wasn't very powerful; it was only level 0. But it'd be enough if the bot's controller wasn't in range. For a few moments, my goggles filled with ones and zeros. Then the bot's red lights flickered pink.

[Good Thinking! +1 Cunning Point]

I grinned. "Alright, Pink Panther, back to the Grant Building! We're saving our minions and conquering the Student Supervillain Society once and for all!"

"Understudy, recalculations show an increase in breakdown to 52%. Recommendation: switch Costumes back to Understudy."

"Not happening, TA-1LZ," I said. I pointed back toward Weber Quad. "If we lose the bot, our odds of success drop back to, what'd you say? 13%? Not acceptable. And I'll do whatever it takes to win."

"Just be judicious in your power use."

"I don't think this is a good idea," Fursona said.

"Okay, I'll be careful."

"Who are you talking to? Me or your cat?"

"Uh, yes."

The dog-bot strode across the Weber Quad toward the TUEAS Building, and I jogged to follow it. A few student Extras, curious about the robot and brave—or stupid—enough to risk it, had reeled up some of the taser shots' wires. They looked at the robot and clearly powerful villainess and started running.

I let them flee. I had bigger fish to fry than a handful of insignificant Extras.

The bot crashed back through the twisted steel-and-glass doors, with me just a step behind. I had enough time to reflect on the déjà vu feeling before Fursona hopped through the doors, too. "Where are Sara and Springlock and the rest of the team?"

"They probably got captured." I shrugged and headed straight for the stairs. "We'll check for—"

WHAM!

A metal bench catapulted out of the engineering wing's doors. It knocked me off my feet and into a plexiglass wall.

[HP 4/7]
[Gritty Recovery: +1 Grit Point]

As I picked myself up, the dog-bot sprinted toward Springlock, Fursona in hot pursuit. "Springlock, stop!" they yelled futilely, rounding a corner just behind the dog-bot, which opened fire with its tasers.

"Shit," I muttered, picking myself up and dusting off my lab coat. If the bot attacked Springlock, one of them would lose. Either way, I'd lose the Episode shortly after that. Peter *must* have built some way to control his Panic Pals in these damn goggles. Maybe I could use it to call off the dog-bot.

I peered into the goggles' corners and found a simple set of commands. Attack, Defend, Scout, and Patrol didn't seem helpful right now, but Stand Down looked promising. Three others—Seek, Point-to-Point, and Overdrive—were all grayed out with a number under each: 1, 3, and 5, respectively. I smiled a devilish smile and selected Stand Down. My plan was coming together.

"Villainous breakdown increased to 58%," TA-1LZ said.

The bot clomped back, with Fursona scolding it. I laughed. Heroes were so stupid! Then I took a cautious step into the engineering wing, hands up like I was surrendering. I wasn't. It was all a trap for Springlock.

And it worked. A minute passed, and Springlock stepped out of one of the labs. Her blue bodysuit sported a big tear on one arm, and her helmet was dented.

She pointed at the steel crate she'd suspended behind her, ready to launch, then pointed off to the side, then at the floor in front of her.

I remembered *that* one from the barbecue, and I walked over until I stood a couple of feet from her. She held a hand in front of her face, fingers spread, then repeated it.

I cleared my throat. She'd said lip-reading was tough at the barbecue. "We're winning this. Where's Iron Fist?"

Springlock shrugged, and I repeated the question. Springlock touched the side of her head and angled her palm toward me. Then she pointed back at the hall we'd come in through.

I nodded and walked the dog-bot to the stairwell. Then I looked at Springlock and Fursona. "I'm sending the dog-bot in first. Fursona, find the heroes and free them. Springlock, you and I are support for the bot and a distraction. Stay back."

She shook her head pointedly and made a mouth-closing signal with her hand, glaring at me. At me! This was my evil plan, and she needed to follow my lead, dammit. I thought about using my **[Maniacal Reveal]**, but I needed that for later.

Besides, she'd already disappeared down the stairs.

I selected Defend and followed her. The bot and Fursona dashed down behind me.

Springlock kicked open the first door, shook her head, and froze another bench. Then she threw it through the next door, which crashed in and hung, squeaking, from one hinge. Before she could rush through it, an identical bot to mine rushed *out* instead.

"Fursona, stick with the plan!" I screamed as another bot and Iron Fist rushed out. I counted to five as Fursona hopped down the hall. Then I started laughing. Maniacally.

"Ahahahahaha! I have a **[Maniacal Reveal]**, Iron Fist! Just by attacking, you've fallen into my trap! Even now, my lieutenant is freeing our minions. Soon—"

"Actually, I've got a **[Maniacal Reveal]** of my own," Tearjerker yelled from inside the door.

[Show-off! +1 Flamboyance Point]

"**[Beep!]** Shit, shit, shit!" Tearjerker had **[Maniacal Reveal]**, which must've been powerful enough to override my own. I'd *never* had that happen before, and I made a note to ask Rocko or TA-1LZ about it later.

[Rating Warning #1! Episode Rating - PG-13! Limited Censor in Effect]

"The reveal is me! I'm the reveal! Ahahaha!" She pointed at me, ready to make me cry uncontrollably again, but Springlock clobbered her in the face with a fake planter.

With all the **[Maniacal Reveals]** broken, Iron Fist roared and chased after Fursona. Hopefully, her head start would let her find the heroes before Iron Fist found her. Springlock tried to close the gap to Tearjerker, but before she could, the red dog-bot fired its Gatling taser, and the blue-suited heroine had to duck and dodge instead.

I gave my pink dog-bot the order to Attack. It complied, though it flashed red briefly as it did. I paused, concerned. Was that going to be a problem?

Not right away, at least.

The pink bot slammed into the red one, disrupting its Gatling taser and stabbing with its vibrating blade. Springlock also piled in against the bot, throwing chairs, a backpack, and herself at it. And Tearjerker started retreating.

That didn't work for me. I charged up my **[Hypercompression Cannon]**. *BANG!*

[Dramatic Damage! +1 Drama Point]

My airburst slammed into Tearjerker, knocking her to the ground, but a red glow filled the room and hallway before she could get up.

"I'll never stop 'til I've won, and I'll step over any too weak to stop me. My minions will crush TUSSA, take over the university, and propel me into the major leagues. This I swear!"

I froze as my pink bot's glow flickered, then faded. A moment later, it flashed, glowing a brilliant scarlet. I couldn't see the newcomer, but I recognized an oath when I heard one.

Was the "dealer" a Dark Magical Girl?

57

Dark Magical Girl

Thanks for bringing my bot back," the mysterious Dark Girl said. As she stepped over Tearjerker, I got a good look at her. Just like the goth villainess on the ground, she wore fishnets, a red skirt and black top, and a more-than-healthy dose of mascara. But instead of black, black, and more black, a reddish glow surrounded her like a halo around the sun.

I stepped back, away from the newcomer. Springlock did, too. Both bots were much worse for wear after their duel with each other. *My* bot's blade had bent, and its Gatling taser spun uselessly. Its plating was dinged and dented, but not as badly as the other. Its front leg—not the one with the blade, but the other one—had shattered, and it staggered as it tried to turn to face us. Both bots were also tangled in taser wires.

I laughed maniacally despite myself. "Yorkston Robotics wouldn't be proud. My ex could do better than this!"

"Your ex is probably some worthless Extra," the Dark Girl said, almost spitting.

I had a choice to make. We could fight, obviously. We'd almost certainly need to. But the longer I could stall before that fight, the more time my lieutenant had to free the "heroes" and turn the tables. And I needed those heroes if I wanted to win.

"Alright, you've got me. He's just some Extra from back home," I lied. "These bots are quite something, though. Did you build them yourself?"

"No. I didn't even design them. Our dumbass supplier said they were finished, but they wouldn't start. I had to use—"

"Enough, Anima! If you tell them more, I'll make you remember when Damian broke up with you," Tearjerker interrupted, picking herself up. "Now, let's deal with these two!"

Springlock's eyes were locked on the two bots. The moment one of them moved, she threw a soda vending machine at them. It clobbered *my* bot, sending it skittering into the room and blocking the door with its bulk.

With one bot and both supervillains stuck in the room, Springlock held one hand out and stabbed under it with the other pointer finger. When I shrugged, she froze a bench and pointed at the remaining bot.

It didn't have a Gatling taser anymore, and it wasn't fast, but it was coming right at *me*. I started running as the bench caught the bot's back leg. Then I turned and aimed at its damaged front leg.

BANG!

[Dramatic Damage! +1 Drama Point]

With two legs damaged, I cheered. But my victory was somewhat dampened.

"Villainous breakdown percentage is at 80%, Understudy," TA-1LZ reported.

"80%? How'd it get that high? That's unacceptable!" I shouted. If it kept climbing, I'd have to switch—either Costumes or sides—and I needed **[Speed Hacker]** to turn things around.

Or did I? I wasn't sure I really did. Dark Girl Anima's power seemed to override my **[Speed Hacker]**; either it wasn't powerful enough, or her power ignored it. I tried to take over the badly damaged bot. If I could just **[Speed Hack]** it for a couple of seconds . . .

[Good Thinking! +1 Cunning Point]
[Playing with Powers Beyond Comprehension! +1 Drama Point]
[Warning: Red Rover Antivirus Activated!]

It felt like a dog biting my nose. I screamed and tore the Lab Assistant Panic goggles off, whirling as the bot flickered briefly pink, then went entirely red. My eyes watered, and I squeezed them shut and rubbed to get the tears out.

[HP 3/7]

CRASH!

The bot inside the room slammed into the vending machine, sending what glass hadn't shattered when it got tossed spraying into the hall. "Alright! Everyone freeze!" Tearjerker yelled.

"**[Beep!]** that, Tears. I'm kicking their asses!" Anima said. The vending machine gave way, and *my* bot thumped into the hall. I went for **[Hypercompression Cannon]** again.

BANG!

The golden bot froze for a second, knocked back by the wave of compressed air. It also tossed the two villains back since there wasn't anywhere for them to dodge in the narrow doorway.

[Dramatic Damage! +1 Drama Point]
[Dramatic Damage! +1 Drama Point]
[Dramatic Damage! +1 Drama Point]

I grinned as the notifications came in. Then I yelped. Springlock pulled on a handful of my sleeve, dragging me away from the door and the two bots. She dragged me off-balance just as a blade buzzed over my head, missing by inches. I watched it slice a lock of hair free.

"Let me go! We were winning!" I yelled, but of course, she couldn't hear me. Even if she could, I doubted she'd stop dragging me, so I activated [**Hometown Heroine**]. She was *ruining* my plan, and I was *going* to fight back.

I mean, I was.

But then, a fresh robot pushed through the door behind Anima and Tearjerker, and I gave up on *that* plan. We'd have to stall until Fursona freed the rest of the TUSSA assault team. She was an unwilling lieutenant for my evil plans but a competent underling.

Springlock half dragged me up the stairs, Tails following behind. I ran too, but I looked over my shoulder in case there was another window to use [**Speed Hacker**]. But it wasn't any use; Dark Girl Anima was too close to the bots, and her [**Red Rover Antivirus**] was too aggressive for my hacks. "It's not fair! Real antivirus isn't anywhere near that good," I whined to no one.

Springlock ran around a corner, let go of me momentarily, and pointed back toward the oncoming villains. She made a finger gun with her pointer and middle finger. I nodded and charged up my [**Hypercompression Cannon**].

BANG!

[Dramatic Damage! +1 Drama Point]

The shot caught an off-balance, badly damaged robot, throwing it backward. Before I could celebrate, Springlock dashed into an open classroom in the Applied Sciences wing. I followed her, and we clicked the door shut.

A second later, I heard the first bot clatter and whir around the corner. I pointed at the door and put my finger over my lips. I had no idea if that was even a sign, but I'd always used it for "quiet" or "silent," and I didn't have anything better. When this was over, and I'd won, I would force Springlock and Milo to teach me to sign.

"Understudy, you're at 93%. I recommend you switch back now," TA-1LZ whispered in my ear. I shook my head. If the villains didn't know where we were, I could turn this around, but *only* if I could use my Lab Assistant Panic powers.

I kept my hand on Springlock's arm until the sound of the robot's servos faded around the corner. Without the bot, TA-1LZ had said we had a 13% chance of a win. Then I ran to the whiteboard. Springlock followed me. She grabbed a marker.

'What's ur plan?'

'Fursona saves the others. They beat Iron Fist. We fight the villainesses and bots together and win.'

'Thats it?'

'Lab Assistant Panic hacks a bot and evens things out. But Anima . . .'

'Yeah. Anima powers inanimate objects. If she's gotta do it the bots don't work. Incomplete? Broken? No power? Dunno.'

'Makes sense. Bot ran out of energy at Felsic statue'

'Anima is key. Take her down fast'

'Got it'

We walked back to the door. I pressed my ear against it. A bot's messed up leg scraped against the tile floor, and it was getting louder. That meant they were getting closer. I nodded toward Springlock, held up a hand, and started counting down.

Five. Springlock froze a desk.

Four. I tensed next to the door.

Three. The bot passed by, foot scraping. Another bot's joints whirred behind it.

Two. I heard footsteps in the hall.

One.

As I opened the door, Springlock shot the desk through toward Tearjerker. It caught the villain in the shoulder, knocking her over.

"That wasn't the plan," I muttered as I ducked through the entry. We were supposed to take out Dark Girl Anima. Instead, she was focused on Tearjerker! Well, if she wasn't sticking to the plan, I would.

The Dark Magical Girl looked shocked as I charged her. She started to say something, but I spun and kicked her in the stomach. She doubled over momentarily, then stood straight as I tried to punch her in the face.

[Stylish Strike! +1 Flamboyance Point]

"You . . . you punched me in the tit!" Dark Girl Anima looked at me incredulously. "What the hell?"

"Uh, sorry?"

"[Energy Beam]!"

Anima threw herself into the air, sending a wavering beam of crimson light at me from the red teardrop symbol on her dress. It washed over me, burning like acid. I rolled to avoid it, but it stopped almost as quickly as it had started.

[HP 2/7]

As Anima pointed at one of the bots, I took stock.

To my left, Springlock had pretty much finished off Tearjerker, but two bots had closed in on her. One of the damaged bots—the one Anima was giving orders to—stomped toward me. I couldn't use my Lab Assistant Panic powers; I needed to take over a bot to have a chance, and I couldn't do that if Anima was still conscious.

And I couldn't switch back to Understudy for *actual* combat powers. It'd take too long. I only had seconds before the bot attacked.

As it closed in, I rolled away from it. My roll took me right under Dark Girl Anima, so I did the only thing I could think of. I kicked her in the shin.

"**[Beep!]**" Anima crashed to the ground, and I rolled on top of her, pinning her between my legs and sitting on her stomach. I punched her in the nose, then in the wrist when she got a hand between her face and my fist. She tried to use her energy beam, but I hit her again before she could get the words out.

[Badass Brawler! +1 Badass Point]

The bot clomped and whirred closer. It was the fresh one, still armed with a Gatling taser and vibrating blade. I felt the red heat pouring off of it, more than should be there in an electric engine.

I punched Anima again. This time, she punched back, and I struggled to pin her arms so she'd *stop*. I had to get away from the bot. No. I had to stop Anima so I could hack it.

[Badass Brawler! +1 Badass Point]
[HP 1/7]
[Gritty Recovery! +1 Grit Point]

Something hit me from behind, and I screamed in agony. My shoulder was on fire—no, my whole arm was on fire—as the blade vibrated deeper. The bot pushed me off of Dark Girl Anima. Its Gatling taser whirled as it prepared to blast me in the face.

[HP 0/7]

A hero leaped over my head—something red and white, with cloth that flapped in the wind. Another figure in a purple super-suit ran up, pushing me off Anima and pinning me to the ground, even as a green-clad super took over my job of punching Anima in the face.

I relaxed for a moment, even though Grapple had me pinned better than Gourmet in the weight room. Fursona had come through! I couldn't wait to enact Phase Two of my evil plan and depose that idiot pretender, Monologue!

"Understudy, you're at 99%! You need to switch back immediately!" TA-1LZ yowled, running up to me on metal legs.

Oh. Shit.

Grapple let up on his pin, and I half whirled free. I spun on the floor as I rattled off my ridiculous oath. "Never fear. Magical Girl Understudy is here!"

I didn't know if I'd be able to finish before the breakdown—or before Grapple got a hold of me again!

58

Got a Hold of Me Again

I woke up in a room . . . somewhere—I didn't know where, but there weren't any windows, and a fluorescent light hummed on the ceiling. My arms weren't tied to the chair or anything, but the door was locked when I checked it. I banged on it a little. "Hey! Hey, I'm in here!"

No one answered.

I was Magical Girl Understudy again. Tails sat on the floor next to my chair, which I flopped back into. If the villains had won, I was their prisoner under the Grant Building. And if the heroes had won, was I their prisoner in the TUSSA Cave?

"H-Hi Tails," I said. My voice cracked slightly, and I wished I'd kept one of Rocko's water bottles. "Did we . . . win?"

<Sort of. It's hard to tell right meow,> Tails replied from her place on the floor. <TUSSA won. Fursona caught Iron Fist after they freed the assault team when he ran into them on their way back to us. Neither Dark Girl Anima nor Tearjerker could stand up to Punch, Grapple, Springlock, and Milo; the robots couldn't hold them off either. TUSSA wasn't in any shape to check out the lair, though. That place had Genius written all over it, and they never have untrapped lairs.>

"So if they won, we won, right?" I asked.

<Nya. You were a villain at the Episode's end, and Lab Assistant Panic's plan didn't work. Or, more accurately, it could have worked if you hadn't lost control. We're waiting for TUSSA to finish their end-of-Episode camera talk; then we'll see what the System thinks.>

"Oh." That made a lot of sense. I'd never *finished* an Episode as Lab Assistant Panic, so maybe getting knocked out as Lab Assistant Panic counted as a loss. After all, my faction wasn't TUSSA when I was a villain, and it definitely wasn't the SSS.

Screw those guys.

While I waited for the end-of-Episode message, I debated what to do with Lab Assistant Panic. She was too dangerous to keep around. I'd had delusions of grandeur the entire Episode, from the moment I changed into her until the end. I hadn't *acted* on them while I had control, but I still didn't know what I'd tried to do after. Plus, the thought of it reminded me of Peter. I fidgeted in my seat while waiting for someone to tell me what was happening.

The only good news was that I was TUSSA's prisoner, *not* the SSS's. Who knew what those villains would've done with me?

No, I thought as I twiddled my thumbs and waited. Lab Assistant Panic *was* dangerous. But the Costume had special powers. Powers I needed access to. So I couldn't get rid of it. I just couldn't use it all the time. I needed a way to turn it off quickly.

A camera drone hovered in front of me, and I grinned half-heartedly. "Hi, fans. Remember, it's *Heroics 101* to do what you have to do to stop the bad guys! Just don't get your friends and neighbors hurt to do it, okay? Lab Assistant Panic is a bad example." That ought to make Rocko happy.

[Episode Finished!]
[Investigative Episode: Grand Building Dogpile - PG-13]
[Penalties: 1x Rating Warnings - No Penalty]
[Episode Finished! +3 of each Style Point]
[No Decision! +2 of each Style Point]
[Role Focus: Cunning+Drama - Goal Met! +10 Focused Style Points]
[Alias - Understudy] [Archetype - Magical Girl] [Community Rank - 440/523]
[HP 4/7]
[Styles and Skills]
▶ Archetype Skill - Transformation Sequence
▶ Badass (56) (Skill Roll Available)
▶ Cunning (68) (Skill Roll Available)
▶ Inkling 1
▶ Drama (26)
▶ Hometown Heroine 1
▶ Bit-Part Barrage 1
▶ Flamboyance (44)
▶ Signature Skill - Adaptive Armoire 1
▶ Stored Costumes: (Rainy Day)
▶ Flickerform 1
▶ Spotlight Strike 1
▶ Starwave Sail 1
▶ Grit (24)

Before I could roll my skills, the door opened. I groaned; I wanted to *know* what I'd gotten. But Springlock and Milo crowded into the room. She glared at me briefly, rubbing her shoulder, and I winced. "What'd I do?"

Milo started interpreting as Springlock's hands flew. "You punched Grapple in the face. Then you shot me with an air cannon. Milo and Punch beat you up, and we dragged your ass here. You're in the TUSSA Cave. We need to talk about this Costume."

"Okay. What do you want to say?"

"That Costume—Lab Assistant Panic—is scary. If it gets too powerful, you'll get branded a villain."

"Yeah, but it gives me powers I can't get anywhere else. I thought about it, and I can't put it away for good, even if it's . . . bad for me."

"Just be careful," Milo interpreted for Springlock. "It's your decision, but understand the risks of letting that Costume get out of hand. In the meantime, we won! That means it's time to celebrate! TUSSA after-party!"

That last bit was all Milo; I could tell by Springlock's eyeroll and the smack to the arm he got. The two turned around and opened the door, nodding at Ikenga, who I hadn't realized was still standing there. He nodded back. "Welcome to the TUSSA Cave, Magical Girl Understudy. It's good to have you back."

"I've been here before," I protested. But the sheer noise from the rec room proved the lie in that statement. Hephaestus, the Tokyexico City Student Superhero Society's resident Genius, stood behind the bar, pouring an almost undoubtedly illegal drink for Punch. I'd drank back in my place with Bianca and before college with Peter, but this was a school function, wasn't it?

The Genius waved me over and handed me another illegal beer, which I accepted. Pulsing music echoed in the TUSSA Cave; a few heroes were pretending to dance, but most were standing around talking about their favorite Episodes. I avoided both the dance floor and the various conversations. Something felt off. Like eyes were on me. Distrustful ones.

Fursona sat in front of the *Ms. Pac-Man* game, fiddling with the controls. They didn't have a beer. "Hey," I said.

"Hey." They ran from all the ghosts, but I didn't see how they could escape without power-up circles. Sure enough, the ghosts caught up, cornered Ms. Pac-Man, and ate the yellow circle's last life. "Damn, I was so close to a high score!"

"Are we good?" I wasn't sure.

"Yeah, we're good. I almost high-scored, but you didn't distract me or anything," Fursona said. They looked at my face. "Oh, about the Episode? Maybe we should come up with plans in your Understudy Costume. It was a good idea to send me after the prisoners, but I *really* cut it close with Iron Fist, and I didn't have any backup, and there's no way I could fight him one-on-one. He's way stronger than Theseus, and that guy wrecked me."

I winced. I'd learned from the knife that in the minor leagues, the weapons hit harder—much harder than even in the Orientation Episode. That whole Episode must've been toned down a bunch. Maybe even to little-league levels. I'd put my sidekick—my friend—in the path of a full-blown minor-league villain and just left her there.

Peter had been completely wrong when he told me I couldn't be a villain. I definitely could be.

"Hey! Underoos!" I looked over my shoulder as Punch walked up with Grapple in tow. Both were bruised, with dust and grime still covering parts of their Costumes. More importantly, neither looked happy. Punch felt downright hostile, while Grapple looked more apologetic.

Punch downed his beer and crushed the red Solo cup in one hand. "*Your* plan got us caught. *Your* Costume almost got us all the loss. What the hell gives you the right to call the shots? You're lower than *us* on the rankings!"

"Hey, chill," Fursona said, standing up from their spot at the *Ms. Pac-Man* machine. "Understudy didn't come up with the plan. She just gave the information to Ikenga, and *he* came up with it."

"Yeah, but she's a villain!"

"No, she's not."

"Punch, I don't think she is," Grapple started, but a look from Punch shut him up. I could *feel* the irritation pouring off Punch, like a hot wind.

I looked over at Milo and Springlock, looking for backup, but they were busy at the pool table. I gulped. I was on my own. "I got the plans from *your* teammates in Superpower Ethics. Flare and The Crumb. You heard the same plan I heard from Ikenga, but he didn't *see* the robots in there until it was too late."

"Whatever, Underoos. I'll be seeing you around." Punch spat on the floor and stalked off.

"Hey, good hit back there. You're no Punch, but if he gets over this, maybe he could teach you how to really do it, Underoos." Grapple grinned a stressed-out grin and followed his twin.

"Don't listen to them. They're just upset you turned the Episode around, and they couldn't," Fursona said. "Why don't you finish your—"

"Nah, I'm heading back to my place," I interrupted them before they could continue. "I'm tired of all this."

"Alright. I'll walk you to the elevator in case someone's revenge minded."

"The boys? They won't do anything." I stomped toward the TUSSA Cave's door, leaving my drink behind. "But thanks."

We walked through the tunnels in silence. Fursona kept clearing their throat awkwardly, like they were dying to say something, but then they'd fall silent again.

After the fourth time, I turned toward them. "What?"

"Nothing. Sorry. I just . . . never mind." They shoved their hands into their kangaroo pocket. "Sorry."

"Fine." We got to the elevator, and I climbed on. "I'll see you in class Wednesday, yeah?"

"Yeah," Fursona said. Then they paused. "Shit. We missed our afternoon classes."

"I'm not worried about that. I'm crushing mine."

"Yeah. Me too." The elevator door started closing as Fursona waved.

I rode up quietly and then sat down on my couch. I had two skill rolls, and I'd get to them soon. But not right away. I was too stressed out about Punch and Grapple's anger, even though they'd probably cool down soon. And about something else. Something was bugging me about the Episode, but it took me a few minutes to put my finger on it. It was the bots.

They weren't Peter's style, but Dark Girl Anima had said she wasn't the supplier. I had to know for sure. I pulled out my phone and looked at the last message in my texts with Peter. I'd been asking him if he was on his way to our video call. He'd never responded.

I gulped, squeezed my eyes shut for a second, then opened them and started typing.

<Hey Peter. Checking in. How've things been? - Annie 4:14>

While I waited, I untransformed and stepped through the door to my apartment. The algebra book was sitting on my coffee table; I swore under my breath and started working on one of the problems Su-Bin had shown me how to do.

<What do you want? Skip the small talk - Professor Panic 4:19>

I sighed, heart pounding. So that was how it was going to be? He wasn't anywhere near as over this as I was if he couldn't even text with me as Peter. Shit.

<Just got done with an Episode. Some robots glowed red. - Understudy 4:20>
<Do you know anything about that? - Understudy 4:21>
<Why would I know anything about that? - Professor Panic 4:21>
<You're pretty untrusting sometimes - Professor Panic 4:21>
<It's not me - Professor Panic 4:22>
<Is there anything else? If not, stop wasting my time - Professor Panic 4:22>
<No. Thanks. Bye - Understudy 4:24>

I put my phone away and grabbed Tails. I hated to think it, but it was a relief that Peter wasn't the mysterious robot supplier. I hadn't *really* thought he was, but I'd had to be sure.

[50 Badass Credits Used. Rolling Skill!]
[50 Cunning Credits Used. Rolling Skill!]

The Episode was over, I'd plugged *Heroics 101*, and Peter had . . . well, not filled me with confidence, exactly, but at least it probably wasn't him. How would he get robots like *that* to Tokyexico City anyway?

[New Skill! Doom Ball: Get all your claws in on the beatdown, dealing massive damage to an opponent in melee.]
[Skill Upgrade! Inkling ▶ Check the Script: Forgot your lines? Check the script for a hint.]

PART SEVEN

59

Cramming

How can time move so fast *and* slow at the same time?" I muttered to myself, turning my phone screen off.

"What?" Su-Bin grabbed my math paper and shook her head. "No, bring the *x* across, not the *y*. The *y*'s got exponents, and it'll go negative, but if you isolate it, you can start breaking it down."

The late-November weather was so much colder than Riverside had ever been. Outside the Student Union Building's windows, a near-blizzard whipped snow up from the sidewalk and piled it in drifts. It felt like the semester was rocketing by; it'd *just* been sweater weather, or at least warm enough not to be miserably cold in an evening gown. Now I was bundled up, and even in layers, the wind outside had made my walk to history class painful.

I groaned and did as Su-Bin asked, checking my phone again—ten more minutes. Ten more stupid minutes of math time, then I could disappear back home, get changed, and brave the long, cold walk—or flight—to Superpower Ethics. I just had to survive math time with Su-Bin.

"Hey, how's the roommate?" I asked. It'd been a good subject change in the past.

"Fine."

"Fine? She hasn't been fine all year."

Su-Bin stared at my homework and nodded. "Now try that on the next problem. Decide whether to work on the *x* or *y* first, and explain why. Then you can try it. Veronica broke up with her boyfriend."

"They broke up?" I started working through the next problem.

"Yep! Now she just cries a bunch, like it's his fault she was a shallow bitch who was only dating him because he was a sports star or something. Serves her right. It's so much easier to fucking sleep when she's just sobbing or sniffling, though. I hope she stays single until after Christmas break."

"Uh-huh. Alright, so I'm going to work the *x* on this one?" I half asked.

"Why?"

"Because, uh, it doesn't have exponents?"

"Okay, go for it."

I started working on the math problem. But just as quickly, I realized I straight-up didn't care. Sure, finals were only a couple of weeks out. And yeah, Su-Bin had been super helpful in keeping me afloat in math. But it had been almost a month since the TUEAS dogpile Episode, and I hadn't heard anything about a TUSSA or SSS follow-up. TUSSA's lack of response wasn't surprising; Ikenga seemed, for the most part, like someone who wanted the status quo preserved—and was good at that.

But the SSS *had* to be up to something.

They'd lost the Episode, but their lair was still intact unless the minor-league heroes had gone back. I had a bad feeling the SSS wasn't done yet. But I couldn't mix it up with minor-league villains. Not by myself.

"Hey! Are you even trying anymore?" Su-Bin interrupted.

"No. My next class is on my mind," I said. "Sorry."

"It's fine. I've got my own studying to do, so when you're ready to listen, I'll help, but I can't spend time on you if you're daydreaming." Su-Bin stood up, gathering her tray. Her face didn't look angry, just matter-of-fact. I half sighed. At least she wasn't pissed at me.

I packed up my math book, dumped my dishes on the rollers, and bundled up for my walk home.

It was cold as hell. Honestly, that expression had never made sense to me, but it did now. It was so cold that the snowflakes almost burned as they melted on my cheeks. To distract myself, I thought more about my three builds.

I'd slotted [**Bit-Part Barrage**] into my Understudy build to give it more damage and a ranged option. As good as [**Stellar Ray**] was, I didn't need the consistency; I needed something burstier to close out fights, and if I was rotating between Lab Assistant Panic and Magical Girl Rainy Day, I wouldn't always have that option. I'd also added [**Starwave Sail**] in for [**Rejuvenation**].

I'd moved [**Check the Script**] over to Rainy Day, ditching [**Light as Vapor**], and grabbed [**Rejuvenation**] for [**Cloudy Disposition**]. [**Rejuvenation**] was too powerful to abandon, and I didn't need [**Light as Vapor**] if I was running [**Starwave Sail**] on Understudy.

I wasn't thrilled with how many of my Understudy abilities were Drama or Flamboyance, but I didn't have other options. [**Doom Ball**] didn't fit in at *all*, and without a decent Badass skill, I'd be relying on [**Spotlight Strike**] for melee damage, which wasn't quite the same power level as a full Badass power.

There was . . . one other thing on my mind. Tonight was Friday night, and that meant date night with Bianca. We were going to the sushi place my parents had taken me to if we could get off campus safely with all the snow.

The cold burned inside my nose, the kind of cold that felt dry and that made my nose bleed in the winter if it went too long. I was happy to duck inside Walnut Tower and board the elevator.

"Hey, Anika," Avan started as I pressed my floor's button.

"Not today. Got a date tonight," I said. It wasn't even a serious question anymore—just a game between him and me.

"Where are you two going?"

"Sushi, then back here." I shivered a little. "We're getting an early start; hopefully, we'll be done before the roads freeze too badly. If not, we'll figure it out."

"Alright. Have fun."

I transformed as soon as I stepped into my room, then jogged through the green room and up the stairs. I hadn't flown in a long time, and there was no way anyone would see me in this blizzard. "[**Starwave Sail**]!" The windsurfer materialized under my feet, and I zipped off toward the Mister Felsic statue, buffeted and battered by the storm.

"'Series Finale: Burning Curiosity!'" the announcer said, his voice echoing from the screen. The giant television showed Mister Felsic glaring at Mindstorm, who was wearing a lab coat. I winced. I hadn't seen this one, but when Mindstorm was an active villain, she'd been close to the perfect counter to most nonmeta/nonmind heroes.

Dr. Jackson cleared her throat as the opening credits started, muting the show. "There's one type of Episode where an ethics code is both more important than usual and much more likely to be abandoned. That's a series finale. How many of you have been through a series finale? Not a season, but a series."

Theseus raised his hand. So did Gourmet. And, shockingly, so did The Crumb.

"Just three this year? Okay. No introduction. No assignment on this one. Watch Mister Felsic and note where he struggles to maintain his code of ethics and where he overcomes incredible adversity. Don't worry about Dr. Mindstorm. At this point in her career, she only had one tenet: win."

The Episode started, and I glued myself to the screen. She was sneaking onto an old missile base; the Ilneats had conveniently added a ticking Geiger counter sound to show that it was still radioactive. With her were a handful of men and women in heavy-duty hazmat suits. They hurried past a mostly demolished sign labeled *Alpha-01: Lindburg*.

I'd heard of Alpha-01. It was a missile base just north of here. The base had come up in high school pre-Launch history classes during the Cold War lessons and in discussions about Launch Day. It had taken at least eight missiles during Launch Day, though most were airbursts and EMPs, and the Ilneat cleanup crews refused to touch it; anything past the fences was a hot zone.

Mindstorm didn't seem to care. After a moment inside, her skintight black-and-white leotard started sparking. So did her skin. She was using some power to shield herself. The camera passed in front of her, showing a bead of sweat. She was working hard. Then it hovered in front of one of the researchers, whose suit was labeled Matthew Franks. His eyes were swirling blue portals to nothing.

"Hey, Snack, the SSS told us you went vil," Gourmet said, leaning over and grinning.

I glared. "Nope. I have a Costume that's . . . antiheroic."

"That's what I thought, too." Gourmet took a bite from her apple. "But then I watched your Episode last night. You've got *it*, kid. The spark."

"No, I really don't." I tried to focus on the Episode onscreen instead of the one Gourmet wanted to talk about. Mister Felsic arrived. He was off camera, but the suddenly red screen and shaking cameras announced his presence all the same. A moment later, there he was: two lava-throwing gloves and a red-and-orange Costume on full display. He stopped at the gate and started coating himself in shining black obsidian.

The second he walked through the gate, the camera cut to Mindstorm. She and the research crew ran through a sequence of buttons and codes in one of the bunkers. One researcher—Matthew—kept flipping through binders. Some weren't marked with the radiation symbol but with a nasty-looking bio-weapon warning.

Then the whole bunker started rocking. Mindstorm waved. "Keep digging. We want any records from Launch Day. They *had* to have done something fishy. Even if they didn't, we need to know how they moved us all. *I* need to know how they did it. Such power . . ." She stalked down the hall toward the bunker's exit. The researchers didn't even flinch.

"Snack, Snack, Snack," Gourmet chided. "There's nothing wrong with giving in to your criminal urges. Just put on your pretty little lab coat, join up with the SSS, and—"

"Enough." Theseus snapped under his breath. "I'm trying to pass this damn class. Harass her on your own time."

That had to be the first time I'd felt grateful toward Theseus. I settled back in my chair and watched as the action picked up.

Shit hit the fan fast. Whatever the obsidian armor Mister Felsic was wearing did, one of the biggest advantages seemed to be resistance to Mindstorm's thought control. Not immunity; he tripped on nothing a few times and couldn't aim his lava jets correctly. The two fought back and forth, the ruins of buildings exploding around them and molten, cooling lava coating everything.

Eventually, though, an alarm went off inside. Klaxon sirens started wailing across the facility, though most only went off once or twice before petering out. The launch tubes' doors opened.

"Fuck, fuck, fuck!" Mindstorm yelled. The cameras following the two dueling major leaguers switched to a view of the four researchers. Three panicked as Mindstorm dropped her control, but Matthew Franks grabbed a double-armful of the bioweapon binders and started running not up, but down.

Mindstorm vanished. I knew one of her powers was to mentally *will* herself to be in another place. She landed in her secret lair, cursing. A camera drone had been waiting for her.

But Mister Felsic couldn't leave. He *wouldn't* leave. Instead, he started riding an eruption that weaved back and forth across the missile launch tubes. Whole feet of lava poured into the tubes, tearing at the ancient, worn-out fuel tubes. The timer ticked down to ten seconds, and the superhero started covering himself in layer after layer of molten rock. Then he stared into the camera. "Alright, super-fans. Remember to stay solidly on the side of good."

The lava covered his face.

The timer hit zero.

A white flash enveloped the camera drones, all except for one.

As the credits rolled, a man in a tattered hazmat suit limped out of the emergency shelter. He coughed as poisonous fuel fumes poured past his destroyed mask. The camera zoomed in on the half of his name tag that hadn't gotten destroyed. "Matt."

"Alright. Compare notes with your teams about what you saw, or work on cleaning up your codes. And in case you're worried, Mr. Felsic lived. He and Mindstorm both retired after this Episode, though. He wanted anonymity, and as part of Mindstorm's legal settlement for almost nuking the world *again*, she agreed to retire and go into teaching. And break!"

We worked on removing the parts of our code where we'd been arguing, fighting, or otherwise messing with each other. As we worked, I couldn't help but be distracted. The Episode stuck with me, and Gourmet kept bothering me even though both Theseus and Fursona were on my side; we needed to try to focus.

Code of Conduct: November 21
We will not involve Extras
When Extras must be involved, they must be clearly informed of danger
Destruction of non-corporate/non-government property is unacceptable
Property damage must be directly related to the Episode's goals
Medical Extras are off-limits. Healing heroes are not a target unless they directly engage
Neutrality will be respected
Finales?
We'll talk about those later.

The code was finalized, most of the way at least, when Dr. Jackson cleared her throat. "We'll meet two more times. Next Friday will be a workday to finalize your codes. I recommend you talk to other supers about things they wished they had on theirs. And the Friday after that, you'll present your codes and justifications to the class as your final assessment. We'll have a few Extras in attendance next Friday to review your codes from their perspective. I'll see you all next week."

I headed for the door, Fursona right behind me, and launched onto my **[Starwave Sail]**. I could hardly wait for Intro to Drama to end, because after that? After that was a sushi date!

But instead, I got a text.

<Hey Understudy, its Honey. I've got Jumper's next plan! - Honeycomb, 12:05>
<Be there or be . . . a hexagon? God, that's stupid - Honeycomb 12:06>

Shit, I thought as I typed a quick response and looked for Fursona. The sushi date would have to wait.

60

The Sushi Date
Would Have to Wait

<Gimme a minute - Understudy 12:07>

Well, shit. I looked around for Fursona, but the kangaroo was already hopping toward another building. We'd crammed an Episode between Superpower Ethics and Intro to Drama before, but . . .

<What's going on? What time? - Understudy 12:08>
<Multiple burglaries. All across the University district - Honeycomb 12:08>
<Should be kicking off soon. No casting call yet, but any minute. - Honeycomb 12:09>

Alright. Okay. I could do everything. I texted Fursona to get their butt back here, then hesitated, finger hovering over Bee's number.

<Hey, Bee. Some stuff came up. Might miss ItD - Annie 12:11>
<<3 you! See you after. If Im a minute or two later, sorries - Annie 12:12>
<Thats fine. Imma ditch it, too, then. No point if youre not there - Bianca 12:13>

Alright. My bases were at least a *little* covered. It felt wrong to put Bee off for superhero work, though. Almost like I was Peter. But . . . this was different, I just wasn't sure how. I twiddled my thumbs and waited for Fursona to show up. While I did, I texted Honeycomb again.

<Where? - Understudy 12:15>
<Corner store on Independent and University. I'll be there. Thanks - Honeycomb 12:16>

As soon as Fursona showed up, I explained what I knew. Which, admittedly, wasn't much. The kangaroo nodded thoughtfully. "So, we're going after Jumper again? What's different about this time? Other than that you'll be on the lookout for vans?"

"Honeycomb knows what's up, so hunting her down won't be as hard." I hurried toward Independent and University, wishing I could fly but not wanting to lose Fursona in the blinding snow. I glared at them; they were probably *warm* in that suit, and I was freezing my ass off in a dress and tights!

As we got close, a familiar message popped up.

[Casting Call]
[Episode: Short: Jumping from Crime to Crime - PG]
[Role: Backup! Do you accept the role? (Yes/No)]
[Role Focus: Flamboyance+Drama]

We accepted the [**Casting Call**] and arrived at the corner store tucked below some off-campus apartments. Honeycomb stood outside the store, shivering and rubbing her hands together. I waved. "Hey, Honeycomb. What's up?"

[**Short: Jumping from Crime to Crime: Act One in Progress**]

"Well, Jumper's making the rounds with S again. The buzz around town is that they've got a new van, and they're looking to fill it up with stuff. He's going to start, uh . . . Y'know what, I'll show you." Honeycomb started wiggling, her Costume's wings fluttering as she wiggled back and forth.

"What . . . what are you doing?"

"I'm . . . using my [**Bee Dance Map**] power," she replied, a little breathless and flushing red. "It lets . . . lets me *show* where things are instead . . . of trying to explain it."

"Ooookay." I waited for her to finish her dance, and oddly, a picture of the University District started to form in my mind. By the time it was over, I could "see" the buildings Honeycomb thought Jumper would hit.

"That's it." Honeycomb frowned. "The problem is that . . . I can't cover them all, and she moves faster than me."

"We can't make a great plan here. You stay near the Quik-Mart. Fursona, remember the art gallery?" The kangaroo nodded, and I continued. "Great. You're there. I'll circle above and try to spot the van or Jumper. The snow is going to be a problem, though."

"You don't have to tell me twice," Honeycomb said. They opened the Quik-Mart's door, then turned around. "Text if you see anything."

"Will do. [**Starwave Sail**]!" The windsurfer took off, with me on it, squinting against the snow. I had to stay low over the streets, but luckily, the weather was bad enough that most people weren't out and about. It wasn't long before I found what I was looking for.

<Got a white van heading your way Honey - Understudy 12:42>

<Copy that. You going to buzz it and see whos driving? - Honeycomb 12:43>

I snorted and dipped the windsurfer toward the snow-covered street below—and the white van covered in white snow. It all blurred together as I rocketed forward, and before I knew it, the van's top loomed out of the blizzard.
Crunch!

[HP 6/7]

I slammed through the van's skylight and landed in the cargo bay in a crumpled pile. The shocks squealed in protest, and the van rocked. A camera drone followed me through the shattered safety glass. A moment later, I shot forward as the driver stomped on the brakes, smashing into the viewing window between the bay and the cab. The van's wheels slipped in the snow as it spun midroad.

I had a moment to think about the absurdity of it all. I'd been hit by minion-driven vans twice during Episodes; at least I'd had my revenge when I hit this one!

[Gritty Recovery! +1 Grit Point]

I peered through the window, preparing to punch through it as the van slid to a stop in the snow. A very, *very* familiar mask turned back to look at me. I couldn't hear him through the window, but S's exposed lips mouthed the words, *Oh shit.* He reached for the radio.

I used **[Spotlight Strike]** and slammed a fist through the plexiglass window, popping it out of its frame. S shouted into the radio, "Jumper, that magical girl is—"

I dragged him through the window frame. The van's engine idled, but he'd grabbed onto the e-brake for a moment, so it wasn't *going* anywhere.

[Bull in a China Shop! +1 Badass Point]
[Stylish Strike! +1 Flamboyance Point]

As far as earning the right types of points went, I was not off to a good start. I used **[Spotlight Strike]** to punch him in the stomach and make him double over on the floor. "Do you surrender?"

[Stylish Strike! +1 Flamboyance Point]

"Yeah, yeah, whatever, just leave me alone!"
"Alright, on the floor, and don't move!"
The henchman complied, and I climbed through the window. I had an idea.

<Honey, FS, I have the van. - Understudy 12:45>

<Heading toward Quick-Mart - Understudy 12:45>

My phone buzzed twice as I corrected the van and drove it toward the Quik-Mart. I didn't honestly think the battered, clobbered van would trick Jumper for long, but we didn't *need* long—not with three of us and one of her. We just needed to bait her in. She cared about the van; after all, she and S bought it and paid to fix it. She'd want to make sure her investment was in good shape, especially after hearing the incomplete message from S.

As I turned onto University, something bounced off of an apartment building's walls. I grinned. Jumper. The young woman's green hoodie and tan jumper were soaked with melted snow. She stared at the white van momentarily, then kept running and jumping higher and higher up the building.

Then, a block and a half from University and Independent, something crashed into the back of the van, almost like I had. I checked the mirror; Jumper stared back at me. "What the [**Beep!**] You again?"

"Yep! I'm Magical Girl Understudy, and I'm here to save the—hey!"

Jumper tried to . . . jump . . . through the hole I'd made. I pulled on the steering wheel and slammed the brake.

Thump!

[**Good Thinking! +1 Cunning Point**]

Jumper slammed into the van's roof and fell back inside. I floored it, tires kicking up snow before they bit into the cold asphalt below. Alright. One block. If I could keep Jumper inside the van until the Quik-Mart, Fursona and Honeycomb would be there. I buckled my seat belt.

This was going to be a bumpy ride.

I glued one eye to the road and one to the rearview mirror. Jumper grabbed S by the collar and got ready to jump again. I whipped the van to the right the moment she did, putting it into a nasty spin on the cold, snowy road. I cranked on the wheel, the sounds of Jumper and S bouncing around in the back competing with the van's engine.

[**Merciless! +1 Badass Point**]

"[**Beep!**]" I looked back into the mirror. Jumper was still up, but S flopped around, unconscious. "Sorry about your henchman!"

[**Rating Warning #1! Episode Rating - PG! Censor in Effect**]

"Screw you! Stop breaking my vans!" Jumper dropped S as I pulled the van into a parking space outside the Quik-Mart. She had a point; white delivery vans *had* to be pricey. The second I threw the van into park, I unbuckled my seat belt and leaped out the door.

But I wasn't as fast as Jumper.

She sprang up like a . . . well, spring, sailing through the van's broken skylight. "I hate you so much. There's gonna be *water damage*," she whined, glaring.

"[**Honey Spray**]!" Magical Girl Honeycomb said, pushing through the Quik-Mart's glass doors. A wave of amber goop flew from her flower-shaped wand as she rushed the van. It splattered across the metal side and the roof, but Jumper hopped off, her power propelling her almost all the way across Independent Avenue toward the art gallery.

Unfortunately for her, Fursona hopped out of an alley right as she landed. The kangaroo took one look at Jumper and, balancing on their tail, kicked out with both feet. Jumper went flying, and Honeycomb cheered.

So did I, but not out loud. We were winning, sure, but Jumper was a full Speedster, and if she—

She jumped.

The camera drone exited the van; I had no idea what it'd been doing in there, but its lens flashed onto me. "Jumper, it's time to play your [**Bit Part**]!" I jumped into the air, spinning, and threw my arms wide.

I froze midair. A gigantic spotlight shone along the street, improbably bright against the washed-out, cloudy day. I moved a finger to point it at Jumper, and the barrage began.

It was like a [**Stellar Ray**], if instead of one, there were a dozen smaller ones. And if they cast about every half second. Rays of pinkish-blue light caromed off the snow-packed road, slammed into buildings' brick facades, and in all the flashing lights, a few hit Jumper.

[**Dramatic Damage! +3 Drama Points**]

Even as my power set me down, Jumper picked herself up and kept on jumping. Honeycomb flapped her ridiculous wings, taking off like a bumblebee in a wobbly pursuit path. Fursona hopped after her, too, though they didn't have much chance of catching the villain, especially once she started bouncing off the walls.

I summoned my [**Starwave Sail**] and took off, flying just a few feet above Jumper. This time, she wouldn't get away.

She jumped through a window, but I leaped off my sailboard and into an old lady's bedroom just a second behind her. The old lady screamed. I didn't blame her one bit, especially when a pair of camera drones filled up the rest of the room.

Jumper dashed into the living room as the tenant threw a pillow at her. I followed but couldn't keep up. I heard the door open, then a twanging sound. Then a curse. Then someone shouting [**Honey Spray**]!"

When I came around the corner, I couldn't help but laugh.

Honeycomb must've broken through a different window. I had no idea how she'd had enough control, and she'd definitely taken superhero damage in the crash, but she'd ended up in the living room. A moment later, Jumper had dashed through and gone for the door—which the old lady had locked with a door chain. That one moment to loosen the chain was enough for Honeycomb to finally—*finally*—defeat her nemesis.

Jumper was covered in honey. It dripped off her green hoodie and covered her face. The whole apartment building smelled sweet to the point it was almost gross. "Fine, you win this round, Honeycomb," the villain muttered.

[Episode Finished!]
[Episode: Short: Jumping from Crime to Crime! - PG]
[Penalties: 1x Rating Warning - No Penalty]
[Short Finished! +3 of each Style Point]
[Winner Winner! +3 of each Style Point]
[Role Focus: Flamboyance+Drama - Goal Partially Met! +10 Drama Points]
[Alias - Understudy] [Archetype - Magical Girl] [Community Rank - 432/523]
[HP 6/7]
[Styles and Skills]
▶ Archetype Skill - Transformation Sequence
▶ Badass (14)
▶ Cunning (25)
▶ Inkling 1
▶ Drama (45)
▶ Hometown Heroine 1
▶ Bit-Part Barrage 1
▶ Flamboyance (52) (Skill Roll Available)
▶ Signature Skill - Adaptive Armoire 1
▶ Stored Costumes: (Rainy Day)
▶ Spotlight Strike 1
▶ Starwave Sail 1
▶ Grit (31)

I didn't have any new powers to roll, but Honeycomb's beaming face more than made up for it. A camera drone hovered in front of her, and she looked at it, then at me. "Do you two want to say something?"

"No, this one's all yours. I've gotta go," I replied.

We apologized to the resident and gave her the university studio's contact information; they'd agreed to pay for damages, and covering an entire living room in honey certainly counted. Then, as I squeezed past the honey-stuck door and went looking for Fursona, Honeycomb started giving her speech.

"It looks like Jumper finally found herself in a sticky situation. That's okay; she'll learn that crime is sour, not sweet. Now . . ."

I grinned. Honeycomb's excitement felt like a physical lift. I'd felt it dozens of times after big wins, but this was probably her first time. I hurried down the hall and texted Fursona. If we hurried, we could still make our next classes.

And then? If the roads weren't much worse, I still had a sushi date!

61

Sushi Date

You'll like this place. Trust me," I said as Bianca drove her two-door beater through Tokyexico's streets and parked outside *No More Mr. Rice Guy Kaiten-Zushi*. The building's obviously fake facade was covered in blown snow, and I had to pull hard to open the door. The moment I did, snow started eddying in the entryway, and Bianca and I hurried inside.

"Yeah. Probably." Bianca looked more like her normally nervous self. I chalked it up to the weather; she'd had to drive in it, and it'd be dark and snowing by the time we were done here. The same table I'd sat at with Mom and Dad was open. Actually, most of the seats were empty; no one was out tonight despite it being Friday. Food on the buzzing and clattering conveyor belt passed by as we pulled off our jackets. Neither of us was dolled up like we had been for the theater. I wore a skull T-shirt with some band name across it and jeans, while Bee had opted for fuzzy tan leggings and a gray turtleneck sweater.

She smelled like green apples again. It competed with the smells of soy sauce and fish, a light, snappy scent. We sat down at the table. Bee eyed the clattering, rolling sushi plates dubiously.

"So, here's how it works." I explained the rules and scooped a plate with a California roll off the belt. Bianca grabbed something filled to the brim with reddish fish and green paste. She sniffed at it.

A moment later, Callie bustled over from another table. "Hi, I'm Callie, and I'll be taking care of you two tonight!"

"Hi, Callie," I said. She'd been part of the Orientation Episode; I hoped she didn't still remember me as Toilet Girl. Or that she didn't remember I'd kind of/sort of ditched her with the SSS. "How are classes?"

"Hey, TG!" Callie said, and I winced. She *remembered*. "Oh, they're good. Almost done at TU, then it's off to the real world. I'm taking a flight to Yorkston and going into marketing after Christmas. I've got a paid internship with one of the big non-Ilneat studios. It looks like you two know how Kaiten-Zushi works already, so I'll be back with some drinks. Want anything?"

We ordered sodas, and Callie disappeared.

"Tell me about home?" Bianca choked out after gulping down a bite of sushi. Her face reddened; whatever she'd just eaten was spicy, and the drinks weren't here yet. She started coughing into her napkin.

"Oh, Mom and Dad are both super-supportive," I said.

Bianca fidgeted as I explained how Dad supported everything I did while Mom was more concerned about me "making it" and doing better than they were. I wasn't sure how to get into their attitudes toward superhero work without revealing my secret identity to Bianca, and we weren't at that point in our relationship yet. After talking for a while, I popped my California roll into my mouth. "Wha' abou' oo?"

"Well, I told you my parents wanted me in—"

"Hey, here's your drinks. Enjoying everything?" Callie set down two dark-brown sodas, and Bee started sucking on her straw. The waitress laughed. "Spicy salmon roll? You've gotta respect the heat here."

"Yeah, I figured that out." All three of us laughed a little. Callie left, and Bee continued. "So they want me in bioengineering. I'm not sure what I want, though. I thought something in science would be good for me, but there are so many options. Mom's an archivist in Tortuga West, and Dad's in construction."

"Oh, did Tortuga West have a MIRACLE program?" I asked.

"Yeah. Dad's pretty well-off. His company did a bunch of work on the sea walls around the islands. He doesn't run the company, but construction is . . . well, you know?"

I knew all too well. Ever since Launch Day, construction, rehabbing buildings, and remodeling were the biggest businesses in North America. I'd done my share of destroying things, and Rocko Productions had always paid the damages, plus extra. Even when the Ilneat studios wouldn't pay or couldn't pay enough, heroes like Tele-Portal and The Triad sometimes threw money at problems if damages were dire.

"But they both encouraged TU for me. I haven't gotten into any of the bio-engineering classes yet, but the school's got a good reputation." Bianca grabbed a couple more dishes off the belt, and I followed up my first California roll with a plate of fruits. "I'd love to get into some of the work Allegiant Labs is doing on megafauna reversal. For all that Father Thyme got Kudzu-Zilla under control, Allegiant came up with the real solution."

"Yeah, but their goats rule the Gulf Coast now."

"Still easier to manage than Kudzu-Zilla." Bee started eating her new sushi rolls.

I should have expected it, to be honest. Bianca was a fast eater, and her sushi vanished before I'd even started my fruit. She sat there, tapping my foot with hers and watching me eat. Eventually, she cleared her throat. "So, what are you doing later tonight?"

"Thinking about having *someone* over after this date. Maybe watching some Man vs. Nature or something."

"Sounds fun. I'm in." Bianca grabbed my hand across the table and rubbed my knuckles with her thumb. "But maybe we could skip the show and, I don't know? Do something *else?*"

We chatted for a bit before I paid for the meal. It was just habit; I'd paid for every meal with Peter after the very first. Still, I felt Bianca's funny look as I slapped the bills down without even asking. I shrugged and smiled apologetically, but she still seemed annoyed. I'd have to . . . explain somehow. Later. Once I'd come up with a viable lie about why I paid.

Callie smiled at the tip and waved goodbye, and we headed to the car. The sun hadn't gone down, but it was way, way colder than it had been, and the flurrying snow was piling up in the parking lot. "You were right, Bee. It's getting worse."

"Told you." She slid into the driver's seat and started the engine while I pushed snow off the windshield with her scraper brush. When I'd done enough to get a thumbs-up, I hurried into the seat next to her, putting my freezing fingers under my armpits.

Bee laughed but got serious as she started driving across the increasingly slick roads. Her brow wrinkled. I winced and grabbed the armrest as the car started sliding, but she corrected and kept moving back toward Walnut—just a little slower than she'd been going. She cleared her throat. "Why didn't you ask if I wanted to pay?"

"I, uh . . ." I froze up. Of course this was going to be an issue. Why hadn't I thought about it before? "My, uh, ex . . ."

"Peter?"

"Yeah, Peter. He usually didn't have much money he could spend, so I ended up paying for most things. It was just habit." I paused. "Do you want to split the bills, then?"

"Yeah, I'd like that." She reached back for her gigantic backpack, steering with one hand. The car started to spin out again as she struggled.

I tensed again, fingers hurting from squeezing the armrest on the door. "How about later?"

"Yeah, later. Listen, you're my girlfriend, and I wanna spoil you, not just get spoiled *by* you," she said, grinning stupidly.

I smiled back. Bee was very, very different than Peter. "That'd be nice," I said.

Saturday, November 22

I awoke to something warm pressed against my back, which was wonderful against the cold late-November chill. I wriggled against Bianca. She kissed the back of my neck, and I shivered, but not from the cold.

Neither of us wore much clothing, but shockingly, we hadn't drunk anything last night. We hadn't watched any Man vs. Nature or Power Wars either. We'd just sat around and talked until I . . . made a move. An awkward, hesitant move. But Bianca had reciprocated, so all's well that ends well, right?

After that? I wasn't going to share that. A girl didn't kiss and tell, or something.

"Hey," I said stupidly.

"Hey." Bee shifted under the blankets and started rubbing my shoulder blades as I melted into the bed. I turned my head so I could see her face; she had a dumb, half-asleep look to her eyes, her curly black hair was a mess of tangles, and her makeup had smeared across her face because . . . reasons. She looked gorgeous.

"You never took my money," Bee said. She flipped the blanket off us, and I whimpered and curled into a ball as the warmth vanished. She climbed out of bed and covered me up again, leaving me to admire the view. She kept talking while she tracked down her clothes. "Why don't you just let me make you breakfast instead?"

I nodded. "Yeah, that'd be nice." I didn't have much, but surely Bee could find some eggs or something? Or frozen waffles. I had to have frozen waffles.

Bee sniffed her bra, shrugged, and put it on. She finished dressing and walked over to the bathroom. I heard the sink running and her muttering over it. "Alright, it's a good thing I've got the car. It'd be a cold, miserable walk of shame this morning." She splashed the water—maybe against her face.

"Turn on the heater," I whined.

"You think it's bad for *you*? I'm from Tortuga West."

I saw her curly black hair, which looked like it'd be hell to untangle, stick past the doorframe. She stuck her tongue out at me. "Why don't you get dressed and tell me where you keep your breakfast stuff?"

"Some breakfast in bed this is!" I took a deep breath, trying to psyche myself up. Why wasn't it hard to crash my windsurfer through a third-floor window or fight a minor-league villain, but I couldn't handle a little cold? I flipped the blankets off, wrapping my arms around myself, and started my own search for clothes.

"How are your finals looking?" Bee asked.

"Uh, I'm probably going to pass Algebra. Su-Bin's helping me a ton with it, so even if I don't get full points on the harder stuff we're learning right now, I'll do well enough on the beginning-of-year parts of the test. Same with Biology," I lied. Comfy sweatpants and a long-sleeve shirt would have to do for now. I started pulling on the pants. "Ilneat Studies should be easy because I've always been curious about them, and obviously Intro to Drama's fine. I could miss that one and still pass. How about you?"

"Well, I've got Fencing and stuff. They're having a tournament for the final. All you have to do is show up, but I wanna win. That's the Friday classes' end, the same as Intro to Drama. Then I have a couple of science classes that I'm hopefully gonna be ready for, but we'll see. Oh, found your pans. You can go back to bed."

"Shit," I mumbled. I heard the crashing sound of pots and pans falling out of the cabinet as I flipped the blanket back over me.

Then something flashed green outside the window. A bright green, even against the morning light pouring through the shades. I blinked. Bright green. That was . . .

Another crashing sound filled my ears. Through it, Bianca screamed.

62

Bianca Screamed

Bianca kept screaming as I burst out the bedroom door into my living room. She'd dropped the pan, and half-cooked eggs covered my kitchen. The window had shattered inward, covering my couch with glass shards, and the coffee table lay in splinters. As I took in the scene, I saw another green flash. This one kept glowing as LABRAT—freaking *LABRAT!*— stood to its full height, almost hitting my ceiling with its glowing green mouse ears.

"I told you I hated you, Understudy," it monotoned at me, leveling its **[Hypercompression Cannon]**. "The Professor sends his regards."

BANG!

[Casting Call]
[Episode: SERIES FINALE! Absent-Hearted Professor: Part One - PG]
[Role: Teen Heroine! Mandatory Acceptance Required]
[Role Focus: Drama+Flamboyance]
[Absent-Hearted Professor: Part One: Act One in Progress]

As the super-compressed air blast slammed into me and launched me into my bedroom, I got a good look at the LABRAT. Three Panic Pals had already launched from its back, taking to the air. Blinking, pulsing green lights reflected off the steel appliances in the kitchen. Bianca screamed again, ducking below the island sink.

Then I hit my bed's footboard and flipped onto the mountain of blankets I'd been buried beneath a moment before.

I waited for the HP notification, but as my thighs burned where they'd slapped the footboard and my back spasmed from a funny twist just before the landing, I realized I didn't have superhero damage to help me out. I cursed under my breath. This wasn't how the sushi date and aftermath were supposed to go!

Then I picked myself up, wincing, and ran back toward the door.

Bianca was in there with the bots, and she needed my help. I didn't have time for a transformation, but dammit, I was a heroine!

A pair of chrome camera drones slammed through the other living room windows. One of them zipped into the kitchen and hovered over Bianca; her screaming had died down, but she was still *definitely* the most dramatic person to watch, even if she was an Extra. The other got right up in my face.

"LABRAT, why are you here?" I needed to stall. My secret identity was definitely blown, but that didn't matter right now.

But even as the robot started talking, its **[Hypercompression Cannon]** was already whining, and the Panic Pals had spread through the room around me.

"Magical Girl Understudy, you hurt Professor Panic a lot a few months ago. Now he's returning the favor."

BANG!

I threw myself to the side, landing hard on the living room floor. The couch all but vaporized behind me. Bits of glass and splinters dug into my arms, but I was already up and running before I felt them.

So was Bianca.

She threw herself out from behind the island sink and ran toward the hall. A Panic Pal swooped down at her, but I had bigger problems than a single flying robot. I couldn't help but hear its stupid rap, though!

"PROFESSOR PANIC IS PREPPED FOR PAYBACK!

EVERYONE FREEZE! WE'RE ON THE ATTACK!"

Bianca slid under the attacking bot, blood flying as its arm clipped her temple. Then she was at the closet. She ripped her gigantic backpack out and spun, smashing the Panic Pal with it. The bot wobbled in the air, then careened toward the ground. I didn't have time to watch any longer, though.

BANG!

The last living room window came apart, spraying shards onto the snow below. I winced; hopefully, no one had been down there. LABRAT stomped after me as I ducked into the bedroom again. Behind me, I heard a door slam.

Good, I thought. Bianca was safe, or at least safe-ish. She'd made it out into the hall, so she'd gotten away. "LABRAT, Professor Panic told me he wouldn't seek vengeance!" I yelled, trying anything to distract the bot and slow it down.

It worked. The robot halted. "Professor Panic said you'd say that. I have a recording that proves otherwise."

From a speaker on one of the remaining Panic Pals, I heard my voice, then Peter's, digitized a bit. It was from the night we'd broken up. Peter had edited it a bit, but only to remove his secret identity.

"I don't want it. I appreciate it, but I don't want it anymore. I just want to be done."

"Fine. Fine, then. We're done, Magical Girl Understudy. I'm an honorable villain, so there's no need to hide. I swear I won't seek revenge on your family."

Well, shit. The robot was right; Professor Panic hadn't said anything about not seeking revenge. He'd only promised not to take it out on Mom and Dad. I rolled over the bed, grabbed Tails, and fell to the floor.

BANG!

Alright. It was definitely more dangerous dodging LABRAT's cannon without superhero damage to spare, but since I wasn't looking for an opening, I could—

"Ooof!" A Panic Pal surged toward me, whacking my back. I crawled under the bed, past a discarded bra from the night before. I didn't think it was mine.

The Panic Pal dropped lower, slapping at my feet, and I heard LABRAT's **[Hypercompression Cannon]** spool up for another shot. At the same time, the last Panic Pal kept pounding away on a door. I took a deep breath, getting ready for the inevitable.

Peter—Professor Panic—wouldn't push this too far. LABRAT would probably knock me out, and I'd wake up tied to a chair in the center of some alligator-infested room deep underground or something. Typical supervillain crap. He was a theater kid at heart, even if he'd quit to focus on his Genius work. At least, I was pretty sure that was how it'd go. Not 100% sure, though. The villain had *clearly* not taken the breakup as well as I'd thought.

Either way, I couldn't stop what came next. LABRAT spooled up its **[Hypercompression Cannon]** again as the Panic Pal grabbed at my ankles and tried to drag me out from under the bed.

BAM!

I raised an eyebrow as I kicked at the Panic Pal. That wasn't the **[Hypercompression Cannon's]** normal sound!

"Have no fear! Justice-Roo is here!"

"What the **[Beep!]**"

[Rating Warning #1! Episode Rating - PG! Censor in Effect]

I barely even saw the rating warning. Something orange, blue, and fuzzy crashed into LABRAT, and though they bounced off the machine's metal armor, the cannon arm turned up toward the ceiling.

BANG!

Ceiling tiles rained down on my bed. I clawed out from under the bed to see Fursona spin on one foot and plant the other—plus their animatronic tail—straight into the Panic Pal that'd been yanking my ankle. I had no idea how they'd gotten here so fast or gotten into my apartment—unless—no. No, I didn't have time to go down that line of thought.

I got to my feet and ran, sliding past LABRAT's claw arm. My thigh burned as it rubbed against the carpet, and I blinked back tears. But then I coasted past the bot and regained my feet in the hall, with Tails in my arms. My key to the maintenance room sat on the kitchen counter. I grabbed it, shoved it shakily into the door to my secret lair, and slipped inside.

As the door slammed, I took a deep breath, trying not to shiver. I'd just been bailed out of whatever Peter had planned for me. It would be fair for me to take a break for a second.

Instead, I held Tails up in the air. "I swear on my family, who I love very much, that I'll stand up against Professor Panic, his minions, and evil all over Riverside— and Tokyexico City! I'll fight for justice, peace, and hope! And I'll never stop 'til evil does first!"

The choral music and lights kicked off, accompanied this time by the sounds of LABRAT, the last Panic Pal, and Fursona destroying my apartment. I screwed my eyes shut as something large and wooden crashed against a wall; hopefully, Tokyexico's insurance or Rocko's studio was paying for this mess. Bangs and thuds and "Eat **[Double Kicks]**, bot!" came through the door in a muffled, endless wave of sound.

As the last bows and mask secured themselves to my head and I sat back down on the pastel-pink green room's floor, something crashed into the door. I jogged toward it.

<Are you going out there?> Tails asked. <Wait for it.>

"Wait for it? My sidekick is out there!" I half screamed.

<Wait for it.>

I waited. The unspoken last part of my oath weighed down on me like the blankets just . . . five minutes ago? Less. Yeah, like the blankets, but less comforting and more oppressive. Crashes, thuds, and rap lyrics filled the air.
BANG!

<Meow!> Tails shouted in my mind.

I pushed the door open. "Don't fear! Magical Girl Understudy is here! I swear to defend the weak against evil and uphold truth and love!"

[Dramatic Entrance! +1 Drama Point]
[Stylish Reveal! +1 Flamboyance Point]

My apartment was a war zone. Shattered glass littered the ground, and every window in my living room stood broken in its frame. LABRAT had crushed my coffee table, and its wreckage lay in the hallway next to the front door. Either Fursona had kicked it or LABRAT had tossed it at her—them. I couldn't tell. A fire alarm blared, and I could hear Extras from the nearby dorm rooms running down the hall and into the stairwells, but I couldn't smell smoke except from burning egg splatter in my kitchen.

The robot itself looked worse for wear. No parts were missing, but its minimal armor had been dinged and battered, and its claw arm kept catching as it moved it. My sidekick's suit was crumpled, and they reached up to adjust their head during the momentary pause.

It only lasted a second.

Fursona hopped across the room and punched the last Panic Pal just as it started up another rap song. It spun out of the empty window frame and crashed into a window below. I heard someone scream. LABRAT turned around, cannon warming up, but I beat the robot to the punch.

"[**Bit-Part Barrage**]!"

BANG!

As LABRAT's cannon blast crashed into me, I spun into the air; I was an easy target, but it was too late for the bot to stop my power. Even as the air slammed me into the wall, the power aimed me back the way I'd been facing. The spotlight covered LABRAT; from this distance, it wasn't hard to hit it with the rippling barrage of bright beams.

The bot's armor took some of the hits. But not all.

[HP 6/7]
[**Dramatic Damage! +4 Drama Points**]

Four beams slipped through. One took the massive bot's claw arm off. Another two burned holes into its leg. And the fourth slammed just below a greenish light on its shoulder.

A chunk of that shoulder flew off toward the window. I blinked incredulously. It was the Lil Pal—the goddamned little robot that Peter had gifted me when I went to college. But . . . how? I hadn't *finished* the thing! Its propellers wouldn't work together! I dashed toward it, trying to catch it before it could esca—

BANG!

[HP 5/7]

The airburst slammed me into the shattered, battered bathroom door. I caught a glimpse inside as I rolled off it.

Bianca's backpack. I pushed the growing suspicion out of my head. I had a fight to win.

"This is my hometown now, and I'm a [**Hometown Heroine**]!" I shouted. As the blue aura shimmered around me, I dashed toward LABRAT. [**Spotlight Strike**] highlighted a hip joint, and I kicked the robot. My boot took most of the impact, and the leg popped loose. LABRAT fell forward onto its front side.

[**Stylish Strike! +1 Flamboyance Point**]
[**Dramatic Assist! +1 Drama Point**]

I stared at its back just before Fursona ran up and stomped into the three open docking ports. Its green eyes looked up at me as they faded, and its monotone voice crackled as it said, "I still hate you, Magical Gi . . ."

The room went silent for just a moment. I took a deep breath, blew it out in a sigh, and started taking another. I had no idea how to explain what had just happened.

Fursona wrapped me in an iron-gripped hug before I could inhale. "Holy crap, Annie! I was so scared, and then I was so worried you wouldn't get away, and then—are you okay?" They let go of me, and I sucked in a quick breath before they could get me again. Annie. They'd called me Annie. Shit, shit, shit.

Instead, they reached up to their neck and unhooked their head. A curly black mop of hair, now drenched in sweat, peered out of the neck hole as Fursona—no, Bianca—wrapped me in another crushing hug and gave me a quick, half-panicked kiss. I blushed. The camera drones were having a field day.

[End of Act One! Act Two in Five Minutes! No Skill Rolls Available!]
[Alias - Understudy] [Archetype - Magical Girl] [Community Rank - 432/523]
[HP 5/7]
[Styles and Skills]
▶ Archetype Skill - Transformation Sequence
▶ Badass (14)
▶ Cunning (25)
▶ Inkling 1
▶ Drama (51) (Skill Roll Available)
▶ Hometown Heroine 1
▶ Bit-Part Barrage 1
▶ Flamboyance (54) (Skill Roll Available)
▶ Signature Skill - Adaptive Armoire 1
▶ Stored Costumes: (Rainy Day)
▶ Spotlight Strike 1
▶ Starwave Sail 1
▶ Grit (31)

63

Field Day

I blinked stupidly at Bianca as she pulled away. My brain needed to reset, and my jaw hung slack; I probably looked like a goldfish out of water. I definitely *felt* like a goldfish out of water. As the gears in my mind started turning again, I stared at the black-haired Extra—no, super—inside the kangaroo fursuit.

In retrospect, it'd been so obvious. She *always* had that backpack, and she'd always disappeared whenever superhero stuff happened. I'd never seen her so much as carry a fencing foil or anything that could hold one. And she'd never been in the same place as Fursona, but the kangaroo had usually shown up a couple of minutes after she left. Alone, that last bit didn't mean much, but taken with the rest, it should have been obvious she was a super. So why hadn't I noticed?

Well, that was obvious, too. I'd never *been* around other supers before. Peter and I had confessed to each other early on, and Collidus had told me right away. Like, within minutes of linking up with me. That kid had no filter. So yeah, my superhero radar wasn't the best, and clearly, my ability to hide my identity was . . . lacking.

"What the fuck? How long did you know?"

"Understu . . . Annie . . . you really want to know?" Bianca fidgeted awkwardly inside the Fursona Costume. I nodded, and she continued. "You told me your address after our first Superpower Ethics class. Then, later that week, you told Fursona. It wasn't hard to figure out your secret identity from there. Plus, you weren't subtle with your emails and stuff, and I kinda liked snooping around your place. Sorry."

"And you never told me?" I wasn't sure whether to be angry or impressed.

"Well, no. Pataki and Rocko said—"

"That secret identities had to be protected." Of course they had. A reveal like this had to be worth a fortune in ratings. The kiss would be blurred locally, but it felt so perfect . . . so . . . superhero-movie. It'd play well in Ilneat space.

"Yeah."

I stood there for a minute, feeling dumber by the minute. My whole web of lies to keep my Anika persona separate from Understudy hadn't mattered at all. I'd blown my cover on the first day of classes.

"Yeah, it was pretty dumb," Bianca said. She laughed nervously. "Lucky you've got a *very* trustworthy girlfriend and a sidekick who values your privacy, huh?"

<We don't have much time for small talk right meow,> Tails interrupted. <There are more Panic Pals outside. One minute.>

I wasn't worried about my face or name being on camera. The Ilneats would edit such a small oopsie for the Earth audience, and the galactic audience would enjoy the reveal.

"Yeah, it's pretty lucky. We need to talk about this, though. Later. Right now, we have a problem. My evil ex-boyfriend has to be in Tokyexico. Or more likely, he sent bots over, but he's still in his lair back home." It made sense. He'd been building LABRATs that could travel the distance. The only reason he'd be here would be revenge.

Actually, I thought, *he was definitely here.* "Either way, his robots are on campus, and we need to deal with them."

Bee sighed and pulled the Fursona head back on. "Alright. We'll talk about it later. For now, let's get out there and kick some butt." She dashed for the door, opened it, and headed for the stairs as the fire alarm blared.

I shook my head. Things were happening too fast. Professor Panic was back. Bianca was Fursona. What was next?

[Absent-Hearted Professor: Part One: Act Two Beginning]

I ran to the roof. It would have made more sense to head down the stairs or take the elevator into the tunnels, but either was painfully slow. "Holy crap, it's cold!" It wasn't snowing; the clouds had cleared out, making for a bright, sunny morning. But, somehow, that was even *colder.* The slight breeze bit my skin. I wondered if I could have a winter uniform.

<No time to complain, Understudy. You need to deal with the bots.>

Tails was right. I looked down as Fursona jumped out a window, landed on the ground, and started hopping toward a swarm of Panic Pals. "**[Starwave Sail]**!" I took off after her. A crowd of students in pajamas and jackets stood around, marveling at my room's broken windows, and one of them pointed at the blue-and-pink streaks my sailboard left behind. That wasn't good; they knew my secret base was in Walnut.

[Show-off! +1 Flamboyance Point]

I rolled to the soft, frigid snow between Walnut Tower and Weber Quad. Fursona hopped up a moment later, a swarm of Panic Pals buzzing right behind her.

"MAGICAL GIRL UNDERSTUDY ACTS LIKE A WITCH!
BUT IN REALITY, SHE'S JUST A —"

"Hey! Rude!" Fursona kicked the offending Panic Pal while I shook my head in disbelief. Peter wasn't ready to make the minor leagues. What was he thinking, teaching the Panic Pals cursing lyrics?

A Panic Pal swooped down at me. I spun, using **[Spotlight Strike]** and punching it in the glowing green "eye." It shattered inward, and the bot collapsed around my fist. I shook my hand, flinging the bot to the fresh snow. Oil leaked out, staining the snow blackish brown.

[Stylish Strike! +1 Flamboyance Point]

Then there were only two bots in that pack, and two Panic Pals hadn't even been a problem for me a year ago. Fursona smashed one while I swung the other by its legs as it tried to deploy its speakers.

In seconds, we'd pulverized the first pack of Panic Pals. Another squad of them zipped overhead, rap music playing. I watched them dive down into Weber Quad. "Are they heading for the engineering building?"

"Looks like it," Fursona said. She started hopping after them, then turned. "You want to tell TUSSA?"

"Not . . . No. This isn't a TUSSA Episode. This is about Professor Panic and me. If the SSS shows up, we'll let Ikenga know. Otherwise, no." I took off toward the Panic Pal squad, watching as they docked onto the back of a LABRAT—one that looked identical to the robot on my living room floor. I barely suppressed a shiver. Peter had finished the 1.6s he'd told me about during our breakup. He'd probably finished the 1.5s, too, and if he had, he'd had plenty of time to work on the FEAR Power Armor and get it up to speed.

He was *here*. On campus. Somewhere. Probably in the Grant Building's basement.

As each Panic Pal docked, its green lights flashed yellow, and the docking ports lit up. The LABRAT backpedaled into the Weber Quad. I used **[Hometown Heroine]** and slid across the icy concrete on my knees just as—

Bang!

Snow sprayed out from the LABRAT as the airburst passed, coating me in icy crystals. Fursona jumped across the quad, cutting the distance quickly. The new LABRAT kept backpedaling, avoiding her flying kick. I sprinted—carefully—across the courtyard, trying not to lose control and slip.

Ding! Ding! Ding! Ding!

The lights on the LABRAT's back flashed blue. The four Panic Pals that'd docked on its back took off again a moment later. The second they did, one opened up its speakers.

"HE HAD A PLAN, BIG RISKS AND BIG DARES!
TO CROSS THE MAN VS. NATURE, BUT SHE DIDN'T CARE!"

"What the [**Beep!**]" Had Professor Panic written . . . a breakup song? Or was this a diss track? Either way, it was *not* mature. "[**Spotlight Strike**]!" The LABRAT's whole back lit up, and I spin-kicked it.

[Rating Warning #2! Episode Rating - PG! Censor in Effect]
[Stylish Strike! +1 Flamboyance Point]
[Dramatic Assist! +1 Drama Point]

It would be easy to just [**Bit-Part Barrage**] it and be done, especially if it turned around. But I could only use it once per act, and I wanted to save it. Besides, Fursona was right next to me, kicking the seven-foot-tall robot and all but knocking it down.

The remaining Panic Pals buzzed us, and I peeled off to fight them while Fursona circled the LABRAT. It kept stepping back until it stood against the Grant Building's doors. I only had time to keep track of Fursona's fight with the bot. Instead, I was busy breaking up Panic Pals.

[Stylish Strike! +1 Flamboyance Point]
[Dramatic Assist! +1 Drama Point]
[Stylish Strike! +1 Flamboyance Point]
[Dramatic Assist! +1 Drama Point]
[Stylish Strike! +1 Flamboyance Point]

[**Hometown Heroine**] fell off before the last one crashed to the ground, and by the time I was finished, so was Fursona. She kicked the LABRAT into the glass doors, which shattered. I winced. TU would hate us; this was the second time in less than two months that supers had broken that door.

I grabbed one of the Panic Pals I'd just destroyed. It seemed . . . lighter . . . than the ones I'd fought in Riverside, and when I looked at it more closely, I could tell its body was smaller. Not by a lot, but most of the batteries had been removed. Fursona kicked the LABRAT's chassis, breaking off a chunk of something black from its shoulder. "Is that a solar panel?" she asked.

"I think so. Professor Panic must've de-armored the LABRATS and stripped the batteries from his Panic Pals to make them lighter and support recharging. It's the only way he could have gotten them from Riverside to here."

Fursona nodded. She pointed at the door. "So, you're pretty sure he's holed up inside the SSS lair?"

"He has to be. The bots seem to be defending the building or something." Even as I said it, though, I wasn't sure. Peter was tricky at the best of times. There was a chance he was still in Riverside. After all, he could be running the show from his computer. Hell, he could be asleep, and his bots would still earn him points.

I used [**Check the Script**]; it said to slow down for a moment and think, so I pulled out my phone. "We'll wait out here for a minute. I've got valuable intelligence to gather."

<Hey Dad. Has Peter been at work the last couple of days? - Annie 9:15>

While I waited for a response, Fursona stood in the building's entryway, fidgeting with her pouch. We waited; I could hear something clanking around inside for a moment, then it was gone.

<Nope. Think he took sick days. - Dad 9:18>
[Good Thinking! +1 Cunning Point]

Crap. He was here. I took a breath and composed myself, getting back into character as a camera drone hovered nearby. "Alright. He has to be here. We're going down there and checking out the basement. Maybe he built a lab down there or something."

"Are you sure? Lair assaults are always tough, and we had TUSSA with us last time," Fursona asked.

She wasn't wrong. Lair-assault Episodes rarely worked out perfectly. Some of Golden Goose's only defeats were against Genius-defended lairs, like in "The Doomsday Device," when she went up against The Mind's fortress. He'd had so many traps that even Golden Goose's frankly ridiculous powers weren't enough to breach it, from self-replicating defense drones to laser walls to a forcefield I was pretty sure was pure Ilneat tech.

Lord Destructo's fortress wasn't much better, though it was crawling with henchmen and lieutenants, and any attempt to break it would result in a dogpile. Stella-Lunar had built a team of a dozen major leaguers to crack *that* egg, and it had taken three Episodes before they finally won.

So, yeah. Fursona had a point. This could suck—a lot. A Panic Pal buzzed toward us, so I used [**Spotlight Strike**] and punched it. It skidded across the tile floor and crashed into a wall.

[Stylish Strike! +1 Flamboyance Point]

"Yeah. It'll just be him. He doesn't work with others. He probably had his bots set up the lair and sold the dog bots to the SSS from there, so it might not even be an official SSS lair. Either way, if it's a Series Finale, the Ilneats won't want interference."

"What about me?" Fursona asked worriedly.

"Sorry. You're involved in this mess. Professor Panic is my ex."

"[**Beep!**] Seriously? You're neck-deep in drama, huh? Accidentally dating your sidekick is one thing, but a villain?" Fursona teased.

"What can I say? I'm a theater girl." I ran toward the stairs, feeling the camera drone's eye on me. Down below, somewhere, was the SSS lair. Or, I was pretty sure, Professor Panic's lair.

64

Professor Panic's Lair

"...And the itsy-bitsy spider went up the spout again!"

Fursona laughed as I transformed into my Rainy Day Costume. "You ready, Squirt?"

"Yeah, yeah, make fun of the kid," I said. "Let's go."

Fursona led the way down the stairs into the Grant Building. We'd agreed that having two melee-focused superheroes in such tight quarters didn't make sense, and even though [**Bit-Part Barrage**] was extremely powerful, I'd built Rainy Day for this exact situation. My wand had shifted, turning blue aquamarine instead of its usual pinkish tourmaline.

It wasn't just that Fursona was tougher than me or more suited for melee fighting. I let her lead for another reason; she knew where to go. Since she'd been here before, I followed her down the hall and over to . . . a maintenance closet? "Are there *any* maintenance doors on campus that aren't secret lairs?"

"I bet most of them are real. The maintenance and custodial people need to work, right?" Fursona turned the handle. It didn't move, and she shook her head. "I figured it'd be locked, but you've gotta try, right?"

"Right. So now wha—"

Crash!

I flinched as Fursona kicked the door on its hinges. It twisted, the hinges' screws tearing out of the frame. She kicked it again. The whole thing ripped free this time, slamming into the ground with a screeching, thudding sound.

I glared at her, arms on my hips. "A little warning next time?"

She laughed. "Sure, Squirt. This is the right door. The lights were red last time, though."

Sure enough, the "maintenance room" behind it was instead a long, dim tunnel lit by a few green-tinted lightbulbs. Fursona pushed inside, shaking her head. "Your ex has style."

"Shut up." She was right, though. Professor Panic had always known how to set a scene. I couldn't help but approve of the green lights; they flooded the room, turning Fursona's suit and my skin a sickly pallor. It felt sinister. Intimidating.

Evil.

Goddamn, he was good at this.

"THE MAD PROFESSOR GAVE HER A GIFT!

BUT SHE NEVER FINISHED IT, NOW HE'S QUITE MIFFED!"

"Behind us!" I didn't have time to squeeze past the half-unhinged door as the Panic Pal swarm rushed me. Their tiny arms flailed around, pounding on me, and one bit my shoulder, teeth gnashing into the Rainy Day Costume's poofy sleeve. At least they weren't swearing at us.

[HP 4/7]

Fursona started to push back through the door, but a steel wall slammed down between us before she could. I had just enough time to read the sticker on the wall—*Professor Panic's Portable Panic Room*—before the bots looped around to fight me again.

"Professor Panic, stand down!" I shouted as I got back to my feet. With four bots, including the speaker bot hanging back, and my superhero damage approaching half strength, Rainy Day didn't mess around with [**Stellar Ray**] or anything. I used [**Ride the Lightning**], filling the hall with a thunderstorm.

[**Electric Lightshow! +3 Flamboyance Points**]

As the storm abated, the last remaining bot retracted its singed speakers and swooped toward me. I waved my wand. "[**Stellar Ray**]!"

The familiar, bright beam wasn't what I got. Instead, a wave of bubbles zipped across the ever-closing gap between the Panic Pal and me. As each hit the bot, they popped, tearing at its thin metal plating until, just a few feet from me, it ricocheted off the floor and into a wall.

[**Dramatic Damage! +1 Drama Point**]

I checked the hall leading to the stairs; no more bots, at least not for the next few moments. However, I could hear a hip-hop beat and something thumping against Professor Panic's Portable Panic Room's walls. After a moment, it stopped. Then the door opened, revealing a panting Fursona, her hands on her knees, and a few broken bots.

"Well, shoot. I didn't expect a trap *that* soon," she said.

"There's no way he moved in this fast. Dad said he'd only been missing work for a few days."

"Yeah, he had help. He had to have help." Fursona helped me across the busted, shattered maintenance door—I was too short to get over it easily—at least as Rainy Day. Then we started down the hallway.

We hadn't gone ten feet when the lights flickered. A screen activated, and Professor Panic's face filled it. His voice echoed down the empty hall, slightly staticky. "So, Magical Girl Understudy, you've found my Tokyexico outpost."

"Yeah. Look, Professor—"

Before I could finish my sentence, the screen spoke again. "Don't interrupt my speech, Understudy. I gave you a gift, and we were going to finish it together. I made plans to visit, and you told me not to. You had a Costume you could have worn. We could have spent time as Professor and Lab Assistant and ruled the world . . . together."

"I told you I didn't wa—"

"But that opportunity is long past." It wasn't *him*, I realized. He'd recorded this. When had he moved in here? Had he been here during the "Grant Building Dogpile" Episode? Or had his bots been here getting ready? "Now, there is no Professor and Lab Assistant. There is only the Professor . . . and revenge!"

The screen changed to some words in bright red. "First LABRAT in 0:20." The timer started ticking down—19, 18, 17—as Professor Panic's Portable Panic Room closed on either side of the hall. "Magical Girl Understudy, prepare to lose."

"Your ex is a real charmer," Fursona quipped.

"Yeah, but he's *so* good at Drama. Professor Panic, I'm still the [**Hometown Heroine**]!" I said, posing as heroically as I could in my kid-sized body. The familiar blue glow covered me and my The Cloud–themed outfit.

9, 8, 7

"Not much room," I muttered. The hallway had a few doors on either side, and we needed more space for a proper fight. I pointed. "Can you get that door open?"

3, 2, 1

"You got it!" Fursona headed for the door. As she started kicking at it, a different one popped open just below the screen. A LABRAT stomped out. This one did *not* have an accompanying swarm of Panic Pals. What it *did* have was a second [**Hypercompression Cannon**]. It started charging them up as the timer reset to forty seconds. 39, 38 . . .

Bang! Bang!

I threw myself onto the floor, ducking one of the shots. The other shoved me into the Panic Room wall with a thud, but even before I hit, I was already moving, waving my wand and pointing it back at the LABRAT. "[**Stellar Ray**]!"

[HP 3/7]
[**Gritty Recovery! +1 Grit Point**]

My fight against LABRAT in the Riverside Bank's safe-deposit-box room had proven that [**Stellar Ray**] didn't have the punch it needed. I couldn't beat LABRAT 1.4's armor. I expected the beam to dissipate on its chest plate or something.

That's not what happened.

[Dramatic Damage! +1 Drama Point]

Instead, as the bubbly beam started popping against its armor, something else popped too. The LABRAT's right cannon dipped toward the ground for a few seconds, green lights fading across its whole side. Then it lit back up and kept charging.

This wasn't, I realized, a LABRAT 1.4. Even with the flight module on the 1.4, it couldn't possibly have the power to fly from Riverside to Tokyexico. I thought back; just before we'd broken up, Peter had been rambling about the 1.5s, about dropping weight, adding solar collectors, and reducing armor. That had gotten the LABRATs to Tokyexico alright, but it had turned them from juggernauts to . . . less-armored juggernauts? Yeah, to that.

31, 30

Bang!

"Fursona, help me take it down! [**Stellar Ray**]!"

[Dramatic Damage! +1 Drama Point]

The next bubbly burst caused a similar reaction; the gigantic robot staggered. Off-balance, it struggled to recover, but before it could, a mass of faux fur and fury slammed into it. Fursona kicked and thrashed while I, as Magical Girl Rainy Day, looked for an opening to cast another [**Stellar Ray**].

23, 22, 21

Bang!

At point-blank range, the LABRAT couldn't miss, and Fursona went sailing. She crashed into the screen, which fizzled out. Then she slammed into the floor. I heard her groan as the air got pushed out of her lungs from the impact; superhero damage helped, but it didn't stop everything.

Worse, I was sure the timer was still running. We needed to not be here.

"[**Stellar Ray**]!" I blasted the LABRAT again, then grabbed Fursona by her Costume's collar. [**Hometown Heroine**] was still running, and the door that the LABRAT had been waiting behind was still open. If I could—

[Dramatic Damage! +1 Drama Point]

Bang!

The LABRAT fired again, and the airburst slammed into my back. I kept hold of Fursona's Costume, and we slammed into a wall. I struggled to my feet—so did Fursona, who'd recovered enough to start moving.

[HP 2/7]

[Gritty Recovery! +1 Grit Point]

The door was *right* there. We took two steps and dipped through it into a small room; this one *could* have been a maintenance closet if it wasn't empty. Fursona slammed the door shut and leaned against it as the first airburst smashed into it. The door shook in its frame, but it held.

"So, what now, Squirt?" Fursona asked.

I thought about our options. There were four doors, and I didn't like our odds against four LABRATS at once. The door shook again as another **[Hypercompression Cannon]** fired. A moment later, even more stomping filled the air. A second LABRAT entered the hall.

We couldn't stay here. And we couldn't wait too long. I started transforming back to Magical Girl Understudy. She had the power set to solve this problem—or at least dig us out of the hole we were in. As soon as I transformed, I pointed at the door. "Open that on my count, and get ready to fight."

[Rejuvenation Activated: HP 5/7]

Fursona nodded.

"One . . . two . . . three!"

The door flung open. I was already spinning, using **[Bit-Part Barrage]** on the two LABRATs stomping forward. Their cannons fired in a long volley, and bursts of air slammed into Fursona. She was using her body to shield me!

Then **[Bit-Part Barrage]** fired.

[Dramatic Damage! +7 Drama Points]

The LABRATs had nowhere to go. They were both stuck inside the door, trying to get to Fursona and me, so almost every beam in the barrage slammed right into their spotlight-covered frames.

As ray after ray slammed into it, a flash of green light filled the hall and room. Its torso burst into flames a moment later, then tore itself apart as my feet hit the ground.

My jaw dropped, and I looked away from the ongoing explosion. I'd never made something the size of LABRAT blow up before.

[Don't Look at Explosions! +1 Badass Point]

I'd hit the second LABRAT hard, too, and Fursona hit it even harder, slamming a pair of kicks into its chest. It collapsed, and a moment later, the kangaroo heroine was on top of it, slamming punches and kicks into its armor, which buckled and popped. Its lights went out.

The green lights overhead flickered, then went white-yellow. A moment later, Professor Panic's voice filled the hallway. He sounded . . . panicked. "Understudy! Quit breaking my bots!"

65

Quit Breaking My Bots!

I had to spend half my lifetime earnings on the power converters and solar rechargers. Then it took two *days* to fly them here, and you're just . . . breaking them!" Professor Panic continued. This wasn't a recording. I could tell by the barely detectable deranged tone; when you fought someone repeatedly for years, you started picking up on the little things.

"No, I won't be doing that," I replied. He could see us, so he could definitely hear me. Where were his cameras and speakers? He'd moved in fast—either that or his bots had been here a *while.*

"Then I'm done messing around! Come in . . . to your doom!"

I heard a beep through the speakers, and a door opened. It led farther into the lair, and I could hear machine engines running inside. These weren't the gentle hums and whirs of the Panic Pals or even LABRATs' louder, deeper vibrations. No, these sounded crude—less like one of Professor Panic's creations and more like . . .

. . . I couldn't quite place it. But something big and immobile.

I dashed toward the open door, Fursona right behind me. We sprinted down the stairs and took a right through the unlocked doors. I punched a Panic Pal as we ran, for Badass points, then kept running, always toward the sound until it filled my ears. Then a sharp left.

[**Badass Takedown! +1 Badass Point**]

I skidded to a stop and sidestepped as Fursona catapulted past me. The cavernous room we'd rushed into was filled with clanging, thudding assembly lines. Near us, one line riveted tiny motors into the Panic Pals' bodies to run their arms, while a few lines away, a claw installed batteries into the robots. A few stalled, silent machines in the back held half-finished golden dog bots—the same kind we'd fought a few weeks ago.

But the room hadn't always been an assembly line. A half-assembled conference table stood shoved against a wall in one corner, and a pair of walls had been smashed in to make space for the assembly lines, but before that? They'd clearly been locker rooms. A few helmets with decorative spikes sat on the changing rooms' benches or strewn across the floor. The rickety scaffolding and corrugated tin sheets attached to the machines' sides made me think the whole operation was slapped together, not a longer-term project. This hadn't been Peter's lair for long. Was he working with the SSS, or had he just moved in after the last Episode?

My money was on the former.

A squad of Panic Pals swooped at us, and Fursona and I sprang into action. If I could shut the factory down, finding—and beating—Professor Panic would be simple. The machine's controls had to be somewhere in the SSS's former lair, but where?

I'd taken a dozen steps into the maze of conveyor belts when I realized Fursona wasn't with me. I looked over my shoulder. She was fighting the Panic Pals. A chomping, rapping robot slammed into a painting machine, and Fursona waved for me to keep going. "I'm fine. Just shut it down!"

"Okay, just keep them off me!" I looked around. There! A steel walkway halfway up the lair's wall looped around the room before turning into a catwalk. The suspended catwalk cut the room in half, and right in the middle, where someone could see the whole room, was a tiny control panel.

Two LABRATs guarded the stairs up to the walkway, but I didn't need to fight them. "[Starwave Sail]!" I leaped onto my board and rocketed away toward the factory's controls.

A Panic Pal rushed me as I landed a few dozen feet away from the controls. I used [Spotlight Strike], punched it, and kept running.

[Show-off! +1 Flamboyance Point]
[Stylish Strike! +1 Flamboyance Point]

The two LABRATs clunked up the stairs; their thrusters were too powerful—too out of control—to get them onto the platform safely. They charged their [Hypercompression Cannons] and fired.

Bang! Bang!

The catwalk rocked back and forth. I clung to the railing and pulled myself forward. The machine below me stamped steel plating into thin, shining armor, and I realized that landing on *that* conveyor belt would chip away my superhero damage pretty quickly.

The rocking, bucking catwalk stopped momentarily, and I lunged for the controls. I grabbed them and started trying to read them. Then I stopped. "Professor Panic, you [Beep!]" He hadn't labeled anything, and nothing looked like a standard keyboard.

[Rating Warning #2! Episode Rating - PG! Censor in Effect]

There was *something* I could do, though. I [Checked the Script]. After more pondering, the power highlighted a pair of buttons. One was bright red. The other was a toggle on the control panel's bottom.

A 50/50 chance. That wasn't so bad, especially because Peter was a drama queen. He'd definitely have a self-destruct button, and it'd absolutely be the big red button.

Or . . . would it?

Nope. Peter knew that I knew he was a drama queen. He'd switch stuff around. But if he knew I knew that . . .

"Hey, hurry up! They're coming!"

Bang! Bang!

Fursona was right. I didn't have time to second-guess and puzzle through Professor Panic's line of thought. The two LABRATs clomped onto the catwalk, which creaked from their weight and the airbursts that rocked it back and forth.

I slapped the button.

An alarm started sounding, and a steel door slammed shut over each exit. The two LABRATs stopped, and so did the assembly lines below.

[Good Thinking! +1 Cunning Point]

I breathed a sigh of relief. I'd stopped the factory. If we could get to Professor Panic before—

"UNDERSTUDY THINKS SHE'S SUCH A GENIUS!

BUT IN REALITY, SHE'S JUST THE MEANY-EST!"

I punched the Panic Pal. I didn't even need to look at it. That rhyme didn't deserve attention.

[Badass Takedown! +1 Badass Point]

Anyway, if we could get to Professor Panic before—

"Magical Girl Understudy, you think you've won?" A screen popped on, revealing the face of the FEAR Power Armor. It seemed thinner than the one I'd fought on Flat Top Hill, with less armor; Peter had cut every bit of weight he could from his machines.

"You haven't won anything. LABRATs, we're leaving. Delay the heroes. I'm starting the self-destruct sequence manually. This factory will implode in one minute." A timer appeared next to the FEAR armor's face, which opened. Professor Panic grinned maniacally. "Fifty-nine. Fifty-eight. Goodbye, Understudy."

[Episode Update! Rating Change! New Rating: PG-13]

I froze for a moment as the timer kept dropping. I'd *never* seen an Episode rating change, but the self-destruct-with-the-heroes-inside trick wasn't a little-league move. Professor Panic's picture disappeared from the screen. Clearly, he wasn't sticking around for the explosion.

The moment he did, I realized something. "You motherfucker!" I shouted.

That's right. I could swear now, and there was *no* way Fursona or Professor Panic was taking the big one from me!

The two LABRATs kept stomping after me, but I had no intention of fighting them. "[**Starwave Sail**]!" I flew off the catwalk, which groaned ominously under the two bots' weight, but stayed up. At least for now. Fursona glared at me as I landed next to her.

[**Show-off! +1 Flamboyance Point**]

"Dammit, Understudy, that was supposed to be my swear! I even had it planned out for when we met back up. How are we getting out of this?"

I wasn't sure. "Can you kick down a Panic Room door?"

"Probably not." Fursona shook her kangaroo head. "Other ideas?"

37, 36, 35

I [**Checked the Script**] again. "Okay, we need a bathroom or something. A room that's pretty much cut off from the rest of the place. There's a chance we can get through the floor and into . . . tunnels."

"What kind of tunnels?" Fursona said. She was already looking for a bathroom.

"Uh, probably sewer lines or a monorail."

"Oh man, it's gonna get in my fur!"

"Cheer up! It could be the monorail. If it is, we'll have to run in case a train's coming." I spotted a bathroom; the good thing about college campuses was they were everywhere, even in a supervillain club's basement lair.

25, 24, 23

We slammed through the door. Urinals lined the wall, but it'd been cleaned recently. I started tapping on the floor. Fursona joined me. "We're listening for a hollow spot!"

13, 12, 11

"There *is* no hollow spot!" Fursona shouted at me.

"Keep looking!" I ran toward the sinks. Surely, there had to be one in here. Somewhere. Anywhere.

2, 1, 0

"Goodbye, Understudy!" Professor Panic's voice echoed, and the whole lair started to collapse. So did the bathroom, falling twenty feet as the floor gave way.

[**Good Thinking! +1 Cunning Point**]
[**Absent-Hearted Professor: Part One: Act Three Beginning**]

Water rained down on my face as I woke up. For a second, it felt good. Then I realized it had a chance of being sewage, and I jumped to my feet, pushing rubble off of me as I did. The shattered, wrecked porcelain fixtures lay strewn around us, but a quick sniff showed it was clean water. I felt around until my hand felt fuzz and started helping Fursona up.

"Did we win?" the Justice-Roo asked.

"No, but we didn't lose either. Act Three is starting now, and we need to get out of this . . . bathroom and figure out where we are. We did miss our intermission, though." A tiny bit of light trickled in from above; it seemed like the whole TUEAS Building had collapsed, but somehow, we hadn't been crushed. Even more luckily, a camera drone had gotten trapped under some rubble. We moved the twisted pipe and tiles off it, and it took to the air, filming us.

There was, in fact, a way out. I held up a pipe for Fursona to squeeze through, then waited for her to lift it while the camera drone zipped into the dark passageway. Once I was safely across, she let it go, and a whole mess of concrete rubble collapsed over the entry to the bathroom.

The tunnel we found ourselves in . . . wasn't a subway line. And it wasn't a sewer system either. It was natural—or at least, it wasn't something people had made. The tunnel cut through the dirt in an uneven, twisting path, but it was tall—and wide—enough for Fursona and me to walk through it easily. The wall looked like it had been . . . brushed?

"Your ex-boyfriend is crazy," Fursona said as we wandered the tunnel.

"Har har. He wasn't always like this."

"Really? You sure about that?"

I was. Professor Panic had always pushed the limits, but Peter . . . we'd had . . . something. Even if it wasn't great at the end, we'd had something that lasted a while. The ending—and Professor Panic's bullshit—didn't necessarily mean the rest was bad.

And to be honest, I missed Peter. Not as a partner; I hadn't had any interest in that *before* he started a Series Finale about revenge. I definitely didn't now. But I did miss him. Or at least, I missed him when he wasn't going Genius mode or running an Episode I didn't want to deal with. Which was . . . most of the time.

"Maybe not."

"Shhhhh!" Fursona held up a hand as the camera drone zipped around a corner.

I listened, dramatically holding a hand up to my ear even though the drone was gone. As Fursona and I silently stood there, I heard a snuffling sound up ahead. Then something moving against the tunnel walls. Whatever it was, it was big.

"Quiet. We've gotta get past it . . . whatever it is," I said.

Fursona nodded, and we crept forward and peeked around the corner.

"Shit," Fursona said.

"Shit," I agreed.

The creature's rear end filled the tunnel in front of us, its thick brown fur rubbing against the wall. Its long back legs ended in sharp-looking claws, which dug into the ground and ripped the dirt and rocks apart with each step. It was shuffling away from us. We ducked around the corner again, holding our breath as the sniffling sound stopped and a low growling filled the stale tunnel air.

We'd gotten out of the metaphorical frying pan . . . and straight into the fire.

66

Into the Fire

We retreated down the tunnel, back until we ran into the rubble piled against the bathroom's wreckage. The creature—a D-wolver, a gigantic, mutated wolverine—didn't follow us, and the growling subsided. I let out a breath I hadn't realized I was holding. "So, I'm pretty sure Professor Panic got away. That's a megafauna."

"Yep." Fursona fidgeted with her pocket.

"And we're stuck in its tunnel under who knows how much rubble." The TUEAS Building wasn't very tall, but we'd been down below the basement. Professor Panic had laid a trap for us, and while we'd avoided it, his intent had been . . .

His intent had been revenge. To end our rivalry on his terms with a win. Had he planned to kill me?

Yeah, he planned to kill me.

That was a chilling thought. But I pushed it down because now wasn't the time. I cleared my throat quietly and whispered to Fursona. "So, there's probably two ways out of here. We can stay put and hope the D-wolver doesn't find us . . . or try to get past it. Either way is risky, but I think we should fight. The school will be investigating, and this Episode just got a lot more dangerous. If we can stop the dire wolverine *before* some Extra gets eaten, that'd be better for everyone."

"It *wasn't* more dangerous when your ex tried to blow us up?"

"No. I mean, yeah, but we're solidly in the minor leagues for danger now." The little leagues had always had a tinge of goofiness, whether it was rated-G shenanigans or the PG serious-but-silly fights with Professor Panic. Blowing up buildings and running into megafauna? That was minor-league danger; it wouldn't get *too* much worse until the majors, when the danger zone spread to everyone in the city. Or worse.

I cleared my throat again. Even minutes after the collapse, dust filled the tunnel. "We're supers. Sure, we got flattened by Theseus, but we've got new moves and more power since then."

Fursona shook her head. "If you really think we can fight it, I'll give it a go with you. But if we die, I'm killing you."

I laughed. Quietly. "Fair. Alright. We'll open big and try to take it down fast. It's just one wolverine, right?"

"Right."

Dozens of animal species had mutated after Launch Day, but thanks to the Ilneats' assistance, most species hadn't gone extinct. I'd heard that there were even *real* wolverines somewhere near the Great Lakes. Oddly, most of the mutated animals didn't grow extra limbs or two heads. They just got bigger. We'd gotten an email briefing on turbo-buffalo and D-wolvers in case one made it past the wall. Wolverines were solitary animals, and while the real deal was more of a scavenger, the mutated dire wolverine *had* to hunt for its food.

The bad news was that as soon as it realized we were here, *we'd* be its food. The good news was that it'd almost certainly be alone.

We crept back down the tunnel. The creature's snuffling and growling had gotten quieter, and as I poked my head around the corner, its long legs and bulky hindquarters waddled down the tunnel and into the darkness. I signaled Fursona to wait before attacking; if the monstrous mammal kept moving, we might be able to avoid a fight. Carefully and slowly, we walked down the tunnel, following the gigantic carnivore.

The dark, dank tunnel never went pitch-black, though. Before the dim daylight leaking through the TUEAS Building's wreckage could fade completely, Fursona tapped my shoulder and pointed ahead. "Light," she whispered.

"Shit," I whispered back a few seconds later. The light she'd picked up wasn't much, but it glowed the friendly yellow-white of electric bulbs. "We *have* to fight it now."

The D-wolver's tunnel cut into a subway line near one of the campus stops. That *should* have been detected; if Riverside had a sensor network, TU *had* to have its own. Why hadn't it gone off the moment a megafauna breach happened? Was Professor Panic to blame for this, too? I shook my head to clear it. It didn't matter. If the D-wolver was in the subway tunnel, it was here to hunt people. We *needed* to do something.

I pointed at the subway tunnel's light. "It's in there. We have to take it down fast before a train comes. It'll rip through any Extras that get off."

"Uh-huh. Okay, right." Fursona bounced on the balls of her feet like she was psyching herself up. Then she hopped toward the lights.

I sprinted behind her, feet slipping slightly on the loose dirt, then crunching on gravel. The gigantic wolverine's claws scrabbled on the concrete platform as it pulled itself up off the track. It turned, saw us, and roared, sending a scream of fetid-smelling breath right at me.

I used **[Bit-Part Barrage]** before it finished its feral-sounding scream. The aiming spotlight overlapped with the gigantic predator's body. A moment later, pink-and-blue beams started pounding into it. It screamed again, this time in pain.

[Dramatic Damage! +3 Drama Points]

I'd gotten three good hits in, but shockingly, I'd seen at least eight beams make contact. Was its fur that thick?

I didn't have time to think about it. I'd only barely landed back on the track's gravel when the D-wolver *moved*. Its claws slammed into me, knocking me into the subway's faux-tile wall and driving the wind out of me.

[**HP 3/7**]

The subway's charging line crackled high above my head as I rolled. The wolverine's huge claws had ripped across my stomach, shredding my Costume and knocking off two points of superhero damage. If it weren't for that, I'd have been in trouble.

[**Gritty Recovery! +1 Grit Point**]

"Dammit," I coughed. The wolverine jumped down onto the tracks and sprinted at me. I *was* still in trouble. I pushed myself back to my feet and braced for impact.

"[**Ground Pound**]!" Fursona shouted. She shot up into the air over the oncoming monster, inches from the sparking charging line, then slammed into its back. Something cracked, and she fell off its back and onto the platform.

She *did* stop the wolverine's charge, though. It skidded toward me, legs no longer under it. I turned and ran. Gravel smacked against my back. I could hear its paws churning as it struggled for purchase right behind me. "I'm a [**Hometown Heroine**]! This overgrown weasel isn't going to run me down!"

I'd reached the station's far side before the wolverine stopped sliding. It growled again, a guttural, room-shaking sound, and I leaped onto the platform. Any distance I could get was good. I didn't have a ranged damage power left in Magical Girl Understudy, and I'd fucked up my build to get to Rainy Day. I didn't have [**Flickerform**]. There weren't *enough* power slots.

Something knocked the monstrous mammal sideways, and it whirled, back turning toward me. Fursona kicked out again, then ducked a claw swipe. Now that she had the monster's attention, the Justice-Roo seemed more focused on staying alive. She backed away from a whirlwind of claws, kicking and using her tail when she had openings.

I had an opening, too.

"The itsy-bitsy spider went up the waterspout.

Down came the rain and washed the spider out."

I was halfway through my transformation to Rainy Day and fully committed to it when claws hit Fursona for the first time. I bit back a scream as fuzzy armor ripped off of her arm, exposing bare skin. "I'm okay, keep going, dammit!" she shouted and kicked the D-wolver's front leg. It slammed into the ground, roared, and kept attacking.

"Out came the sun and dried up all the rain,

And the itsy-bitsy spider went up the spout again!"

The transformation was complete—and not a moment too soon. "Run!" I shouted and dashed *toward* the D-wolver. It roared after Fursona.

But not for long.

I [**Rode the Lightning**]. But it wasn't a normal-sized [**Ride the Lightning**]. Instead, as I used my power, it pulled electricity from the charging line up above. The yellow-white lightning arced into me, then into the D-wolver, ripping across its back and head. The lightning ripped across my Rainy Day Costume, too, but it hurt the D-wolver more than me.

[**Environmental Combo! +1 Cunning Point**]
[**Stylish Strike! +1 Flamboyance Point**]
[**Stylish Strike! +1 Flamboyance Point**]
[**Status Effect: Feedback 1**]
[**HP 2/7**]
[**Confirm Combo Continuation?**]

I could keep going? "Hell yeah," I whispered, and the lightning continued, zapping both of us. The [**Feedback**] *hurt,* but tore into the D-wolver, which sizzled and smoked as the combo kept running. It was a good trade-off. I hoped.

[**Environmental Combo! +1 Cunning Point**]
[**Stylish Strike! +1 Flamboyance Point**]
[**Stylish Strike! +1 Flamboyance Point**]
[**Status Effect: Feedback 2**]
[**HP 1/7**]
[**Combo Collapse**]

The combo collapsed, and so did I, crumpling onto the platform as my power finally ended. I picked myself up, still twitching from being a conduit for a combo'd [**Ride the Lightning**], and looked over at the D-wolver and my sidekick.

[**Tough Girl! +1 Grit Point**]

The monster twitched, too, as it pulled itself onto its feet. It started clambering down the tunnel, slowly at first but quickly picking up speed. It'd had enough, and I got ready to pursue. If we could stop it, that'd go a long way toward my quest for the minor leagues. But Fursona was in even worse shape than before. Her duel with the wolverine had shredded her Costume, and she wouldn't be much use in a fight.

In fact, she probably had less superhero damage left than *I* did.

I made a choice. I couldn't chase the D-wolver—not while Fursona was out of the fight. The Episode was probably a draw anyway since it was *supposed* to be Professor Panic against me. Drawing with a gigantic, minor-league-level threat like the wolverine wouldn't hurt me too much.

I transformed back to Understudy, helped Fursona to her feet, and started walking up the stairs. Neither of us was particularly quick—we'd taken a beating, and even with [**Rejuvenation**] triggering, a real fight wouldn't end well for either of us.

[Rejuvenation Activated: HP 4/7]

So we both groaned as a *different* supervillain sprinted down the subway stairs right at us. I got ready to use **[Spotlight Strike]**—not that it'd help against a fresh supervillain.

"What the **[Beep!]** are you two doing here? And did you already use the f-bomb?"

It took me a minute to recognize the villain. One arm was paper, and it held a gigantic, McHammer-esque mace like it was a feather. The other was . . . a gun. And unlike my previous encounter, the villain had replaced both legs, this time with what looked like sprinters' legs. I didn't want to know where he'd gotten those.

"Hi, Theseus," I groaned. "Yep, I got it this Episode."

Theseus would either beat us into the ground if he wasn't on duty or hunt the D-wolver if he was. Either way, there wasn't much we could do against the minor-league villain, so there wasn't much point in getting ready for a fight.

"We got an alarm trigger just after the TUEAS Building collapsed. Where's the megafauna?" Theseus was, as usual, all business.

I pointed down the subway tunnel. "Are you armed for the job?"

"Har har. I'm on duty, so I'll tell you how it went in class tomorrow. Do *not* attempt to help. Little leaguers aren't supposed to get involved in Man vs. Nature fights unless it's an emergency." He sprinted off, moving faster than I did with **[Hometown Heroine]**.

"Good luck. We did a lot of damage to it," I called as he left.

It didn't take Theseus long. We'd barely made it up the subway station's stairs when the notification came in.

[Episode Finished!]
[Episode: Series Finale: Absent-Hearted Professor: Part One - PG-13]
[Penalties: No Warnings - Episode Rating Shift - No Penalty]
[Episode Finished! +5 of each Style Point]
[Call it a Draw! +2 of each Style Point]
[Role Focus: Drama+Flamboyance - Goal Met! +10 Focused Style Points]
[Alias - Understudy] [Archetype - Magical Girl] [Community Rank - 405/523]
[HP 4/7]
[Styles and Skills]
▶ Archetype Skill - Transformation Sequence
▶ Badass (24)
▶ Cunning (37)
▶ Inkling 1
▶ Drama (85) (Skill Roll Available)
▶ Hometown Heroine 1
▶ Bit-Part Barrage 1
▶ Flamboyance (89) (Skill Roll Available)

▶ Signature Skill - Adaptive Armoire 1
▶ Stored Costumes: (Rainy Day)
▶ Spotlight Strike 1
▶ Starwave Sail 1
▶ Grit (42)
[50 Drama Credits Used. Rolling Skill!]
[50 Flamboyance Credits Used. Rolling Skill!]

I rolled my skills, and another notification came in as the Style System's letters spun like a slot machine. A **[Casting Call]**. Fursona got it, too. She glared at me—I couldn't see it, but I could *feel* it. "There's a Part Two?"

[Casting Call]
[Episode: SERIES FINALE! Absent-Hearted Professor: Part Two - PG-13]
[Role: Teen Heroine! Mandatory Acceptance Required]
[Role Focus: Drama+Cunning]

67

There's a Part Two?

Bianca lay sprawled out on the chaise lounge in a pair of shorts—mine—and a T-shirt—also mine. Neither of us was talking much. We both had skills to figure out. Mine had rolled well. Really, really well.

[Rank Up! **Adaptive Armoire 2:** Store a second Costume for your Adaptive Armoire.]
[New Power! **Science Has Rules?:** Experiments don't need proper planning or procedure. They just need tension. Experimental weapons work if you can describe why.]

I was over the moon. The second rank in [**Adaptive Armoire**] meant I wouldn't have to choose between Rainy Day and Lab Assistant Panic. I could have both, and I'd need to build with that in mind. The Lab Assistant could become a full support/investigation Costume, but Rainy Day felt like it was slipping behind. It hadn't gotten a single power increase yet, and that was going to be a problem since I didn't *really* need it as a fight finisher with [**Bit-Part Barrage**] on Understudy, and I couldn't switch quickly enough to use it as a ranged damage dealer consistently.

Bianca grumbled to herself. She'd pulled off the wreckage of her Fursona suit as soon as we'd gotten to the green room; it sat by the door to Rocko's, but though we hadn't said as much, both of us knew we had a lot to talk about before she dropped it off.

"So, your ex, huh?" Bianca asked, breaking the silence. I was glad she'd started because I wanted to go in a different direction. "He seems like a *real* winner."

"Okay, first of all, ouch! Being the only supers in a small town is tough, so we ended up together. For emotional support reasons. And other than Professor Panic, he was mostly a nice guy. Mostly. Second, yeah, he's definitely overreacting. We broke up; it's not like I killed his favorite pet."

"Well, now I'm stuck in this Episode, the same as you are, Annie, so I've got some questions. What's his power set? Does he have any major weaknesses? And, if he's in Tokyexico, is he going to stay? Is he the kind of villain who's going to strike again soon, or will he wait it out?" Bianca sat up on the lounge and stared at me, waiting for an answer.

I told her about his power set; she'd already seen the robot army but not the FEAR Power Armor. It was a wild card. I couldn't beat it without some luck the last time we fought, but I'd gotten some new tricks. Plus, Fursona was a much more reliable sidekick than Collidus had been. The kid was probably stronger, but getting him off a battlefield for a few minutes was surprisingly easy.

"As for whether he'll stay? I don't know. I'm not even sure he *can* get home. He'll bide his time, find a place to work on what LABRATs and Panic Pals he has left, and probably convert them back to the 1.4 model. It's tougher—a lot tougher." I sighed and slumped on the couch.

"As tough as the dire wolverine?"

"Probably not. That thing took *too* much punishment. But he's been powering up his Cunning powers, too. He could have something new. He'd never seen **[Bit-Part Barrage]** before, and he *probably* didn't know much about Rainy Day, but we'll be up against stuff I haven't seen before too."

<**That's correct. Based on how many Style Points you two got, he could be building something new right meow!**> Tails spoke up from her perch on the makeup table. I relayed what she'd said to Bianca.

"So, to sum things up, we don't know all his powers, we don't know where he went, and we're stuck in this Episode with him until he decides to start up Act One?" Bianca frowned and adjusted her glasses. "Does that seem right?"

"That's about right," I said. I twiddled my thumbs, then coughed. The thing I wanted to talk about was right there if Bianca would just open the conversation. But she fidgeted just as awkwardly as I was. Which meant it was up to me to start it off. I'd have to be gentle, but I couldn't let it slide.

"How long did you say you knew?"

Bianca blushed. "Like I said, the first day we met. I didn't tell you because, uh, I dunno. I guess I thought secret identities needed to be respected. Besides, it seemed like you really, *really* valued having yours be private, so I couldn't tell you I knew. And it was so cute—"

"Hold on—"

"—when you told me your lies about Biology class and when you believed I was in Fencing. I mean, I *am* in fencing, but it's a once-a-week club, not a class. One of the things Pataki told me when they fixed up the Fursona suit was to *not* tell you, anyway. They said secret identities were super-important, and that you'd made a mistake, and that—"

"Wait a second."

Bianca stopped rambling. It was a return to the incredibly awkward freshman from Intro to Drama, not the ever-more-confident girlfriend Bee or Fursona. But I didn't care.

"I don't need excuses or anything. It's fine. We're partners, right? So I'm not mad, just . . . annoyed and embarrassed I did such a bad job hiding. Just, like, tell me next time, okay?"

She snorted and started laughing. "Next time I discover your secret identity?"

I started laughing, too. Then she squeezed me tight, and we laughed for a while on the lounge. After a while, she started getting restless.

"Annie, my arm's asleep. Get off me."

Still laughing, I climbed off the chaise lounge and helped her up.

Once Bianca left to drop her suit off with Pataki, I called Dad. The phone rang and rang as I paced the green room. Maintenance and repair workers were already swarming my apartment, and I'd probably be in a hotel tonight, but LABRAT hadn't made it to my secret base, and I didn't want to leave home just yet.

"Hello, Annie." Dad's voice came across the speaker, and I breathed a sigh of relief. "How you doing? We're still on for the video chat tomorrow, right?"

"Yes." I took another deep breath. "Peter's not sick."

"Huh. How would you know . . . oh." Dad stopped talking for a minute. "He's in Tokyexico, huh?"

"Yep." I started tearing up as I explained the last couple of hours. "So, anyways, there somehow wasn't anyone inside the TUEAS Building, and only one wing collapsed. There should be an email about it later, but it'll probably be months of repair work. There's probably enough extra classrooms on campus, but I don't know what the students who had project finals are going to do. Their projects are buried under tons of rubble, and they can't redo them without labs."

"What about you?" Dad asked sharply, cutting me off.

"Oh, I'm okay. They're fixing my room. It should be a week or so, but I'm trying to decide on a hotel or Bee's place."

Dad didn't say anything for a minute. I opened my mouth to keep talking about the Episode and how much damage Peter had caused. Before I could, he cleared his throat. "I don't mean about your space. Your ex-boyfriend is a maniac, and he won't stop."

"I know. He started up a Part Two as soon as the Episode—"

"Anika."

I stopped. He *never* called me Anika.

"I don't mean as a superhero, *Miss Understudy*. I'm talking about real life. It doesn't sound like he gets it that you're done with him. I'm not sure what the legalities are, but if you weren't supers, what he's doing would be stalking." Dad hadn't been this serious since the night I'd broken up with Peter. And worse, he was right.

"So what should I do?"

"I'll talk to Peter's dad on Monday. He's my boss, but maybe that'll help. If I were you, I'd let the Tokyexico police know your ex is out there, or I'd talk to any adult supers you know for advice. They've probably been through something like this, and they might be able to help. At the very least, it'll give you something to go off of. Other than that, I'd let Bee know you might have some bullshit coming your way, so you have someone to check on you."

I nodded even though he couldn't see me through the phone. "Uh-huh. Thanks, Dad."

We talked for a while longer. There was drama at Dad's work. Something about a big order that had come in for Angel City expansion, but without the materials to get started on the drills themselves. They'd done all the prep, and the work floor was ready to make the gigantic foundational drill bits, but without the materials, they couldn't. Worse, they couldn't refit the work floor for other jobs, so Dad wasn't working.

Mom was okay, according to Dad. She was training a new girl at the diner, so she wasn't around much, but the work was easier—for the most part. He said he'd relay the drama to her. We said goodbyes and love-yous and goodbyes again, then hung up.

I had business to take care of—first, an email to Dr. Jackson.

Subject: Supervillain Drama
Hi Dr. Jackson,
So, I screwed up. My ex-boyfriend is a supervillain, and today, he came to Tokyexico City for revenge. I'm not sure how to handle this, and I was hoping we could meet in the next couple of days to discuss what I'm supposed to do.
Thanks,
Understudy

After some hesitation, I also cc'd Dr. Mindstorm and sent the email. She'd probably have some terrifying but effective advice on how to deal with Peter. Another email came in before I could do too much wallowing. I read its subject line, then opened it.

Subject: TUEAS Damage, Campus Super-Security Protocol, and Campus Response
To All Students,
This morning, a superpower-related incident destroyed the Tokyexico University Engineering and Applied Sciences Building's engineering wing. The supervillain responsible remains at large but was not a student at TU. An unrelated incident caused damage to several dorm rooms in the Walnut Tower dormitory. Three superpowered students investigating the collapse discovered a dire wolverine infestation in the subway lines and, working together, were able to clear the megafauna from campus.
We take student safety very seriously, and as such, the Board of Directors, Faculty Senate, and Campus Police held an emergency meeting shortly after the incident. As this isn't the first such incident in TU's history, we successfully implemented the Campus Super-Security Protocol from the guide to TU. The following accommodations, consequences, and responses are in effect on campus.

—*Students who had classes in the TUEAS building may take their grade as of Friday, plus all assignments their professors can safely grade, as their final grade. Alternatively, classes will be held in alternative classrooms. Note that project work may still be required in this case.*

—*A campus-wide curfew is in effect. The Student Union Building's noncafeteria services will close at 7:30, and students are required to be in their dorms or on the major paths only at that time. This restriction is in response to the dire wolverine sighting and will last for two weeks after the most recent megafauna sighting on campus.*

—*Super students are prohibited from joining or participating in Episodes on campus until after finals. Those found engaged in non–Man vs. Nature Episodes will be penalized in their superpower studies classes.*

—*Finally, TU has arranged with both The Triad and Magical Girl Stella-Lunar for additional campus security and to help enforce the No Episodes rule above. Due to the dire wolverine infestation, these superheroes will run patrols and have part-time duty stations on campus.*

Thank you for your cooperation,
Helen Barber
Vice President of Student Services
Tokyexico University

PART EIGHT

68

That's So Extra

FRIDAY, NOVEMBER 28

Professor Panic is *out there,* and I can't do *anything* about it," I complained to Fursona for the five-hundredth time in a bit over a week. The snowy, blizzard-filled weather had continued, which had its pros and cons.

It was great because the turbo-buffalo herd was slowly leaving for greener—or at least less snow-covered—pastures, which meant the dire wolverines would hopefully follow. All the signs had pointed to them leaving before, but they'd stayed, sometimes going so far as to scratch themselves on the wall. And now that they were moving, it'd take months for them to clear out.

But it was bad because we still had to go to classes.

Fursona nodded as we walked. "Yeah, and I'm getting tired of hiding this stupid Episode all the time. He sticks us with it and then won't even start Act One? Unbelievable."

"That part makes sense. He wasn't ready to fight again, and by the time he was, he'd have to deal with a major leaguer. *I* wouldn't want to fight Stella-Lunar, especially when she's been freezing her ass off. She's probably pissed."

"Yeah," Fursona laughed.

The professors knew about the Series Finale—at least the first part of it—but I hadn't told them about Part Two. At this point, they'd probably fail me in Superpower Ethics or something if I did. The major leaguers' eyes were on me after the Grant Building fiasco, too. Like it or not, it was Peter's move.

We walked down the ramp and into the theater room. Dr. Jackson had already set up pods of six chairs. Fursona and I sat down with Gourmet and Theseus—and two unpowered students. As soon as the movie theater was full, Dr. Jackson cleared her throat.

"Students, you should have a more-or-less final draft of your code of ethics. Next week, you'll present them for your final grade. Your final task is to set aside your egos. Each of your teams has two temporary members. These are juniors and seniors in

Superhero Law. They're also Extras, and they're here to poke holes in your codes of ethics from a legal and unpowered perspective. Listen to them, consider their advice, and then finalize your codes. Break!"

"Hi, I'm Magical Girl Understudy," I said, offering handshakes to each Extra. They introduced themselves as Jennifer and Robert, then shook hands with each of my teammates.

"Alright, let's see it," Jennifer said.

I looked at Theseus nervously. This was the first time *anyone* outside our team had seen our code. Even Dr. Jackson hadn't looked at it except in passing, and she'd refused to give us advice. That had struck us as odd, but we'd continued soldiering on. Well, we were mostly arguing about it, to be honest. But yeah, soldiering on.

Theseus pulled out our code, scowling at me. "Here it is."

Code of Conduct: November 28
We will not involve Extras
When Extras must be involved, they must be clearly informed of danger
Destruction of non-corporate/non-government property is unacceptable
Property damage must be directly related to the Episode's goals
Medical Extras are off-limits. Healing heroes are not a target unless they directly engage
Neutrality will be respected
Finales?
We'll talk about those later.

As Jennifer and Robert looked at it, faces twisting in disgust, my heart plummeted even more. Finally, Jennifer cleared her throat. "I'll take one and three, you take two and four, we'll team up for five?"

"Yeah, sounds good," Robert said.

"Okay. Robert and I developed similar codes for our Dilemmas in Superhero Law course. We did it without any superhero input, and it's a 300-level class, not a 100 like this, but the principles are the same. And, uh, as it stands, you're not passing this class," Jennifer said.

"What? That's bullshit, we worked hard on this," Gourmet interrupted.

Theseus held up a hand. "Let her talk. She's an expert."

"Thank you." Jennifer continued. "I'm not trying to be a downer, but there's a lot you haven't thought about here. According to your professor, there's a group like this every year, and they usually pass if they get their shit together. So it's time to get your shit together. 'We will not involve Extras' is unrealistic. We're stuck with your Episodes, so figure out how to deal with that. Is murder okay? What about involuntary manslaughter? What about if the paparazzi gets in your face in the middle of the Episode?"

"Oh," Fursona said through her modulator. "I see."

"You don't have to solve every problem here, but this is both too general and too absolute. It means less than if you'd stuck a bunch of 'as possible' and 'unless necessary' in it. How do you plan to inform Extras of danger? You need to think these things through or change your code. Over to you, Robert."

"Thanks. So, which super was responsible for leveling the Grant Building?" Robert stared at each of us, and I could see Fursona fidget. I almost raised my hand but decided against it.

"All that damage they caused meets this requirement. Good job on the second part. But the first bit, frankly, sucks. Think about government housing and dorms. Or a lot of social work buildings. They're government property, but only a lunatic like Mister Twister would have gone after them, and he spent time in Almhurst for stuff like that. Clarifying information is important. Be specific, otherwise APPEAL will shred you in the media."

On and on the beatdown continued. Jennifer liked most of the "medical Extras and healers" section but wanted more details about what "engagement" meant for medical Extras and healers. We agreed to look more closely at it if we had time, but Robert's face told us we wouldn't. He spent almost ten minutes talking about corner cases where neutrality needed to be violated, like in the "Almhurst Anarchy" Episode, when McHammer declared Neutral Fields while his henchmen took a school hostage. Ultimately, he recommended we talk to a major leaguer for that one. I decided I'd link up with Tele-Portal sometime for advice.

They also recommended a different set of rules for finales, but we'd have to finish the rest first, which would be the priority. As the Extras finished talking, Dr. Jackson cleared her throat.

"By now, you've all realized your codes of ethics are terrible," she said. "That's normal. Our unpowered guests are willing to spend time over the next week working with you. They'll be available during class time, should you choose to use it, on Monday and Wednesday next week. I'll have the room unlocked, but I'll be in my office grading Villainous Endeavors finals. You present on Friday."

Theseus looked ready to strangle her, but he'd have to do it with his own hands— the weightlifter's arms wouldn't work on her. Gourmet, for the very first time, looked sick to her stomach. I understood *that* feeling, but someone had to take charge. I turned to Robert and Jennifer. "How about Monday?"

Behind me, Gourmet groaned.

When Dr. Jackson finally dismissed us, I hurried toward my next obligation—a meeting with Dr. Mindstorm.

"I don't get it," I complained to Fursona. "Why's she my advisor, anyway? You got Mays. Lucky!"

"I'd rather have Mindstorm. She seems serious, just less interested in the rules. Dr. Mays is a total goofball unless he's upset, like with The Agent at the job fair." Fursona gave me a quick hug outside the Beaumont Administrative Building. "I'll get you some pizza and drop it off in the green room, alright?"

"Alright. You should be able to get in." I gulped. Last week, when I'd talked to Dr. Mindstorm, she'd demanded I do nothing about Professor Panic . . . yet. Her advice had been sound—so far. Still, I felt like I was wasting time following the administration's rules, and the finale's weight bore down on me. My only other solo meeting with my academic advisor had been during the Orientation Episode, and she'd taken over my mind. I shivered. "Wish me luck in there."

"Good luck in there." Fursona squeezed my shoulder and headed for the Student Union Building while I stepped into the admin building's lobby.

"Have a seat, Magical Girl Understudy." Dr. Mindstorm said in her usual curt voice. She typed on her computer while I quickly sat in the straight-backed chair across the desk. "There will be no mind-sharing during this advisory meeting. Consulting your current grades . . . you'll most likely pass all your classes if you figure out Superpower Ethics, but if you're considering a career in math, you'll need to work harder. What career path are you interested in?"

"Superhero work. Isn't that what most supers say?" I asked, confused.

"Obviously. You're minoring in that, but you'll need to work toward a major as part of your cover." Mindstorm typed for a while, letting the silence grow oppressive. Then she typed a bit longer. "So, what do you want to learn?"

"My parents think superhero law. I've always wanted to go into theater, though."

"Those work well together, believe it or not. Practicing courtroom lawyers—and those who work with supervillains—require acting skills. Both will also be . . . practical in your career as a superhero or villain. As a second-semester freshman, you'll need to cover certain prerequisites. A foreign language, psychology, and a language arts or English class. We'll use language arts as your cover class for Combat Style."

"Combat Style?" My next superhero class was going to be about combat? I was thrilled!

"I'll tell you more . . . later. I recommend Ilneat 115: Intro to Ilnean Language, and Theater 143: Prop Design and Manufacturing. They're building-block classes for the Superhero Pre-Law major and Theater minor, respectively. Human Growth and Development is a solid basic psychology class. And . . . let's see . . . Ilneat Politics with Dr. Quailman."

I groaned, and Dr. Mindstorm narrowed her eyes. I immediately stopped complaining. "Sorry. He's not very exciting."

"I am . . . aware. However, Ilnean Politics is better. There are guest lecturers who are more . . . intimately familiar with the political situation in Ilneat space. You'll also sign up for Creative Writing One. It's your cover class. The real treat is Combat Style. One day of Combat Style Forum on Mondays, during which time you'll learn minor-league-level skills in preparation for your . . . hopeful . . . league-up soon. And one day of Combat Style Practicum on Fridays to practice minor-league skills and powers with other students."

"So I'll fight other students? What about Theseus? Will he be there?"

"No. Theseus will be in a class about supervillain organizational management. As an aspiring lieutenant, that is his best choice for the second semester, and his power level is sufficient to skip Combat Style."

I confirmed the classes Dr. Mindstorm had selected for me, then fidgeted in my chair while she stared at me. Her eyes bored into my brain, but it didn't *feel* like her power. Then she nodded slowly and stood. "That should do it. As for your . . . other problem, think outside of the box you've been put in. Be creative."

I opened my mouth to say something, but she put a finger to her lips. She held the door open and I slipped out. The moment the elevator doors closed, I had my phone out.

<Collidus, break into Professor Panics room - Understudy 12:25>

<Hes in Tokyexico. See if you can find out where - Understudy 12:26>

<Im gonna need some time, Understudy - Collidus 12:27>

<Three days. Maybe four. You dont just break into a supervillains room - Collidus 12:28>

<Fine. Ill wait. Patiently. - Understudy 12:29>

69

Patiently

Collidus was *not* true to his word, and it was pissing me off.

It'd been four days, and we were deep in finals week. I'd texted him daily asking for updates, but he kept putting me off. Apparently, and uncharacteristically, he kept saying he was "scouting" or "planning."

<Who are you and what did you do with Collidus? - Understudy 5:24>

Whatever he was planning, I hoped it worked, but the waiting was killing me. We'd tinkered with the code of ethics on Monday. Only three teams had shown up—Punch, Grapple, The Crumb, and Flare were confident in their code. In any case, Jennifer and Robert were *not* more chill with Dr. Jackson out of the room. It took almost two hours—Gourmet left to get us lunch twice, apologizing after she ate it all the first time—but we had something that the two pre-law students agreed was . . . not great, but at least serviceable.

It'd have to do. Superpower Ethics was just one class of many, and Dr. Mindstorm *had* stressed the importance of passing all my courses. Academic probation—mandatory weekly meetings with my advisor, enrollment in a twice-weekly study hall class, and constant email checkups on my classes' progress—sounded miserable. Between studying for and *taking* my Intro to Drama final, I'd been too busy to hunt for Professor Panic myself.

With nothing much to do, I found myself—*gasp*—studying for Ilneat Relations. I'd be taking that final Thursday, and—

My phone buzzed.

<Hey, Understudy. Im in Prof Ps lair! Wyd? - Collidus 11:37>
<I told you to break into his bedroom - Understudy 11:37>
<Did you find anything out - Understudy 11:38>

He'd done it. The little shit had followed through. He was inside Peter's *lair*. How the hell had he pulled that off? I'd hunted for that damn lair for months! My stupid Ilneat Relations textbook vanished into my backpack.

This time, my phone rang.

"Hello?" I stood up from my place in the library, smiling apologetically at the other studying students as I fled outside.

"Hey, so Professor Panic has *way* too much security on his computer. When I messed up the password, I got attacked by Panic Pals. Then, I tried again, and the whole thing melted. Like, actually melted. It looks like metallic mac and cheese now. But I did find something interesting."

"What? What'd you find?"

"You and Professor Panic were in *love*! Panic and Understudy, sitting in a tree!"

I took a deep breath. "Collidus, what about where he is?" He was being a brat, and I *needed* Professor Panic's location.

"So, the computer melted down. The rest of the room was pretty much empty, but I found a sticky note on his desk. Most of it was charred and scorched, but there's something about a submarine. I don't know why he'd need one of those; we're in the middle of North America."

"A sub? I have no idea why he'd be looking for a—" It hit me like a ton of bricks, and I stared down the concrete path. Dozens of students walked back and forth from the dorm towers to the short, squat Student Union Building. And somewhere below it, Professor Panic lurked, plotted his next move, or waited for me to mess up with all the superheroes on patrol. "Thanks, Collidus."

"No problem. When are you—" He didn't have a chance to finish. I'd already hung up.

<Do you have finals today? - Annie 11:41>

I was already running toward Walnut Tower. They'd finished my room two nights ago, and they'd added reinforcements to the windows so they'd break less easily. It was good to be home, even if the bed wasn't quite the same or if my new coffee table needed a folded-up piece of paper under one of the legs to stop it from rocking. I had a lead for the first time all week, and it'd be enough. I was going to end this Series Finale. Tonight. Once and for all.

<Yeah one this afternoon. - Bianca 11:42>
<Meet me at 1301 at 630. Bring your backpack <3 - Annie 11:42>

The Third Ilneat Compact, as it's commonly referred to on Earth, allowed limited Ilneat presences in all major Earth cities. In exchange, continued post-Launch cleanup efforts continued in the Everglades, near former Alice Springs, Australia—which, for some reason, attracted a disgusting number of nuclear strikes for a tiny town—and the Ganges

Watershed. While those cleanup efforts were important, the real benefit from the TIC was the cultural exchange with the Ilneats themselves.

I did not want to write this stupid essay. I was supposed to argue the significance of the Third Ilneat Compact, but Peter was *so close*. All it'd take was me turning in what I had—I was confident I'd nailed the multiple-choice section after all my time with Rocko and Pataki—and taking the loss on the essay. My hand was writing, but I wasn't really thinking.

Bianca—Fursona was the one I needed, but Bianca all the same—was in a science final, putting the last bits of data in from some experiment. She wouldn't be done for another hour, so there wasn't any point in rushing. Instead, I kept writing.

Elephants react similarly to seeing humans as humans do to kittens and puppies. They think we're cute. Similarly, the Ilneat Empire thought humanity—or at least human media—was cute, cool, or entertaining. The continued Earth-wide contract as a studio world represents humanity's part of that cultural exchange, but Ilneat contributions to humanity's culture have an understated but profound impact on the theater.

One of the major impacts on theater (and also on music) was hyperacoustic coating. Though expensive and fragile, hyperacoustic materials, and especially coatings, allow for unique, nonacoustic theater and auditorium shapes. They can also be used to make certain sounds, like those common in Ilneat music, audible to human ears. Hyperacoustics have opened up a whole new level of depth in music and new theater productions, both musical and traditional plays.

I kept writing. Every few lines, I stared at the clock as it crept closer to the end of the day, or I glanced at Teaching Assistant Smith to see if she was as bored as we were. She stared at her computer, typing, then reading, then taking a quick look over the room. No one else had gotten up, so I kept writing.

The sun was descending below the wall by the time I finally finished what I *hoped* was a viable final essay on the Third Ilneat Compact. I turned it in, ignoring Teaching Assistant Smith's shocked look at how quickly I'd finished, and left the classroom. Pass or fail, whatever happened would happen, but I had other things on my mind.

"Hey, sorry I'm late," Bianca said. She gave me a quick kiss and started unpacking the Fursona Costume.

"It's fine. Let's get ready." I was already suited up as Understudy, this time with both Rainy Day and Lab Assistant Panic equipped and ready to go. I'd made a few adjustments to each build. Both Costumes now carried **[Check the Script]**, while, with a ton of regret, I'd changed out Understudy's **[Hometown Heroine]** for **[Flickerform]**. I wasn't *happy* about it, but there weren't enough power slots to cover everything, and with two **[Adaptive Armoire]** Costumes, I needed the flexibility. The minor leagues would open up a slot or two, I hoped.

I watched and talked while Bianca pulled off her coat, sweater, and fuzzy leggings, stripping down to shorts and a spaghetti-strap top.

"He's in the Student Union Building. I'm pretty sure SSS members are helping him out. They have to be—he's in too many on-campus lairs. So, what we're going to do—here, let me help you buckle in—is break in, take him down quickly, and try to get the police there for the arrest anonymously. We need to move fast and hit him before he can get into the FEAR Power Armor."

"That buckle attaches to my head," Bianca said. She pulled the head on, and I saw how it worked. I strapped her into the suit, and Fursona stretched. "Thanks, Understudy."

"No problem."

We stepped into the elevator; the moment we did, the Style System hit us with a message.

[Absent-Hearted Professor: Part Two: Act One in Progress]

"So, Professor Panic probably posits our plan," Fursona quipped.

"Shut it. It's still going to work." The elevator door opened. "We'll head to Ash Hall and go from there. If we're lucky, we'll be able to sneak out through the curfew."

"Sure." Fursona and I hurried furtively down the hall. I kept looking over my shoulder, and so did Fursona. As we exited into the Ash Hall basement, she paused. "Which major leaguer is on duty tonight?"

"I'm not sure. Hopefully, it's Stella-Lunar." If it was a Triad member, we'd be screwed if they caught sight of us; they'd call the whole team in, whereas Stella-Lunar—hopefully—wouldn't be able to summon backup. Maybe we could outrun her or find a place to hide. But ideally, we wouldn't run into the guest security on campus or, worse, a superpowered professor.

We ducked out Ash Hall's door, nodding at a couple in the common room who were . . . being wildly inappropriate for a public space. He nodded back while she blushed. "Nothing wrong with what you're doing, but maybe take it back to your room?" I suggested.

Then we were outside. Somewhere out here, a major-league hero was on patrol. And I was becoming increasingly certain that the Student Supervillain Society was plotting with Professor Panic.

We couldn't use the main path; that much was obvious, so we crunched through the snowdrift-covered grass. About halfway to the Student Union Building, in the middle of darting from one tree to the next, Fursona held up her hand and pointed. "They look familiar," she said.

I followed her pointing paw. A faintly glowing figure dashed across the quad ahead of us, leaving behind melted footprints in the crusty snow that steamed. "Is that Flare?" I whispered.

It was. Fursona and I followed the Speedster as best we could, creeping a few hundred feet behind him as he headed toward the Student Union Building and an oddly placed delivery entrance.

"That's where he is," I said. "Let's take Flare out and break in before any other villains appear."

As the spark-themed little leaguer arrived at the delivery door and started typing a code into a keypad conveniently hidden in a power outlet, I used [**Bit-Part Barrage**].

I'd say he never saw it coming, but the spotlight gave it away.

[**Dramatic Damage! +4 Drama Points**]

Fursona leaped across the freezing-cold field a moment later and crashed into him. I darted forward, activated [**Spotlight Strike**], and started looking for an opening. But before I could find one, a portal opened before us. A pair of hands reached through, grabbed Flare, and pulled. Then, before I could scramble away, one grabbed Fursona's wrist, the other grabbed my outfit's collar, and I found myself yanked onto a warm, tiled floor.

Tele-Portal stood over us, hands on her hips, glaring. Flare moved to escape, and she fired a portal under him, another above him, and dropped him into an endless loop. Then she turned her gaze toward us as if daring me to try something. I held up my hands.

She cleared her throat. "Understudy, I'm disappointed. You're in so much trouble."

70

In So Much Trouble

I was in so much trouble.

"Sit," Tele-Portal said. Fursona and I sat on one side of the Superpower Studies office waiting room; Flare found a seat on the other, and she blooped a portal into existence and disappeared. All three of us stared at the ground. My stomach felt like lead; we were screwed.

"What's the plan, Understudy? What do we do?" Fursona asked. She sounded as nervous as I felt, even through her voice modulator.

I shrugged. "We got caught red-handed breaking the rules. I don't think there's much we *can* do."

"So, what? You two are just gonna come clean about attacking a supervillain during a lockdown? You think that's going to work? Ha!" Flare crossed his arms and glared sullenly at us. "You two are the worst, you know that?"

"At least we didn't get beaten by us three times," Fursona said.

Flare flushed, anger flashing across his face. He looked ready to start something for a moment—right here, in the professors' waiting room.

I shook my head at both of them. "Chill out, Flare. We can still get out of this if we're honest about our actions. Or at least, maybe not fail Superpower Ethics."

Flare breathed, screwing his eyes closed. Then he half groaned and half screamed. "Augh! You're so fucking hateable! Fine, you win. We'll settle this shit later."

I sat back in my chair, pretending to relax even as the camera drone—why was there *always* a camera drone around when I didn't want it—spun slowly between our faces. My heart felt like it was going to pound out of my chest.

The portal flared. Tele-Portal stepped back through, this time with a *very annoyed*-looking trio of professors. Even this late, Dr. Jackson wore most of her pantsuit from teaching, but with a sweater instead of the jacket. Dr. Mays was in a T-shirt and jeans, and though he'd cleaned up a little, flecks of sawdust covered his arms. And Dr. Mindstorm wore footie pajamas, not too much unlike my favorite ones still stuck in Riverside. Fursona stifled a giggle.

"You two, my office, now," Dr. Mays said, pointing at Fursona and me. He opened the door, and we filed in with Dr. Mindstorm. The two professors took the seats, leaving us standing awkwardly in front of the desk.

"Why . . . am I back here right now?" Dr. Mindstorm started. I stared at her. She'd *encouraged* this play!

Neither Fursona nor I said anything for several seconds.

Mindstorm glared. "Look, I have fifteen Episode Manipulation essays to grade. I'd rather be doing this than that, but I'm on a deadline, and . . . my show starts in twenty minutes. I'll figure out the truth . . . one way or another. Talk to me."

Dr. Mays scowled at Mindstorm. "What my colleague means is that this is incredibly inconvenient for all of us. What's going on?"

"Okay, here's what happened." It took almost ten minutes to explain everything; somehow, neither professor interrupted me while I talked and talked.

By the end, Dr. Mindstorm looked incredibly bored. She suppressed a yawn. "I *get* it. You're a young super with big dreams and no idea how things . . . really work, and no ability to *think outside the box*. It takes a while to grow out of that."

"Some of us never do," Dr. Jackson said, joining the others and staring pointedly at Mindstorm.

"But we can't have a bunch of little leaguers running around campus *openly* flouting school rules. I'd recommend you take a 20% hit to your ethics grades, but Dr. Jackson runs the class as a pass/fail, so that won't work, will it now?"

"No, that won't work at all. However, I want a small essay from these three students on Man vs. Nature events and why it's important to follow policies from the Tokyexico Council of Heroes or TU staff. That's now required for you to pass the course, and I've already assigned it to Flare."

I swore under my breath. The nice thing about the rating having gone up—which I hadn't told the professors—was that I could do that. I didn't have *time* for an essay on authority and Man vs. Nature. I had finals, and I had to make plans for winter break.

But there were three professors here, plus Tele-Portal in the waiting room. And to be honest, I'd fucked this up. I'd been in such a rush to go after Professor Panic and stop whatever he was doing under the Student Union Building that I hadn't put any thought into planning—just like when TUSSA had attacked the SSS under the engineering building.

So, after a minute to compose myself, I nodded. "Fine."

"Tele-Portal has also volunteered to escort you all to and from your finals for the next two days in lieu of more restrictive measures to keep you out of trouble. Here's her phone number. Please text her your schedule for Thursday and Friday," Dr. Jackson said. She handed us business cards with Tele-Portal's logo and smiling face.

"Fine. Can we get back home? Arianette's introducing Rojireck to her parents in fifteen minutes, and I was supposed to be done grading by the time it started." Mindstorm didn't seem put out at not messing with my brain.

Dr. Mays cleared his throat. "Yes. You two wait in the lobby with Flare. Tele-Portal will be by soon to drop you off at your elevators."

The camera drone, which had been following us around, zipped away. As it did, I got a Style System message.

[End of Act One! Act Two Soon! No Skill Rolls Available!]
[Alias - Understudy] [Archetype - Magical Girl] [Community Rank - 405/523]
[HP 7/7]
[Styles and Skills]
►Archetype Skill - Transformation Sequence
►Badass (24)
►Cunning (37)
►Drama (39)
►Hometown Heroine 1
►Bit-Part Barrage 1
►Flamboyance (39)
►Signature Skill - Adaptive Armoire 2
►Stored Costumes: (Rainy Day, Lab Assistant Panic)
►Spotlight Strike 1
►Starwave Sail 1
►Flickerform 1
►Grit (42)

"Fuck, fuck, fuck!" I screamed into my pillow. I was out of Costume, just regular old Annie. It was easier to be furious this way—easier to be upset and frustrated. Magical Girl Understudy didn't lose control. She did dumb stuff sometimes, but never lost control.

Anika DuPont, though? I punched the bed as hard as I could, screaming into the pillow again. It took a while to calm down; I hadn't been this pissed since just before the Peter breakup. Somehow, that thought was calming. If I could stop reacting to Peter's bullshit, I could make it through the semester, then flatten him afterward to end this Episode.

My phone rang. I stared at the number—it wasn't my parents, Bianca, or Tele-Portal. It wasn't one of the professors. The area code wasn't for Tokyexico *or* Riverside. I wasn't sure it was from *Earth.* I picked up the phone.

"DuPont. Studio. Now." Rocko's voice sounded soft, without their usual fanfare and aplomb. He was furious. He hung up before I could even *start* explaining things to him.

Well, shit. This wasn't just *my* Series Finale, or Peter's. It was Rocko's, too, and they probably had a lot riding on this. I hurried toward the Backstage entrance in my secret base, opening the star-festooned door and stepping into Rocko's studio.

[Welcome to Rocko's studio. System Disabled. Now arriving Backstage.]

Rocko had not one but two cigars in their mouth. Bianca was already there, sitting and drinking from a water bottle. I grabbed one of my own as Rocko started gesturing wildly, four hands—and cigar ash—flying. "DuPont! Marino! What is going on? Your professors stalled out my Series Finale!"

I opened my mouth to explain, but the Ilneat got in my face, standing on their desk. "No, DuPont, listen to me. I've got two payments left on my house. Then it's done and paid for. So give me some ideas here because we're on a knife's edge, and Professor Panic won't pick up his phone! If this flops, Rocko Studios is ruined!" They sucked in a gigantic cloud of cigar smoke; the cloying smell lingered in the room, a hint of something tropical in the middle of the too-hot office.

"Rocko, I don't know what to tell you," I started.

"Then don't tell me anything. Just listen. 'Absent-Hearted Professor: Part One' had ridiculously high ratings. *Small-Town Super*'s Episode last week beat out half the minor-league shows. I've got three factories—three!—working on LABRAT toys, and the Fursona pajama is sold out in two systems!

"So, I'm thrilled, right? Part Two is gonna be even bigger, like the pre-Launch Day movies. Merchandise deals like you wouldn't believe. But it just . . . doesn't happen." The Ilneat put out one of their cigars on their desk and sat down behind it dejectedly. They weren't crying; instead, they shook slightly, three arms wrapped around their body while the last one held the cigar. "A little tension and anticipation is good, but our target demographic doesn't have the patience. We've gotta get Part Two going again."

They'd gone all-in on the Series Finale. They'd bet everything on it, and they'd probably gone into debt buying merchandising contracts. Which meant they had a very, *very* big stake in getting this Episode rolling. It'd ruin them if it failed. It might even ruin them if it got delayed.

"Why don't you call up, uh, Mindstorm's old studio? There's gotta be something they can do," I asked. Mindstorm was on my side—kind of. Maybe her studio would be, too.

"'Why don't you call up Mindstorm's studio?' You think I hadn't thought of that. They don't wanna talk to a little-league production. They're busy working with, I don't know, Golden Goose's producer, or McHammer's, or someone worth their while. They don't have time for us."

"It's worth a shot." I *had* to get them to try it. Otherwise, I only had getting escorted around and essay-writing to look forward to. "What would you do if Ed called for help?"

"Ed? I'd tell him to take a spacewalk. Ed and that Bouncer supervillain, they're competition. Sort of. But, hmmm . . . Yakko *did* call last week about you two showing up at Tottergarten over your winter breaks, and I said I'd check in with you. It'd be good publicity to line it up with the holidays. What do you say?"

I felt a flash of anger for a moment. What were they doing, trying to get me to commit to something? But . . . Rocko needed me to say yes. Maybe to convince Mindstorm's producer to pay it forward. "Fine. I can't go home anyway, so Christmas Eve?"

They clapped their hands together, lit another cigar, and reached for a phone. "Now we're talking! I'll see what I can do. Give me eight hours."

71

Eight Hours

THURSDAY, DECEMBER 4

Aaaaaaaayyy! DuPont, good news! I pulled some strings for you and got the major leaguers out of your hair for an hour—*maybe* two—this afternoon!"

I groaned. It was too early for this shit, but Rocko *had* said eight hours, and his call was right on time. "That's great. What'd you have to do?"

"Oh, nothing, nothing. I owe favors to Phil and Lil, Zim, and Yakko. You have no idea how many strings I had to pull to make this happen. But forget it. Just be ready, alright? And don't tell anyone until, say, 1:36 this afternoon. Oh, and you owe Tottergarten a Christmas special. No danger, just stolen presents and shenanigans."

"Thanks for the heads-up. I won't let you down."

"You better not." Rocko's voice sounded serious. "I'm not joking when I say I owe Zim *and* Yakko massive favors. Getting The Narrator's villain to move ain't cheap, kid. Now, DuPont, go get 'em."

They hung up the phone, and I stared at the blank screen for a few seconds. I'd hoped Rocko could pull something off, but I hadn't *really* thought he'd be able to move the major leaguers. I'd have a window to finish this with them out of the way. But first, I had an Algebra final. I started texting furiously.

<Tele-Portal, Math final this morning. 9. 15 minutes away - Understudy 7:11>
<Majors will be busy this afternoon. Finals schedule? - Understudy 7:11>
<Great. C U @8:55 @ ur elevator - Tele-Portal 7:12>

I snorted into my milk glass. She texted like my parents, or like someone from *way* before Launch Day, when they, supposedly, had to pay by the text and had max text lengths. I guessed she'd set up a portal jump to get me to the Algebra final, or at least close. Either way, I had an hour and a half to plan my attack on Professor Panic this afternoon. Not that I was much of a planner.

<Final in Chemistry. Done by 12:30 - Fursona 7:17>
<Perfect. - Understudy - 7:17>
<Here's the plan - Understudy 7:18>
<We run it just like the TUEAS Building lair - Understudy 7:18>
<Didn't we fail that one? - Fursona 7:19>

My waffle sat on the kitchen counter, forgotten and drowning slowly in syrup. I was too busy typing.

<We know where the entrance is. We go fast as soon as whatever Rocko has planned happens. Get inside that door and take Professor Panic down before he can suit up. If we get stalled, you keep the SSS off me and I get Professor Panic - Understudy 7:21>
<I think itll work. We can make it work. 1.5 and 1.6 LABRATs. Weak armor. Panic Pals are nothing. Maybe Flare, but only if he gets out without TP catching him - Understudy 7:23>
<The big thing is speed. Gotta go fast. Rocko only gave us a few hours - Understudy 7:24>
<Ok. Im in. See you at 145 outside the SUB - Fursona 7:25>
<And if were not fast, the Triad or the professors will flatten us - Understudy 7:25>
<Thanks <3 - Understudy 7:25>
< <3 - Fursona 7:26>

I turned on my phone screen and stared at it. 1:33. It'd been 1:33 the last three times I'd checked, too. My Algebra final had been the most challenging test I'd ever taken. It wasn't the questions; I thought I'd executed *the plan* well. The problems I knew how to do, I'd worked hard on, and the ones even Su-Bin couldn't teach me? I guessed where I could and skipped where I couldn't.

Just like planned.

1:34.

The issue with Algebra wasn't the test. I wanted to get out there and finish this Episode, and the test felt in the way of that. But I'd done my best; that was all I could do.

I dipped into the bathroom. Before I'd finished washing my hands, a loud, echoing voice boomed across campus. It sounded a little like The Narrator's, but deeper and rougher. "It was a lovely day. You were minding your own business in a little park by the wall. Then, suddenly, a storm blew in from the mountains. You could practically feel the electricity in the air as the Poudre Districts descended into . . . Gothic Horror! The bats were on their way."

I looked out my window; a sinister-looking black-and-red pallor had descended on the two districts to Tokyexico University's north. *Something* flew through the air toward Tokyexico, massive wingbeats echoing against the wall loudly enough that I could hear them from here. "What. The. Fuck." I almost called Rocko to have them call off . . . whatever was happening, but as I reached for my phone, I received three new text messages.

<Aaaaaaaayyy! Go go go! Make me proud- Rocko 1:35>
<I'm assuming that's the signal right? What the hell is that? - Fursona 1:35>

Then, a minute later . . .

<This is an automated emergency SMS message. The meta-powered supervillain Fanfic has launched an Episode in the east and northeast Poudre Districts. All minor-league and lower supers are required to stay out of the Poudre Districts. Unpowered citizens in the Poudre Districts are urged to shelter in place. All major-league heroes and villains in Tokyexico City not currently on Man vs. Nature duty must respond. Repeat: lower-league supers must stay out of the Poudre Districts. Unpowered citizens, shelter in place. - TCoH 1:36>

I texted Fursona to let her know that, yes, this was the signal. Then I started transforming. That lunatic had pulled strings to get *Fanfic* involved, of all things? The fifth meta-powered super, and possibly the most powerful; Fanfic's power worked similarly to The Narrator's, except that they controlled genre and character actions as well as the plot. They weren't as deadly as Lord Destructo, but their rambling, half-baked stories were impossible to get out of, and they'd destroyed enough supers' careers that everyone usually banded together to stop the IP-violating villain.

Plus, they didn't care about collateral damage in their Episodes. At all. They needed a code of ethics.

But I didn't have time to worry about that. The transformation finished, and I sprinted for the stairs. The time was 1:38. According to Rocko, there wouldn't be any major-league heroes or villains on campus for a couple of hours.

It was go time.

"**[Starwave Sail]**!" I threw myself off the roof and windsurfed through the air, straight toward the Student Union Building. As I got close, I got a new notification.

[Absent-Hearted Professor: Part Two: Act Two in Progress]

I landed on the snow right outside of the delivery door. It was locked, but that was fine; I'd wait for Fursona, and she'd kick it open. In fact, I could hear her crunching through the crusty snow as she bounded closer. She rounded the Student Union Building's corner and waved.

A moment later, something slammed into her, moving fast. A fiery explosion threw her into a tree; I started rushing over, readying **[Bit-Part Barrage]**, but she stood up and waved me down before I could finish my power. "Ah, Flare, we meet again. I'm surprised you were brave enough to come out after our last meeting," Fursona said.

"I'd have beaten you if I had a better sidekick. The Crumb is worthless!" Flare shouted. He danced sparks across his knuckles and dove toward Fursona.

I wanted to help, but the loading bay door opened, and a pack of Panic Pals and a LABRAT came out. By the charging docks on its back, it was a 1.6, which meant it didn't have the armor to tank my attacks.

"IT'S PANIC TIME! EVERYBODY LOSE IT!
THE MAD PROF OF TOWN'S GOT CRIMES TO COMMIT!"

Bang!

The flying robots swarmed me, and the airburst kicked up a cloud of snow that covered my Costume. I ignored the Panic Pals, instead running straight toward the LABRAT before it could recharge its cannon. I had a trick up my sleeve this time.

I **[Flickerformed]** into **[Speed-Hacker]**, targeting the **[Hypercompression Cannon]**. Its lights flickered pink, and it fired another airburst—

Bang!

—Right into the Panic Pals closing in behind me. One catapulted backward, detached arms landing in the snow as its body rolled.

[Good Thinking! +1 Cunning Point]
[Smarty-Pants! +1 Cunning Point]

The speaker-bot was still up, and with the **[Hypercompression Cannon]** out of commission, the annoying robot was my next target. I had enough time to see a fiery explosion on the quad and Fursona kicking Flare in the chest as I turned and ducked a pair of Panic Pals' metal fists. One bit onto my shoulder, but I punched it.

[HP 6/7]
[Badass Takedown! +1 Badass Point]

My friend the LABRAT stomped after me. "We all hate you, you know. It's in our programming."

I didn't even respond. Instead, I used **[Spotlight Strike]** and caught the speaker-bot right in its open mouth, exactly where the spotlight highlighted. The bot sparked, shorted out, and slid off my arm onto the snow as I spun.

[Stylish Strike! +1 Flamboyance Point]

Bang!

The LABRAT's cannon fired into the ground this time, knocking the whole bot off-balance as it followed me around the snow-packed field. It reached out with the hijacked cannon arm to catch itself. Its weight worked against it, and the arm twisted with a spine-tingling screech. It sounded like fingernails on a chalkboard.

With a moment of respite from the LABRAT, I turned my attention to the Panic Pals. A pair of punches knocked each of them out of the fight. I didn't get any Style Points—they weren't particularly great punches, and I hadn't used a power, but then it was just the LABRAT and me.

"I'm getting inside that door, LABRAT," I said, turning to face the robot as it leveraged itself up. Its [**Hypercompression Cannon**] trailed behind it, attached only by a pair of sparking wires, and its pink lights had burned out.

"No, you're not. I only have to delay for a few minutes for Professor Panic to . . . well, you'll see." LABRAT lunged toward me, clawed arm grabbing for my wand, and my skirt flared as I spun out of the way. I [**Spotlight Struck**] it in the shoulder, then right in a charging dock, which sparked and started whining.

[**Stylish Strike! +1 Flamboyance Point**]

I couldn't switch Costumes to Rainy Day and [**Stellar Ray**] it down. The nursery rhyme was too long. But I didn't need to. I had more options than ever; I even had another use of [**Flickerform**].

I used it, this time for [**Ride the Lightning**]. I didn't have an environmental combo going, but I didn't need one. The electrical tendrils wrapped across LABRAT, and its charging ports shorted out one after another in a series of popping explosions. I dodged backward, landing on an oak's root that bumped out of the grass. It drove the wind out of me. A moment later, the LABRAT went up in flames, screaming dramatically in monotone.

[**Intense Finish! +1 Drama Point**]
[**Electric Lightshow! +2 Flamboyance Points**]

With the LABRAT destroyed, I had a moment to breathe and look for Fursona. However, another two Panic Pals zipped out the door before I could find her or Flare. They took up posts on either side, rolled out their speakers, and started blasting rap music.

"TELL 'EM, PANIC PALS, WHILE WE'RE ALL JUST CHILLIN'!
WHO DO YOU THINK IS THE ULTIMATE VILLAIN?"
"THE FACTS ARE IN, THE TRUTH IS OUT, PANIC'S THE BEST!
HE PUTS TOKYEXICO TO THE ULTIMATE TEST!"

Another voice, not Professor Panic's, a LABRAT's, or a rapping robot's, boomed out over the Student Union Building's loudspeakers. "Attention, students and faculty! I apologize for interrupting your finals, but I need a moment of your time! We've got a revenge story on our hands today, and vengeance can't wait!"

The rap music swelled, and so did the voice on the loudspeaker. I couldn't move. No one could, and I realized it was Monologue! He was [**Monologuing**] on the speakers!

"On the field is the treacherous, fickle Magical Girl Understudy and her sidekick Fursona! I've personally had my plans disrupted by these two, so I know how it feels! They're here to fight a man Understudy wronged repeatedly before kicking to the curb! But will their powers be enough?"

I started to move as Monologue stopped talking about himself, only to freeze up again when the villain continued. "Hailing from a small town and here for revenge, it's a man I consider a personal friend and colleague. My experience with him goes back a few months, and he's proven as good as his word at almost everything I've asked him for. Coming out of the tunnel, piloting his brand-new creation, it's the *Small-Town Super* villain himself."

Something was moving inside the cargo bay. The sounds of screeching metal filled the air as the Panic Pals kept rapping.

"HE'S HERE FOR REVENGE; HIS NEW BOT'S GIGANTIC!

PUT YOUR HANDS TOGETHER FOR PROFESSOR PANIC!"

72

Professor Panic

Peter's new mech—it wasn't the FEAR Power Armor I'd grown familiar with, that was for sure—shoved its way through the cargo door and rose to its full height. The mech no longer qualified as power armor; its blue-and-black paint job was the only allusion to the FEAR ever having existed. A pair of familiar-looking Gatling tasers spun up on the machine's back while an absolutely massive [**Hypercompression Cannon**] took up the entire left arm. At the top, almost fifteen feet off the ground, sat Peter.

He smiled as Monologue kept talking, even as he—and the mech—froze. "Professor Panic wanted me to say a little bit about this new machine, and—well, Tokyexico University, you all know me. I'm more than happy to talk. This is the TERROR Mech, a spiritual successor to the professor's old FEAR Power Armor. We at the Student Supervillain Society helped him out with space to build it, access to materials, and, of course, labor in exchange for some . . . services! Ready? Fight!"

The [**Monologue**] effect dropped, and I sprinted right, toward some trees in the quad. Monologue rambled on and on about the Trepidation-Enhancing Rack-and-Ruin-Oriented Robot's design, carefully avoiding telling me anything *useful*.

WHUM-BANG!

The enormous [**Hypercompression Cannon**] fired, tearing a line in the snow down to the brown, dead grass. Twigs and branches rained down on me as I ducked behind an oak tree, which shook from the air's impact. Snow blew upward between the mech and me, and I took a deep breath and dashed toward a different, wider tree.

"Professor Panic, stand down! The major-league heroes will be back soon!"

"No, they won't. Do you think you're the only person who asked Rocko for help last night? I wanted this as much—no, *more*—than you did. I've been begging him to help me get started for weeks. Now that they're off campus, we can finally end this!"

"I already ended it!" I dashed out from behind the tree, sprinting toward the mech.

As I got closer, I realized it was bigger than Underdelver's mech but that, once again, Peter had sacrificed mobility for armor. It ponderously turned toward me, Gatling tasers spinning. The two cannons howled and popped, and a moment later, dozens of wires sailed through the air over me, clattering harmlessly to the ground in my wake as I kept running.

"You miss—oh shit!"

The wires draped over me, then tightened, pulling the tasers back toward me before I could yank free from all the cables. One hooked into my skirt. Another caught a tight, zapped me, and then tore free.

"Surge time," Peter said. Sparks arced from one wire to the next as I tried to free myself from the tangle.

[HP 5/7]

I screamed. The electricity ripped through me, and I flopped to the ground. The *stomp, stomp, stomp* sound of the TERROR Mech's feet filled my ears. A shadow covered me, then disappeared. I yanked wires off me, tearing my Costume and ripping tiny cuts into my arms.

I'd almost freed myself and struggled to one knee when I heard a whining sound. *WHUM-BANG!*

The heavy [**Hypercompression Cannon**] threw me through the Student Union Building's glass windows, which shattered around me. I slammed into the ballroom floor. The impact drove the breath from my lungs; the airburst was like being hit by a hammer, and the floor itself was an anvil.

[HP 3/7]

<**You should run meow,**> Tails said cheerfully in my head. The cat glanced pointedly at the strewn, shattered glass shards. <**You've seen it fight. Now, you need time to make a plan.**>

"Why are *you* so chipper?" I asked, pushing myself up onto my feet. The two-tailed cat was right. I could hear the TERROR Mech's feet crunching glass and concrete below me. For a moment—just one—I let my brain go into self-pity mode. Sure, I'd gotten some cool powers, but Professor Panic got a killer mech? It wasn't fair. Then an Extra's scream from the hallway snapped me out of it.

[**Gritty Recovery! +1 Grit Point**]

I couldn't stay here, and I had to be obvious about leaving. Professor Panic would tear the building apart looking for me, unless he *saw* me go. "[**Starwave Sail**]!" I said, taking off and zipping right over the TERROR Mech's glass dome.

WHUM-BANG!

The airburst pushed my windsurfer to the side but didn't knock it off-balance. I pulled up, gaining a few feet of altitude. The Gatling tasers started firing a moment later but arced through the air harmlessly below me. "Missed, for real this time! I doubt you've got a trick to fix *that*!"

I *really* hoped he didn't have a trick to fix that.

I tore across the sky, looking back. The gigantic mech couldn't fly. Either that or Professor Panic was holding out on me. It stomped slowly through the snow, pursuing me. My first destination had been Walnut Tower, but I changed my mind. Instead, I circled above the TERROR Mech, taking a breather.

Tails ran through the air next to my windsurfer. **<Right meow, I see two threats. The air cannon is bad but manageable. Your real problem is the two shock guns.>**

"Yeah. I have an idea." I whipped the windsurfer into a long, wide arc around the Student Union Building and flew hard for the Mister Felsic statue.

My first thought had been Walnut Tower, but I couldn't put other students at *that* much risk. Not everyone was in finals; some Extras would be studying at home, and as much as I hated it, we *had* agreed not to put Extras in harm's way intentionally. I'd have a few moments to warn anyone at the Mister Felsic statue to leave, and the massive mech behind me would signal I was serious. Deadly serious.

[Show-off! +1 Flamboyance Point]

There were, inexplicably, a dozen students hanging out by the Mister Felsic statue despite the cool weather and snow—and the text message warning to shelter in place. A familiar smell—cigarettes—filled the air as I landed. One of the dudes looked at me, raising an eyebrow. "Hey, babe." It was Avan from history!

"Hey, I don't want to break up the party, but—"

"Aaaaaah!" Avan screamed.

[Terrible Timing! +1 Drama Point]
[End of Act Two! Act Three in One Minute! No Time for Skill Rolls.]

"Yeah, that," I mumbled as Avan and the other students started running. The Drama point was welcome, but not the TERROR Mech's appearance. Neither was the second message saying I wouldn't get to roll skills. That'd happened before, usually—like now—at the worst possible times.

It was still far away—far enough that its tasers probably wouldn't hit me. "Alright. Gatling tasers. I can do this. The itsy-bitsy spider . . ."

[Absent-Hearted Professor: Part Two: Act Three Beginning]

By the time the TERROR Mech arrived at the Mister Felsic statue, I'd concocted a foolproof, three-part plan to win this Episode.

Part One: Take out the Gatling tasers. The damn things rotated quickly, covering for the rest of the mech's ponderous movement, and worse, Professor Panic had too many tricks engineered into them. I'd have to fight him from range until I got lucky hits on them or they ran out of shots.

Part Two: Disable the **[Hypercompression Cannon]**. It was slow, telegraphed hard, and I knew how to manage it from my dozens of fights with Peter. I'd try hacking it; that was a good trick, and it'd worked in the past.

Part Three: Turn it into a kite fight again, just like the FEAR Power Armor. No glory, sure. But I couldn't afford a stand-up battle. Once the TERROR Mech stopped working, I'd drag Peter's ass out of it and beat him up personally until he stopped.

"Come out, come out, wherever you are!" Professor Panic taunted from the plexiglass cockpit.

WHUM-BANG!

I took a deep breath, steeled my sixth-grade self for battle, and whispered to myself, "I'm a **[Hometown Heroine]**. I'm a **[Hometown Heroine]**. I breathed again as the blue nimbus surrounded me, then threw myself around the corner.

"There you are!"

"**[Stellar Ray]**!" My bubbly beam went wide, splashing against armor instead of the plexiglass dome or a stun gun. I scrambled back. Gatling tasers sparked against the concrete a moment later. They kicked up a still-warm cigarette butt. I watched it fly through the air, squeaking when it bounced off my leg.

I'd half hoped Professor Panic wouldn't recognize me as Rainy Day, but that'd been a foolish hope. I'd wrecked some of his bots on camera as the diminutive dynamo, and he was smart enough to put two and two together. Instead of subterfuge, my plan was speed—that and hiding like a scaredy-cat.

I pressed against one of the statue's giant granite pillars.

WHUM-BANG!

Snow blasted on either side of me, and I waited three heartbeats, then started running left. The two Gatling tasers tracked me. As they fired, I stopped on a dime and sprinted the other way. "**[Stellar Ray]**, you big bully!" I shouted.

[Dramatic Damage! +1 Drama Point]

I'd hit something, but I couldn't see what. Tasers clattered against the granite pillar—and against Mister Felsic. One caught my arm, and I pulled it back with a hiss. I got ready to duck out and fire another **[Stellar Ray]**.

WHUM . . .

Preoccupied with where to aim, I didn't realize the **[Hypercompression Cannon]** hadn't fired until I was halfway around the corner. I stared straight down the barrel; I hadn't realized Professor Panic could hold charged shots!

BANG!

It caught me right in the face. I screamed as I flew back, but it cut off when I slammed into Mister Felsic's chest and slid to the ground. My head spun, and my back howled in pain. I closed my eyes.

[HP 1/7]

When I opened them, the TERROR Mech was pushing against one of the granite pillars in a vain attempt to get to me. I rolled to my side and climbed sorely to my feet. "Dammit, Professor Panic, stand down!" I shouted. My voice felt whiney and wavery, so it wasn't a shock when he laughed it off.

"Stand down? Surrender? I'm winning, Understudy! Why would I do that?"

I grinned and dodged a much-lessened rain of tasers, rolling past Mister Felsic and hiding behind him. The extra second of taunting had bought me the time to escape. The second the shots stopped, I ducked between the statue's legs and fired another **[Stellar Ray]**. It missed the camera drone that filled half my vision but didn't miss the other Gatling taser.

[Dramatic Damage! +1 Drama Point]

It exploded, sending sparking shrapnel raining across the snow. The whole mech seemed to flinch as Professor Panic jerked reflexively. I cheered in victory. Then I dropped onto the ramp leading down into the tunnels below. I didn't go all the way inside. Instead, I started rapping.

"PROFESSOR PANIC IS UP TO NO GOOD!
TIME FOR THE ASSISTANT TO TAKE OVER THIS HOOD!"

[Rejuvenation Activated: HP 4/7]

I'd gotten pretty good at freestyling, I thought, as I spun and transformed. The TERROR Mech stomped around the Mister Felsic statue, closing the angle to blast me with the **[Hypercompression Cannon]**. My transformation finished, and I started up a **[Maniacal Reveal]**.

But before I could, Professor Panic started his own! "You thought that was all I brought to our final fight?"

73

Our Final(s) Fight

I've got more than just one mech! Panic Pal Platoon, get her," Professor Panic's voice boomed from the loudspeakers. A hatch opened on the TERROR Mech's chest. Four Panic Pals surged out, flying straight for me.

I relaxed just a touch; I'd dealt with dozens of these flying wastes of metal. The first one zoomed at me, jaw opening and closing, and I ducked. Before I could recover and stand, something slammed into me, knocking me back to the ground. I couldn't hear any rap music. None of the bots held back or unfurled speakers. Instead, they were all on the attack!

[HP 3/7]

I rolled, curled into a ball to cover my head and goggles, and started [**Speed-Hacking**] a Panic Pal. The lights flickered pink, and the newly christened Pinkie Pal grabbed one of its friends, dragging both toward the ground in a flurry of punches, chomps, and beeping.

[**Good Thinking! +1 Cunning Point**]

With only two Panic Pals left, I felt more confident, but every punch and chomp still *hurt*. I reached out, grabbing the closest one by the arm and swinging it into the other. The explosion knocked me off my feet, but both Panic Pals were gone. They left behind only crushed, half-scorched wreckage.

[**Badass Takedown! +1 Badass Point**]
[**Badass Takedown! +1 Badass Point**]

WHUM-BANG!
The TERROR Mech's [**Hypercompression Cannon**] ripped the air apart over my head. The backdraft tore at my lab coat, and I laughed hysterically. "Ah, Professor! A worthy challenge!" I [**Checked the Script**], which highlighted the two destroyed

Panic Pals' wreckage. Lunging out before the TERROR Mech recharged, I grabbed the scrap and returned to the statue's cover.

A quick glance showed the Pinkie Pal winning its fight, but not by much, and TA-1LZ lurking at my feet. I had an idea—a terrible, villainous idea. "TA-1LZ, get over here! Want to find out if [**Science has Rules?**]

I'd gotten this power after Part One, and I'd had *no* idea what it did. But [**Check the Script**] had given me an idea; where Professor Panic was a plotting, scheming Genius, Lab Assistant didn't have time for that! I was a mad scientist; I'd have to build something on the fly!

Pinkie Pal won its fight, and I sent it on a suicide mission against the TERROR Mech. Then I grabbed TA-1LZ. "Sorry about this, robo-cat!"

The mecha-cat yowled as I popped open a panel on her back. "Put me down! Me-ouch!"

I didn't. Instead, I grabbed a handful of wires and ripped them out of TA-1LZ's back. She shut down with a pitiful meow. But I didn't care. I needed her to beat Professor Panic and claim my rightful place as the most powerful Panic.

As Pinkie Pal buzzed around the gigantic mech, holding on surprisingly well, I grabbed the wreckage and built an armored turret atop TA-1LZ's back. Then I fed the wires through it. I needed one more part, though. And, unfortunately, I'd need to leave the safety of the Mister Felsic statue to get it.

Pinkie was still running. Peter had stopped using the [**Hypercompression Cannon**] to shoot it down. Instead, he swatted at my tiny bot, which buzzed around, fly-like. I had time. I started running, counting the seconds. One. Two. Three. Four. My hand wrapped around the mostly broken Gatling taser on five—the exact moment Professor Panic swatted the pink-tinted robot out of the air.

WHUM-BANG!

"Ahahaha! Too slow, Professor!" I jammed the Gatling taser onto my mecha-familiar's brand-new turret. Then I stepped out from behind the Mister Felsic statue. "It's time for a [**Maniacal Reveal**]!"

"Goddammit!"

"That's right!" I held the jury-rigged cat mech up in the air. My [**Science has Rules?**] power said I had to explain how my invention worked, so I cleared my throat, thought, and got started. It was just improv, right? "This is the C1-AW5 Fast-Attack Robot. It uses a Gatling taser salvaged from one of my battles—"

"This battle! That's *mine.*"

"—as its primary weapon and runs steel battle armor and a, uh, neo-nuclear micro-point reactor with enhanced, um, wobbly-flop processing. I wired it into the original frame to create an agile combat assistant, and with its power, I can take you down!"

[Good Thinking! +1 Cunning Point]
[Sinister Speech! +1 Flamboyance Point]
[Pseudoscientific Mumbo-Jumbo! +1 Drama Point]

As I finished, TA-1LZ—er, C1-AW5—powered up and leaped into battle. The cat's new form was *fast*! It wasn't as fast as the unarmed mecha-cat, but it fired off tasers in a rippling barrage as it weaved between the TERROR Mech's legs. I laughed, on the edge of losing control. Peter couldn't keep up, or the mech couldn't turn fast enough, and even though the tiny cat wasn't doing *much* damage, its cannon kept rattling, and more and more wires hung from the mech's undercarriage by the second.

The TERROR Mech jerked away from C1-AW5's attack, handling shakily as it pulled away from the tasers. My evil plan was working!

[Speed-Hacker] activated, and I had control of the [Hypercompression Cannon] for just a moment. Then an antivirus kicked in—Peter had *learned* from our fight on Flat Top Hill, just like I had. I backed out of the hack before I could get hurt like I had against Dark Girl Anima; I didn't have the superhero damage to give.

CRASH!

Peter had given up on the cat. The TERROR Mech slammed into a granite pillar. *There's no way it'll move it*, I thought, just before the pillar tipped slightly. As the massive mech pushed into the heavy pillar, it started to fall on its own—right toward me! I turned and dashed down the ramp toward the tunnel door.

I made it inside a moment before the stone pillar smashed into Mister Felsic, raining granite, concrete, and rebar down onto the courtyard. The rubble filled the ramp, blocking the doors. I was cut off, which meant I had a moment to breathe.

Lab Assistant Panic had done her best. I shifted back to Magical Girl Understudy and jogged down the tunnel toward a different exit. Behind me, I heard the [Hypercompression Cannon] fire; whether he'd shot Tails or the rubble, I couldn't tell. I couldn't do anything about Tails either way. She'd have to find me—or safety—on her own.

[Rejuvenation Activated! HP 6/7]

I'd seen weaknesses, though. Just before I'd disappeared into the tunnel, C1-AW5 had activated the dozens of tasers, sending a jolt of electricity through the TERROR Mech. Its non-cannon arm had flopped to the ground, unusable. I had no idea if that was permanent or if Professor Panic could fix it, but if it was broken, I could finally press the attack. It wasn't all according to plan, but when had one of my plans *ever* worked out so far, right?

Yeah. Basically never.

I ran up some stairs, through a dorm common area, and out the front door. "[Starwave Sail]!" Good things happened when I improvised—like Bianca, my internship, and Tottergarten. I wasn't a good playwright, but I could improv like a champ. So that's what I'd do.

Peter—and the TERROR Mech—were both still at the Mister Felsic statue's wreckage. The bot shoved rubble aside, trying to dig its way to me, but I flew high above it. A tiny figure darted between the mech's legs, trying to get its attention.

Tails was alive, in spite of me ripping her back open. I had an incredibly dumb but cinematically awesome idea—something Professor Panic would never see coming.

I deactivated [**Starwave Sail**].

[**Leap of Faith! +1 Drama Point**]

I fell. The wind whipped my hair and skirts as I rocketed toward the ground, and I squinted my eyes inside the domino mask. Behind me, a camera drone whistled and hummed, filming my descent. I started counting down.

Five.

Four.

Three.

Nope, not enough time. Now!

I stopped with a sudden jerk, twenty feet over the TERROR Mech's domed plexiglass cockpit. Even through my superhero damage, I felt muscles tearing, and I screamed. I'd never, *ever* taken so much superhero damage at once.

[**HP 2/7**]

Peter looked up, and the [**Hypercompression Cannon**] started ponderously aiming at me. His face screamed disbelief and, for the first time I could remember, fear.

My spotlight stopped, centered on him, and [**Bit-Part Barrage**] went off.

[**Dramatic Damage! +5 Drama Points**]

Plexiglass snapped. Electricity sparked. The mech's controls took hit after hit. It wobbled on its legs but stayed upright, even as its lights flickered and shut down.

And I plunged toward the earth again. I landed on top of Professor Panic with a bone-crunching smack.

[**HP 1/7**]
[**Stunt Woman! +1 Drama Point**]

"Oooow!" Peter bellowed.

"Ugh," I muttered, shaking off the damage and getting to my feet shakily. I got my bearings.

Professor Panic squirmed backward, pressing up against the ruined control panel. He reached for a tiny [**Hypercompression Cannon**]. "Time to die, Und—"

I used [**Spotlight Strike**] and punched him in the face before he could lift it.

[**Stylish Strike! +1 Flamboyance Point**]

Something crunched under my punch, and he slumped to the cockpit's floor. I sank down beside him, breathing long, deep breaths as sirens filled the air.

A campus police officer grabbed Professor Panic by the cuffs and shoved him into a waiting patrol car's back seat. "I almost had you! I almost had my revenge!" he shouted from the window.

I ignored him. It seemed like the right thing to do. Instead, I focused on giving the campus police—and a furious-looking Dr. Jackson—a rundown of the Episode, which hadn't ended yet. Usually, they were over when the police showed up, but not this time. The camera drones hung around, recording my interview, and Tails weaved back and forth around my legs. Her seams had torn and stuffing leaked from the hole, but she was fine. Mostly.

Fursona hopped up, dragging a kicking and screaming Flare with her. "Here's another one," she said, dropping him off at a different car.

Seeing Professor Panic cuffed in a patrol car filled me with relief. Sure, the Episode wasn't over yet, but Monologue was the only loose end I knew about, and as soon as I'd mentioned his part in things, Dr. Mays had promised he'd hunt him down and get to the bottom of his—and the SSS's—involvement.

Still, the camera drone wouldn't stop hovering overhead. It was looking for a resolution.

I walked to the patrol car and leaned down to stick my head in. "Hello, Peter," I said, keeping my voice low and quiet so no one but the drone and Peter could hear.

"I was so close! Goddammit!"

"We both played our part in this whole mess, but it's over now. It's time to let go and move on. Maybe, in time, we can be friends again, but I can't deal with this right now. *Small-Town Super* is over; I'm done fighting with you." I turned my back and started walking away.

[Episode Finished!]
[Episode: Series Finale: Absent-Hearted Professor: Part Two - PG-13]
[Penalties: No Warnings - Episode Rating Shift - No Penalty]
[Series Finished! +10 of each Style Point]
[Winner Winner! +3 of each Style Point]
[Role Focus: Drama+Cunning - Goal Partially Met +20 Drama Points]
[Alias - Understudy] [Archetype - Magical Girl] [Community Rank - 352/523]
[HP 1/7]
[Styles and Skills]
▶ Archetype Skill - Transformation Sequence
▶ Badass (40)
▶ Cunning (54)
▶ Drama (84) (Skill Roll Available)
▶ Hometown Heroine 1

▶ Bit-Part Barrage 1
▶ Flamboyance (59) (Skill Roll Available)
▶ Signature Skill - Adaptive Armoire 2
▶ Stored Costumes: (Rainy Day, Lab Assistant Panic)
▶ Spotlight Strike 1
▶ Starwave Sail 1
▶ Flickerform 1
▶ Grit (level 2; 56) (Skill Roll Available)
[50 Drama Credits Used. Rolling Skill!]
[50 Flamboyance Credits Used. Rolling Skill!]
[50 Grit Credits Used. Rolling Skill!]
[New Skill! Thunderhead 0: Charge up power for a stronger Elementalist finishing move. Earns drama points and adds damage.]
[Upgrade! Flickerform ▶ Quick-Time Change: Nail the dance moves to quickly switch Costumes! Activates triggered powers.]
[New Skill! TA-1LZ Size Boost 0: A combat robot? Science can make that happen! TA-1LZ is tougher in combat with this power.]

"Understudy," Professor Panic—Peter—said from behind me. His voice dripped with desperation and pleading, and the maniacal edge had disappeared. "Understudy, before you go, I did this for us. I just wanted *us* one more time. One final battle."

"Well, you got it. But there won't be more." I walked back to the patrol car and leaned in again. "I talked it over with the campus police and Dr. Jackson. There's no way they can get you home. They're going to ask your lawyers to okay moving you to Almhurst until the end of Man vs. Nature Seven."

"No. No way." Peter went pale. I didn't blame him. Almhurst was where incorrigible villains—villains like Mister Twister and Haze-Matt—went, and we both knew it. But what Peter didn't know, and I did after Dr. Jackson's explanation, was that there was another wing—one for holding lesser villains who just needed a place to be where they wouldn't be in trouble.

"They've got a special place for you. A nice, safe wing, away from the real monsters," I said. Peter relaxed, and I sank in the final dagger. "Maybe they'll even work on rehabilitating you. You have a spark of good; someday, you might make a good hero. Maybe even a sidekick for someone. But not me."

I turned and looked for Fursona. Peter spluttered, trying to think of a snappy retort. I'd won. Once and for all, I'd won.

Still, something he said bothered me. As Fursona came in for a superhero hug, I played it over and over in my mind. One final battle, he'd said. One final . . . Blood rushed from my face, and I felt a chill. "What time is it?" I asked my sidekick-girlfriend.

"About 2:55."

"Fuck!" I cringed, waiting for the rating warning, then tore myself from her embrace and started sprinting across Tokyexico University. I had five minutes to get to my Ilneat Relations final!

Epilogue

I wasn't going home for winter break.

It sucked, and I'd held out hope even through my last final—the code of ethics presentation. But deep down inside, I'd known. The turbo-buffalo were leaving, but the herd and the D-wolvers were still too dangerous for convoys. If Peter couldn't go home—if his lawyers had agreed to house him in Almhurst until the passes cleared—there definitely wasn't a bus or a ride-share across.

Instead, I'd spend Christmas at Tottergarten—a couple of the kids' parents had to work holidays—and eat dinner with Su-Bin's family. Everything about it sucked. But I couldn't be too pissy about it. The Cloud would probably be *thrilled*.

Speaking of the code of ethics presentation, though . . . honestly, I owed Theseus my life if we passed this. I hadn't practiced my lines—that was *fine,* though. It fit with my new "Understudy is an improviser" mentality. But Theseus? He'd showed up *ready* to present. He'd borrowed Monologue's suit, or at least the jacket's arms. Would that give him Monologue's speech-making powers? I didn't know, and honestly, I didn't want to find out.

"Alright, next up is Theseus's Ship," Dr. Jackson called from the back of the lecture hall. All four Superpower Studies professors were back there, and so was another man I didn't recognize. He wore a business suit, and he and Dr. Mays stood in the back, arguing quietly as we filed to the podium and started our slideshow.

"Here we go, everyone. My name is Theseus, and you'll find our code of ethics is head and shoulders better than it was a week ago," the villain started. "We broke our code into four sections, then made subsections for heroes and villains. With help from our Extras, Jennifer and Robert, we were able to take into account some serious issues our first draft didn't. So, without further ado, here's Magical Girl Understudy to take it from here."

I swallowed and took a deep breath. It was just like being on the stage or in an Episode. "The first category we focused on was how heroes and villains interact with Extras. As you can see on the screen, heroes have many, many more rules than villains."

Dr. Catherine Jackson had taught Superpower Ethics for five years. Before that, she'd been the lowest-earning but most successful superhero in the major leagues. And if she'd learned one thing from all that time, it was this. There was always *that group*.

Whether it was 3V1L, the In-You-Endos, or just another day of teaching, one team never clicked. There were always two members making out or batting eyelashes at each other, another slacking and goofing off, and a "leader" who, despite all their efforts, couldn't make anyone do any actual work at all. And, unlike the In-You-Endos, who made that brand of chaos their *thing*, most teams couldn't handle it. On day one, she'd bet twenty bucks on The Crumb's team being *that group*. She'd already paid Dr. Mays for her mistake.

She poured herself another glass of wine and sat on her couch. She'd graded every essay on "League of X Logistics and Problem-Solving," every self-recorded Episode for the Studio/Super Dynamics class she'd created over the summer, and every code of ethics. Except for *that group*.

It was time to grade *that group*.

Her wine smelled nutty, with a hint of cherry—something from the Pacific Coast. She sighed. The code of ethics was right there. It'd take ten minutes to grade—maybe less. But *that group*, and *that girl*, gave her a migraine. After the "Study in Black and Scarlet" Fanfic Episode in the Poudre Districts, she'd hurried back to campus to find the Student Union Building's ballroom windows destroyed, the Mister Felsic statue toppled, and, worse, *her* classroom's electronics damaged. The one to blame? Magical Girl Understudy.

The wine was half-gone already? How had that happened? Catherine topped off the glass and rubbed her temples. Then she opened the folder, helpfully labeled "Theseus's Ship - Theseus, Gourmet, Fursona, Magical Girl Understudy." Where did kids these days *find* team names like this?

Code of Ethics: Final Draft

Extras

Heroes will make every realistic effort to avoid harming or involving Extras in combat.

Pragmatism is fine. If one Extra getting involved saves lives, it's acceptable to enlist Extra help temporarily.

Volunteer Extras, the press, and emergency services will involve themselves.

When Extras are combative, removing them as threats is acceptable but should be done nonlethally.

Minions are not Extras. They are hostiles until they surrender.

Villains will not kill or injure Extras without Episode-based justification.

Extras' involvement must directly relate to the villain's goals for the Episode.

Property

Property damage must be directly related to the Episode's goals.

Heroes will make efforts to avoid damaging residences and small businesses except where not doing so would put Extras in harm's way.

Corporate-controlled and government buildings should be analyzed on a case-by-case basis.

Villains will not target residences unless the Episode's goals relate directly to the resident.

For example, see the Episode where Danger Close kidnaps the mayor to force his team's release from Almhurst.

Other properties must be evaluated on a similar case-by-case basis as heroes.

Neutral Fields

The spirit of Neutral Fields is a pause in the fighting. Therefore, neither heroes nor villains will use Neutral Fields as cover for a teammate or henchmen to carry out a plan.

Action happening during a Neutral Field meeting is cause for the meeting to end immediately.

McHammer's Gambit, where his henchmen took a school hostage to shift the balance of power during Neutral Fields, is an example of poor-spirited Neutral Fields.

Finales

The following changes are in effect for Series Finales

Heroes:

Extras will be involved more frequently. Make good decisions and keep them as safe as possible.

Nonresidential structures are fair game if their destruction relates to the Finale.

Neutrality can be used strategically in Finales.

Villains:

Collateral damage happens. Avoid hurting and killing Extras when possible.

Accidents happen. Don't target civilians.

Neutral Fields can be used strategically.

"Fine. *Fine.*" The wine was gone again. Why was the wine always gone when she needed it most?

That group's code was a pleasant surprise compared to where it'd been a week before. Of course, they'd missed the key messages, and it wouldn't hold up in the major leagues or the upper minors. They'd omitted details Catherine hadn't explicitly pointed out, like the rivalries between Lord Destructo and Magical Girl Stella-Lunar or the ethics of heel-turns in the Tapdance vs. Outrider fight.

Still, Dr. Catherine Jackson thought, *it might not be an A, but it'll pass—barely.* And Superpower Ethics was pass/fail.

Rocko shivered in their studio's oppressive heat. The Ilneat finished the final cuts and edits to "Absent-Hearted Professor: Part Two" and pressed play from the beginning. Pataki sat next to them, staring at the screen as Fursona and Magical Girl Understudy charged across the snow toward the Student Union Building.

"This could have ruined us, you know?" Pataki asked.

"Yep. We got the Episode done, though. It ships to Ilneat-Three tomorrow."

"To quote a pre-Launch Day film, what did it cost?"

The Ilneat producer took a long drag from their cigar. The Tele-Portal portal opened, and Rocko and Pataki both grinned momentarily; free cameos were the *best* for ratings. But Rocko's glum mood returned soon enough. "Everything."

Pataki laughed, then hacked out a couple of coughs. "Not *everything*. Just the rights to Collidus's spin-off, Professor Panic's contract, and favors to be named for Phil and Lil, Zim, and Otto."

"Yep. I'm still ruined unless I can find a primo villain for DuPont, and thanks to the networks, I can't negotiate for a new villain until next summer. Until then, *our* heroes are gonna have to share Episodes with other studios, and that means splitting royalties! And the merch. The beautiful, beautiful merch sales all but dry up unless they guest star in big-time shows, and, of course, they're scheduled for *Tottergarten*." Rocko grabbed a new cigar as their old one sputtered out. They chewed on it. "If we're lucky, Part Two pushes the same ratings as Part One, and we can recover financially. But there's no way around the networks. It might still cost us everything."

Rocko's phone rang. "Pause that," they snapped at Pataki.

The TV flipped off.

"Rocko Productions, producer of *Small-Town Super* and *Heroics 101*. Rocko speaking. How can I help you? . . . An opening, you say? I see, I see . . . Yes, we can be ready by the first . . . mid-May? That's doable. Low budget? Yeah, look, I'm running on fumes here, Dexter, you gotta give me something! Who's the rival? . . . Who's the girl? A boy, huh? Oh, that'll be dramatic. Yeah . . . Yeah. Thanks, Dexter, you're a real pal, you know that? You ever need anything . . . *anything* . . . let me know, okay? . . . You too. Buh-bye."

The Ilneat steepled their four hands, chewing on their cigar. Rocko Productions was saved! Well, not yet. It wasn't up to them. They stared into a mirror on their desk, running a grasping hand through their otter-like fur.

Pataki said something, but Rocko didn't hear it. All they could hear were gears turning and cash registers ka-chinging.

Pataki held up the remote. "Hey, we watching here? Proof-watch is prudent, you know?"

"No, watch it yourself. I'm busy."

The news they'd gotten changed everything. They just had to tell Magical Girl Understudy, and she'd do the rest herself. They and Pataki would be rich, and she'd be a minor-league hero. And with the human Christmas holiday coming up, they had the perfect chance to tell her the good news.

Author's Note

Hello, Aest here! Thanks for reading Magical Girl Undergrad: *Heroics 101*. Three more books are coming in the series, but if you can't wait, check out AestBelequa.com for more of my work.

Please leave a review; it means a lot to me.

I'm usually on Discord in Walnut Tower, Room 1301 (Discord.gg/xvkfnNMzfe). Come say hello, tell me your favorite superpowers, and meet the fantastic community!

You can find the work of several talented authors at Linktr.ee/coteh.

Check out Zenkarn's book, *Reincarnated for an Apocalypse Store*, available on Amazon!

If Discord isn't your favorite, you can keep up with LitRPG through these Facebook groups:

LitRPG Books

LitRPG Forum

GameLit Society

Acknowledgments

Thanks to the Council of the Eternal Hiatus. Without them, I probably would never have written this book.

Also, thanks to Zenkarn, whose help with brainstorming and rubberducking was essential to this book's planning.

Finally, I want to thank my family for putting up with me while I learned how to be an author.

About the Author

Aest Belequa is a LitRPG and progression fantasy author, play-by-post RPG game master, and former teacher from Colorado. He grew up loving fantasy and science fiction and tries to bring that same energy to his writing.